Praise for *Popisho*

"Fantastic . . . This bold, iridescent l[...] landed on anyone's shoulder but Ro[...] Ross's lyrical, rhythmic writing is sor[...] sings out loud and pure."
—Eowyn Ivey

"Intensely absorbing . . . [Exploring] love, second chances and fate, with razor-sharp postcolonial satire, this love story has already drawn comparisons to Gabriel García Márquez, Toni Morrison and Arundhati Roy."
—Layla Haidrani, *Cosmopolitan* (UK)

"Mesmerising . . . A madcap, freewheeling ride through surreal and supernatural territory."
—Michael Donkor, *The Guardian*

"[Written] throughout with such juice and verve . . . *Popisho* will please and excite anyone who appreciates literary ambition and risk-taking."
—Wendy Smith, *The Washington Post*

"In recent years, a clutch of incandescently talented writers . . . have reminded us that fantasy is one of the oldest and most imaginative branches of human storytelling. Ross has her own 'cors,' a gift for creating an unforgettable world, and with this book, she takes her rightful place at that table of writers."
—Nilanjana Roy, *Financial Times*

"An ode to the soul, to food, to Caribbean myth and to magic."
—Jessica Morgan, *Refinery29* (UK)

"[*Popisho*] carves out a place in the canon of memorable works of magical realism alongside *Midnight's Children* and *One Hundred Years of Solitude*, but it's also totally itself, a raunchy, sly, colorful exploration of individual and collective identity. A novel that suffuses the senses."
—*Kirkus Reviews* (starred review)

"Wondrous . . . Passing reminders of the works of Gabriel García Márquez and Alice Walker serve to establish Ross firmly in the global storytelling tradition of bold and beautiful narratives . . . A stirring literary experience."
—Shoba Viswanathan, *Booklist* (starred review)

Hayley Benoit

LEONE ROSS
Popisho

Leone Ross is a fiction writer and an academic. She was born in England and grew up in Jamaica. Her first novel, *All the Blood Is Red*, was long-listed for the Orange Prize for Fiction, and her second novel, *Orange Laughter*, was chosen as a BBC Radio 4's Woman's Hour Watershed Fiction favorite. Her first short-story collection, *Come Let Us Sing Anyway*, was nominated for the Edge Hill Short Story Prize and the Jhalak Prize. Ross has taught creative writing in London for twenty years and worked as a journalist throughout the nineties. She lives in London but intends to retire near water.

ALSO BY LEONE ROSS

Come Let Us Sing Anyway

Orange Laughter

All the Blood Is Red

Popisho

LEONE ROSS

PICADOR

FARRAR, STRAUS AND GIROUX

NEW YORK

In memory of Shaka

For Marjorie
Because of Joan

Picador
120 Broadway, New York 10271

Excerpt from *Conversations with Audre Lorde* © 2004 by
University Press of Mississippi.

The Library of Congress has cataloged the Farrar, Straus and Giroux hardcover
edition as follows:
Names: Ross, Leone, 1969– author.
Title: Popisho / Leone Ross.
Description: First American edition. | New York : Farrar, Straus and Giroux, 2021. |
Published in 2021 by Faber & Faber Limited, Great Britain, as *This One Sky Day*.
Identifiers: LCCN 2020050641 | ISBN 9780374602451 (hardcover)
Subjects: LCSH: Magic—Fiction. | GSAFD: Love stories.
Classification: LCC PR6068.O836 P67 2021 | DDC 823/.914—dc23
LC record available at https://lccn.loc.gov/2020050641

Paperback ISBN: 978-1-250-82963-4

Our books may be purchased in bulk for promotional, educational, or business
use. Please contact your local bookseller or the Macmillan Corporate and
Premium Sales Department at 1-800-221-7945, extension 5442, or
by email at MacmillanSpecialMarkets@macmillan.com.

Picador® is a U.S. registered trademark and is used by Macmillan Publishing Group, LLC,
under license from Pan Books Limited.

For book club information, please visit facebook.com/picadorbookclub or
email marketing@picadorusa.com.

picadorusa.com • instagram.com/picador
twitter.com/picadorusa • facebook.com/picadorusa

1   3   5   7   9   10   8   6   4   2

Pain is important: how we evade it, how we succumb to it, how we deal with it, how we transcend it.

AUDRE LORDE

Old fire-stick easy fi ketch

JAMAICAN PROVERB

Popisho

I

On the first anniversary of his wife's death, Xavier Redchoose got up before light and went downstairs to salt the cod. He sat in his kitchen, green notebook in hand, rubbing his left thumb along the stained pages, waiting for delivery. Through the restaurant window, he could see the golden stalk of a fading moon. Around him, the Torn Poem was silent, except for the morning wind, making the front doors shiver.

It was going to be a trying day, of that he was sure.

The local fisherman arrived promptly, his adolescent son trailing behind him, father genuflecting, son's eyes downcast and fixed on the backs of their silver-blue catch. It was this same boy who had found Xavier's wife floating in the sea, limbs tentacled, and carried her corpse onto the beach. He said Nya's dead voice sounded like rotting pineapple: sweet and grating as she tapped his chest.

You can put me down now, boy. It gone bad, already.

The fisherman's son watched her walk down the sand until he couldn't see her anymore.

Why you never hold her there? snapped Xavier. *Call for me? Something.*

I never know how, the boy whined.

Take me two day to get him up here to tell you, macaenus! the father said. *Damn fool go hide in a bush!*

When people died alone, without proper burial rites, the carcass wandered for years, rudderless, rotting and shrinking. They had all seen these ghosts, rebuilding their bodies with bits

3

of rubbish, hanging on, half-maddened. People who died alone: heart attack, stroke, old age, sleep-and-dream-and-dead. Fall and lick your head on a rock. Poverty. Murder. Suicide. Drowning. People whispered behind their hands. *All of them dead of the same thing, you know. Loneliness.*

It hurt Xavier, to think of his fierce wife, so.

Xavier paid for the fish – two thick bellies and a sack of velvety cod livers – and watched the youth's trembling mouth as he hoisted it onto the kitchen table. He didn't forgive the boy. How hard was it to restrain a dead woman, when so much was at stake?

'Blessings, macaenus,' said the fisherman. He patted the cod. 'Walk good today, you hear?'

Xavier nodded.

He leaned against the kitchen door, listening to them make their way back through his cliff-top garden, imagining every plant they passed: his pearly bougainvillea; the night-blooming cereus clambering up the mango tree; his pawpaws and twin almond trees; his hot pepper, pumpkins and white roses. He liked flowering plants between the herbs; they attracted the right kind of insect. Down the sheer steps they went, calling softly to each other: *mind how you go*. He liked the fisherman's voice. It reminded him of being young. *Before you got so very speaky-spokey, macaenus*, his brother Io liked to say, grinning all over his face. Xavier sucked his teeth. He wasn't too fancy, whatever his elder brother said. He still knew how to curse a man in the language of their ancestors.

He rubbed his palm-heel across his jaw. His beard needed trimming.

Chse, Io's seven-year-old daughter, would be in here soon, demanding breakfast from him. She was an early riser, too. In the months just after Nya died, Chse was the only person who dared come to his room without invitation, jumping into his hammock and swinging her legs. She told him he looked far too tall, and why didn't he do something about it, and when the room smelled – *ooh, so bad!* – she'd stretched her arm to open the window and turned his face towards the sunshine.

You going out today, Uncle?

Not today, Chse.

She pulled his nose until he gave in and tossed her, giggling, into the air.

Don't drop me, Uncle Speaky-Spokey!

★

Xavier took a deep breath and stepped out into his yard. The dark garden poured out in front of him, and beyond that, the islands of Popisho. The Torn Poem was perfectly located on Battisient: right inside the capital Pretty Town but still private, on the cliff above the harbour. Up here, he could see his diners snaking across the sand towards him, then away afterwards, a silvery line of nourished people stretching back to the sea, like foam.

After he fed them, some swam, some danced.

An orange sliver climbed the horizon, no more than the peeping eye of an egg. He closed his eyes and began turning a single, slow circle, back straight, arms out and palms up. Beaches east and west, at the end of his fingertips; the old-gold bay and its harnessed fishing boats splintered across the soft water; the tall, thin schoolhouse; Bend Down Market; the solemn chiming Temple – why, his finger might just touch it; one of the toy factories, painted ugly green, like something you found up your nose after a bad cold; squat, creamy cottages

5

spiralling into the hills, lit by front-yard cook-fires at night. Sometimes he visited the owners and offered them fire-dye in particular colours, so that his diners could admire the light. *Yes, macaenus*, they said, smiling at his quiet face. *Of course, for you, and the gods that chose you.*

He stopped circling and opened his eyes. Battisient's sister island, Dukuyaie, glimmered in the distance, its thick hide grainy in the dawn. You could see the Dead Islands if you looked north and squinted: like a spray of wet, blue pebbles. It had been so long since he'd walked them.

The world was stirring awake again, and he had a list of things to do today in his green notebook.

1. Fish delivery
2. Fuckery

★

They didn't have Nya's body to bathe or bind, so he had prepared a ceremony by the ocean. He stood, linking arms with his mother-in-law, their family and friends crowded around them, silent obeah women in golden robes scattering herbs and making rum libation in the water. *Tragic*, people muttered, too loud for his liking. *She was never a strong swimmer.*

She going come to you Xav, Mamma Suth said, standing composed in his day room, patting his shoulder. *You know they haunt the one they love the most.* He kissed her forehead. Her eyes were dry. She'd screamed when she heard her one-child was dead, and pitched herself backward, only caught by her husband, who wrapped his arms around her waist, clutched her belly and shook it fiercely.

6

She will want her mother, Xavier murmured. But they both knew she was right. Nya would come back to him, looking freedom. And the only way to free a ghost was to . . . *dispense* with whatever was left.

He was ready to do what was necessary. What the fisherman's son couldn't do.

After the funeral he'd changed into work clothes and begun preparations for evening service. He hadn't neglected a single one. Even in those early months when he slept whole days, his back to Nya's empty hammock, he had still gotten up and staggered into the kitchen when the sun went down, eyes slitted, hoisting slabs of goat and coney on his shoulder, eating crusts and vegetable ends, needing to break bone and use his knives.

His sous-chef Moue came into the kitchen in her funeral whites to ask what he was doing.

Xavier paused over the sputtering pans, noticing absently that his hands were shaking.

It wouldn't surprise Nya, he said.

No, macaenus. Moue didn't blink. *But I not talking surprise. I talking decency.* She was a reticent woman, but she'd been very fond of his wife.

Xavier sucked his teeth and turned back to his stove. Moue sucked hers right back and turned on her heel. He'd tried out eleven cooks before he found her, with her sensitive nose and her crochet-bump hair – such a little-girl hairstyle! The way she skimmed the stockpot was like conducting a choir. But she didn't come back that evening, and he was left with the pot-washer and one of the waitresses, roped in to brush mushrooms and slide the cakes out, to follow behind him wiping plates and moving *wrong*. The waitress burnt herself twice and actually complained about it. Did she not know that chefs' backs were worn

7

and flayed things? His hands were criss-crossed with scars from twisting sinew and boiling syrup and someone in the kitchen walking into him with scalding gravy; scars from pig bristles and fish scales; from being tired; from picking up a hot pan, roaring: *What, nobody never hear me when I said dust down the handles with flour so everybody can see they hot, raaaaaaaaaass!*

The memory of Moue's disapproval still irritated him. He expected his second to understand her duty. He had a scant twenty years to cook a meal for every single adult man and woman on Popisho. To delight a whole *nation* with his food. It was an entire life's work, training for it, then doing it. Finding his own replacement, his acolyte, and training them to begin again. Failure was inconceivable. Only one macaenus before him had ever failed and that was because he'd died.

Nya's death reminded him that nothing was promised.

As the weeks passed, he became consumed with the idea that he'd be out when Nya returned. At market when she came looking for him in the shelter of their bedroom; in Temple with Chse while Nya waited in the garden. Out, out, out, while she rotted and searched for him. Asleep when she arrived; that seemed the cruellest possibility of all.

Did ghosts cry? No matter. He had to stay inside and wait.

Flex his hands and shoulders.

Do it quick, I beg you, Mamma Suth had said.

Months then, not a toe outside the Torn Poem, not even to soothe the garden. Sitting in his bedroom all day or circling through the building late at night, he'd felt his own potential madness. He found old notes she'd left for him before she died, slipped down the back of the stove, unread and oily, or caught under a plant: *meet me here, Xav*, and *why don't we go . . . ?* and

8

he stood holding them, whispering: *wife, wife.* The word turned into a crimson shadow and blew through a crack in the wall, down the sea-cliff and into a neighbour's house, where it made the children gag and paw at their mouths.

But in all of a year, Nya never find her way back home.

✱

Io arrived at the front door two weeks after the funeral, all his corroches stuffed into three battered valises and a yellow chicken under each arm. He had his own calamities: an accident on a building site the year before had left him twisted and limping; the convalescence ruined his marriage.

Xavier grunted, let him in and went back to his room to wait for Nya.

Io declared himself Grand Concierge, in charge of all comings and goings at the Torn Poem, and promptly began a lunch-hour catering business. Simple chicken dumplings and coconut water. He nailed a sign at the bottom of the cliff.

You only get macaenus food
once a lifetime
But you can buy dumpling here every day!

The venture was an immediate success: three days of neat, warm packages passed briskly through the kitchen window; scrupulous cleanliness; extra work for the Torn Poem staff; union wages; everything cleaned up *tight*, so the macaenus didn't have to stress when he came downstairs.

Every day!

Xavier didn't notice the brazen campaign until Moue pointed out the large and outraged group of citizens arriving with a petition for the removal of the sign. Irritably, he sent a message for them not to be so sensitive and watched the crowd dispersing from his bedroom window, all lip-biting and head-hanging. He understood their loyalty to him; he also understood Io's sense of humour – his brother was a true egalitarian. Xavier suspected Io didn't believe in *any* god, much less the idea his baby brother had been chosen by them. What Io knew how to do was work hard and go on long, halting walks.

Want to walk, Xav?

No, he wasn't ready.

Macaenus better wear red drawers. He'd overheard the waitresses. *'Case she come back for him dicky.*

After service, when the night was deep and their backs were raw and Chse put to bed, the brothers sat together on the veranda and Io knew when to be quiet and when to talk, swapping low, funny, outrageous stories of the day, each absent-mindedly trying to outdo the other. If you passed by, you'd have heard nothing more than grunts and half-sentences, in that way of people who have known each other for years.

Except recently, Xavier saw the restlessness in his brother's eyes.

★

Everything but Nya had arrived that year: fresh milk from the goat-man; pomegranate season; a woman trying to sell him hand-carved buttons for his robes; another with one breast bigger than the other who wept at the door to think of him widowed, Moue shooing her with a dish-rag; Chse's constant band of playmates;

and the Governor's letter, nearly three months ago, printed on thick, expensive, imported paper.

It was that letter started off the *particular* fuckery scribbled down in Xavier's green notebook. Sent from the home of Governor Bertrand Intiasar and His Wife, the letter informed Xavier Laurence Redchoose – four hundred and thirteenth macaenus – of the recent and glorious engagement of their one-daughter, Sonteine Melody Ignoble Intiasar, to Dandu Abraham Brenteninton.

It also said the Governor would be *delighted* to welcome the macaenus into their home to cook a traditional wedding-night meal for the newlyweds.

Xavier snorted and ripped the thing in half. Wedding-night feasts were a common thing, said to confer good fortune and sweet life on happy couples, along with various other long and complicated steps and blessings. But Bertie Intiasar knew better than to ask *him* to do it. Send a letter indeed!

He hated letters.

★

His first meeting with the Governor had been in this same kitchen, ten years ago, Ascension Day, the day he took up his title, the garden stuffed with people for the ceremony. He and Nya had been in residence for less than a week; the restaurant didn't even have a name yet.

Xavier hovered in the kitchen, waiting for an obeah woman to come and present him formally to local dignitaries, and make him do *something* – wave? – at the crowds packing the beach below. He had been expecting the Governor of course, as guest of honour, but he didn't like the way the man bounced in. Intiasar was surprisingly sweet-faced; everybody knew he'd spent time in foreign, off-island; it charmed far too many.

Don't bleed me dry and don't cause no scandal, that was the first thing Intiasar said, leaning against the good-good stove and eyeing the garlic bulbs. Not even a good afternoon, to rass. *And when time come to cheat on that pretty wife, keep it quiet. The men will appreciate it, but the women won't.*

Xavier regarded him patiently. Things had become slack with macaenus in recent years. Bad reputations. Too many parties for attention and clout. It wasted time, lacked dignity and made poor people nervous to come and eat, 'sake they never have the right party frock. His place was going to be different, but only a fool told a powerful fool he was a fool.

I only have one thing I want, Xavier said.

And what is that?

A randomised guest list. No one skips my line. No special treatment.

The Governor looked amused.

Aren't you a self-righteous creature.

Not even you.

Intiasar put a hand on his own cheek, a curiously feminine gesture. *You mean I going have to wait my turn to eat from your hand? My beating heart.*

He knew the Governor would need dishes bursting with vegetables when his time came, and moisture: gravy, goat's milk, syrup, ice water, sap, marrow, rum.

Alright. I have to respect any man who fucked Des'ree De Bernard-Mas and lived.

His master-teacher. First woman macaenus. Sitting outside with the other guests of honour, her nipples visible through her soft green robe. Incorrigible woman. Nya had looked sour, ushered in next to Des'ree. They *had* met before. He had hoped it was nothing more than the sunshine slamming into her face. Des'ree would have told him to punch this fool, quick o'clock. *And ascend, boy. Hurry up.*

She wouldn't have liked sitting next to Nya, either.

✱

Three days after he threw away the Governor's letter, Xavier was making bread in the kitchen when Salmonie Adolphus Barnes burst in, Io one rickety step behind him. Salmonie was a well-preserved man in his late seventies, with a huge red nose like a half-capsicum. He identified himself as Governor Intiasar's houseboy and began to read from a series of papers in a loud and self-important voice.

Xavier attended to his bread. He needed to add pimento berries and goat's cheese at the right time and in the right amount, which was an act of love, and therefore concentration.

What a blessed duty, bleated Salmonie. *To speak of the most romantic meal in the world! Seven dishes, as predicted auspicious for the couple. I am sure we could find Temple tales foretelling this special meal, macaenus!*

Xavier ignored him.

Naturally, explained Salmonie, the macaenus would be paid well, much in excess of his annual stipend. *Someone going come and take your measurements, sah, so luxurious robes can be made for the occasion.*

Not for this *macaenus*, said Xavier. His temper was gathering at the edge of his left eye.

Salmonie jumped as Moue swept past him with a sizzling pan of pink and purple octopus. Xavier nodded at three tentacles.

Five seconds more on two, and seven on the other.

Moue whisked the pan away.

The capsicum nose twitched. Salmonie looked beseechingly at Io, who was sitting in the corner on top of a very large upturned cook-pot.

Io gazed back. Vivid blue butterflies rustled in the milkweed bush outside the open window.

Salmonie began reading again. The Governor was *enchanted* that the holy macaenus had agreed to do a traditional walkround on the day before the wedding! Give the ordinary people a chance to choose the wedding-night feast ingredients.

What? roared Xavier. *What you said about ingredients?*

Io shook his head.

Salmonie spluttered. *You know what a walkround is, macaenus! You journey through Popisho and buy food and recipes from the masses and from that you make a menu—*

I know walkround!

Then you should be pleased *the Governor choose to honour the tradition!* Salmonie reached through the window and tried to catch an aqua butterfly. He missed, sucked his teeth and chuckled nervously. *Governor Intiasar has decided the food for his daughter must come from the land and the people. He not interested in any* elitist *meal.* He looked pleased with himself for saying so.

Get out of my place, said Xavier.

Your . . . The old man's chin wobbled. *What-what?*

Xavier tasted the cheese carefully, scattered a handful onto his dough and added hot pepper from his left palm.

Get out of my place before I kill you dead until you die.

Your – your – this place was purchased for you by the government of the islands of Popisho. By the people who pay taxes!

Tell him no-one-skips-my-line.

You – but – I—

Get out!

The man scuttled away, glancing at the sharp knives hanging on the blue kitchen wall, forgetting his papers on the table.

Xavier passed his hands over the bread. Moue broke chicken joints, *crack-crack*, and plunged pieces into three different marinades. Io unfolded himself and picked up Salmonie's notes.

Xavier tasted again.

Fool, he said conversationally.

Crick-crack.

Io tapped the papers.

He right, you know.

Crack.

It used to be part of a macaenus duty to walk round for all kind of rich wedding and celebration. The people's contribution increase the chance of the young wife breeding. Io laughed. *Ah, the fecundity of peasants! You been getting off light, Xavier Redchoose.*

Xavier didn't like people telling him things he already knew. Des'ree had dishonoured the walkround enough for one generation.

I told him ten years ago I wasn't working for no rich people, he snapped. *Why he bothering me now?*

Nothing more than election he trying to win.

Crack.

Xavier oiled the dough and placed it on a baking tray. The smell of the bread would greet diners at the door and make them think of their mothers and aunties. Old tricks. Food, it was nostalgia.

Hm, said Io. *I wonder why he trying so hard.*

Moue grunted. *Somebody coming for him. Twenty-odd years*

far too long for any man to be in power, but people don't like try
nothing new and clean.

That would be one hell of a change. Io squinted. *You going do*
this foolishness, Xav?

Xavier sagged. Intiasar hadn't put his mouth in macaenus
duty once, not for all this time; many would say he'd gotten
off lucky. A rebellion would look petty. People *wanted* the most
romantic meal in the world.

Since you taking his money *an' thing,* said Io.

He'd turned to retort, but his brother was gone, and all he
could hear was chuckling down the hall.

So the next morning, when Moue ran out of tomatoes, Xavier
had surprised them both by putting his knife down and stepping outside for the first time in seven months. Shuffling
towards the tomato vines, skin throbbing in the sun, marvel-
ling at what seemed like the garden's new-green loveliness,
he'd felt breathless and overwhelmed, as if peeled. He stroked
a sandy almond tree. He'd seen Moue drying the leftover
almond kernels, feeding them to the chickens and the staring
school children loitering on the beach. Applying aloe to Chse's
fingernails, to stop her biting them.

Moue was one of many who stood for him while he broke.

When he got back, she snatched the warm fruit from his
hands, her eyes wet.

About time, she said. *Don't stop now. Go down to the damn*
beach.

He felt as if his ankles were tied together, heart shrieking,
perspiring ferociously, clambering towards the pink sand. He
managed twenty minutes, the heat too bright on the back of his
hands, astonished to be trailing through a gossamer sea he'd

almost forgotten, when a man passed by, lugging a bundle of brilliant tie-dyed cloth. The colour so reminded Xavier of Nya's favourite robe, he had to sit down in the shallows and pant.

*

He forced himself out every day now; had done, for nearly a fortnight. Men whispered, excited at his return. Women flirted shamelessly; he didn't see them. The walks were longer each time, wading to his thighs in the sea, gulping the air and contemplating the old harbour where the local canoes had once delivered Leo Brenteninton's toys. He remembered running down there as a young boy, pushing like the others to catch a glimpse of the unloading, scooting back to his parents to beg a few coins. The government put a stop to all that. These days, it was a vast operation: hundreds, even thousands of toys, the gossips said, straight from the factories, over to a big warehouse on the Dead Islands and the foreign ships swooped in three times a year to empty it. Some people didn't remember it being any other way.

Had Intiasar never run to the shore and towards the boats, when he was small?

You going be alright, Io murmured each time Xavier staggered back to the Torn Poem, swallowing mouthfuls of thick, panicked spittle, rearranging his sweaty clothing.

Xavier attempted a laugh; coughed instead.

Absolutely, said Io firmly. *You soon see. And when you go walkround next week, I come with you.*

And still, Nya had not arrived.

Wah, the gossips said. *Macaenus come back to us, but he wife still heavy 'pon him.*

Dawn was due.

Xavier walked out of the garden and back towards the restaurant in the new light. The cod was calling: salt grains gathered in the lines of his palms. A thin stream of music echoed out towards the water. Three radio stations were playing the national anthem, seconds behind each other.

He only listened to the radio when he had to, but it was hard to avoid. There was one in every house and on every street corner, blaring noise and gossip; merry but dull interviews with local musicians; maddeningly obsequious chats with government officials, thanking the gods for this year's crop and that year's blessed Temple chorus. They used to try to get him on, these people, but his permanent answer was no; was he to be reduced to a recipe, asked what *inspired* him? How to answer these questions?

He knew he was being impatient: people *did* try to be honest and brave. They called up to complain about the way that things were all the time; old-timers rang to showcase their clever grandchildren. *This child can talk, boy. Listen him! How many egg you give me for twenty word out of this child mouth? Fresh, mind you! Fresh!* But discussions inevitably devolved. He could hear the exact moment an argument frayed, when it became about feelings, still pretending to be facts.

Argument was in his people's blood, their history; they should do better than this.

Popisho
o islands we adore
every day and more

In the kitchen, he placed his hands on the fish. Salt thickened under his clean fingernails, sifting down his wrists and filtering out onto the fish belly. He closed his eyes. Too much: he must concentrate, to slow the flow. Take his time. He'd weight the flesh with a smooth, flat stone and leave it in the sun and wind behind the restaurant.

One whole cod side covered. Saltfish, like his ancestors made it, to preserve scarce protein sources. Salt grains falling from his hands, thick on the work surface, falling onto the floor, making it white, falling onto his bare feet. He flipped the fish.

Behind him, a crackling sound.

A tipping-tapping, creaking.

The hairs on his neck, prickling.

Xavier?

A wet sound, like something dragging its teats across the floor.

O, Xavier, come see me, nah.

He whipped around, fists salt-encrusted, crouched and panting. The fish slipped, hung, half on, half off the table. He gulped air; hiccuped violently.

The kitchen echoed back at him, empty.

Beneath his bare feet, he could feel the stones warming with the imminent heat of the day.

Xavier Redchoose sat down on his kitchen floor, closed his eyes and let his hands dangle.

He didn't miss his wife at all. He thought of her, often. But it was hardly the same thing.

✱

Everyone in Popisho was born with a little something-something, boy, a little something *extra*. The local name was cors. Magic, but more than magic. A gift, nah? Yes. From the gods: a thing so inexpressibly your own.

The Council of the Obeah Fatidique was made up only of women, who existed solely to curate magic. The gods made no mistakes, but they *were* notoriously mischievous, and their messages could be confusing. Obeah women were ancient, even when young, and they *smelled* conception, an instinct passed on through centuries. Some women only realised they breeding when a local obeah woman hintfully invited herself for supper; this same golden-robed woman might have come to their family for generations, mother after mother; would have identified their own cors, when they were small.

No one watched a pregnancy like an obeah woman: counting new hairs on the back of the hand; walking curious fingers up the thigh to new port wine stains; commiseration with early leaking nipples; bringing perfumed fruit for that metallic taste in the mouth; reassurance when orgasms turned the belly a pointy shape; melasma on the cheekbones. And oh! when that baby push out and navel string was cut, the hunt was on for cors.

Some kinds of magic were immediately obvious – multiple limbs and prodigious strength, an extra row of teeth or the kind of height you could use for a ladder. Other babies arrived with subtler gifts, to be deciphered slowly: permanently pleasant breath, hair like thick silk with never a tangle, the balance of a cat, or look, my child can turn coconut water into any other taste you want! Xavier's old friend Entaly had musical earlobes and three buttock-cheeks. Moue got tipsy on butterflies one night and told Xavier her cors – a row of extra taste buds, and try as she might, she was immune to the nefarious effects of liquor. Xavier wondered which look-close obeah woman had found *that* on her.

Mental accoutrement was rarer, but it happened – the ability to tell the future; time-juggling triplets; toddlers moving objects with a careless thought or setting angry fires. All this mind-cors made good money, but parents had to use extra discipline in the rearing. One act of youthful rebellion could be unfortunate – a girl down Dukuyaie killed her mother with a spiteful thought after the mother banned her from dancing with her belly-skin out-of-doors. Thank the gods, her sister was standing right there with her cors to restart a heart like a putt-putt engine.

New mothers wept when the process was over and the cors named and the golden robe didn't whisper through their rooms so regular. But Temple was open all day and all night, and the sound of obeah women singing was as perennial as birdsong.

It took the obeah women a long time to work out that Xavier could flavour food through the palms of his hands. At first he'd displayed no magic at all, despite everybody turning him over multiple times and peering into his orifices; much to his mother's anxiety. His mother Treiya Redchoose was the pragmatic daughter of a clumsy fisherman and could calm storms at sea. No stranger to poverty, she wanted *useful* cors for her sons, more than most mothers.

Io's gift wasn't too shabby: he could change the colour of things with just a touch, and he was very strong indeed. By the time Xavier was born, his brother was already charging a few coins here and there, sprucing up the walls of people's houses, refreshing the faded robes brought over by their mothers' friends, and hoisting machinery, sugar barrels and shark carcasses. Their father, Pewter, was the proud owner of a long black-and-silver prehensile tail that fluffed up when he spotted injustice. He used it to build schools and temples and to climb scaffolding without a ladder.

When Xavier was nine, and still not showing a single sign of magic in any part of him, Pewter was underpaid by a crooked employer. Pewter whipped the man with his tail and then his fists until the fool bawled out. No matter the injustice, Pewter developed a bad reputation and work dried up. Treiya fretted about feeding her sons and let her husband know about it. Io missed school, changing the colour of putt-putts, old shoes and flower arrangements for anyone who could pay him. Treiya said her children needed education. *No*, said Pewter. *They need to be men.* Treiya sucked her teeth loudly and went to work long hours with the fishermen at the local beach. Pewter had no regular work, but he still expected supper.

I tired, said Treiya. *Come here, Xav, let me show you.*

So Xavier took over the family cooking. He surprised himself by easily mimicking Treiya's movements over the fire, using the limited cupboard as she instructed, and enjoyed tending her modest but very well-kept garden. Pewter muttered about it being a woman's work, but he sure did suck the bones in the fried chicken-back, make a pile of bone dust in the corner of the plate, and hug Xavier under his armpit. It was Pewter, belching contentedly, who first asked if anybody else notice that the fish have plenty flavour even when no hot pepper not in the house and wah, you don't notice the honey jar never finish . . . ?

He fell silent. The whole family sat up and stared. Xavier looked back solemnly. Io beamed and Treiya took a breath.

Go fetch that damn obeah woman, Treiya said to Io.

When she arrived, the obeah woman seized Xavier's wrists.

You never notice?

What? said Xavier. The flavouring thing happened like any other bodily function. You didn't report spitting or defecation to the obeah woman. It felt . . . private.

Oh my gods, said Treiya.

The obeah woman sorted through their pantry, taking out a pack of Treiya's precious corn flour and sending an obliging Io to buy some very cold butter.

Quick-bread? asked Xavier.

The obeah woman smiled and nodded, cutting butter into lumps. She let Xavier rub it into the flour. *Don't add no salt, now.* He had to think about that hard, to stop the cors. When the dough was done, the obeah woman rolled it out and cut five rounds. She greased a skillet, ignoring Treiya's sighs at her temerity, just come take over people kitchen.

Alright, boy. Give me five different flavour.

Xavier hesitated then passed his left hand over the first quick-bread. Everybody squinted as the corners of his already brown hands became browner.

Cinnamon, Xavier said and chose another round. *Cardamom, that big seed one. Um.* He liked the sudden smiling in the obeah woman's eyes.

The whole family gawped at him from the dining table.

Do crab, Xav, called Io.

Xavier snorted. *I can't do animals.* What might an obeah woman like eating? *Ginger, lime and sugar.*

Well, kiss my neck, exclaimed Pewter.

Hot Jack pepper. He felt confident now. There was only one more piece of dough, so it needed to be good. *Cocoa seed and mint leaves.*

The obeah woman shook her head. Family sometimes spotted cors before the Obeah Fatidique; however it happened, it was wonderful to see magic reveal itself.

Look at the light in your face, she said.

Xavier said he could put garlic in a chicken's bottom if she wanted him to, which was quite rude but also witty, because everybody knew that people who ate chicken bottoms talked too much. Io dissolved into laughter. The obeah woman cuffed Xavier playfully.

You going make an excellent husband for some lucky woman, she said. *Cooking-cors rare as hell in a man.*

Treiya snatched back her skillet and fried up the quick-bread. They ate the five rounds warm, murmuring at the clear, delicious flavours, but not before Io made each piece a different colour, so they'd remember which was which. Everyone seemed pleased, Pewter rubbing his son's back and saying it was *he* seen it first you know, *yes, baba!* and his mother, her cheeks all swollen with pride.

Looking very thoughtful indeed.

2

Anise slept badly and woke to the sound of splintering wood. She rolled over to the middle of the cold pallet. The room was dark, and Tan-Tan was missing. She sat up.

'Tan-Tan?'

No answer. Just the muffled sound of panting and sawing and the great mass of her husband on the other side of the bedroom. She knew it was him, better than she might have known herself; ten years lying back on this pallet, enjoying him moisturising his stomach and legs. He used to come over to her, smiling and nudging.

Do my back, Anise.

Gods, Tan-Tan! Make me sleep now, man!

Him, laughing: *You not sleeping. You watching me.*

Her arms outstretched: *Come and kiss me.*

Even during those early days, he rarely slid back into her arms once he was out of them. He was a self-contained man. Punctual in his work, and everything else. She'd admired his responsibility. It made her feel safe. But what might happen to the world, 'sake of a single act of spontaneity?

'Tan-Tan?'

Scrape. Snap.

'What you *doing*?'

She searched for the oil lamp next to the pallet. Struck a festering, weak light, applied it to the wick, and lifted the lamp so she could see him better.

He was kneeling on the floor, ripping up the wooden boards.

Anise stared, her scalp tightening. He didn't want the whole floor, he wanted a single plank – and he was destroying its neighbours to prise it free. Before she knew what she was doing, she was on her feet and across the room, shivering in the early morning chill, clawing at his shoulders.

'No! No!'

Tan-Tan shrugged her away, hands twisting, jaw straining. She stumbled backward two paces. He was bare-chested and she smelled his morning breath. Straight out of bed then, and to this task. Had he even taken time to piss? There was something frightening about a man so inexorable. She sprang on him again, pulling and panting. It might be too late to save the precious wood, but she would not stand and watch it happen.

'Leave it, *leave* it!'

Tan-Tan got to his feet, cradling pieces of gouged wood, holding her at bay with the other arm. He moved towards the heavy window. She followed him, snatching at the jagged edges of the plank. Perhaps she could salvage a tiny remainder, could run far away from here with one sliver. If she fought hard enough, she could even stop that heavy tread.

'Don't do this, Tan-Tan! I said no! *Please!*'

She clung; he dragged her behind him. She might have been a fly. Surely someone would hear her crying out and come. Mas' Bucky and his two sons, from over the road. But even if they trampled through her front garden and up the veranda steps this minute, it would still be too late to stop Tan-Tan flinging the wood through the window.

She had to stop the very act of discarding. It would hurt them too much.

Silver light hissed around her fists. She was fully awake

26

now and concentrating. She wasn't strong enough to hold him back, but she could do something else.

Anise Latibeaudearre-Joseph reached up for the back of her husband's neck and stroked her fingertip across his tender skin.

Tan-Tan jolted to a halt. His throat quivered like a cockerel's comb.

Outside in the yard, a crackle of ball lightning bounced across the grass, illuminating the mottled orchid plants.

Tan-Tan took another step forward. She pressed liquid energy into his body. She felt it bubbling out of her and into his flesh.

'Don't *do* this.'

Silver light ran up the back of his skull, haloing his dark hair. His thin laughter shook them both.

'What is *wrong* with you, Tan-Tan?'

He dropped the pieces of wood and she scrabbled through them, trying to touch all of them, ignoring the bite of splinters.

✱

Her first pregnancy had been in the cool season, seven years ago. Tan-Tan threw warm patches of air across the house, where they floated like seaweed, and she had pulled them around her shoulders when she felt a chill. By the time the sun came back, she'd grown bulbous and irritated, so he massaged her knees and shaved her hair low, because that was the way she liked it and the pregnancy made it grow thicker and faster than usual, sitting on the veranda, all soaped up, Tan-Tan making theatre, flourishing the straight razor, people going by and smiling and calling out.

Gyal too pretty to bald-off her head! the men called and Tan-Tan told them watch it now, boy.

She had smelled different. Gamy, which was not to say unpleasant. She felt compelled to show him her teeth and flash her eyes and hold grudges. Her mind filled with guilty thoughts she knew were normal, from listening to the secrets of so many women clients. Fantasies of eating the baby, like the local cats, afterbirth and all. Of dropping it, losing it, compressing its head between her thumbs. In the last month she wouldn't let her husband near her stomach, nipping when he tried, once drawing blood in the web between his second and third fingers. When he remonstrated, he seemed the most foolish man in the world, then minutes later, she found herself apologising, healing the bite, puzzled at her own behaviour. How would she be at birth, getting on so? Howling, chuffing, sweating? As quiet and dangerous as she felt?

In the meantime, she enjoyed him admiring her. *This is a mother*, he announced to their friends. *Watch her, nah!*

Labour surprised her: the depth of it, the high smell of her armpits, the concentration necessary. These things were less familiar and more frightening than the pain. Too long: she knew. As day and night stretched on, fear crept into the room. Her master-teacher Ingrid huddled with her anxious, praying mother, murmuring. Anise could feel her lips cracking. Had some part of her warring, defensive self known there was something wrong? Tan-Tan sat in the kitchen, gripping the edge of the table. She felt his anger under the blanket with her and wanted to kick it away. How could he, how dare he blame her?

It was Ingrid who found their child in between the rocking chair and the pallet, as small animals and twilight drew closer to the house. Holding the dozing Anise's hand, chanting low under her breath, Anise's mother on the other side, head nodding sleepily, the young obeah woman felt herself watched.

Ingrid Durande decided it was a girl-child because the eye-balls were so big and luminous, sitting disembodied in a pool of liquid, sinking into the wooden floor. The eyes blazed once, twice and were done. Ingrid used a clean rag to sop up as much of the strange child as she could, then cradled the eyeballs in her hands and went down to the beach. She buried them under a sea grape tree and cried.

Four of them pass through Anise: these wet things that will not hold. They leak out of her and across the bedroom and sink into the same plank, until the wood buckles, and each time, Ingrid takes what is left. Fingers. A piece of skull. She buries them under the sea grape tree and tells Anise not to worry. *Trust me*, she says. *Let me bear it for you.*

Anise, she trusts her teacher. Her closest friend.

She wonders what they lack, she and Tan-Tan. Some vital chemical or core belief? Is there a poison they synthesise together? Are the gods screaming advice from somewhere in the sky?

She tried to sit at altar to hear them, but the silence was absolute.

No, she said, when Tan-Tan asked if she would try a fifth time. Over a year ago, now. It took most of her to say so. *Alright*, he said. He didn't fight her. And she is grateful. But he is *angry*, oh, so angry and quiet and what, o gods, to do about that?

✱

Anise sat on the ruined bedroom floor, listening to her husband in the kitchen: stoking the fire, the hiss of fire-dye. He liked to make morning prayer over it, feeding handwritten blessings to the flame, then smoking honey bush with his mug of black chocolate and his right leg crossed over his left leg, looking out at the mountains above Lukia, the capital town of Dukuyaie. He generally sought privacy for his ablutions, but these days his morning movements made her want to scream: the scraping sounds, the clinking, the ring of his lip-piercing against the mug, the poker stabbing the fire, punctuating the silence between them. Her girlfriends put their hands on their hips and said selfish, and some days she wanted to shake him, but despite the size of her pain, she couldn't pretend it was she-one mourning for these children.

She examined the decimated floorboards, considered lying down and putting her cheek against them; wrestled her attention back to the kitchen sounds. There was something quite correct and *right* about a man so sad he made bad decisions.

Is that so?

That angry little voice inside her head only crept up when she was tired. Answering usually sent it away again.

Hush, now.

She opened the bedroom door. Paused, tiptoed, listened again. She was like the halves of two women glued together: paper shoulders, stinging-wasp waist, small breasts. Sitting down, people were drawn to her huge, dark eyes, the thick eyelashes so exposed by her bald head. But when she stood up, the men smiled at her hips. Rounded and flared they were, juicy thighs rubbing together as she walked, everything as heavy and tight as when she was a girl. Run, dance, slap, not a quiver; her cellulite was like ripples on water. She used to wear suck-on skirts in bright reds and greens so everyone could appreciate the contrast between her waist and hips and wonder about the secret triangle in the midst of it all and Tan-Tan could think, *mine, all for me*. He came home to kiss her ripples. She was privately gleeful when he sprouted a pimple because she liked to squeeze them.

All before they began to breed water children and Anise changed into funeral white and never stopped wearing it.

He worked too hard, weaving cloth for boat sails, for dolly-baby clothing and yellow school uniforms and indigo-blue factory worker uniforms and check-print maid uniforms and sheets and tablecloths and at his part-time foreman job at the Dukuyaie toy factory. He used to be so happy at the loom, now he snapped the thread and sucked his teeth and didn't appreciate beautiful things.

She found him sitting on a stool on the front veranda, puffing clouds of white smoke into the air. She slipped onto the floor next to him and waited.

'What?' he said, eventually.

She looked up, without speaking. What should her first question be?

'What,' he said again, as if it was not an enquiry at all, but something harmless, like aubergine or ambergris.

'Why you did it?'

'What?'

'Tan-Tan.'

'*What?*'

She struggled to remain kind; he was the sort of man who thought there was no good from feeling too much and what did he allow himself anyway, besides rage?

She put her cheek on his knee, and he shivered, as if threatened by an ocean undertow.

They looked out at the dark spines of the mountains.

She pressed her cheek into his knee, no cors this time, just trying to love him. He shook and shuddered. She couldn't remember their last lovemaking. There had been none of that since she said no to his children. When she reached out for him at night, he smiled into her neck, kissed the corner of her mouth, shifted his pelvis so her hands slid away, turned his back, and she was left in the company of his untouchable shoulders.

She could see him watching the wooden floor in the moonlight.

The celibacy had dried her skin and made the ends of her hair brittle as old leaves. She handled her body as if it were wooden, washing it without noticing its smells or textures.

She reached up for his hands and placed them on top of her head. They lay there like dead things. She kissed them; anything to move him past this dreadful storm shaking.

'Tan-Tan,' she whispered, again and again. If only he could speak, they might begin to heal.

'What?' he said and neither of them found an answer and the day moved on and he shifted her half-dozing head from his knee and stepped over her and away, trailing through the yard, the snick-shut of the gate behind him, heavy work bag on his shoulder.

She sat sleepy, watching him leave, her chin pressed against the stool. Occasionally she stroked her own scalp. She would get up very soon and shave her head. It was too bad, lying around like this.

Move your lazy self!

That snappish voice.

Still, she sat.

A light came on in the house next door. Her old woman neighbour trundled onto the dark veranda, swinging a lit red lamp. She hung it on a nail and began to examine the silky milkweed on her trellis. Anise sat up. She *was* a one: fuchsia robe, heavy

and rich, skirts set out a-plenty, vulture neck, a chignon of thinning, glossy hair. An early riser, but then old women usually were;
would she eventually get up so early she never went to bed? Anise
wondered if she might look so magnificent at the same age.

You don't look so good now.

Her own thought startled her with its cruelty.

Her neighbour glanced up from the milkweed and waved.
Anise waved back. The old lady was tremendously house-
proud, regularly cleaning with rags or sweeping, but that didn't
change the overgrown madness of her passionflower vines,
heavy and ripe for hummingbirds and bees, or the state of her
snaggle-toothed porch steps. She'd offered Tan-Tan's help more
than once, but the old lady merely shook her head and pressed
sorrel tea and slivers of goat's cheese into her hands. *I don't
get no children*, she said. *And a woman with no children learns
to accept many things.* Anise could almost see the pain sitting
between them, like a corporeal thing, making the hot air shiver.

The old lady – and it was ridiculous that she never remembered her name – was the only one who truly understood, unlike
her girl cousin Bonamie, so full of advice and stories of miracles.

This one try six times, Anise, and then she get a baby!

If somebody buy the right kind of poultice . . .

Relax, just relax.

Bonamie didn't say the word: *mule*. That colloquialism for
barren women. Mule. A short jook of a word. Anise didn't want
to hear about miracles; she wanted to rip apart the streets, looking for mules. What did *they* have to say about poultices and
the right number of times to try before you told your husband
no, and about how that word on its own was so big it could lock
down all the other words in a house?

Light curved over the hills. The old lady's shoulders clicked and clacked, moving across the veranda. Dogs barked. It was time to get up and greet the day.

The old woman sat down heavily and began to spread something in front of her on the porch table. Busy, sweeping, mosaic hands. Anise squinted.

The old woman had picked sleeping butterflies out of the crevices of her trellis and out of the corners of the stone porch wall and laid out what she found like breakfast: delicate pink and white wings, antennae, black thoraxes. She began to eat them, like sweets, smiling and swallowing rapidly. She waved again.

Anise waved back. It was too early in the morning for butterfly, and sleeping butterfly at that, but she supposed the woman *was* just a little bit lonely.

Butterflies were like alcohol. The heat of good wine in a burnt orange butterfly. The cool swallow of rare ship-bought vodka in clear, white and blue beauties, the kind that skimmed the waves until you didn't know where water began and insect ended. It took practice to pluck them from the sky and eat them alive. If you didn't know how, you found yourself coughing dust, a puzzled creature beating wings in your throat, scales sticking to your teeth. But when you developed the knack, butterfly warmed the stomach and spun the room. If you took too much, they made you vomit, crashed you into bushes and doors, made you alternately merry and lachrymose. When you pulled a butterfly from the air, there was something jaunty about it, something *fun*.

Not like deep-cured moth, from indigent hands.

Most normal moths were safe, if bland, nobody bothered with them. The danger was in the bigger ones: eight or ten inches

34

across, elaborate, hung for weeks, flaking and dark, bred in the Dead Islands. That kind of moth killed you over time, like revenge.

But before you died, you were sanctified.

So said the moth eaters.

She'd seen moth eaters and it wasn't pretty.

She stole a last glance at her neighbour. She'd eaten all the pink and white wings and was napping contentedly in her chair, mouth ajar, hand dangling.

Five years ago the government had tried to eradicate all Lepidoptera, but the insects fought back as if the cull had birthed a consciousness. They bred at a terrific rate, six hundred, seven hundred per cent the usual amount, and in even more splendid, eye-singeing colours and patterns. It was a ridiculous and joyful time, butterflies thick on the streets, racing up and down the skies, like soldiers in rank; gathering on quarrelsome radios inside people's houses, so impenetrable they drowned out the music; rare day-moths prancing on washing lines, on the knobbly knees of grandmothers, following the *scroops* of sandals, each one crushed beneath a heel replaced, it seemed, with ten more; butterflies landing in ladies' church hats; thousands of tiny moths balancing on waiters' trays in the evenings. Children reached out into the air to try their first blues and blacks and aquamarines; young men romanticised the beautiful chaos, bursting through clouds of multicoloured butterflies to declare their passions. Anise had loved the abandon and pomp of it. It was only when the cull stopped that the insects reduced their ranks to normal.

She laughed softly at the memory.

They would be alright, in time, she and Tan-Tan. Let more time pass. She had the skill necessary to care for a man in grief.

35

Old people said the gods didn't send you more than you could handle. Adversity was good for a marriage, surely? It would make them stronger.

If you say so.

She pushed the sarcasm away. An owl skimmed above her, on its way home after hunting. The old lady's head came up off her chest.

'O-Anise, oy.'

'Morning.'

'I have something for you, child.' The woman's teeth sawed, as if the words were granite. She thrust handfuls of fruit forward: fat, green limes it looked like. Oranges. Yellow guavas. A good reason to rise up.

'How you always have such beautiful things?'

'Come, nah.'

Anise walked across. The fruit smelled wonderful. The old woman piled it into her hands, pushing Anise's palms back into her chest so nothing fell, wrinkling her nose and speaking rapidly, the smell of butterflies on her breath.

'Your husband have another woman, alongside you.'

Anise's ears burned. It was a curious sensation, as if deafness was due but delayed on the road. The limes felt smooth in her hands, the guava rough.

'What?'

The old woman said the next sentence even faster, as if the words were strung together with netting rope.

'Tan-Tan have another woman, and she pregnant to bursting, like a plum.'

'Oh,' said Anise.

She liked to think of herself as a rebel insect when bad things happened.

3

'Romanza, get up.'

Grunting, sniffling sounds.

'Romanza, man. Rise up, nah!'

The sniffles were coming from him. The voice calling his name was familiar, but he was so *very* nauseous from the poison last night. He opened gluey lips; his voice seemed far away from his mouth.

'Romanza, I *neeeeed* you!'

'Mmm.'

'*Zaza!*'

Romanza Intiasar raised his head and peered down through the branches of the mango tree where he was lying. The young woman standing underneath scowled up at him. Sonteine. He groaned. What foolishness now, so very early in the morning?

'Romanza, serious things. Come down.'

He tried to obey. After all, his twin was the only person in his family who still spoke to him and he was very fond of her. He sat up carefully, balanced in the tree's fork, forty feet up. Arms like elastic bands. His knees felt mildewed. He coughed, grimacing at his sore throat. Pilar would have something to say about that, he could hear him now.

Mmm-hmm. Gallivanting the streets all night. Mind people hold you and give you more than a sore throat.

He smiled; despite Pilar's dire warnings, he knew the man was proud of him.

Below him, Sonteine stamped.

'Wait, Sonte. Gods.' The words were impatient, but he wasn't.

'Your bumbo. I coming up to get you.'

She seemed to mean it, alright.

He had taught her how to climb, so he wasn't concerned about her falling, although she did look remarkably oily this morning, if he could trust his eyes in the brightening light.

'I don't believe you making me climb and scratch up myself, especially right *now*!'

Up she came, smooth and steady, talking to him and the tree. He fought sleep. Sometimes he was tempted to tell his twin about his late-night trips into town. The audacity of his mission would delight her. But he also knew she'd talk it out the minute she left the bush – certainly to Dandu. He couldn't have that.

Women liked to put their hands in his long black hair, pulling out the golden strands as gifts, thinking him young and harmless, telling him their business. *Look how he eye dark*, they said. Generally, men told stories to boast, but women were different. They wanted to look at their words in the air and extract the meaning, and if you shut up and listened, they'd tell you very interesting things indeed.

Nobody would take his messages seriously if they knew who and what he was. He grinned sleepily. Most of the fun was in the secrecy, and he certainly didn't want the attention. Unlike some bastards, who just deserved it. Like Pony Brady.

Christopher 'Pony' Brady was councillor for the second district of Dukuyaie, and well known for his campaigns to protect young women from the sins of men. He'd once set his henchmen on a couple found kissing on the steps of Pastor Latibeaudearre's church. Said she looked too young for such slackness. Broke the boy's back and nobody complained when it came out later that the girl was a youthful-looking twenty-four years old and the boy's family too poor to raise a fuss.

Romanza had long smelled something on Pony. The councillor was a liar, and violent, so he'd kept his ear out for the man's business. Someone must know and eventually talk; last night, a woman with three arms did.

She told him in the corner of a dancehall, where black-kohled musicians played low every second day, on guitars that sobbed like women. She worked for Pony Brady, and she drank too much and mumbled so Romanza had to bend closer to hear her. *Shhh*, he crooned, as she fell asleep, arms stretched out across the table. She was lighter after she'd confided; people were better afterwards.

He knew she was telling him the truth, born as he was, knowing the difference between the truth and a lie.

He'd painted what she said across the courthouse and the town hall and oh, the streets and sides of houses, and on trees, everywhere, before he got tired, these brilliant orange ribbons.

PONY RAPES CHILDREN

Sonteine reached him, panting and shaking her head. She arranged herself on the sturdy branch opposite and tried to lie on her side like him, talking fast. He'd taught her better than that: you arranged yourself in the tree *before* you did anything else.

'Zaza, you hear about the—'

'Sonteine. Slow *down*.'

'Oh.'

She wobbled slightly and closed one eye to concentrate. Dimples and shining skin and frizzy dark hair and nineteen years old and no cors at all. That shocked people, but he thought it made her something rare.

She took a deep breath, equilibrium regained. A cloud hovered next to her ankle.

'You look tired,' she said.

'Yes.'

'You hear what happening in Lukia?'

'Is you wake me up.'

'You know Christopher Brady?'

'No.' He told lies like everyone else, but he didn't like to do it.

'You know him, man.'

'Do I?'

She scratched her oily shoulder. 'Big-time politician. Papa have him at the house a few years back.'

'Pony Brady. Mmm.'

'He been raping a nine-year-old *girl*. Zaza. I feel sick.'

'Yes.'

'Papa said they taking him in. Is that graffiti boy paint it all across the place.'

'Which graffiti boy?'

'You know, he paint all kind of scandal. Is him mash up that thieving bakery down in Pluie that was selling puss meat in their patty. He giving Pap a warm time. That boy is in the middle of everything.'

'How them know him not lying?'

'Everything he put his mouth into seem to work out. Pap say he sending police chief to go haul up Brady. Two witness come forward, as well as the girl mother look like she find the courage to talk out, and it might be even more children, have mercy. Pap cussing, say he don't have no time for this now, but I tell him he better see to it.'

Romanza nodded. 'I hope he does, Sonte.'

He was not convinced by their father or the police; what he

hoped was that someone else would take Pony into a private corner and beat him, pause to rest, then beat him some more.

'Anyway,' said Sonteine. 'I break out the house to come spend an hour with my brother before madness take over today.'

He tweaked her nose. 'Good.'

'Before *light* this morning them old lady and Mamma come wake me up to oil me!'

He winced: she was lying somehow, and it made his sore throat worse. Most people lied: for shame, fear, expedience. He didn't hold it against them, but Sonteine generally tried to avoid hurting him. It was probably a lie to soothe herself, then: a minimising. One of the worst kinds. He fixed his eyes on the cloud near her. He'd dreaded this whole conversation.

Her face fell. 'You not coming to my wedding tomorrow, are you?'

He coughed so hard they both had to cling to the tree. Momentarily, he wished he was something else.

'I didn't plan to come, no.'

Sonteine pulled her ear. He wondered if their mother noticed she did it when she was confused or sad. He doubted it.

'I guess Pap wouldn't let you in,' she sighed. 'Not even Temple *steps* though, Zaza?'

He didn't want her angry with their father the day before her wedding. Papa was a fool and a bigot, but he loved Sonteine. Some people learned best through love.

'How you feeling?' he asked. 'Frock ready? You ready?'

'Yes.'

He closed one eye at the acid shock in his jaw. '*Ow*. Sonte, man!' He prodded her waist. 'You think I could let a big *rass* lie like that pass? What *happen* to you?'

Her mouth turned down. 'Nothing.'

41

'*Ooooow*. Is what? You and Dandu fight?' He liked Dandu.
He would know what it meant when Sonteine pulled her earlobe.
She was silent, looking down.

'I was joking. You and he really in disagreement?'

'Noooo . . .'

The complicated lies made him dizzy. There was a problem
between them, but perhaps Dandu didn't know about it. He
coughed.

'You need to tell him if you have a worry.'

'I know.'

'Secrets can mash up love, Sonteine.'

She glared at him. 'I know, I *know*! Stop looking at me like
you know everything.'

'I do know everything.'

'Shut up.'

'You come here in my owna tree, come tell me to shut up?
Mind I fling you out.'

'Your tree? Not you say tree don't have no master?'

'When I said that?'

'All the *time*. Damn mad indigent!'

His mouth twitched.

'Girl, you don't even know.'

'Mad poison eater.'

She would laugh like this when she married Dandu; he was
quite certain of it.

'You better listen to me,' he teased. 'Long time I have a man,
you know.'

'You think man-and-man business have something to do with
woman?'

'Of course. Tell me what happen. Dandu don't like the frock?'

42

'Romanza!'

'The frock ugly? It make you look like a cake?'

'Idiot boy!' She laughed harder.

'He look at another pretty girl?'

'I kill him dead!'

'Ahhh, that is it! He look at another giiiiirl . . . !'

'You *know* is not that!' She was crying with laughter.

'The girl look better than you?'

'I hope the poison kill you.'

'*Ow!* Lie.'

'I hope you drop out this tree one night.'

'Sonte, that hurt like hell, you know!'

'I hope you fall in love with a *woman*.'

'Stop it!'

A lizard paused at the foot of the tree, looked up at the laughing siblings then trotted away to do lizard things.

✳

When they were children, his father took him away from the women after weekly Temple, leaving a pouting Sonteine with their mother and the maids. Over to Uncle Leo, Pap's best friend. They'd arrive at the rotund shack in the late afternoon. Leo usually saw them coming and called through the window.

Boy pickney, you want to see what Uncle Leo make today?

New toys, always! The acrid, warm smell of paint. Romanza would lie on his stomach in the single room, pushing boats under the chairs and between his father's feet, Intiasar teasing and complaining of tickling, the men drinking hard rum, eating butterflies straight from the air, talking business schemes. Romanza raced out into the yard, pulling toy carts behind him, Uncle Leo urging him on. Leo was the best adult he'd ever met, with his bushy beard. He could tell Uncle Leo only lied when he absolutely had to, and usually to avoid hurting someone's feelings. He was very gentle and listened to you quietly, not like most adults.

Faster, Zaza!

Popisho people don't like things too fast, his father snapped. Sometimes he took too much butterfly.

Lord, Bertie, give that a rest.

Who the rass you think you talking to?

Romanza crawled back under the table and sat cross-legged with his hands on his jaw and his fingers in his ears. He didn't like it when his father was mean. Uncle Leo said it was time for Bertie to take Zaza home, now, don't he think?

What you know about child? his father jeered. *I don't see Dandu anywhere.*

Bertie, man. He with his mother people. Best place for him. I can't grow a boy alone.

On their way home, his father held his hand.

So which toy you like, special boy? You think I could sell them to the whole world?

Romanza looked up at him, still worried.

Smile for me, boy. You have the best smile, make Papa feel good.

Old-time proverb said: *stones on the river bottom think the sun is wet*. For years, he'd thought of his father like that. Not bad, just stuck in a river-stone space, unable to see the world any other way.

Until Pilar came.

★

44

The lizard came back to watch Romanza, lying with his head on Pilar's chest. The morning sun played tricks with the leaves above them, casting golden spots and dappled stripes onto their skin, tearing through holes bitten into them by insects. Sunlight pretending to be rain, dripping off the branches. Pilar pointed his toe towards the lizard, and it bit him gently. Romanza watched him. His eyes were far away, as they often were; it was because he spent so much time with his ear to the earth. Sometimes you could wait half a day for Pilar to consider his words. His voice reminded Romanza of a crow, and his hair was glossy like the crow.

'Something happening today,' said Pilar.

Romanza curled a lock of Pilar's hair around his finger and tapped his nose gently. Pilar's eyebrows were like a bird, flying.

'Something important. You going to have to be wise.'

'Just *me* have to be wise, in the whole of Popisho?' Romanza teased him. 'That sound heavy.'

Pilar kissed him quiet.

'You not telling me no more?'

'I don't know it.'

Like screaming, that was.

'*Pilar.*'

'Sorry, lie drop out. What I mean is I *suspect* things, and because is suspicion, I don't want to tell you everything in my mind.' He smiled. 'I know I can't stop you, beloved, walking the road and into people business. But remember what I said.'

Romanza kissed his forehead. 'You never really said nothing at all.'

The lizard watched them from a sun patch.

4

Xavier got to his feet in the kitchen, shrugging off the imagined sound of Nya's dead voice. The front doors of the restaurant banged open for the arrival of four young women, all led by Moue, laughing, squabbling and moving around the house in avid formation. The sounds of routine whisked away the haunting, and he was grateful.

He needed to tend to the things of life today: the creak of Io's footsteps on the second floor with Chse; Moue's sharp commands; the sound of singing as the women began scrubbing every item they could get their hands on, very hard, yet carefully.

His place had to shine, oh yes. He'd do it himself, if need be.

He liked to think of people rising from their beds, picking up fire fans to stir the hearth stones for bread. There were three town bakeries and you could even get ship-bought bread over in Dukuyaie – the high-hill snobs snapped up that rubbish – but most people still made their own in the morning. The rumble of grinders for maize and the slip-slap-clap of the dough, flattened and passed from hand to hand, by women like his grandmother and her mother before them, clap-trapping the dough, pausing to plait up their hair, so it was dusted in flour and young women looked old. He often got maize flour in his dreadlocks, like a woman, and so many disapproved. Only homeless, worthless men choose 'locks.

He tried to ignore it all: the worship and the disapproval and the expectations.

He slipped out of the kitchen and headed upstairs. The

46

anthem and morning prayers and weather reports would be finished by now. He sat down in Nya's hammock and snapped on the radio. It was probably time to listen to what they were saying about him.

'Good morning, Popisho. I am Hah, daughter of Lus. Blessings on this new day! Gods waking up the sun! You ready for me?'

He'd overheard people in town talking about this woman running a radio show for the very first time, asking what the rass was the world coming to? He thoroughly approved of women doing what they wanted to do. *Fire in her belly though*, said the chatterers. She'd need that.

Hah sounded like she was smiling, not just pretending.

He moved restlessly, got out of the hammock.

'All kinds of things going on, baba! Everybody excited about wedding tomorrow! So much freeness Governor Intiasar putting on, I can't even count! Free food! Party and music! Presents for all the pickney-them! I never know a man so happy his daughter getting married! I hope Sonteine Intiasar gladdy-gladdy like her daddy!'

Xavier smiled. She was a dissenter, talking like a peasant on the radio. No speaky-spokey here, a rass.

'The day before a woman wedding day is a good day to think, Sonteine Intiasar!' Hah laughed wickedly. 'You still got a whole day and night to consider if that man is the *right* kind of somebody for you. Don't watch all the noise we making out here about your business! Man know what them getting when them married – a woman to run them house. Is woman who have to watch themselves, 'sake pretty frock and wedding party cloud judgement. Ladies, I *know* you all understand me! How much of you wish *you* did think twice?'

Xavier decided he liked this woman very much indeed.

'. . . while Sonteine thinking, everybody make sure you take advantage of Governor Intiasar and his largesse today, you hear me? I talking: eat hearty and drink deep.'

Except here it was, now.

'And watch out for that macaenus. Imagine, that *pretty-pretty* man doing old-time walkround today! What you know about *that*, ladies? Coming to a neighbourhood near you!'

Xavier sighed. Maybe he didn't like her that much.

There was a knock on his bedroom door.

Maybe he shouldn't go and do any of it. Maybe today of all days, Nya would finally come.

'You going know Xavier Redchoose when you see him. *Strapting* fellow, I hear.' More merry laughter. 'After Sonteine Intiasar done eat up her wedding feast I going to read out that menu right here, so all-you can know how to cook like macaenus.'

He snapped the radio off and stood, stroking the top of it. Glanced at Nya's hammock.

More knocking, harder this time.

He murmured yes, then said it louder.

The door cracked open. Much giggling, then a small hand bent around the door, holding a piece of paper. It was swiftly followed by a long thin arm, whipping almost six feet across the room. The paper waggled.

'Guess who, Uncle Xavier?'

She liked this trick. She'd started doing it after he told her running into his kitchen could be dangerous. Now she did it when she wanted to cheer him up.

'Now who is that? With such a lovely brown arm?'

More giggling. She had company. Then in a breathless rush: 'We can come? Olivianna mamma said she can eat breakfast here but first you have to wash her.'

'Come, come.' He'd done this washing before.

Chse entered, arm retracted and normal, followed by a dark girl with pink lungs slung on her hips like fleshy sacks.

'They get dirty this morning,' she said.

Xavier smiled. The child stared back, solemnly. One of the indigent people from the Dead Islands. You knew them by their scant, frayed clothing and steady gazing; most had lost their capacity to blink and live in houses. Theirs was a heavy consideration, as if a stone had decided to look at you, with all its knowledge of soil and sap and mineral and heat. He hadn't seen this little one for weeks and she'd become thin in too short a time. Hollow chest, stripped collarbones. He frowned as she walked towards him. Her belly looked swollen.

He helped her wash her lungs at the bathroom sink, hands unsure under her remorseless eyes. Could this be . . . *starvation*? On Popisho? The elders spoke of such travesty a very long time ago, when their ancestors forgot how to care for the land. The earth had protested: with tremors and ferocious drought. Hundreds died. Or so people said. How could this indigent girl be starving, with an abundant bush so open to her people?

And him, spending the day indulging fripperies?

Olivianna flapped her lungs and reminded him it was best to air-dry.

Perhaps she was eating too much poison. The indigent ate fruit, vegetables, tubers, insects, occasional meat – and poison. They built up slow immunity in their children: a single flake of blowfish dissolved in river water; one eighth of a manchioneal berry; a fingernail of green ackee. He'd asked Des'ree why.

Nobody know, she said.

He knew what to feed this child. He always knew. Cors was a

49

gift from the gods; so was he. As strange as that always was to think and to say and to feel.

He couldn't remember the first person who had whispered *macaenus* in his presence, only that once his mother began selling his food, his instincts had become legendary. He was ten when Miss-Mercy-down-the-road's headaches were stayed all to completion by his coconut cake with otaheite applesauce and twelve when mad Anastasia Brown stopped shitting on people's doorsteps after a dozen of his tamarind bonbons. *Nothing going sweet you like that young Redchoose boy food*, people said. Provided you could bear that look when he came into your kitchen. Like he was cooking not for your appetite, but your failings.

★

He took the children downstairs and hooked one of Moue's fresh-baked sweet potatoes out of the lit fire. Chse was set down at the table with a big half-potato of her own, topped with avocado chunks, crushed almonds, fresh tomatoes and fine-chopped, crunchy broccoli. He crushed the other half of the potato with cardamom seeds and added the oil from a lady-tears plant – both good for stomach upset – with a spoon of the peanut butter he'd made fresh yesterday.

He fed Olivianna himself, sitting on his lap. He wanted her to take her time. She needed to feel encased, protected. Her lungs swung. Chse pointed her foot into the air, chewing and stretching her leg until her sole was close to the ceiling, narrowly missing a large pile of ground yam and carrots. Xavier patted the mad leg and she lowered it.

'Uncle Xavier. Yesterday Olivianna help me pick the guests for next week!' It was her proud weekly task: practising her penmanship by copying twelve random names out of the cors record at the town hall, so he could invite them for their one macaenus meal.

Xavier grinned. 'Yes?' Oliviana must be a *special*-special friend. No one else had been given *this* honour.

Oliviana flapped the lungs. 'I get a name-o!'

More delighted arm-elongation from Chse. She waved a small bag, where she carefully kept the names. The vegetables trembled as the bag brushed them.

'Chse, behave.'

His niece pouted, and he waved a finger at her. She lowered the bag without mishap.

'I get a *name*!' said Oliviana.

'What is your name? Read it for me.'

Slips of paper dumped out and unfolded proudly. Oliviana read first.

'Jeremiah Jason Joaquin Jameson, thirty-two, of Pluie. Cors to make fire.'

'Very good. So we going send an invitation to Brother Jameson and hope he like the food and don't burn our flowers. Chse, you write down a name for me?'

'I give Oliviana more to choose because she is the guest!'

'Very good! But you have one?'

'Louise Sidony Heron, fifty-five. She is very old, Uncle.'

'Not so old. And what does her cors do?'

'. . . fifty-five of Lukia Town and her cors is to adjust her height to . . . to . . . *maximum* eighteen feet at time of record and minibrum fourteen inches.'

'Minimum. Well, we hope to fit her into our place or maybe she will get very small and we can save on food!'

Chse kicked out gleefully. Three burgundy carrots tumbled free.

'He said not to kick,' chided Olivianna. 'Sonteine Melody Ignoble Intiasar, nineteen, it don't have no cors for her.'

Goose pimples ran along his arms. He cleared his throat.

'Somebody tell you to say that name, Olivianna?'

'A man did come and said is a *special*.' The child looked pleased with herself.

'I give her the *special* name!' Chse embraced her friend; her arms flicked loose across the room, like fishing rods, smashing the carrots and the yams, yellow and purple skitter-scatter.

Beautiful arms.

Well, now. Intiasar was *all* kinds of serious, today. Just in case Xavier was tempted, as the old people might say, to try mash up Miss Sonteine's dolly-house.

I see you. I see who special to you.

Xavier sent the indigent child back to the bush with a letter for her mother, to come see her macaenus when she could, and talk about food.

✱

He didn't know why the gods made them chefs. He'd argued the matter with Des'ree. *If our purpose is to give our people pleasure, we could have been anything. Sculptors. Musicians. Puppeteers.*

Don't be silly, said Des'ree. *The first thing a obeah woman ever did was clean your mouth so she could jam you on your mamma titty. Nothing is as basic as food.*

Dancers?

Boy, I can't dance, and neither can you.

She could dance. She could do most things. He was a grown man and he still might tremble under her gaze.

All he could do was cook.

Most diners arrived at the Torn Poem alone and holding their breath. He went to the roof so he could see them coming in. Feel what they needed. Each guest could bring another, but most preferred to wait for their own special time, so people often ate alone, or gravitated to other chosen ones in the dining room. He'd seen the beginning of long-life friendships; irresistible affairs; deep conversations and women holding hands earnestly, telling old secrets. Love. Oh, so much laughter! Some had been known to faint at the doors of the dining room, or to stomp and complain, refusing seating until they touched his hand. He ignored the foolishness, though he did occasionally leave the kitchen to pass along the balcony during the evening, much to excited mutterings below. He hated it, but a certain amount of theatre was necessary. People could see he cared, and he could check the fresh white hibiscus were floating perfectly in earthen bowls on each table and make sure the burning citrus oil really was chasing away the mosquitoes.

This year, a man had come three times as guest to three different women, puffed up and winking at his staff, Io hanging by the kitchen door, restraining his amusement. *That lucky bastard reach again, Xav.*

Xavier believed the philanderer was at a disadvantage. The experience was meant to be singular. You dreamt macaenus food; you ate the dream; you dreamt of eating it again. But he admired the man's gusto: for life, for love. The women looked happy.

He barred the man when he tried for a fourth.

He could have served anytime, but he cooked at night because he liked the quiet; many and many plates, with time for good digestion. Dishes like lagoons, slopping rich with gravy and

excess; in the next hour, a single perfect square inch of something, and the waitresses whispering hush, so diners might concentrate on mouth and tongue. There was privacy in his place,
and calm. A tinkling, two-woman band in the corner: sitar and
a wall-drum, almost imperceptible, like insects he'd let indoors.
He only hired musicians who were lovers. It affected the sound.

Above it all, the torn poem tree branching across the ceiling,
its bright blue fruit dangling like ripe jewels. From the balcony
he watched the waitresses gesturing up at the tree at the end of
the evening, hushed and speaking with reverence.

And now we invite you to pick a poem.

The laughter and the exclaiming was his favourite part.

He had found the brown, flat seeds walking in Battisient
west, on a small, rocky beach that no one liked because it was
all rocks, just before he and Nya moved in. He didn't know
what they were, but as was his habit, brought them home anyway; pushed them into the soil by some old tomato vines and
forgot them. But Nya noticed.

*Xavier, there is a tree in the yard growing fast and growing
poetry. Come see.*

He went with her the third time she asked. The blue fruit was
surprisingly juiceless when peeled, a sentence in its belly.

eat honey goddess raw

What it mean?
I don't know. Nya's eyes danced.
All of them have words?
Yes! You ever see such a thing?
They sat together, breaking fruit open, reading the nonsense,
some stranger than others, laughing until her mouth turned

54

down. *None of them are finished.* She was suddenly inconsolable. *Is like the gods tried to write poetry, then tore it up and threw it away.*

Alright.

You don't see what I mean?

He wished he did, truly.

He replanted the tree in the middle of the dining room, hoping it would amuse her. When he announced the restaurant's name, she sighed.

I should change it?

Please yourself.

I thought it would please you.

Sighing.

Sometimes he found her peeling fruit and trying to finish the poetry.

★

He stood in the kitchen, watching the waitresses twisting and twittering in the garden, the last of the watery dawn turning their arms and shoulders grey. They were joined by several young men, all stamping and chattering together. He liked the sound of them. The path down to the beach looked even longer than usual. He could hear someone chopping wood round the back of the building.

You going to get love, Xav, Io said, when he'd started going out in public again. But facing this trek across Popisho, he wasn't so sure. What kind of macaenus hid away in grief and trembled under the sky?

He turned to watch Moue, feeling for a single imperfect chunk of onion, slicing it identical to its brothers. She was calculating,

55

he knew, given the larder contents, the ovens, the preparation time for ingredients she couldn't predict, how best to pack anything to go over to the Intiasar compound.

Serving was sacred work, he had no problem doing *that*, but Intiasar intended humiliation.

Moue would probably slip in a compress to mop his angry brow, knowing her.

The day was inevitable. He couldn't fight it anymore.

He turned the kitchen radio on. Moue only turned it off when he was there.

'—don't worry, sir.' Hah was still on. 'Governor Intiasar say he speaking to me on this very show soon-soon, and I going ask him about goat tax for you.'

'Wicked rass government not even taking no down payment.'

'Siiiir, beg you, take time with the *cursing*,' moaned Hah.

That sounded more like a radio host, doing what they did. Keeping people *polite*.

'And I want to know what the government going do with the crayfish in the river behind my house. You bite them and is like sugar. Intiasar coming down to my place to test the fish? Eh? You ever hear anything so, Miss Hah? Fish not to sweet.'

'Well, that is very strange, yes . . .'

'I need more Jack pepper,' Moue said. She wiped her hands on her apron and nodded at a paper-wrapped item near the sink. 'And the fisher-boy come back. Said to give you that, with his respect.'

Xavier picked up the package. It was surprisingly heavy.

'I think he outside. He still feel bad about Nya, macaenus.'

'You think I care how he *feel*, Moue.'

She lowered her head and slipped away, leaving the door behind her trembling.

The bag was creased and covered in fingerprints. He unplaited dried banana leaves and turned the object over, allowing himself a moment of excitement. It was a large, chipped rock. Perhaps it was something he'd never tasted before: something interesting, something elegiac. Such moments were rare, but they happened. There were edible rocks and soil, but this didn't look good to eat.

Xavier frowned.

A small, flat envelope fell free of the final leaf, onto the floor. He bent and picked it up, using his other hand to pull a burlap satchel from a nail on the wall and sling it across his body. It was all he would need for the walkround. People would happily deliver any other produce he chose.

Please gods, let it be more than rocks and nonsense.

Xavier tipped the contents of the flat package into his palm, hissed, dropped it and backed across the kitchen.

The fisher-boy had gifted him a moth.

He saw moth all the time, thick in the evening with mosquitoes, crickets, flying cockroaches, dangling lizards: all the small creatures of a Popisho night. He hardly registered them.

You had to take yourself and go and get the kind of moth *he* liked. Moth like this.

He crept forward, groping, peering at it. Nine-inch wingspan; a fat thorax. Butterflies clasped their wings together when resting; moths spread them out, inviting admiration. He picked it up. Yellow-brown scales flecked onto his fingers. It was a honeydew, would have lived on sugary liquid from particular leaves. How long had the boy saved money for this? Did the father know? He placed the insect on the kitchen counter. Ten years free of the damn things, and still people thought him lost.

He sucked the spittle off his bottom lip. He was salivating.

It was a great gift; a king of moth.

He began to move swiftly. His thick, battered notebook, four sharp pencils and a small, red leather pouch on a string he found in the back of a cupboard. He slid the book and pencils into his satchel, twirled the yellow moth tight – deft as a man rolling a cigarillo – and slipped it into the pouch. Pouch into right pocket.

He stood very tall, back straight.

'Xavier?'

Io calling.

✷

In the garden, most of the young people were gone. A single waitress sat on a bench, peeling the flesh off the fisher-boy's shoulder, the way another person might attempt seduction. Xavier saw a flash of white bone, heard a tap-tap sound as she flicked bone with her first finger and thumb. The boy grasped her waist; saw Xavier watching them; pushed her away so hard she gasped.

'Macaenus!'

Xavier kept walking. He could hear Io, muttering, 'Not *now*,' but the boy was blocking their way.

'*Macaenus!*'

He had a sense of Moue's arrival; her wide-eyed efforts to stop it all. Of legs and arms and flurry. If he just listened to the sea, all would be well. You couldn't go anywhere in Popisho without hearing the sea.

'Macaenus, you get what I leave you? Lady, you said you would give him – ! I *sorry*! That's all! *Sorry*, macaenus!'

Perhaps he felt the boy's fingertips, brushing his own shoulder, reaching into the bone.

He thought of his mother-in-law, pounding his door, one year ago today. Calling for him, and he'd never heard that sound in a person's voice before: how the fisher-boy found Nya in deep water and how small white fish come out of her ears, and sadness like weeds and *oh Xavier, she talk to you, she* talk *to you before . . . ?*

He and Io walked down the steps carved into the cliff side, towards the muttering ocean. Xavier slowed his stride to suit his brother's limp. They stood in front of the water. The dawn had finally burst, like squeezing a bruise: a yellow-violet light that made the white sand sparkle. Above them, the fisher-boy stood alone on the cliff, charcoal sticks for legs and arms.

The pouch. In his pocket, so Io couldn't see it. Holding. Moth. Yes.

So here he was, again.

✱

He was sixteen when he put himself forward for the testing, mostly because he couldn't take the nagging at home anymore. Nothing could have convinced his mother he wasn't macaenus. If Des'ree had ended up not saying so, Treiya Redchoose would have burst into her house and told her she was a liar.

Better you go ask, said Io. *Make her happy.*

Life with an unhappy mother was not good, they agreed that much.

So he went to Des'ree's restaurant over on Dukuyaie and asked in the bakery she ran and went back to the restaurant and asked the staff, who teased him. *Des'ree always have the young boys looking for her!*

He couldn't believe they were so disrespectful. Everyone

knew Des'ree De Bernard-Mas charmed in all flavours of the rainbow, ripped shark from the ocean, that she wore slivers of amber sewn into her underwear.

He found her on a day he wasn't looking, buying guava cheese and sucking a bag of ice like a street urchin. She was reaching for the same guava cheese as he was, and he was so startled, he dropped the suck-suck.

She eyed him.

The cheese seller, recognising the moment, looked as if he might vomit in anxiety for the boy.

Xavier cleared his throat. Everyone said the same thing when they applied; that was a mercy.

O macaenus. I can sit by you?

Des'ree put down the guava cheese, picked up a white onion and smelled its root.

Mm, she said, like she might kiss the onion.

O gods, said the cheese seller, and fanned himself. Xavier hadn't realised a grown woman could be so soft-eyed and succulent, especially this one, who scared grown men. Des'ree took a large bite of the onion and chewed calmly. Xavier and the cheese seller grimaced. Des'ree looked at Xavier like he was a scavenging thing of the sea.

I have all I need, boy. They beat you to it.

He turned away, flushed and hot, screaming at himself. Relieved? Astonished? It had not occurred to him that he would fail. At least to enter the testing. Everybody *said*. He didn't believe what everybody said. But at least to try?

She called after him.

Ask me again.

Heart in his throat.

What?

He deaf too, nah? She winked at the hyperventilating guava cheese man.

He couldn't. He'd given her all he had. But she was waiting.

I . . . can sit by you?

Cho, boy, you don't know what you asking.

Cho was an old word. It could be used as a compliment, to trivialise, to dismiss, or tenderly: coaxing a baby to eat or a man to lie down. She was making fun of him.

I can sit by you, macaenus?

She crunched the onion and laughed in his face.

He turned away again, wanting to piss and to hit something.

Is so you give up easy? You not going to handle my kitchen if you short a backbone. She was suddenly serious, even angry. *Ask me again, boy. And this time, think about how I look* good *and how you all sniff-sniffing me, like puppy dogs, reminding me how time passing. Ask again. Make it excellent.*

He didn't understand. He looked down at the brown freckles in her neckline. There were tiny lines at the top of her breasts, and he wondered if anyone could see them besides him.

I—

Well?

I don't know what you want.

She sighed, flapped a hand at him and threw the rest of the onion into a bush.

Sit by me, boy, or don't. I don't give a rass.

Yes?

Yes.

He walked away, swelling. Then turned back: *But you* said . . .

She shrugged. *I lied. You is the first little doggie to brave it.*

Rumour said Des'ree had chosen sixteen first-level acolytes from the archipelago, many more than usual. Five were from the Dead Islands: five! It was unheard of, even the *possibility* of an indigent macaenus. There was terrible grumbling.

But they were the chosen; her decisions were those of the gods.

They spent a year scattered among the obeah women, learning basic skills, before entering kitchens across Popisho. Four more years: washing dishes, cleaning floors, waiting tables, taking care of animals, cooking with scraps first, then better produce. Nobody told the diners their water was poured or their mess cleaned by a young person in macaenus testing. The cooks they worked for barely seemed to know.

The obeah women said humility was important.

He met no more than seven of his rivals ever; worked side by side with four. Only three-buttocked Entaly became a friend, when they were posted to the same kitchens repeatedly. He was content: young and strong and patient. Calm, he decided, whatever the outcome. He felt most himself in a restaurant, threading his way between tables, watching diners take their first mouthful, smiling when they were happy, like at home.

He'd not forgotten Des'ree – how could he, they whispered about her enough – but he tried not to *think* about her, or about the day she would cleave through them, leaving behind the tattered and wide-eyed who'd laboured just as hard. She came one afternoon: no drama, no warning. He looked up from roasting garlic and spotted her leaning on the counter, watching him, Entaly trembling next to her, Morris the chef-patron fawning. Morris had sneered when he first arrived: *You? Too skinny and quiet to be a macaenus, boy!*

Des'ree crooked one finger at Xavier. *Come, nah.*

He dropped his knife. He could hear Entaly gasp and her anxious chiming earlobes.

Des'ree glanced at her.

You, too. You're splendid.

Me? Entaly squeaked.

We going walkround.

Sweeping out, the three of them past a sweating Morris, Xavier felt lighter, despite his sticky garlic hands. Outside, Des'ree insisted he wipe them clean on her skirt. Entaly's eyes grew wider. Xavier tried to protest.

Why?

Because I said so, boy. She seemed to have grown younger. She didn't know his name.

That astonishing, hot afternoon: collecting the six she believed had a chance. Three boys, three girls. Xavier and Entaly. Dominique and Persemony. Martin and Sisie. He recited the names at night, like a small dirge. Which one? Who was fated, special, who had put themselves forward, for the best of reasons? They'd started out knowing it could be anyone in their generation. Now, it could only be one of six.

Was it him? He felt unremarkable, except for his mother's glee.

Des'ree made them walk all day. *We must walk with the people*, she said. *Be a song for them. A reminder the gods don't leave them, nor do they sleep.* They burst into small communities, fanfare through the streets – *macaenus come!* – Des'ree grasping women's elbows, roaring into their houses: *SHOW ME YOUR WOMEN!* Pushing aside the men, who were puffing up and holding their groins: *Don't puff your chest on me, boy – you know my chest better than yours. SHOW ME YOUR*

WOMEN! scattering children and goats, coming to a screeching halt in some hapless Battisient kitchen. *Sis, what you cook good in here?* Wiping banana draws – a kind of cornmeal pudding – off her lips; sticking a spoon into cook-pots; the lewd and whooping gestures. And how they loved her! So many jokes, and so much call-and-answer. He felt too quiet indeed, standing in the back of the others, taller than everyone else, watching pumped fists and celebration. Entaly had recovered from the shock, was brave enough to slap his back gleefully, he trying to smile but feeling no fun at all, and was this what you had to be? Des'ree, barking orders, beckoning the handsome bearded Dominique who had not forgotten to bring his knives with *him*, showing him off to the crowd: *Come over here, see my acolyte, he have a good hand!* Winking lasciviously. Dominique, flirting back. How could he *be* that brave? Des'ree preening and whispering: *Sis, show me how you mince your pepper so fine, how you chop so fast, girl?* and all the time, her swift fingers in the pot she really wanted, and braps, before you knew it, new taste or style on Des'ree's menu.

She was such a beautiful thief.

People knew the stories. Of macaenus who cooked not for love, or honour, but profit and pride. Each one brought their own sins to the kitchen.

Not him.

Years later, after he was named macaenus, he did a monthly walkround, creeping out under Nya's encouragement, feeling the title as if branded to his back, a wound only just healing. He was more confident, of course. Older. But he could not make himself loud. Stoosh, the peasants called him – the Torn Poem, the food – stoosh, meaning fancy and fanciful. Their haughtiness delighted him.

You eat Xavier Redchoose food? Man and a goat, that boy can cook!

I going try do it your way, you hear, brother? to the man serving him batter-bread, fluffy and dunked in tiny cups of thick, bitter-brewed chocolate on the roadside. *That alright?* Dipping into his pocket for money. Like you should.

Go on then, the man said. *Try, nah.*

He couldn't tell the last time he'd done walkround.

5

Anise hesitated at her front gate, thrumming her fingers along the wooden fence that separated her property from the road. Lukia Town spread in front of her, heaving like a carpet being beaten.

After the old lady had gone back inside, trailing fresh lime and butterfly breath, Anise pared her skull clean, like she did every morning, and slid on her heavy bangles. Her scalp glowed in the early sunshine.

She wanted to see Tan-Tan's eyes when she put the question to him.

Mule make the lady next door mad, or is true you a cheating bastard, Tan-Tan?

She gripped the fence, watching women with gleaming bare shoulders and arms walking past in twos and threes, heading for the town centre. Dukuyaie women were known for their long and supple arms and legs. It was the hills, and the walking up and down them from childhood: it made for length. Battisient women said it wasn't their arms *or* legs that made you know a Dukuyaie girl, but the smell of fish and money. Dukuyaie women pointed out that girls from Battisient always had something to *say*.

It was all true and yet not, in that way that things were.

Perhaps this rumour would break the silence between them. Tan-Tan would say: *no, how you could think that of me?* And she would say: *you shut me out, what am I supposed to think?* And they would talk about their children. He would be kind to her. Touch her hand, her body.

This day could still be good.

She was not a jealous woman. In their first years, when she saw Tan-Tan looking under his eyelashes at a pretty girl, handling his liquor mug nonchalantly, she'd complimented his taste.

Is alright, she said. *People are to look at.*

You *look?*

Some instinct had risen in her. Her mother said there would be small and necessary lies in marriage.

I have you to look at, she said.

Anise rubbed her shining head and stepped out into the thickening crowd. Men joined women, commenting on the day's events. Children cheered and yelled, free from school. Behind her, the fence seemed to flicker, like a river. People called out to her with affection and respect. She smiled back, keeping her head erect. She wouldn't be attending any of Governor Intiasar's propaganda today; he was just trying to sweet-up poor people and get them to vote, and more's the pity they couldn't see that. She'd planned a normal schedule of work. But the old lady's information had changed everything. So now she'd go over to her workspace, cancel her appointments, and visit Tan-Tan at the toy factory. Some things could not wait, and she didn't give one rass if he vex she go to his work and bother him.

✷

Her cors had come through when she was six years old, so fierce her father kept her away from strangers. She was a smiley, dark-eyed child, sociable and curious, the kind who reached out for hugs, ran around her father's church, delighted at the whole congregation patting her hair and face, everybody talking about how Pastor Lati child so pretty and clever. *Fast in other people business*, her mother said, but even she smiled at her little girl's merriment.

Then cors woke up and made itself a problem.

Anise's father stopped taking her along for his daily walk, pushed her hands away from other people, pushed her behind him when she came whirling into conversation: shoving, removing, scowling. It puzzled her, and then it made her sad. Because what was so wrong with telling people things she knew? Pointing out babies in unwed wombs, laughing at men with itchy feet and anuses, following behind strangers, asking if their belly running a two-minute mile? Everyday disorders were easy: the lilac-skinned organ-grinder chucking her cheek, smiling despite his terrible headache; the choir mistress who greeted her with a hug and menstrual cramps; the onset of indigestion, sunstroke, rashes, flu, croup, tonsillitis, sugar-in-your-blood.

You touched her, she knew.

Naturally, she didn't know the *name* for every disorder, but she liked this intimate comprehension of people's bodies, and also of her own body, silver energy sparkling in her chest and around her fingertips. She liked it all, despite her father's embarrassment. He said she was born rude anyway, with her questions and her disagreement and the blasphemous things she said about his faith. *Why you believe in one god, Papa? Most people don't.* Older, stamping her foot: *Why nobody never tell me my day-god? Everybody else at school have one! I bet you she female and you don't like that, do you, Papa?* Flouting his Christian rules, refusing Bible studies, arguing and banging the table at supper, Pastor Latibeaudearre raising his eyebrow and his hand: *You gone too far, now, Anise. Sit still and respect your mother.*

It was clear to her that she needed a master-teacher as soon as possible. Someone brave, who knew the gods intimately. At fourteen, she screwed up the courage to enter the cool of the nearest obeah Temple, mounting the ancient steps, heart beating, the burst of song through the small side door feeling so right and proper she ran the rest of the way in, flying towards the singing obeah women in their tender robes, weaving past disintegrating god-statues with names like Ganzie, Boonoonuhnus and Baxide. She was seized by the waist mid-stride by a small girl who informed her that her day-goddess was Jai, before she even had the chance to ask. The name of the goddess was deliciously fitting: clipped and clean, and Anise found herself babbling; that all she wanted was to heal people and be free.

Jai is very free. Let me show you her statue, Ingrid Durande said. *But* you *going have to learn how to breathe.*

How come you even in here, said Anise. *You're a child.*

I'm eight, but don't watch the age. I am *Obeah Fatidique, which mean is me run this Temple. With the others.* Ingrid stuck her tongue out. *You want to sit by me?*

Anise burst into laughter. Like a girl asking a boy to marry. Quite wrong.

I have to ask you.

Ingrid rolled her eyes. *Then ask and hurry up nah. You know you want to.*

Ingrid was born with the number twenty-nine on her torso. You could see the curve of the number two peeping on her collarbone, the bottom end of the nine when her tunic rode up. The numbers were a slightly darker pigmentation than the rest of her skin.

Mamma say the obeah woman who take me out start cursing

69

as soon as she see it. Ingrid flung her hands in the air and pulled a comical face. *'What the hell this mean, now?'*

Baby Ingrid hadn't been as hard to diagnose as the obeah woman feared; the child just had to learn her numbers.

Seventy-five, two-year-old Ingrid said, over her mother's shoulder, waving at a woman selling extremely fine Dead Island pork. The woman smiled and jabbed at her with one porky finger.

You can count!

Seventy-five, said Ingrid. Her gaze moved to the old woman's husband. *Sixty-four.*

I am *sixty-four,* said the man. *Clever pickney.*

Cute, said the pork lady. *Too early to know cors?*

Way too early, said Ingrid's mother. She rubbed noses with the child and pretended to eat her belly. *Let her be young for a while.*

Ninety-one, chuckled Ingrid. She pulled her mother's nose. *Ninety-one!*

The pork lady's husband died that night, swinging in his hammock.

After some months of this, Ingrid's mother took her to the nearest Temple to urgently consult with the Fatidique. People just dying-dying and pointing at her one-child and surely *that* couldn't be the cors they was waiting on?

After some patience, time and noticing, it was agreed by the Fatidique that Ingrid was merely voicing the inevitable, not causing the deaths. *Don't take her around elders too-too much though*, said the obeah woman who came to deliver their conclusion. *They more likely to be vex with the number.*

Indeed, said Ingrid's mother. *Anything else?* She pointed at the birthmark. They watched the child, playing in the sandy mud and tasting it.

How old she is now?

Nearly three.

The obeah woman looked at her hard; shrugged sympathetically. They stood, nodding together, tears in their eyes. There was nothing to be done; sometimes cors was sad.

She is probably Fatidique, said the obeah woman. *Those who sacrifice sit well among us. Bring her come next week. We train her up.* The mother's tears were falling strong now. The obeah woman put her palms up to the sky. *She come to understand magic, Mamma. Is a good thing.*

I come tomorrow, Teacher.

★

Anise had never met anyone who got into more trouble than she and Ingrid did, calling things out to strangers on the street and running away. Especially fun with the snooty, stoosh people. They learned how to swim in the ocean together and in rivers, which was a different skill, and spent a great deal of time with obeah women, who were strange, blessed, hugging, cheerful, funny women with comforting bosoms and thick hair, as wide and stable as trees, and not nearly as mysterious as everyone else thought.

But there was also work to be done. You had to nurture this kind of cors. Ingrid taught her patience. Gave Anise lists of medical conditions and studied them alongside her because learning symptoms was no fun by yourself. Anise's diagnostic speed and accuracy improved. Hypertension felt like the strike of a heavy peasant drum; syphilis made the earlobes squelchy; toes smelled of cornmeal before a heart attack; squints developed late in life made a screeching sound, like mice in a field. She was more considerate when clients came to see her in Temple, older obeah women standing just a little way off, but close enough to help her with any understandably *human* reactions to bad or surprising news.

Her father was furious that she'd sought acolyte without his guidance, but she was in Fatidique hands now and nobody could fight that, not even him.

You can do more, said Ingrid, sucking her teeth, *stroops*.

Seven months after Ingrid took her as acolyte, her favourite Uncle Coorah, Bonamie's father, arrived at a family celebration with a dripping cold, waving apologetically as family came near, blowing his nose vigorously, skin damp and flushed.

Anise was struck with an urge to hug her uncle right *now*. So she did.

Uncle Coorah said hello and hugged her back, coughing and protesting she'd catch it from him, he knew it was a cold, she needn't double-check, but Anise hugged tighter, caught in a kind of compulsion. Silver bubbles sloughed off her brown skin, translucent in the sunlight, pouring into her slightly alarmed uncle, who nevertheless had the presence of mind to stay still and trust cors.

The bubbles floated around them. The family went *ooooh*, and stared, even her bad cousin Xalam, who could never sit still. The bubbles caught the sunlight and turned pink. Her uncle's phlegm dried, the cough subsided, aches replaced with a delicious tingling, fever cooled.

Uncle Coorah burst out laughing. *What a wondrous cors!*

Pastor Latibeaudearre interrupted before she could answer.

It going have to come with more decorum than that.

Her uncle kissed her cheek – *thank you niecey, don't mind your daddy* – and she was overjoyed. She had *cured* his cold,

72

she hadn't known she could do *that*. It felt revelatory: like an artist surpassing their own expectations. You heard that a lot, growing up, as people lived with their magic and let it settle in. *Eh-eh. I never know I could do that.*

She watched her uncle dancing with his wife, eating rum custard, phlegm-free and smiling. Teasing Bonamie, like he always did. She felt proud.

You get bubbles! said Ingrid. She stuck her tongue out. *What a show-off cors!*

They experimented with ways to deliver the healing: the most obvious was to direct the bubbles through her hands. Hugging strangers, as her father pointed out, might be inappropriate or yucky. But it took practice. The mad silver and pink bubbles filled up a room quick o'clock, and they made people sneeze, or came out of her too fast, soaking her clothes with whatever it was that the bubbles were made of. Plus, almost everybody giggled at the end of her treatment, unless they were in a great deal of pain, and the giggling seemed to encourage some adults to confide much more of their private business than was good for a child to hear.

Pffft, said Ingrid. *Grownups is the same thing as children.*

The whole subject gave her father headaches, which she cured obligingly.

Despite her fine reputation, despite the money she made, despite the hundreds – yes, it was hundreds now – of clients who had embraced her, relieved, sobbing, despite the dozens of lives she had saved, she could not make him proud. Her cors was a vulgarity to him, something he never recovered from. He was scornful of bodies.

Anise shaved her head; the hair was distracting when she worked, and she liked her own face. She attended to her breathing. She learned how to be quiet, how to bear witness. Some

73

days she didn't need cors for her work. Compassion was a kind of magic; listening was at least half the task.

Just leave space for yourself, Ingrid said.

Like you do?

Hmph.

★

Anise tripped over a stone and hopped on one foot, pulling her sandal back into place. If the pregnant mistress rumour hadn't come from *this* neighbour, this precious, hurting woman who took too much butterfly, she would have dismissed it as nothing more than blasted Popisho people love to *chat*. But this lady cared for her.

Sometimes old people see what you don't want to see.

People passed her by, recognising and nodding.

'Morning, Miss Anise.'

'Morning, Mamma Begindorth.'

A horrifying thought spread through her, coming to rest in her solar plexus.

They all know.

News of her babies had spread so fast: she was barely out of labour, and all she had to do was walk market to hear her name. Everyone so very *sorry*. Sorry people filling her house with pots of food and opinions, Tan-Tan across the room, and people-people between them, and the men playing dominoes on the veranda like it was a party. And how things changed! By the time their third child died the sorry people stopped coming, as if they – *she* – were some kind of bad-lucky curse. She'd lost clients. Not many, but enough. She could only rely on Ingrid, her mother, Bonamie. And even they looked at her. No, not Ingrid, who knew her as

74

deeply as another human could. But the rest considered her a tragedy. And now, what sweeter su-su than the sorry mule have a cheating husband?

Is entirely possible that you the very last person to know.

Could Tan-Tan truly betray her so? No. It was impossible to contemplate.

She held her head high; her scalp soft, budding moss.

At the bottom of the hill, she cut through the Clothing District and into a teeming crowd. Everybody in for last fittings for the beauty contest over Pretty Town, tonight. A group of carnival girls passed, their yellow and green costumes winding up the hill: feathers, headdresses, fringes, baby hair oiled and plaits swinging. A few of them waved orange signs. Blue and white butterflies bounced off their heads, like someone grating the sky. It was already so hot Anise had to squint.

All the signs said the same thing.

THERE IS AN ALTERNATIVE

The orange graffiti had thrilled her for months. Tan-Tan had dismissed the Orange Man, despite her argument that the mystery man was the most glorious of rebels. *Cho, mischief-maker*, said Tan-Tan, but eventually even he had taken interest, hushing her when the town crier came down the road with news.

Orange Man say price of banana due to go up-up-up, my friends!

And surely it had, as if the graffiti had its own kind of prophetic cors.

That is one rass *man, keep himself secret so long*, said Tan-Tan. *You know he don't tell no woman him identity.*

A group of smiling girlfriends wiggled past her, apologising, their robes brilliant, virgin cloth, gold and purple and blue. She watched them spread into the crowd, flipping skirts and thigh cuffs at each other, like long-legged jacana birds. Any one of them could be Tan-Tan's mistress, walking across her path.

Last to know! the little voice in her head crowed.

Best friends skipped past, chattering excitedly, hand in hand, no more than nine or ten. Anise watched their eyes passing over her white mourning skirt.

'You see how the bride pretty?'

'I hear is a love match.'

Anise snorted. Sonteine Intiasar was only nineteen, still a child. What did she know about marriage? Tomorrow evening everybody would cheer when they kissed on the steps of the big Temple and sing them off to the nuptial chamber with naughty songs, but nobody would tell them how difficult marriage was, how . . . *long.*

And before you could say puppalick, that young girl would be pregnant, bursting like a plum.

She gripped a nearby wall, surprised by a cold wave of rage.

Don't cry.

I not crying!

She had fallen out with friends, fallen away from the few she had. Become one of those women she didn't like, just all-full of her husband. Busy, she'd been busy, though. So many people to help. She liked thinking of herself as kind.

As important, you mean.

Perhaps she would go and see Bonamie. The last time they visited – she couldn't quite remember when – her cousin had been blunt. Told her that bitterness had filled up her backbone. She'd felt like giving her one *good* thump. They hadn't spoken since, even though Bonamie sent letters.

Was she, gods, was she bitter?

'Somebody tell me that blasted whorehouse giving free service to married man today, can you imagine? As long as they leave their ring at the front door!'

Anise recognised Nelly Agnes Neil, one of her father's deacons, talking to her blue-hatted sister Sherron, who was at forty-four still disgracefully single. Anise thought the hat made Sherron's legs look magnificent, and who the hell cared about married anyway?

'Marshall not leaving my sights come this evening!' declared Nelly. 'Greetings, Anise. You hear this slackness, healer?'

'Greetings.' Her voice sounded squeezed and mean. She cleared her throat and raised her volume. 'No slackness don't reach me, Nell.'

She felt them staring at her.

✳

She'd met Tan-Tan on the Zutupeng quay in Soin ten years ago, she and a group of friends flung hither and thither, waiting for her father's boat back home, pleasantly tired, the dying sun on their head-tops. Someone talking loud about the theatre festival; someone else leaning on her, sharp-elbowed. They were laughing, except for Bonamie, pouting because of the men in the crowd: *You too skinny, gods, how you look so mawga?* Anise prodded her shoulder and reminded her about the boys back in Pretty Town who often strained to see her long waist and slender feet. Bonamie looked relieved. Anise heard new laughter, mingling with her father's voice: man-laughter. She turned to see who it was. Tan-Tan's muscles were popping things, and he was all in proportion and turning to smile at her, too. Pastor

Latibeaudearre caught her eye and spread his arms. *Look what I bring for you*, his face beamed.

Gyal, if you don't want him, I want him, one of her friends hissed.

Hello, Tan-Tan said, and took her hands and helped her into the boat, and she'd liked the calm desire in his eyes, and my, he was one of the healthiest men she'd ever touched.

By the time Tan-Tan turned up, her mother seeming indifferent, but actually insistent, her father so brimming with his own brilliance, she had begun to feel the cause of great fatigue. They were not young. She was their only child. Her father hadn't insisted on a church man; she knew what that cost him. Tan-Tan was a promising, sensible fellow with professional skills and the surprisingly seductive ability to slow down time in a small space, which seemed to warm cold things and had the most amazing effect on their lovemaking. Wah, the man could get money from a bee sting, could wine and dine a client, a child, a coney, a woman, anything that came his way. *You going have the most welcoming home in the world*, her girlfriends said.

Charming, yes, but she'd always thought meeting her husband would feel surer, more substantial.

Of course is your choice, said her mother and put a restraining hand on her father's wrist.

She'd wanted to feel the pleasure of obedience, to show her love for her parents, to stop fighting for just a while.

Hmph, said Ingrid. For a long time Anise wondered if that was jealousy, 'sake as how she was older and due to be married sooner, but Ingrid said hmph about everything Tan-Tan did. She hadn't liked him: hmph was the best she could do. Despite Ingrid's grumpiness. Tan-Tan did make Anise belly-laugh. In company, he was judicious and attentive, although tempted to cards and liquor. In bed, each part of her body was kneaded, the penis broad and firm, her orgasm never neglected. Lovemaking ended with her sweaty and flustered, always physically satisfied; kissed firmly, as if he was placing a full stop at the end of a very long sentence.

He didn't talk excessively, but he never forgot to say goodnight or good morning in a way that made her feel special.

Even now.

Her father fussed, planning wedding tents and the best fish stew and a dark fruit and rum cake with thick icing and a blue formal robe with a long train. She didn't want a commotion. Tents drew mosquitoes, stewed fish lingered in the air and she'd always found rum cake sour. But Pastor Lati and his new son-in-law had planned everything, and men so rarely cared about the details.

She'd worked hard to love her husband and succeeded. But her holy, painful no – *no, Tan-Tan, I can't do it again* – had changed everything. She'd assumed their lack of intimacy was due to his sadness, that he would forgive her, in time. The idea of another woman's frock-tail hadn't occurred to her. Her father had picked this one for her; her father was a good man.

How you really think he could happy with a mule?

She flicked her long white skirt and crunched on through the sandy dust.

*

Someone had tacked a poster to the chalkboard outside her workspace, advertising the Miss Pretty Girl International Beauty Contest. Anise pondered the colourful letters and bad illustrations. This was the second Miss Pretty she'd miss; it was something she and Ingrid had done together and going alone was unthinkable. The contestants were always glorious, decked out in the latest styles by local fashion designers. Sheer pum-pum niceness. Ingrid once told her there were places in foreign where women didn't want to be admired. It had made them laugh.

She transferred the poster to her house wall, leaving her chalkboard clear.

In the thin hallway, she trailed her hands over her altar and its contents: a small, pale blue statue of Jai, holding fire and oil; a heavy bowl of water she hurried to change; a tiny, iridescent purse from an old friend; a letter from her parents in her mother's bad handwriting; still-fresh rhododendron; honey-tea incense cones. She lit one, blowing the smoke through the house and inhaling the comforting smell. This had been her home before she married, and her first altar.

She didn't have much time before her clients arrived. She'd leave a message on the chalkboard outside; she'd done it before. After she and Tan-Tan talked and made up and everything was good again, she would visit them all and apologise in person.

She searched the house for chalk. What should she write? *Called away on business* seemed abrupt. *Family emergency*. No, that would have people down on her by nightfall, fussing. *Closed today – sorry*. Maybe. She had to hurry. She didn't want anyone to see upset in her face or ask questions. She wasn't a good liar. She found a piece of chalk. It snapped between her scrabbling fingers. She cursed, found another, broke it too. A half-sob threatened; she gulped it back.

Gyal, don't even cry.

She sat down on a cushion, taking measured breaths, and put her tongue on the roof of her mouth. She closed her eyes, placed a light hand on her chest, feeling the rise and fall.

Calm.

A soft sound made her look up.

There was a secret stuck to the lamp on the wall.

She got up to examine it. It was the texture of old biscuit. The young, shadowy man the secret belonged to had delighted in it so: in it, and his chronic constipation. But he'd eventually talked enough to let them both go.

People frequently left their secrets here. She did daily checks for them tangled in her hair. Dusted and swept and took them out in the back yard, letting them float into the night air. Sometimes they were old and heavy: the kind that stuck to stars and brought bits down. The stars broke her yard furniture and chipped the roof and covered the ground with sticky white juice.

It was harder to clear out secrets when you were tired, especially the kind that slipped inside your body. If she overworked, she ran out of cors energy quite alarmingly: couldn't move out of bed, had even fainted. She'd once been unable to masturbate to orgasm for three weeks before Ingrid peeled nine secrets off her lungs; sometimes the only way to find them was to listen for the tittering. Ingrid would lay her across warm stones and rub the sludge of other people's secrets out of her, squeeze the blackheads in her back and nose, syringe her ears, pound the knots in her neck, make her stretch and drink water and bathe in bay rum and take good purple butterfly out of the fading sky.

What is that noise? Anise asked, one day last year, when a humming sound had distracted her for the entire treatment.

Just my tumour, said Ingrid.

What? She sat up.

Ingrid pressed her back. *Remember I'm twenty-nine this year.*

She lay frozen. *But how I only hearing it now?*
It start that noise a while ago.
But Ingrid. How I never hear *it?*
Her friend stroked her back. *You don't want to hear it, child.*
Sometimes she called her child. Master-teacher, after all.

She had simply refused to believe in Ingrid's birthmark until she died.

She had to prepare herself for what might happen next. It might be true, o gods. That old lady had watched her belly swell with babies, brought her naseberry fritters, rubbed her feet twice when she couldn't reach them. Why would she tell her a thing she didn't know to be true?

The way he treat you in public. 'Come, wife. Let me bring your shawl.' 'Hey man, you see my wife? She looking good, eh?' Pure guilt. If you look so good, why he don't touch you since—
Married people business is complicated business.
Is that so?
Yes, is so.
He just go and get a grind elsewhere. Not complicated. You would really leave him for that?
'Stop it!' she snapped at herself.

She could hear the Temple song in the distance, pulsating and ancient.

You getting crazy, sitting and yelling at yourself.
Chalk, rass, one piece of dirty chalk, nah.
And another thing.
What, now?
If I was people, I wouldn't trust you to heal not a gingi-fly. Four dead baby and you can't heal yourself.

Anise picked the biscuity secret off her lamp, kicked open

her back door and carried it into the sunshine. Watched as it whirred out of her hands and up. Temple songs chorused louder, almost shrill. She could see the Dukuyaie toy factory.

The sound of obeah women singing usually comforted her, but not today.

6

Sonteine Melody Ignoble Intiasar climbed out of Romanza's favourite tree, did the fifteen-minute walk through Dead Island bush back to the stony beach and waved down a passing fishing canoe with two men at the helm. They negotiated a small fee for the lift back to Battisient.

Sonteine climbed into the boat, annoyed at her still-oily hands. One of the men looked at her curiously.

'Can I help you?' she snapped.

He looked up at the cloudless sky. 'No, lady.'

They kicked off shore; Sonteine pondered what to do next. She didn't want to go home. Mamma would be fussing and cussing about her leaving so suddenly.

She'd meant to ask Romanza how he managed to be so big-chested and boasty, loving Pilar like it wasn't nothing. Living in the bush, like him name mongoose. Knowing that he was scorned in so many ways. He was the bravest person she had ever known, and the most himself. If he could just hand over some of that bravery.

Nobody knew how many men had tried to violate her. Not even Dandu, although she had told him *some* of what had happened. She herself hadn't counted, but she was sure it all had something to do with why she was so scared of her wedding night. When the moment had come to ask Zaza for advice, she'd found herself unable. She would have had to explain *everything*, and she didn't want to make her brother sad.

She would look at the bright side, instead: not a one of the bastards had succeeded.

It started when she was ten, during her morning walk to school: past houses, gardeners in gardens and grown men on their way to work, all baring their penises and waving them around in the air. One of her father's friends played with her knees under the dinner table. During her first kiss at twelve, the boy kissing her threatened to hold her down if she didn't succumb to more. Sonteine punched him in the face. He hit her back, hard. A group of women heard her yelling and drove the boy off with sticks and curses. One kicked like a jackass, which was helpful. The women wouldn't look at her afterwards, and that made her afraid.

You have to fight these fools, the jackass-kicker said, before she strode away.

It wasn't happening to she alone, then.

She didn't kiss anyone after that.

At fourteen, she had tried to confide in her best-friend-then, assuming she had the same problems, but the girl squinged up her face as if she'd smelled something bad and said Sonteine couldn't *possibly* have so much man that liked her, and it wasn't good to show off. She had better friends now, she knew that, but the shame had stayed with her, because maybe there *was* something wrong with the way she comported herself. All the gods knew she had enough things to be worried about, what with being the Governor's daughter, and not having any magic.

The obeah woman told her that what she felt, what she *knew* about herself, was a figment of her imagination. They said it wasn't uncommon for people to want cors they didn't have. *But*, Sonteine argued, *you ever see anybody in Popisho come with no magic at all?*

85

The obeah women admitted that this was strange as the hills, but they had no theories. *She* didn't care what they said: they were wrong. She had wings. She could feel her wings, in the bone structure of her arms and shoulders and in the arc of her pelvis. They were just taking their time to manifest.

Sonteine shifted in the canoe. She wanted to scrape the oil off her body; it was like stinking. Mamma had chosen it: ylang ylang and ginger in fresh almond oil. A three-woman massage, meant to connect you to your past and your future. Traditionally arranged for a bride by her mother, the household obeah woman and her grandmother. She had never met her ama; dead years before she and Romanza were born. A young maid had stepped into her place and they'd been training with the obeah woman for two weeks. She'd thought the maid a strange choice; she hadn't been with the family long. Nevertheless, she respected her mother's wishes.

She'd woken early, seen the lamp in her father's office was already lit and slipped into the kitchen for water.

Her mother and the maid were a dark wedge against the wall.

Moaning, foaming maid, in between her mother's thighs.

Sonteine shrank back, more than embarrassed; she was appalled at the jerking and the animal focus; by the sight of something far too private.

She sat on the floor of her room for a long time, until her feet and calves were numb. She wanted to go to her father but knew he would demand a reason for her distress and try to fix whatever she said. She couldn't go to Dandu; it was forbidden to see him the fortnight before the wedding. Friends were unthinkable: who could say such a thing about your mother, out loud?

★

Later, when the obligatory massage began, she was able to endure the first pouring: the women's arms were like trees, the palms of the obeah woman gentle on her shoulders, their careful murmuring, the oppressive warmth. But when she opened her eyes, her mother was smiling down at her. No, it was more than she could stand, truly. She scrambled up and backed away, overwhelmed, their arms shuddering and reaching for her; put her hands over her ears. *Let me be*, she said, and ran. For her twin and his tree.

★

When she met Dandu last year at an empty local putt-putt stop, she was eighteen, still earthbound, and abidingly irritated with the gods. Why were men *really* put on this earth and where the rass were her wings? Still, she liked the back of Dandu's neck as he shifted from one foot to the other, craning to see if a putt-putt was due: so slender his neck was, and tender. She said hello.

Hello Sonteine Intiasar, said Dandu.

He explained that he knew who she was, and that he'd already kissed her in the scratchy grass in his father Leo's back yard, when they were eight years old, before his mother died and he went to live with his ama.

Uncle Leo! said Sonteine. *I don't remember that!*

I do, said Dandu.

She liked the idea that the horrible boy who hit her hadn't been the first after all, and she *did* remember Leo Brenteninton's son, now she looked closer. He'd been a quiet, big-headed, reading boy and she couldn't believe he was the same person. Tall, and dark and eyes so grey. Tranquil.

As time passed, she was happy to know him. There were no

87

pretty, empty words and no violence. He kept his promises, or tried his very best, and if he couldn't he said why, like a grown-up. He remained calm on the day she told him to close his eyes and kissed him for the second time, and nothing scary happened afterwards. He asked her to go walking the next day and they held hands and kissed some more and still he stayed like himself. He'd agreed to wait until *she* was ready to make love, even if that was on their wedding night. Or even later.

Still, although she trusted him, and already called him husband in her mind, she remained nervous. Even with all the breast-touching they did nowadays.

Sonteine sat straighter in the canoe. 'I going to see him now.'

'Who?' asked the boatman who'd ushered her on board.

'Never you mind,' said Sonteine. 'You can change and go Dukuyaie?'

★

Dandu found himself unable to get out of his hammock that morning, regardless of the climbing sun. There were a whole raft of items to ponder: how many *real* friends were coming to the wedding (four), how many bottles of his favourite vodka they were bringing (thirty), how many lectures his father had given him about married life (two, so far, neither of any use) and how many times his father had said he wished Dandu's mother was here to see this day (only three times and he wished she was, too). He calculated how many preparatory rituals Sonteine would endure (six before tomorrow night, including an examination of her lungs) and by comparison, how many hours he had to himself (a whole heap of hours). He was expected to sit in daily contemplation, which *really* meant recover from the alcohol he was expected to consume. Most grooms would be cotton-mouthed by now, after a fortnight of drinking and debauchery, but he'd remained sober.

Three of his real friends had taken him to an artist's gallery in Pluie last night, where they'd admired the pictures and eaten garlicky chicken legs and got wet in the rain. Many not-so-close friends dropped by and ate butterfly and walked with him through the gardens and left pre-wedding gifts, all to kiss his father's backside. Mostly he *had* spent the time in quiet, if not *silent* contemplation.

Or intense worry. However you wanted to look at it.

Uncle Bertrand's daughter had grown into a hard-hipped, plump young woman who grinned at him like she understood him, and never combed her hair. She wiped his sweat with the edge of her robe, a peasant's love-move, and he was tongue-tied. He could hear the wings creaking under her skin, like scaffolding in high wind, and he appreciated talking and listening to her in almost equal measure. He found that she was the kindest person he knew.

He rubbed his stomach and groaned. Chicken wings or fear, he wasn't sure.

When she said she wanted to wait on lovemaking, he'd agreed. It was enough to become a connoisseur of her burnt-butter breasts, so firm and succulent, so responsive. Her nipples puckered her areolae; he liked the damp in her cleavage, and sometimes when she closed her eyes, he used his teeth to deftly pull out a single thin hair that kept growing out of her right breast. It would embarrass her if she knew.

Breasts, they were one thing. He had no idea what to do with the rest of her.

He'd meant to tell Sonteine he was a virgin. He told her most things that came into his mind. But the more she spoke about a life of pulling and pushing, of stalking and the smell of men on her when she least expected it, the more he felt responsible for her tranquillity. They were both private, the children of public figures. They shared a kind of solemnity. It was clear she assumed he was experienced and, even worse, that she *relied* on the fact. Doubtless, she expected him to take charge when the hour was finally upon them.

He'd seen pig, coney, goat, butterfly, lizard, even the clouds doing it. But what was right and what was wrong with an actual girl? His friends boasted about sex in confident, colourful detail and he mimicked them, feeling a fool. He knew they were exaggerating, but at least they knew *something*. He should know something too, with a nervous girlfriend. Fiancée. Wife. By all the gods in heaven.

His stomach was swollen. He'd developed a bad case of constipation.

'Pssst, boy,' said Sonteine, and he opened his eyes to find her sitting by the window, her mouth a wet pile, wearing an expression he'd never seen before.

★

On the edge of Lukia Town, a ground dove – which in this archipelago is a soft brown bird with a puffed grey breast that makes the saddest and most musical hooting sound – ceased its morning call, sat down and exploded in a flurry of pink-grey feathers. If you had been there, you might have thought there was nothing left, but the black ants scurrying along the beach stopped to pass their feelers over thousands of tiny pink fragments, heaving from the explosion, sweet as coconut drop cakes.

7

Xavier and Io stood in the shade of a jagabat tree, watching people go in and out of Bend Down Market.

Io's face was thoughtful. 'You ready?'

Xavier stared at the open-air arcade. It was *stupid* to begin walkround here. He used to come every morning, and it had seemed intuitive to return to trusted places and habits, but he'd forgotten the deep boom of this market, how frenetic and crowded it was, even this early.

He stroked the leather moth pouch in his pocket, trying to ease the tightness in his chest. He'd once worn pouches around his neck and eaten out of them in public, not caring what anyone thought. His finest pouches still dangled from his bedroom rafters, lay strewn in his day room. He hardly noticed them anymore. It was a matter of accounting: if he could resist picking up a pouch for a day, three days, ten weeks, two years, five, he was doing something real.

But he hadn't had a moth in his hand for a decade. Against the skin of his fingers.

Touching the leather anew, knowing what was inside.

The pouch pulsed.

He was supposed to be better, for Nya, standing at the mouth of the very market where they first met. His fingers traced the thing. What the rass was he planning to do with it? If Nya could see him now, or Io catch him: ah, the shame might kill him dead.

He jerked his hand out of his pocket.

'Xav?' Io touched his shoulder. The ground was trembling

like his hands, and no, he wasn't ready for this market. Suppose he became faint, suppose he crouched, or fell on his face? The day was so bright, and the people were already passing by and noticing them standing here, using their mouths to point, exchanging excited looks and nudges.

'Xav? Maybe you don't have to do this.'

Chse had the same long forehead as her father, the same habit of standing diagonal when she was worried. Except Io wasn't worried, he was grinning. Xavier knew that look. It had precipitated every accident and adventure of his boyhood, whether breaking both wrists falling out of cloud forest trees or walking through old gullies until they were lost. You could go anywhere if Io smiled and talked to you in his calm-river voice.

'Fuck the Governor and his walkround,' said Io. 'We can buy for service and let people see you. That is what is important. Then we go home, nah.'

He could tell Io that Intiasar had threatened his daughter and then flee: climb into his hammock, hide under the Torn Poem, say, *leave me, leave me*. Let his big brother do the job. But Io was liable to climb right up into those Battisient high hills to Intiasar yard and get charged with murder.

'I already close the restaurant for two days,' he said.

'So open it back.'

'No guests.'

'Invite some, Xav. You think they going say no?' Ah, this gentle, turbulent face. 'You was so rass vex you nearly thump down old Sweet Pepper Nose when he come. And now you doing walkround, obedient, so?'

He wanted to sniff his fingers, fresh from the pouch, but that was dirty moth eater behaviour and if he did it, all the gods in the world may as well mock him.

92

'I rethink it, man.'

'I just saying. Maybe I wasn't helpful. I was mocking you. I—'

'I am *doing* it, Io.' His best imperious voice.

Io raised his eyebrows. 'Of course.' He lowered his head and spread his hands. '*Macaenus.*'

Xavier rolled his eyes and shifted the near-empty satchel on his shoulder, feeling the notebook roll inside. Sea breeze gusted in from Carenage beach. They could hear a band tuning up for the next song, its front men teasing each other, half-singing, drums *tam-tam* behind them, *bop-beep-bam.*

So *loud.*

Io was disappointed in him. It couldn't be helped. A man who would threaten a child shouldn't be underestimated.

A warm throng of women arrived, loaded with bag and pan. Xavier watched them stream past: tall women, with rainbow-coloured curls and plaits, beads and tassels, sculptures and shapes. One had perched an old birdcage on her head and the pet quail inside squawked agreeably. Some of them spread outwards from the waist down, like glass bottles; others spread upwards, thin-legged and top-heavy, like baobab trees.

On impulse, he beckoned to Io, stepped sideways and fell in with them, engulfed by their noise and scent.

His first feeling was one of heat and current, as if he'd dived into a whirlpool. The women curved around him, pointing and talking, casting eyes at him, pliable as syrup. There were big brown-leather bellies, exposed, criss-crossed with golden stretch marks; other bodies were thin: would be crispy and delicious on toast. He felt a surge of tenderness.

And so they entered the market.

They moved together, all-a-one, past traders unwrapping their wares, coaching their acolytes and making change, the women's eyes on them, dark as raisins, pointing things out. *Look, macaenus.* Bananas, long as a man's legs, and tiny green melons like beetles. Smiling around him, so many smiles for him.

His hot, shallow breathing eased. He walked faster, moth pouch soft against his thigh, conscious of the increased gap between himself and Io, who had stopped to greet friendly faces, whizzing past pyramids of fresh spinach and heaps of sugar-crusted frangipani; a young boy carving a slab of glistening red gut, hewn from some indeterminate animal even Xavier couldn't identify. Some of the traders he recognised from their bartering technique: shaking their bodies, pounding tables for emphasis, yelling prices, thrusting samples forward. He felt like a dancer, back in the arms of a former partner: old friends with intimate, half-forgotten memories. They worked hard, these people: farmers, bakers, butchers. He'd spent years building relationships with them, for the first pick of their freshest produce.

Xavier gasped: the space between stalls widened and the mass of women broke, streaming right and left, leaving so much space behind them he felt like a child, teetering out of an embrace ended too quickly. Dumped on shore. The imprint of their bodies flickered on him like dying embers.

Radios blared and he could still hear the band playing *neh-neh-neh-plunk!*

He stopped; let himself be still with the produce.

Let people stare, keeping his jaw resolute.

Someone would call out his neglect, surely. Someone would say: *we needed you, and you weren't here.*

He trailed his finger over swathes of green paper for wrapping nuts, accepted a spoonful from a massive corn pudding, rich with cashew, cream and cinnamon. Sellers beamed expectantly, sagging as he passed by their silvery sweetsop and dried lizard meat. He went to admire one man's fine ginger, pimento, garlic, allspice, five spice, mandolin, then moved away, shaking his head, the spice man's face falling. To his right, a toothless wonder made a long *pssssssssst* sound at an elegant woman taking inventory of pillars of yellow butter, like termite nests.

'You look like you have a big brain,' the man said to the butter woman. 'Write me a love letter, do.'

Io had been completely consumed by the crowd; Xavier couldn't see him any longer. Did they love his brother best now, he who'd kept the trade alive? He frowned, impatient with his own self-pity.

The moth pouch bounced. He rubbed his bristled chin. Someone was bound to call a radio station and say how macaenus start walkround raggedy as *hell* this morning, he couldn't do any better than that? It would offend Intiasar, he so dapper and artfully sculpted. It was a small defiance, but worth something. *Pay the people well*, that's what Salmonie said after he'd called him back to the Torn Poem. *But not so well that you vex Bertie.* At least the old man had a sense of humour. The next time he saw Intiasar, he might call him Bertie, too.

'Yes, macaenus!' a voice called.

He didn't turn; young men were always calling out to him, frequently on a dare. He never knew the best thing to do in the face of their posturing. But this was more than that; other voices took up the call.

'Macaenus! Yes, Xavier!'

Cheering. Clapping. He nodded. His heart filled.

'You come, macaenus! Gods, is so *good* to see you.'

He raised his hand in greeting. Let his fingers curl to make a fist.

The crowd burst in jubilation. Suddenly it seemed that

95

everyone was nodding, grinning, lifting a drink, a piece of fruit or a machete in respect. He smelled boiling juvay herbal wine, belching orange perfume. He felt liberated, even triumphant. Where was Io, to share this?

The sellers raised their voices, all hesitancy gone.

'Hi! Macaenus! You need to come over here!'

'My gods have mercy, how you push so? Give him some room!'

He felt skittish, merry; intoxicated with relief. The pouch string dangled down his leg, tickling the skin. There must be a hole in his pocket, or maybe it was burning through? Giddy. Grateful. A woman flirted: 'Macaenus, oy! See me here! You looking handsome like always!'

He stopped in front of a familiar tent, panting slightly. He was very fond of the butcher who owned it, a small yellow man who taught his goats how to meditate and hibernated himself a whole four months of the year. Xavier watched the man winching a live goat skywards, hanging by its sharp heels. It was a fine beast, black-and-white-patched and pot-bellied. It swayed peacefully, eyes closed and numb.

The butcher touched his hand. 'You are well, macaenus.'

It was not a question, so he didn't answer.

'Stay and bless the kill?'

Xavier nodded. He regarded the fine goat's shining hooves and muzzle. He could begin the feast here. Buy this goat, take it home, embroider its body with spice deep in the bone, set it to slow-bake all night in his yard pit, wake up to the aroma reaching down to the shore. But the love and labour necessary! Intiasar and his kind didn't deserve the life of this animal.

People began to congregate. The butcher pushed his acolytes together, like a conductor settling musicians. They hovered, one holding a blue hard-clay bucket, another an array of lustrous knives.

A dark woman wriggled past, murmuring apology, her lime-green skirts swaying and one bare, silken arm grazing Xavier's shoulder. He was impressed by the heavy feel of her skin, so soft it was almost like a pelt, her thick, pliant waist. She hovered, gazing up at the goat, a crocheted bag full of blue crabs swaying in front of her, using the hem of her robe to fan herself languidly. He missed watching women and their skirts: hip knots for wading through the surf; winding skirt-tails around their fingers; the wrinkles in the cloth telling the whole day's story.

Xavier counted one-two-three small warts on the woman's shoulder. All her attention seemed fixed on the goat spectacle.

His hand fluttered around his pocket, palm warming, pulse running along his fingers.

The woman glanced over at him. Her red tongue flickered across her lips. He put his fist into his pocket and closed it over the pouch.

The most romantic meal in the world should be cooked by the most romantic man in the world, nah? What could he feed this woman, with her amazing skin and furling hem? Something so succulent she'd let the juices drip down her chin and neck. And eating it, wouldn't she wonder what else his hands and tongue could do? He imagined her shuddering under him; the sweat between her breasts, the small urgent sounds in her throat. Listening to the tune change, go up, up—

Xavier let go of the red pouch and opened his eyes, startled. He hadn't felt that soaring, hot insistence for years. It was moth arrogance: like you could bring the world to you and be anything you wanted. His nails felt like hot discs.

The green-robed woman sidled a few steps away, as if she

could feel the change in his body and didn't like it. He was momentarily embarrassed: please gods, let her not have cors for hearing the thoughts of strangers.

The crowd called for silence: *hush, hush. Goat going, now.*

The butcher took his place by the animal's head, talking in its ear, explaining he was sorry it must die. The goat listened thoughtfully, as if they were two important men in conference.

The butcher looked at Xavier, as if for permission.

He nodded.

The green-robed woman bit her lip.

The butcher slit the goat's throat in one quick thrust, shifting sideways. A glut of blood arced into the blue air and the waiting bucket; the goat's belly juddered. Each time Xavier saw this man kill he was amazed by the tremendous splash of it and the butcher's ballet.

Ohhhhh, said the crowd.

The butcher brought the dead animal further down and went inside, taking liver, kidneys, heart, brain, turning, sweating, acolytes beside him, washing the body in sprays of salt water, butcher carving with his long knives, sharp and cling-clanging, whittling with sharp, short ones, no more than a penknife for some parts, everything shades of red, intestine blue, yellow fat, gristle, shimmering bone, black eyeballs. One eyeball fell to the ground and rolled under a shaking worktop, coated in dust. The goat hide fell away, all of a piece, and was taken by yet another acolyte; nothing must be wasted. Xavier watched him scuttling and thought of a crab. Turned to see the silken, thick woman standing beside him, running a single finger down her waist to her hip, flicking her skirt open. Surprised, he saw the glint of her soft onyx flesh; saw her thigh cuff as she angled her body to give him the best view. The jewelled cuff reminded him of fresh grass.

The robe fell back into place. She wouldn't show him her cuff twice – that would be desperate. All she needed do now was smile at him, a clear benediction through the smell of goat blood. Her softness was like part of the crowd's earlier greeting and part of the stream of women who had guided him into the market and most of all, it felt like a salve for the goat's beautiful death.

Just one smile, after the cuff flick. He would not pursue her – there were too many things to do and think of today – but he lingered for the final invitation.

Her smooth dark lips parted.

'You come, macaenus?'

Her voice was as sweet as he'd hoped.

He cleared his throat. 'Yes, sis.'

'We are *so* glad.'

She put a hand on his arm. Soft fingers.

'Macaenus, I want to know something.'

He calmed his breathing. 'Yes, sis.'

She smiled. 'Is you *really* drive your wife to kill her own self?'

Outrage threatened to choke him. He looked around wildly, as if the earth might rise and cover them both, for a witness who would confirm he'd heard her wrong. Eyes glimmered; people stared back. He rotated slowly, studying faces. The ones standing closest must have heard her; seemed to be waiting for an answer. Why, they might have drawn lots to decide which one should ask him. Send the pretty woman, they'd agreed. It wasn't the moral indignation some might say he deserved, or the need he'd feared; just simple, naked curiosity.

No one had told him this was what people thought about Nya, why she out dead-walking.

The woman's hand, tugging his sleeve. 'Macaenus, you not going tell me?'

He whipped around, surprising himself with the force he used to push her hand away. She stumbled.

'Don't open your mouth and talk about my wife again, you hear me?'

She fell back, silken no more, perhaps a little afraid.

He shoved through the gaping crowd, towards the yellow butcher. If this was what they wanted, let them have it then: a loud and angry display, some spectacle, a piece of Des'ree? Let them all choke on it. The butcher looked up from his carving table, startled, a red symmetry of guts between them.

Xavier spoke as loudly as he could.

'Sell me that goat, there, brother. Sell it to me for a whole *heap* of Governor Intiasar money.'

The crowd erupted. The band trumpeted. The butcher genuflected: his beloved goat, first. *First for the feast*, people sang and jigged with the band. *Neh-neh-neh. First-first-first.*

It start now.

✱

He was fifteen and the rain so heavy he'd taken a short cut through the empty market, its wooden stalls like the stripped bones of a roast, dripping water. There were two girls standing there, laced between the stalls, dressed in blue-and-white school uniforms, yelling *psssst, hey boy*. Rain ran grooves down his face.

He preferred her friend: her astonishing chest and wide smile. He visited her home twice, but it came to nothing. He'd all but forgotten Nya until she walked up to him months later. *Remember me?* she said. She had very black, shiny hair and even, white teeth.

He went to see her nearly every hot day for weeks, slipping

in when her parents were out working, finally summoning the courage to touch her. He was overcome by the light in her eyes, and her appetite. Her pum-pum was an anthurium. She had perfect, neat eyebrows.

Nya wasn't offended; she kicked her feet in the air and told him how gooooood it felt.

They remained virgins. They were too young, he thought. Not according to the other boys, but according to him. He was used to doing things according to himself.

It was good to be a boy that summer: following Io and his friends when they'd let him, kicking boxes in the dirt, two stones for a goal. Patching bits of their grandfather's canoe. Sneaking the lobsters out of the pots and setting them on the girls to see who would hold their ground. When Nya walked by, he found himself puzzled. What were you to do with the best of riddles, a girl who let you see her whole body? There had to be some special rule. He could feel her watching him, ears pricked and expectant. He didn't know what to do that was right, so he ignored her desperately.

And then more hot afternoons.

Lena Delziel was a girl of a different hue. Tall and brittle and like a long kind of mouse. Her ribcage showed through her clothes. Lena didn't want to play-fight or talk about important things. She wanted to hold hands and kiss with a closed mouth. She wore a ribbon in her hair. He sat at her family table and ate kidney bean stew with pig tails and answered her father's questions about his father. The girls from school sang songs at them. None of it had anything to do with Nya's eager, increasingly skilful hands.

Force-ripe, the old women said about Nya. *And she don't even get a thigh cuff yet.*

It all fell apart on the day Nya found him in Bend Down Market, feeding Lena lemon cake in between chaste kisses and teasing from the vendors. He became aware of someone in his peripheral vision and surfaced in time to catch Nya's bewildered expression. The gods had not come down to jeer and beat drums, but Nya did fix her face and turn on her heel.

✷

The next time he saw her, he thought himself a man. Nineteen and important. Des'ree's acolyte. Tired from sixteen-hour shifts. Virginity lost, not to Lena, but a pretty putt-putt driver with acid in her blood that burned him more than once. People knew him when he walked through town. Strangers drew lots on his face. Would he be the one?

So he was confident enough to walk up to Nya when he saw her getting out of the back of a putt-putt between Pleasure Grow and Carenage beaches, like it was easy. He could expect her to forgive him his childish indiscretions.

Hey, Nya.

She studied his face.

It wasn't the same; the innocence was gone. They looked at each other and made noises with their mouths, and the wanting knocked inside them, distracting them and drowning out words. They'd only known each other in furtive corners, so standing side by side in the sunshine felt strange, he too tall, she too short. By the time they got to the empty home of one of his friends, she was deep in a daydream, and he worried he might frighten her. He poured her bad red wine out of his friend's cupboard. Wordless, she drank, even though she hated alcohol, and sat on the edge of the bed, as there was nowhere else, and the house smelled like dog. They were both sweating in the heat and the knocking inside her was almost imperceptible and the dog hair that covered everything stuck to her bare arms and his face and when he laid her down and kissed her, his head felt as if it might burst. He kissed her over and over, not knowing what else to do, trying to bring back their good and trusting feelings, but her heart shards stuck through her chest and cut him.

He knew she was born with five hearts: chest, yes and one in each wrist, another behind her left ear; the tiniest beating in her third toe. Still the grip and flow of her left him surprised and gasping.

✱

Io arrived as Xavier was examining the goat carcass, twisting and turning it with the butcher, still trying to calm down after the soft woman's offence. His brother was criss-crossed with twelve blood-spattered chickens. A bright glass gourd hung from his hip.

'You want me to take the goat back to Moue?' Io picked the animal off the hook with one hand and hoisted it under his arm. He stopped, seeing Xavier's puffed and angry face. 'Who trouble you?'

'Don't worry about it.'

'Somebody bother you, Xav?'

'Don't *worry* about it, I said.'

They eyed each other. Io tucked the dangling goat closer.

The butcher winced. 'I could send two man up with it,' he offered. 'That is not a problem.'

Io chuckled. 'I can take back Intiasar goat for him.'

'Shut *up*, Io.'

Io frowned. 'Really, is what, so?'

'One *gyal* say is him cause him wife to dead,' the butcher volunteered.

Xavier glared. Why did people never stop talking?

'You should see the nasty bitch, too,' said the butcher. 'Make me want to sleep.'

'Which girl? Where?'

'Lime green!' observed the butcher.

'*Forget* it, Io.'

Io sucked his teeth hard and flung the goat down on the blood-flecked table, ignoring the yellow man's stifled curse. He ducked into the butcher's tent, sternly beckoning Xavier to follow.

Sighing, Xavier obeyed. Io had been good and patient for a year.

Behind the tarpaulin, surrounded by buckets of red water and internal organs, Io examined his feet.

'What?' Xavier kept his voice quiet.

The dead chickens on Io's back quivered.

'I have a woman,' he said.

'Blessings.' Xavier was surprised. This was good news, indeed. Io's marriage had been bad.

Io shuffled, then held his gaze. 'Yes. This one . . .' He softened. 'I too old to get excited about woman. You know. But *this* one . . .' He shook his head, embarrassment and pleasure in equal parts.

Xavier grinned and slapped his back, all anger gone. Their heads bobbed up and down, faces splitting. The chickens bobbed. This was the best he'd felt in a long time. Io looked like a man who was sure about a thing.

'So when you bringing her to the house?'

'Not now.'

'A drink, man, after the wedding foolishness done.'

Io grabbed his shoulder; it hurt. Xavier tried to pull away, but the fingers holding him were iron. His brother began to speak slowly, as if he could see each one of the words.

'All these months I know this woman and I thinking: why I don't bring her to my family? You first, I'm thinking, then Chse. But I never.' He nodded to himself; the grip deepened. Xavier winced; Io didn't seem to notice. 'My woman get concerned. She strong, y'know. But she feeling like maybe I not ready for her, not like I say I am. So I have to ask myself, is what, so?'

It felt as if their entire conversation was booming across the market. Around them, the smell of dead animals thickened.

'You stink, Xav.'

Xavier winced, puzzled, affronted.

'I . . . *stink*?'

'No, no. Not like that. I mean you stink with the *sadness*, Xav. I can't bring people around you. What is wrong with you?'

Rage threatened the rippling white tarpaulin above their heads. Bewilderment, to be so misunderstood, by Io, of all people.

'What you expect from me? Nya *dead* today!' His voice rose. 'And a woman out there talking about suicide? People say that? It was an *accident*, Io!'

'Yes, Xav. We mourn with you. Is a sad, sad thing.' Io loosened his grip. His kindness had returned; perhaps it had never gone away, even in the anger and the woman-softness. 'But you sad the same way you was sad a year ago.'

How could he be truly kind, and say such a stupid thing?

'Why you mourning *this* way for a woman you never even love?'

Xavier opened his mouth and closed it. He felt exposed and foolish.

'The day Nya leave, we all did know where she gone. But you

never notice for *two days*, Xavier. You was in your kitchen. You *realise* that, right?'

'I get *busy*.'

'Everybody else but you *know* she have a man. Alright, a man don't want to know his wife playing, even if he don't love her, is his wife, but she come back and she *tell* you. So what you think you owe her?'

He tried to pick the right words out of the jumble in his mind. That he hadn't known her girlfriends hated him, or that her father had begged her not to marry him. She'd told him years later, screamed it at him.

Io was shaking his head. 'Let her ghost go visit her *man*! Why you have to deal with that? You still not well. Is what, so?'

He could smell the moth in his pocket, as if it was all over his body, more pungent than the blood buckets. He was aware of a small headache, beginning in his left eye socket. He sat down on a small bench beside a pile of sweetbreads.

'Take the goat back to Moue, Io. I beg you.'

'You need to explain this to me, brother. To somebody.'

'I am *begging* you.'

He turned away, heard Io sigh and eventually leave. Touched the book in his bag with his fingertips.

He'd made her sad, her whole life.

✱

Nya went missing for two weeks; neither police bribes nor grass-roots gossip provided a clue. He'd wondered how she walked so silent, macaenus wife and all. Perhaps she'd stowed away in one of the off-island ships. Sometimes people did that, although he couldn't believe it of her.

She came back one day when he was standing in the garden and thinking about her. He rocked back on his heels at her voice. He'd been watching frogs in his pond and flocks of grey birds overhead.

Xavier.

No one else had that poet voice.

Yes.

Is Nya.

Yes. His head hurt.

Is me.

I know.

Silence, then: *You send police on me.*

You alright? He wanted to say more but couldn't.

No.

He leaned against a sweating tree trunk and watched the children on the sand below. He was afraid to turn around. He had the absurd thought that if he did, she might not be there. And in the silence, he began to think he was right.

I not coming back, Xav.

I know.

Suddenly, it seemed he did.

She was crying. *You not going to look at me?*

What you want me to say?

His voice was cold and he hated the sound of it.

Anything! She sounded so disappointed, but he didn't know what she was talking about or what she needed, and it made him feel stupid and sad at the same time. *Anything! Xavier! I leave you!*

He waited. Then *Nya*, a voice called. It was no louder than a sigh behind laughter, but he knew what he heard and what it meant. He could hear her murmuring: *Go, go, go.* Like running wind through a conch shell.

Who you leave me for, Nya?

Nobody at all, she said. Then, as if the conch shell wind had lifted her up: *Somebody who love me, who care about me, who put me first. You know what is like all these years, knowing you never choose me?*

But . . . He didn't understand. She was not well. *Of course I chose you.*

She was on him. Holding him from behind. Hot, hot skin. He was astonished at how unfamiliar her body felt.

I am begging you, Xav. Tell me the truth when I ask you. Even if it burn you, I am begging you.

He could feel her nose and lips along in his spine. *Yes, yes*, he said, in perfect dread and feeling as if something was coming that would answer everything: *Yes.*

I don't know what you call love. But however you understand it. Xavier, in all these years. You ever love me?

Nya . . .

You know what I mean, Xavier!

She was sobbing, and he did know.

No, he said.

He'd married her because she'd wanted it, more than anything else. But it was Anise Latibeaudearre he'd loved.

8

SOON COME, that's what Anise had finally written on the chalk-board outside her workspace. It was a phrase used so often, in so many different ways, it could mean anything at all. She hoped nobody got vex and wiped it off.

She put her hands on her hips and stared up at the factory where Tan-Tan worked. Closed: tight shut like a conch shell.

She had never seen the Dukuyaie toy factory locked or still, this green behemoth rising out of the ground. She was tempted to call out at the top of her voice: *hold daaaaaaaawgg*, like the elders selling jewellery house to house, tapping on gates, trying to avoid excited, noisy yard dogs.

Governor Intiasar and Leo Brenteninton had painted their factories white, blue, even tongue-pink over the years, before this green monstrosity, intended to blend back into the Dukuyaie hills. None of the colours worked; the factories still invaded the skyline, distracting you on your way to work or school or sea. When she was a little girl there was only one toy factory, a small building over Carenage beach run by Leo and his wife. The toys were put on racks and sold early in the morning two days a week, all to Popisho children.

She craned her neck at the silent windows. This was once a friendly neighbourhood, a residential, pretty place, with fami-lies in the yard. But most people had moved out after the factory arrived. There was talk of government money changing hands.

Up and down the road, houses stood uninhabited, creaking and growing mice and weeds like nasal hair. How quiet and lonely these back streets were, with the factory shut up so! If she'd thought about it, she'd have *known* it would close for the Intiasar wedding jollification, like everything else, just that she'd trusted Tan-Tan, pulling his work bag over his shoulder. It was a clever lie. She never came here. And he'd never lied before.

How you know?

Now where could he have gone, eh?

Gone to him woman for breakfast.

She was a bad cook; she came from a line of women who'd been far too busy. Legend had it that when her grandmother Ama Tete turned forty she'd stopped cooking *braps!* and announcing that the quicker wives learned to live on air and spittle, the sooner their husbands would respect them. Anise never felt comfortable in what she thought of as Tan-Tan's kitchen. Maybe if she'd been better at it, a better wife . . .

If a man want a cook, he hire one, nah? Or do it himself, if he have a mind.

Now who had said such a thing to her? The answer was just on the edge of her memory.

She slipped through the factory gates, unsure of what she intended. Closed was closed. What if Tan-Tan came to the doors right now and saw her? Asked her why she was here, interrupting his overtime. *Why we can't just try again with a baby, Anise, you could do it, if you put your mind to it.*

Anise slammed her fist against the green front door. It swung inwards so smoothly she found herself off balance. The bangles on her arms rocked: heavy circles of stone, bone, shell and iron; made of old cart tyres and black seed pods baked in the sun. She'd once clouted a man with her right arm after he'd tried to rub himself against her hip.

'Hello?'

A deserted desk stood sentinel in front of a corridor. She walked past it, almost tiptoeing. She'd never been inside a factory.

'Hello?'

If Tan-Tan was a cheating-lying rass, there might be evidence here. He had an office; there could be a cupboard, a locker inside, the hub of an entire hidden life. She might find them together. Doing overtime.

But she was inside a *toy* factory. Her jaw ached with excitement.

She walked on, past rooms full of brown desks and chairs. There were no personal things and the floor was shiny and cheap, echoing with her footsteps. Maybe she'd find a guard, sleeping under a grapefruit tree at the back. Most Popisho people left their doors unlocked, but this was Intiasar-Brenteninton property and things weren't how they used to be. Who dared invade the heart of island industry?

Me, I dare, she thought.

Now you righteous, said the little voice.

At the end of the corridor the passage split in two. Without thinking she took the right-hand way, mouthing the old rhyme. *Left hand love, right hand mischief.* She wasn't following no damn love.

You saying you don't love Tan-Tan anymore?

Don't be stupid.

You just said it.

I never.

If a man want a cook, he hire one. Or do it himself. The little phrase was in her head now, turning circles. Her grandmother would have approved.

She could smell paint and oil and wood and metal, and hot glass and men and women's sweat.

She was eleven the day she came home from school and her father said Leo's toys were gone: that her big stuffed crow had flown away and her doll snapped. She'd looked at her father hard, felt a sickness in her belly, like he'd taken her navel and said she didn't need it anymore. Because why was he talking to her as if she was stupid?

Thou shalt not lie, was what his Bible said.

Her friends whispered Intiasar's men came and took the toys. And Leo's one small factory, why, it became four and then six, as if the toys they took back swelled the buildings like trapped wind and no one said anything about why the toys weren't for Popisho children anymore. But there was plenty said about Bertrand Intiasar, back from foreign, newly married, Leo's partner, and full of business ideas to benefit the whole community. Running for Governor. They said he was too young, but she'd known even then he was the kind of man who got what he wanted, because what could he have said to Pastor Latibeaudearre to make him lie?

She reached a door at the end of the right-is-mischief corridor, bashed it open, and stared.

The warehouse yawned before her, like church. The walls, a perfect, pale blue. Oh sky, no one sky could be better: towering, sweeping windows, floor to ceiling. She could see the fat white clouds above her, feel the heat outside, sweating against the glass. Saws and other spiky things; conveyor belts, hammers, glue guns, sacks of material, things that made other things. But it was nothing compared to the splendour in front of her.

The toys were waiting for boxing. Row upon row, like fields of flowers.

'Hello,' Anise whispered.

She began to walk through the huge workroom. So much to see! Intricately carved boats with red and blue silken sails that would never sink or blow away; big yellow toy chests, stuffed with knitted mice and parrots, with creaky hinges that made her laugh and sandalwood smells that made her sneeze. She stopped to hold finely woven child-sized hammocks to her lips, mouthing wishes she couldn't hear even inside her own head, much less understand. Wooden alphabets, each letter so elaborate, she could call them nothing but jewellery. Hanging mobiles from which engraved suns and pears swayed in glorious thick strands; dolls with soft tummies, whimpering when she picked them up; little tables and chairs in the shape of animals: not cats or dogs, but goats and wasps and one she'd never seen before, with a soft snout and a curly coat and two tails; long-legged puppets with longer fingernails and black eyes and wooden skins all making crackle-crackle noises when you set them to dance a stringed jig. Boxes of fireworks – she remembered them filling her childhood, at every occasion she could think of, gods, where had the Popisho fireworks gone? Mad swirls of silver-blue lightning and crimson stars. A whole sky of melting yellow moons that trickled into their hair and faces and turned into caramel. A firework whale – she'd seen a real one in the ocean once, but so far away – the firework dove through the trees above their heads, blowing fire-water. The men sending the fireworks up seemed so happy and smelled like sugar water and burning.

Her children – her *daughters* would have loved holding her hands and watching fireworks.

Purple-black crows, perched on the shelf above her head, on the brink of flight.

She held one to her throat, felt the silky feathers, hugged

it to her breasts, blinking back the tears before they started. She tapped a sonorous drum. She'd had one like this too, she remembered now: you could play them, or they could play to you, especially when you were sulking or angry or sad. Hers often struck up a rhythm at supper, as if it had become tired of silence and decided to create a party. The drum confounded Uncle Coorah – when he split it open, he found nothing but air.

Cors, her mother would snort, twisting her head 180 degrees, like an owl, like she did when she was angry. *Too much cors in my house, get it out.*

Anise paused in front of a tray of babies' rattles, like a pile of oranges, and picked up a large blue box nestled in between them. The box had a compartmentalised base and thin layers of fragrant cotton. She peeled them aside. A box of toy butterflies! She turned the box this way and that, admiring the soft contours of the beasts: meaty thoraxes, striped, spotted, brilliant emerald greens and purples and chocolate browns. The wings were striated, filigreed, shot through with sleek veins, patches of cerulean so intense her tongue might burn on the roof of her mouth; so extravagant you might believe they were once alive.

She picked up a sheaf of thin paper lying on top of one of the waiting, empty boxes. It was a list of the cargo to be packaged and taken to the Dead Islands warehouse. Two hundred of this and one hundred of that. Authorised by Tan-Tan Joseph. She rubbed her thumb over her husband's signature. Tan-Tan said every man and woman in Popisho should bow down in front of the factory workers, how they kept the country alive. *You know how much they sell one of those toys for in foreign, Anise?* and she asked how much, but he shook his head and rolled his eyes.

The idea of him in the middle of this cacophony of beauty softened her. How could she forget what she loved about him most? He was a man who made things with his hands. These were more than mere toys. They were works of art and island, and she knew he took pride in being part of that. She stroked the soft silk back of a black crab, tracing the detail of its ruby eyes and little claws. She'd broken into private property, like a mad coney burrowing under the walls o gods. A doll's skirt rustled against her arm and she shivered.

Ama Tete used to shrug and say *man sit down and spread they legs because something in between there.* How man found it hard to show sorry, because their testicles got in the way. Tan-Tan and she, they were not at their best. But to impregnate another woman, and just proud of it, so? No: a man responsible for handling these sumptuous things, he wouldn't do her like that. He'd made mirrors for their bedroom with his own hands. *So you can admire yourself, pretty gyal*, that's what he said into her neck-curve.

She stood, confused. What to do, now? Go home and sit down at his kitchen table and wait on . . . what? More lies? Like an obedient little wife? She didn't know where he was or how long he would be.

If a man want a cook, he—

There was a woman just outside the window, painting.

Anise stared.

The woman looked to be in her early thirties, barefoot, wearing nothing except a brown, open-necked man's tunic over bare and glistening thighs. She was so busy dipping a large paintbrush into a can of paint and applying it to the side of the building she didn't see Anise watching her.

Xavier Redchoose, *that* was who said it. Standing and smiling down at her. Mr Macaenus. Look how much time had passed since she let that tall piece of a man pass through her mind.

She would have let thoughts of him distract her more if the paint on the paintbrush the woman was holding hadn't been so *very* bright orange and if the woman's thigh cuff hadn't looked *so* baroque and expensive, even from here. Was that gold inlay in the weave?

An Orange Man who was actually an Orange Woman in a gold thigh cuff would be a *splendid* thing to find out about.

9

Romanza trotted through the bright-coloured bush and across the dry land. Leaves blurred past him: yellow, blue, orange, red, silver-backed, he saw each one. The poison from last night had worn off, replaced by the whirr and buzz of the new day.

Another opportunity for true things, which meant difficult things. Moments of honesty and risk. Sharing. When people couldn't say their true things out loud – and so many couldn't – he searched for authentic moments to witness instead. A man, bent double, caning a chair. A child singing to themselves. Animals: suckling, defecating, cleaning fur. Someone making lace or touching a musical instrument. Kisses of regret on morning steps. Even violence.

He needed to know the meaning of things, and so he was worried about Sonteine. Perhaps frowning and lying the day before your wedding was normal; he'd never known a bride. Indigent lovers grew together like absentminded weeds, with few words and no formalised ritual. He knew no more than his own way, and Pilar's way. But he couldn't shake the feeling Sonteine had come to tell him something important and lost her nerve. Perhaps she'd decided it was a girl matter, and that he wouldn't understand; he hoped she found a girl to speak to. Their mother wasn't good at such things.

He increased his pace, until the bush became a kaleidoscopic blur. He couldn't see any of the toy factories from this part of the Dead Islands, but he'd find the closest one tonight and go there for orange paint. It pleased him to steal from his father, and to use better-quality paint than the other graffiti boy.

When someone else began writing in orange all over fences and buildings, he had been confused, then angry. People trusted his messages and this imposter was riding his reputation like a mangy cat. But slowly, he became amused. There was mischief in the other messages, a wry tone his own graffiti lacked – it rejoiced in the language of peasants and poked fun at old-fashioned ideas. He approved. This was a comrade, and he'd felt alone too long.

Then three months ago, the messages changed. The criticism became systemic. Run-down buildings exposed. Plans to reduce social funding uncovered. Incessant problems with water, community power, a constant railing against lower wages. Romanza had a clear sense of the mystery artist on his father's heels, snapping, although Bertie was still ahead of the game. His father acted quickly when accusations could be proven and seemed smoothly concerned, even grateful. Heads rolled; people lost jobs. He talked openly of the new graffiti in his unchallenged radio speeches, said it was good for people to speak their minds, although he couldn't sanction this person's expensive and destructive mode of communication.

Nobody argued; it was enough to madden a body.

Then suddenly: this singular missive, everywhere.

WHAT'S YOUR ALTERNATIVE?

He was as eager as the rest to see the man reveal himself. Or perhaps it was a woman. Yes, he liked that idea. Might he discover her one night, dancing down the middle of the thin, silent street towards him? What would they do, to make the moment true? Nod and smile and pass on by? And would it be different, if she knew what *he* was? Would she write his truth on the walls, to remind his father?

✱

When he approached fifteen, his parents, like all families, considered how his cors could make a life. What to do with a child who knew a lie? He needed an exceptional master-teacher, his mother insisted. One with the time and passion, with impeccable reputation.

Most of all, his father said, *the boy need to be useful. You know how these blasted people are, Teacher* – looking hard at the obeah woman in attendance. *If they don't think you have use, life is hell.* Romanza knew his father had already paid this woman much money, slipping it into her hands, pockets, not even trying to hide it. Money, to say his son was strong and could take the reins one day. And how much did a lie cost?

The obeah woman was a pragmatist: she took the money. She also told the truth. *This cors deep. It may take us time to find the right place for him. But he can acolyte with the police chief. Not one fool will get past him.*

So Romanza sat with the police chief. The chief shoved men and women into a seat in front of the boy and asked them questions. Romanza said no and yes when the police chief looked at him.

You thief the man house, you stinking dirty liar?

No.

He lie?

Yes.

The chief smiled and hugged his hands under his armpits and looked at the thief and said: *I did know. Look at how him face scrunch up.* And then he would take up a large implement and beat them around the shoulders, a blow in between every single word: *This – is – for – lying – you – dog – court – going – to – deal – with – you – but – this – is – for – lying.*

And also:

You hold down the woman and touch her breast?

No, sir.

He lie?

He telling the truth.

Boy, you think *about hold down the woman and touch her breast?*

No!

He lie?

Yes.

And then another beating.

At night, his father took him to dice rooms. His father always had two big men with him, and he sat with strangers, debating into the early morning, clinking and drinking and yelling. Himself, dozing in the corner, his father rubbing his shoulders, whispering to keep him awake.

I need you to remember who lie.

A roaring, ebullient man with sour eyes: *Send the boy to him hammock, Intiasar! He not even grow crotches-hair yet and you have him out here?*

Can I trust them, Romanza?

Not the one in the blue tunic, Papa. He is a liar.

Good. Anyone else?

That loud man.

Yes?

He says his wife is sweet-tempered.

And?

He doesn't believe it to be so.

The father rubbed his son's head and rubbed the wrinkle between his eyes.

It will all be well, don't worry.

I not worried, said Romanza.

He knew all that he was.

He hated his job. The obeah woman had made a mistake; the police chief was not his master-teacher, this was not the proper use of his cors. It was dirty and violent. It was dishonest.

Then he met Pilar Tomasz: dragged into the police station and accused of setting spell on somebody's cane field. Pilar, no more than eighteen, rags barely covering. Dirty, but sparkling teeth. Red skin in the days and cool at night. Pure-bred peasant, but the boys look like kin.

You curse the lady cane field, boy?

Pilar won't answer so the police chief applies his knuckles.

On the floor, Pilar spits out blood and hums.

You curse the cane field?

I . . .

Speak!

I . . . Gesticulating. The police chief bends close. *I . . . curse . . . you.*

Good! The chief is merry. *Because I feeling to give a good beating today. So lie right there, boy. I don't see no witness. Stay right there, I going to cut a rope and soak it in salt water for you.*

The boys regard each other across the room when the chief is gone.

Is you curse the cane field? asks Romanza.

No.

Then why you don't tell him?

He is an idiot.

That is not the answer.

I not answering any question like I'm a criminal.

Romanza squinted. *No, that is not it, either.*

I proud like my mother.

No.

I hate cruel people.

No.

He has a look about him Romanza has seen before: a willingness to consider the lies he didn't realise he told himself. This kind of lying gives him thin burning lines in his gums.

Pilar looks at him like he's interesting and hums. They can hear the splash of water outside. The salt water in the rope will dry on the skin and get into the cuts and burn.

Romanza pours water from the chief's jug and Pilar drinks, lying on the floor, one leg hitched over the other.

Why you don't tell him the truth?

I like to look strong.

You like to look strong, yes, but that is not the answer to why you don't tell him.

Pilar hums.

Romanza says, *That's a coney song.*

Yes? says Pilar. *Lizard teach me.*

If you work out why you can't tell him, then you can tell him and I can confirm it and he won't beat you.

No use telling.

Why you won't tell him the truth?

Because beating is nothing.

He pulls his clothes aside to show Romanza the scars, wheeling across his shoulder blades, whipped around his waist, deep into the cleft of his buttocks.

Romanza can hardly breathe.

It will hurt me if he beats you.

The chief is coming up the steps.

Pilar considers. They look at each other, recognising what they share.

I will tell him I don't mess with no cane field.

Romanza touches Pilar's back for the first of what will be so many times.

Master . . .

Pilar smiles.

. . . can I sit by you?

The parents scream. What is this boy to teach him, this nasty indigent, his only friends the moon and the bush? The obeah woman is called back, and three others, for the parents will not be hushed or comforted or trust Romanza's decision. Acolyte indigent. Never. Never. *He will be of no use, no use, no* use, roared Intiasar. But eventually judgement was made: the only important question was whether Pilar had something to teach Romanza. And he did.

He knew the land, and it never lied.

Romanza told the police chief goodbye and thank you. He told his mother goodbye and that he would be back for pudding. He told Sonteine he would send her messages. He told his red-eyed, tight-fisted father goodbye. When Pilar came to fetch him, his father barred the door, half pleading, half shouting.

You not going anywhere boy, don't you see?

For the first time, he let himself be angry with his father, for everything, and perhaps for more than he deserved. Pilar was waiting, with his mouth, and with his hands and his graceful, scarred body and his father was old – he did not understand love.

Romanza wanted to be under trees and close to water, to climb into mountains until his body was bruised, cut and sore; to touch every Popisho tree; to never lie again. To earn his own staring eyes.

He pushed past his father and walked over to Pilar in the yard.

No, Zaza! yelled Sonteine. Ah, his twin knows him. *No, Zaza, don't!* but he'd gone too far to stop.

He put his mouth on Pilar's mouth, head light with his own defiance.

It was only Sonteine, blocking the way, who stopped his father charging; long enough for Romanza to grab Pilar's hand. They run, run, run, fingers clasped and running, amazed and guilty, loving and terrified, each step a rebellion. And long after they are far away, he can still hear his father wailing.

My son cannot be a chi-chi man! My son – !

10

Xavier had not thought on Anise Latibeaudearre for years. Deciding to stop had been like an urgent excision, best for all of them: she, Nya, him too.

Pewter Redchoose had warned his sons, some woman could turn a man mad without even trying.

He met Anise during his time of consideration, three months after the macaenus testing ended. Des'ree had given him a year – not a minute over! – that would end in his ascension and her retirement. For days, Xavier was no more than dimly aware that the duty had been won. He was expected to spend the time embracing his new identity, seeking wise counsel, buying his restaurant, his home. Something. He only knew he felt exhausted and peculiar, much older than twenty-four, desperately grateful it was done. Years of his life, training. Waiting.

He missed the other acolytes: his brothers and sisters. They refused to speak to him, even Entaly.

They'll get over it, said Des'ree.

His mother had been dead three years, leaving his childhood home empty, so he moved out of Des'ree's cavernous house and onto his parents' old pallet, sleeping until he ached. People didn't know what to make of him, or how to be in his company, but perhaps that had always been true. He sought out cold waterfalls, small thick forests, and thought about nothing at all.

Nya came at night. It was good to see her: she was like a helm back into an ordinary life, except nothing would be ordinary again, now everyone knew what he was. He gave her ginger tea, baked three kinds of biscuit: fig, lemon and naseberry, asked for her family, and fucked with her silently until they slept. It was a relief to touch someone besides Des'ree.

Nya never stayed long. She seemed busy. He didn't ask about her life, not more than she volunteered; it wasn't his business.

Perhaps he'd loved that time best of all. Popisho people remained devoted to Des'ree, eating her food as she called them in, touching her hand in the streets, pressing ever more lavish gifts upon her. Her imminent retirement seemed preposterous to most, including him. On the streets, the few who recognised him cut their eyes at him, nervous and angry, then servile if he looked at them directly.

They'll get over it, said Des'ree.

After some weeks of numbed feeling and no ideas, he decided to try his hand at teaching. It wasn't the first time he'd considered the task – communicating his passion would be one of his new responsibilities and teaching seemed a good way to begin. He could offer free cookery lessons to anyone who wanted them. Des'ree said he had his own budget now, but he was still surprised at the unquestioning agreement from the Governor's office – everybody haggled, especially high-hill politicians. Those were the days he was grateful to Intiasar for the unequivocal support, for what he thought of as spiritual leadership.

After a nervous start, he found himself well suited to instruction: patient, enthusiastic, unexpectedly articulate. He might even be inspiring, one day. He travelled across the islands, following demand, returning from each course invigorated, his notebooks full of lists and sketches. A sense of his own impending influence grew.

He took moth every morning and evening. His hunger for it

was like the wings, dark and complicated. He left smudges on people, moth shadows on their cheekbones, a dusting of moth cells in women's hair. He felt infectious, steel-thighed; his core was still and strong. He owned the space around his body. He was beginning to know his own mind again.

★

His fourth residential cookery course happened in Lukia Town in Dukuyaie. He took a canoe over and was escorted from the quay by his shrill, excited hostess, a local philanthropist plucking at his sleeve, gabbling, telling him how blessed she felt. He listened and nodded, spoke low, hoping to calm her.

He asked to be alone in the kitchen so she left him peering into a big-bellied stove and replacing the knives with his own. He listened to the zip of doctor birds at the window and the peach trees in the wind. He heard someone say *sorry, sorry!* and looked up with the vague interest you feel when a stranger speaks too loudly.

She was bald, and it suited her very well. All the better to appreciate her unexpected eyes. What was that expression? Gentle curiosity? Amusement? He felt a tremendous softening and swallowed to allow it to settle through him. She stood, looking: no obvious blaze of attraction or interest, not even a smile. Bangles rustled and clunked on her strong arms. He'd heard men say they knew the moment they met their wives and he'd always scorned the notion.

Are you disturbing our guest of honour? The hostess was back. *No*, the bangled woman said. *I'm not disturbing him.*

Xavier turned away to calm himself. Snuck another look. Yes, just as striking as she'd been seconds before. Dark fuzz on her head, like the belly of a kitten. The hostess swept her off, like laundry. His feelings fell about each other. Minutes later, he was called to a draped purple podium to deliver a speech for students and local dignitaries. He'd decided to talk without taking moth; sometimes it was necessary to remember who he was. But now he'd seen her, he wanted to run to his chambers and his pouch. Without it, he tripped over his sentences and wasn't at all funny.

She stood, listening and serious. He hardly knew how he spoke. He had to grip the ridiculous podium. He fought through the questions, through the sycophantic thank-you speeches. The woman with the beautiful eyes didn't ask any questions; he wondered if he'd disappointed her. He thanked them all, warned of an early start and many onions. Laughing, the students dispersed into the warm evening, some to their quarters, others to take butterflies and light refreshment in the orchard. The woman had disappeared. The idea that she might be a dignitary's wife felt like physical pain.

No, there she was: hesitating at the entrance to the courtyard.

Could she be . . . *waiting?*

His stomach rolled.

She looked back, and straight at him.

Touch me, he thought, and all he could think was: *love me*, and all he could think was: *why I never prepare for this moment better? Look how I had all these years of life to ready myself for your arrival, and what I did with them? Wasted them on other women, and other ideas, and now you here, I not ready.* He wanted to sit in front of her and have her tell him everything she'd ever experienced in all of her life.

He said hello. She said her name was Anise Latibeaudearre.

He followed her and another student to a table and chairs in the peach tree orchard, watching her walk through the grass. She had an amazing backside: he'd never seen its like before. She was clever and opinionated and started her sentences with clauses like 'how about' and 'do you feel' and 'you going love this' as if she was already friends with everybody. He was slavishly grateful for the opinions they shared and ready to dash away anything he'd ever known, in order to properly examine her theories. He spent their first hour together trying not to touch her or fall to his knees, trying to include the other woman – whose name he'd not caught – in the conversation. He wanted Anise in his bed, but also, he didn't want to do anything but look at her face. Her laughter was unspeakably arousing, like it belonged to three people. A kind of giggle-snort-hoot.

Her gaze was steady, open, honest.

When the hostess came to draw the women away to the bowls court at the back of the house – *you trouble macaenus too long now, come* – Anise looked surprised, as if she'd forgotten who he was, or didn't truly know what it meant.

He watched them leaving and sat back, astonished he'd never believed in love.

✳

He got up early the next day, took a handful of moth and headed for the kitchen, palms singing. In less than an hour spices began filtering through the building. Vegetables simmering for soup; spoons dripping stock; sticky ginger running out of his palms into cake. Glistening, sizzling food and such colours! Tasting plates of tiny, moist puddings topped with sugar sculpture. Velvet-green crisp salads; bloody red coney cleaned and cut down; works of art on the sideboard. He hummed as he measured herbs and butter and oil and flour for each student table; rolled pink and purple boiled sweets; deep-fried persimmon slices. Strings of caramel and drinks thickened with avocado, sorghum, cane. He wanted to show off for her.

When the nervous students walked into the kitchen, he was pleased to see Anise clap her hands.

Taste it all, he said.

It was shocking to find she couldn't cook. It was more than inexperience – this was a genuine lack of aptitude. She couldn't tell the difference between the smell of red and black pepper; laughed apologetically when she cut herself chopping root vegetables; burnt a pan and another student in the first ten minutes. The class stirred, sighing, waiting on her to finish a round of simple tasks. He wanted to bellow at their unkindness and had to decide quickly how to apportion tasks, so she didn't hold everyone back. He set her to washing rice, the rest to pastry; felt her gaze on him. Surely her expression was more than that of an attentive student? He was puffed and hopeful until he saw her turn to glazing carrots with the same thoughtfulness. She wore a deep purple robe with yellow spots on it and her arms were nude, the bangles gone, replaced by lengths of thin red chain in the native way. He tried not to watch her frock-tail as it swayed; dare he assume she wore a flirtatious thigh cuff?

He went over and muttered she would have to take off the jewellery to be safe in the kitchen. She looked embarrassed.

Pardon, macaenus.

He felt a pain in his chest. Someone had spoken to her about etiquette.

Xavier, he said.

Xavier, she said.

Eyes on them.

That night the students gathered to take rum custard, butterflies and lime, sitting at tables in the orchard. Crowds hovered around him. Anise chattered with two other women, occasionally looking up, as if she wanted to know where he was. As night deepened, most people dispersed. He found himself praying in her direction. *Don't leave. Stay.* He wondered the hangers-on couldn't hear him calling them names, wishing impalement on the men and excruciating labour pains on the women. Until they were alone, her acquaintances gone like obliging smoke, and she hesitant, like the first day.

Hello, he said.

That smile.

Nine precious evenings they have, sitting bare-footed and telling each other stories, the peaches dropping and bursting. He admired the thin brown scars on her knees as she scooped glistening fruit from the earth and stuck her fingers into her mouth. He'd always been a lumbering man, making splat and booming noises, only manoeuvring through the kitchen with careful practice, but in her company the suppleness of his childhood returned. He could sit cross-legged on the grass and get up from that position without using his hands. His feet were in the right place.

They stayed up each night until their eyes were raw, the red-bearded bee-eater birds in the yard complaining for tired. His moth need doubled; he sent for the indigent moth pedlar and slipped out of bed to meet him in the courtyard before dawn.

Woman bird cry when they see love, his students whispered as they passed on by.

On the final night he was determined to declare his feelings. A man had to be brave, to grab his opportunity, even if he felt less-than. But Anise had eaten too much rum custard and wanted to jump leapfrog over the chairs, skull newly shaven and gleaming and threatening to sing. He might break a sweat at the sight of her revolutionary backside, quivering with laughter. He thought of rubbing moth into her scalp and licking it off. What mysteries might they uncover in the corner of a dark pallet, touching each other's faces?

I think you is a quiet man pretending to be a loud man, she said, finally sitting down.

Alright, he said. *Is that good?*

She giggled and snapped her fingers. He admired the silver spark running across the back of her hand. She had a remark-able cors; he'd seen her heal others repeatedly and quietly since the moment she got here. Put a cool hand into the arc of his sore back and left it normal for the first time in . . . he couldn't remember. He couldn't imagine how it would feel to make love with that cors in the room.

Some woman like quiet men, he ventured.

I hear you find plenty woman, still.

He was appalled. *No.*

Oh, I hear many.

He didn't want to argue. He wanted to say the right thing, worthy of her. The moon pinwheeled above them. She leaned back, her bare legs strong, shining, well-muscled things. He imagined her childhood: climbing trees, falling off putt-putts, playing kiss-chase, mountain-shifting, argumentative relatives. She'd already spoken of some of it. He wanted to grip her hips in his hands: something about the motion would fill the world. He dug his fingernails into his thigh to stop himself. There had been no invitation, and even worse, she was still tipsy. It made him uncomfortable, it seemed unlike her. She was restless, stroking her throat. For him, surely? Soon she'd say goodnight. She always left before he was done looking. He opened his mouth to say all he felt: no, it had to be perfect.

Tell me something, he begged, buying time.

She straightened, smiling. Used her forefinger to scrape up the final bits of rum custard from a bowl.

I hate my name.

Why?

She gesticulated, grandly. *Is better suited to a single-bosomed woman. You know the kind, Xavier – knees together, mouth like a cat bottom, breasts so bound up you can't see it's two of them.*

He protested at the characterisation.

I am not a forest, she blurted. *You know those women like forests, full of surprises? I not like that. I'm solid. Which is good, though.* She sounded troubled.

Anise . . .

Xavier Red*choose.* She leaned forward, waving her fizzing fingers, patted him. *I think we should go to bed.*

He thought he might faint. She smiled. His chest hurt. He leaned forward to take her dear face in his hands and to kiss her, but she was standing up and stretching, yawning and patting his shoulder and he realised electric seconds before he shamed himself that she hadn't meant it as an invitation, but was bringing the evening to an end. He touched his shoulder where she'd left her fingerprints.

Who tell you that foolishness about a forest woman? he croaked at her departing back.

Oh, my fiancé, she said, and hiccuped into her hand.

There is no pain like assumption.

*

When he returned from the cookery course, he found Nya waiting for him on his parents' back steps. She was wearing tea-coloured hibiscus and she'd plaited her hair the way he liked it, so he could bite her neck. He moved restlessly in front of the door, not inviting her in. He felt angry: spiteful. Anise was to be married, and how could he have assumed otherwise? That this beautiful, funny, open human might be alone? She'd come to learn how to cook for *him*: this lucky apparition, this husband-in-waiting. She'd told him the man's name, but the roaring in his ears had been too loud for him to hear it.

He and Nya, and Des'ree: both involvements had been small and inconsequential. Not good, not right. Nya, especially. He was wasting her time. She should go and find a husband, have her children, have adventures, write her heart out. He would tell her so. She would agree with him. He would visit her, and her family. Her success would make him happy. He sat down on the steps. Nya trailed her fingers up and down his thighs. They spoke lethargically, bits of nothing. Nya leaned forward for a kiss. He meant to speak, but he was too late. In the damp of his neck, where she'd been so many times, she caught the new love. It had changed the texture of his hands and the way he smelled, in ways only a lover could know.

Nya drew back, wordless, searching his face. Xavier tried to hold her, horrified at her eyes, but she stumbled to her feet, lurched across the yard, body in rictus, backbone unhinging, her hearts exploding. He watched her go, shocked. In the moonlight, he saw they had the same quality to their hands and faces; now that he was in love, he could recognise it on her. She had been waiting on him.

A man could be a stupid thing.

He went to find an obeah woman when the heartbreak got too heavy. During the years of testing he'd come to think of obeah women as creatures undergoing slow transformation, as if what they seemed to be – midwives, doulas of magic, eating your food, counsel to Des'ree in slow, intense conversation – was nothing more than a stage in a benevolent process, so you could look at them without burning your eyes. To seek them out in their own places was something else: a risk, for who knew how an obeah woman spent her free time?

There were so few of them young, and she was no exception: lumpy and craggy, lying on a mat in her front yard, baking in the sun. Her body made him think of a pile of commas. He didn't make it more than a few steps into her property before she had him pierced in her sights. He could feel the sharpness through his thorax. He hoped she could be discreet.

Greetings, he said.

She remained silent, lying on her side, head crooked, elbows cracked, and he was a little afraid. He should remain formal.

Good morning, Teacher. I can talk with you?

She stayed silent on her blue mat. She looked like a large beetle and he wondered whether she was dead. Then she hauled herself to her feet and skittered into her house. He followed.

Inside, every surface was covered: pieces of cotton wool, small ceramic birds, bowls of fruit in different stages of rot, off-island plastic figurines, long towering candles and golden baubles. God statues, some so old he didn't recognise their faces. The house smelled of olives and cloves. He sneezed, wondering why she had so many cheap foreign things from the ships. It was only when she swivelled around and glared, he realised his mistake. Her small, hot eyes widened. She flung her black arms up.

No, she snapped.

He backed away, horrified. The cloves and the statues and the silence and his own desperation were confusing him, but the weight of his heart stopped him at the door.

I need help, Teacher.

I can't do anything for you. She slapped her palms on her thighs. She seemed to have calmed as quickly as she was disturbed. Her voice was clipped and old.

How you mean?

I can't do anything for you today. But I hope you find the answer.

But . . . you don't ask me what my problem is.

Don't must ask. The answer is no.

But why? He'd expected something: an incantation, a powder, some Oil of Peace and Prosperity. Some performance. She was Popisho, after all.

He wanted a love spell.

He knew the warnings; he knew what people said. Love this way was never sweet, it was not fair, it didn't last. It was an atrocity: love could not be coerced. Their children would be crippled, dogs would howl under their windows, her kisses would run his belly.

He didn't care.

The obeah woman pushed past him and took a seat on the veranda and said it over and over: *I can't do anything*, and each time it offended him some more. Did she know what he wanted? Or was she merely eccentric? She didn't protest when he sat down next to her. They argued through the afternoon, knee to knee; you would have thought them old friends.

Nothing?

No.

Then what am I here for?

I don't know. But I can't do nothing about it.

Please let me ask the question.

Go and ask somebody else. I don't know who you is.

He was reluctant to say; perhaps it wouldn't matter.

You not going to let me ask the question?

You asking the wrong question.

But how you know?

Ask your heart. Who are you?

He tried to answer. *I am a cook-man.*

Is it? Well now. She sucked her bottom lip, as if something made sense. *Macaenus?*

He nodded.

You have that smell on you. But I can't help you today.

Teacher—

Don't call me that.

What I must call you?

Use my name. That is its purpose.

What is your name?

You come to my house, you ask me things, but you don't know my name? Who are you?

I told you who I am. I don't ask you nothing yet.

In your heart, you ask me.

Please say your name so I can respect you.

It wouldn't make a difference.

An hour passed. He opened his mouth to speak again. The obeah woman sighed, seized him by the ears and folded him up. He didn't have time to be astonished. She broke his ankles with an audible, painless snap, pushing up from the balls of his feet so his toes lay flush against the front of his calves, splintering his hipbones, pushing with the flat of her hands. His hips closed. His penis disappeared between his buttocks. She got up and stood over him, snapping the vertebrae along his spine, making little tutting sounds, as if it was all some kind of examination, and she was getting the answers she needed.

The next thing he knew, he was groaning awake on the beach, at the very edge of the shore, unfolding himself like a piece of paper, the sea making his feet wet and only one name in his ears. *Anise, Anise, Anise.*

Instead of a love spell, he took eleven moth, sitting on the sand eating them one after the other, hardly noticing what he was doing, until his breath was coming so fast he had to notice, had to stand up and sit down again, because the folding had made him feel folded and there was blood on his lips and obeah women were irritating, with their folding spells for children who asked too many questions.

★

People told him the ground around Nya's father's crops was boggy, that the banana trees were rotting and the coca plants exploding in the gloomy murk that was once fertile earth. Her aunties kept finding her unshed tears bubbling through the cracks between the kitchen tiles. More than anything else, he was distressed by reports that Nya couldn't write a line of poetry without the page peeling and the ink spreading in the damp. Her voice had changed, they said, because she was gargling, and her five hearts were swollen with the water. She'd taken to caring for insects and breathing through her nose.

By the time Xavier arrived at her family compound, squelching through the spreading mud, her blood was almost completely water. But she could still see him coming towards her, could feel him grabbing her and clinging to her, hear him exhaling in her ear with the breath of a man who had made a decision. Inside her room and inside her, she heard him crying out when he climaxed, he who was usually such a quiet lover, and she could hear him when he asked her, as they lay still and recovering, the bedroom an inch deep in her tears.

Will you?

What, she breathed.

Will you, Nya?

For the rest of her life, she thought of the fact he hadn't been able to say the word: marry.

The sun came up late; Xavier looked down at Nya's sleeping body. There would be old hymns on Anise's wedding day. Fish stew and rum cake, she'd said. He would not have used the love spell on her. He could try to be happy for her. He'd wanted a spell to change his own heart, so it flowed for Nya, but he would have to do his best without it.

Love was an action, after all.

✳

After Io left Bend Down Market, lugging the goat, Xavier laid the moth pouch on the butcher's table amongst the lungs, tails and kidneys. He watched it for a while, then picked it up and slipped it around his neck, carefully pushing it out of sight under his tunic. It felt better there, swaying between his nipples.

He walked back through the market, waving away the ministrations of the vendors; they felt the change in his mood, shrugging and consulting neighbours.

'So him never did want more than goat, then?'

'Don't look so.'

He walked the short beach path towards Carenage jetty and sat down a little way from the other people waiting for transport canoes, swinging his legs above the ocean water. Glanced up at the Torn Poem: you could see it from all over Pretty Town.

He didn't know where to go next, although obviously he should be heading *someplace*.

Remembering Anise was tiring and uncomfortable. The unexpected depth of his feelings for her then, and how unfamiliar it had been to feel *easy*. He could say everything he meant, with no prevarication. There was no need to be different, although he had wanted to be a better man for her. Then the short, sharp ending . . . of what? He didn't know what to call it. Did Anise even remember that time and place?

Surely she remembered. Was she happy?

For the first time since Nya died, he wanted to be with strangers, listening to them talking about themselves, nothing more than a witness. An insect on tree bark. Enough of this *concern*, the crumpled faces, the hanging at his elbow, as if he might break. He wanted to be a person without context, without assumption. Gods, let people stop *expecting* things from him.

He watched the fishermen bringing in the fourth catch, sweating and singing along to somebody's portable radio. How far had the fisherman's son gone for this moth at his chest? Which pedlar? A man? A woman? Long-fingered? Scoop-backed, creeping like a cat through a new home, or facety with it, striding towards the boy? How long had he saved his money?

thanks for the belly of the fish
he gives it

A loud male presenter interrupted the music.

'*Wheeeeeel and come again!* This tuuuuuune so *sweeeeeeet* we have to wheeeeeeeel it back!'

The song was restarted, the host tunelessly bawling along. Xavier rolled his eyes. The biggest reason he disliked radio was fools like this. His name was something-Jones, but he called himself Puppa Gyallis Sweetspeech Mashworks. A gyallis was a man who thought women existed only for his pleasure, and this one was loud, obnoxious and cut people off while they were talking. Especially women. Puppa Gyallis liked to call them hysterical and stupid and to pretend this was a wise thing to say.

His people regularly called with requests for interviews.

Xavier sucked his teeth and stared out at the blue water. The sea was busy in this part of Battisient. Families milled about on the dock, flagging down canoes that passed them by, oars *clip-slap* through the water, headed for ports in Dukuyaie and further up the Battisient coast, occupants rammed shoulder to shoulder. People threw up their hands and complained. Some took to the water to swim about their business, belongings tethered on top of their heads in the traditional way. The boatmen waved apologetically.

He would never make progress, waiting like this. Perhaps he should swim. He felt stronger in his body. Not happy, but more solid. But the notebook might get wet, even on his head. And the moth.

The song played on, Puppa Gyallis mercifully silent.

He watched the dock. Something had twisted in Popisho while he was lying in his hammock, grieving like a boy. People seemed harder. He thought of their hot faces in the market, excited by the soft, horrible woman and her questions. There should be a folding spell to fix all like *she*. He didn't know his people to be cruel. Insensitive, perhaps. Loud-mouthed and fast in people's business. But to thrive on the bad fortune of others was not their way. Perhaps pissing-tail Intiasar's farcical walkround could have some use. To listen and watch Popisho again. People in Battisient and parts of Lukia Town certainly knew him on sight but there were more places where they didn't, or were unsure, unless he identified himself. He grinned. The legends that claimed he was nine feet tall often kept him incognito.

A ruffled man in a dirty tunic waved at a rotund fisherman dragging his writhing nets ashore. Xavier admired the fury of the fish: blue, hoary orange scales, gasping.

'Take macaenus where he need to go nah?' called the ruffled man. 'Disgraceful, him waiting so long!'

The fisherman turned guiltily before Xavier could protest.

'I take you in my canoe after I deliver the fish over Bend Down, o macaenus.'

The ruffled man scowled. 'Take him now. I carry the fish over for you.'

The fisherman looked indignant, haunted, then torn.

'Brother, I know your game, nah?' Xavier spoke softly, so only the ruffled man could hear him. 'You not using me to thief from nobody.' The man's hands became claws of protest. Xavier leaned closer. 'I said to *leave* here.'

The man's loose mouth worked. There was a staring look in his eye; it was best to be careful with this one. He turned to go, then jerked back, defiant.

'Hard times you know, macaenus. Not everybody have what you have.'

'I understand that. But since when we name thief, brother? Open door is everywhere.'

'Who *you* to judge me?'

'I going judge a thief every time.'

'You not *out* here, man. You cooking bits of fee-fee, faw-faw.'

He felt that. The idea that what he did was slight. He tried to speak more gently.

'You come eat by me, yet? I don't remember your face.'

'No, *brother*.'

Xavier offered his hand. 'You need to tell me your name and come.'

The man ignored his hand. 'I might come and eat, but you going to feed my pickney, too?'

He thought of Olivianna and her swollen belly this morning. 'You telling me your child don't have no food?'

The man looked down. 'It getting harder.'

The fisherman grunted, moving closer. 'Goat tax, fishing tax, lamp oil gone up and it cost more to buy school uniform for the child them. They saying this year the factory takings was bad and that is why.'

He hadn't heard much about this year's toy export figures, but he hadn't been paying attention to anything but his own nose-hole.

'Intiasar don't look like *he* having no money problem,' snapped the ruffled man.

'The man trying to help!' said the fisherman. 'Who else you know going to give people a two-day holiday, 'sake of private wedding?'

'So you are a fool.'

'Not one of you would *ever* prosper if not for the Governor and Mas' Brenteninton! We just have to hold fast, like him say, things going to get better.' The fisherman dragged at his net and side-eyed the other man, who was opening and closing his fists as if there was something nasty inside them. 'I going take these fish up, macaenus.'

The ruffled man spun sharply and scuffed off down the beach, bare heels kicking up yellow sand.

Xavier turned his face up to the blue sky, pondering.

thanks for the sea urchin shell
he cries

The song changed, finally. He listened to Puppa Gyallis shrieking about two new music he playing today; rubbed sand grains between his fingers. Popisho songs could be a week long. There was a groan of disappointment as another too-full canoe passed the dock. A gaggle of children waved at him from the pink bow. He waved back.

Smell me, Xavier. Anise was standing on one bare leg when she'd said it, slipping her thigh cuff down the other. He couldn't remember the colour of Nya's favourite cuff, but he could still see Anise in hers, made of wedding silk and red stones. How much it took to stop himself pulling it off with his teeth, to stop himself from pulling her inside him so they could be safe.

144

Man who soft
We don't want no man who soft

'Macaenus! What a shame and a disgrace!'

He looked up, shielding his eyes in the sun. The woman standing over him was gesticulating so madly he thought for a minute she had multiple limbs or faces.

'Is alright, sis. I waiting with everybody.'

'No, *no*. You don't hear it?' She pointed at the radio.

He listened obediently.

It was the kind of popular, mischievous ditty perfected only in Popisho. The small Christian population regularly objected to the bawdiness, but he quite liked this kind of song, even with the sound of Puppa Gyallis' chuckling.

Man who soft
We don't want no man who soft
Man who soft
We don't want no man who soft

Soft in the head (can't work well)
Soft in the bed (curse from hell)
All women cry a thousand tears
Cast all soft man into the sea

That seemed reasonable enough to him.

There is a man
Say him name cook-man
(you know him, you know him)
But he can't fry in the bedroom, no

Cast him out
Suck your teeth
Soft man give the woman wine
But they never get no meat

He was frozen. The woman hovering above him called out to the crowd.

'You see this man singing song about our macaenus?'

A chorus of voices, most of them female, came at him from all directions.

'Nothing wrong with him meat – look how tall him is!'

'Tall with small meat not good! Give me a short man if the bed-part good and strong!'

'Is not *size* he singing about! He say macaenus don't have no *rhythm*. You never have a big man dip down too far and mash up you insides?'

The woman nearest put her hands on her hips.

'He a lie! Macaenus, you can dance?'

Man who soft
We don't want no man who soft

More women were joining in now, tsssking and sucking teeth and calling out and arguing with each other. He thought of getting to his feet, wondered what he might do next if he managed it, aware of his own thudding embarrassment.

'I bet that singing man jealous, he *own* woman want the macaenus, that is all! Everybody know Xavier Redchoose son of Pewter is a fine and decent man. He leave him whoring days behind him, long time!'

Hell and damnation, he'd never *had* any whoring days.

'Still mourning him wife in deep respect!'

'Who say is macaenus he singing about? Is not only him cook in Popisho!'

> *Soft in the head (can't work well)*
> *Soft in the bed (curse from hell)*

'You don't hear the song say we know him? Macaenus, is you vex this nasty singing man?'

> *All women cry a thousand tears*

He couldn't speak. He wanted to. He brought the moth bag up to his nose. What would happen, which gods would cry, if he lifted the thing to his mouth, swallowed the moth whole and cursed them all?

> *Throw all soft man into the sea*

'Gods, the tune wicked, though!'

> *Darling make you come to me*

'Macaenus! I have some bizzi tea for any bedroom problem, set you up right!'

> *Throw all soft man into the sea*
> *Come to me*
> *Come to me*

'Is true what the man saying, macaenus?'

Throw all soft man into the sea

He could barely shake his head, this concrete thing, creaking. Men were looking and grinning, nudging each other.

'Mas' Redchoose, talk up for yourself! Slackness and nastiness!'

Someone turned the radio off, mid-play. Blam. Silence.

The clucking died. The women stared. His throat dry-clicked.

Come here, Xavier. Smell me.

The young man with golden-stranded dark hair who'd turned off the radio flung himself down on the jetty beside Xavier. Legs so long his toes might brush the sea.

'Well, *that* song is a lie,' he murmured.

As if they'd known each other for a very long time, now.

I I

Anise burst out of the back doors of the factory and stood, gulping the air, looking for the woman with the orange paint. There she was: swinging her paint can, marching across the road towards a squat, bright pink, two-storied house. The building reminded Anise of a huge peeled watermelon; she could practically count the seeds.

Anise glanced up at the factory and burst into laughter. The building was glistening, its green walls caked in orange letters: across the doors, still wet, on the diagonal, so neatly done, like taking obedient dictation at school.

WHAT'S YOUR ALTERNATIVE? WHAT'S YOUR ALTERNATIVE? WHAT'S YOUR ALTERNATIVE? WHAT'S YOUR ALTERNATIVE? WHAT'S YOUR ALTERNATIVE? WHAT'S YOUR ALTERNATIVE? WHAT'S YOUR ALTERNATIVE? WHAT'S YOUR ALTERNATIVE? WHAT'S YOUR ALTERNATIVE? WHAT'S YOUR ALTERNATIVE? WHAT'S YOUR ALTERNATIVE? WHAT'S YOUR ALTERNATIVE?

This woman was as bold as Ingrid. It delighted her.

Anise trotted across the road and through the melon-house gate. The low wall surrounding the property was thick with tangled bougainvillea, yard lush with otaheite and custard apple trees. Swarms of box-down-red anthuriums: wet, as if pulled out of some creature's innards. Lizards rustling in the bush, and mice. The wheet-whoot of an unknown bird and the jingle of a backyard river. The acrid mess of an animal. Grass thick with shame-my-lady plants, their miniature green buds closing as she brushed past them.

The paint can sat on the front veranda step; a damp, clean brush laid on top of it, unapologetic. A large bare foot, well shaped and carefully moisturised, poked out of a frayed white hammock, the other tucked underneath the paint-woman's derriere. She was splayed gloriously, her breasts up close to heaven, her thigh cuff as beautiful and expensive as Anise had hoped.

'You bring money?' The foot swayed.

'Money?' asked Anise.

The woman lifted her head, so they were eye to eye. 'You don't come to a whorehouse and get no freeness.' The tunic rode up so high Anise was tempted to look away.

She might have known there'd be whores here, what with the quiet and the privacy and so many factory men. She was one of few healers who worked with them. Tan-Tan liked to talk about their loose morals and idleness, so she'd never told him. He was probably scornful about this place, too; he'd never mentioned it. It annoyed her when he tried to protect her from reality, as if she didn't see nastiness on a regular. She could use *more* whores in her work, truth be told – these days more people were begging credit or offering payment in kind, arriving with bags of avocado, shelled gungo peas and fried breadfruit. Whores paid their bills promptly, with cash-money: duggu-duggu was always in demand, regardless of economics.

'Well?' said the woman with the beautiful foot.

'You get a lot of woman paying for your services?'

'Some.' The woman shrugged. 'Not as many as we should.'

'I don't think is something woman really seek out.'

'That is because some *man* tell them so.'

'Well. I married.' She felt stupid as soon as she said it.

The woman sniggered. 'All the more reason to come here.' Her voice was nasal, a high-hill accent, sentences ending on a soft *uh* sound. Anise was surprised. Most whores were peasants, but this accent meant the woman came from money. Certainly more expensive than her family.

'So why you come?' asked the woman.

Anise gestured at the orange paint can. 'You doing a little painting, sis.'

The woman smiled. 'Don't call me sis, like you know me. You in my place, and I don't even hear your name.'

'Um . . . Mariella.' It was the first word that popped into her head.

'Just Mariella, so-so, no family name, no mother name? You very informal. You think I'm a street girl? That is why you won't tell me your name?'

'What *you* name?'

'Eh-eh! So you can run go police and tell them you find the Orange Man? Tell them Hot Crotches send you – *that* name them will recognise.' Her smile was a beautifully white thing, stretching across her face, so *knowing*. 'But *you* can call me Mistress Mixielyn Establishment the Second, daughter of Esther. Um-Mariella.'

'Mixie, for short?' It wasn't easy, teasing this calm and scornful whore. On the roof, ground doves shuffled and flapped.

'You don't tell me yet which service I can provide for you, Miss Married Lady.'

'I only follow you to ask you about painting up the factory.'

'You know, I revise my original theory.' Mixie wagged her

finger solemnly. 'Is a *special* kind of woman come here to pay for a grind, and you don't look that special.'

'You really not answering my question?'

'*I* think you have a man – excuse me, *husband* – and he have a habit of coming here for a little pum-pum, and *you* just finding out.'

'I – wouldn't – what – ?'

Mixie's grin grew broader and all the more bumptious.

'Mmm-*hm*! I did know it. What him penis look like? If you ever look at it. So many gentlemen come here because them wives don't like them penis.' Mixie was gleeful. 'No, forget that, too! You the *other* kind.'

'*What* other kind?'

'You want lessons! You come to find out how him move and what him *say*. You want to sit down and share wine with us. Tell your friend them how you spend a whole *hour* talking to whore.' Mixie rocked the hammock, clapping her hands together. 'You need me to teach you how to suck a man, Mariella? Only cost a few of your white-robe coins.'

'Who you think you talking to?' She was getting angry out loud, and she hadn't done that for whole heap of time.

'No shame, if you need instruction, my dear. Maybe him bored why him nah fuck you. Don't mean him don't love you.'

'I don't need *lessons*!' Anise's voice rose an octave. Why was it so rass hot today and why them damn dove on the roof and mouse in the bush couldn't shut up? '*I don't need any – lessons – !*'

'You know, time getting on.' Mixie slid out of the hammock gracefully, like a mongoose: *swuuuups*. She was grinning, holding up both hands in a gesture of supplication. 'Is alright. Is fine. You can fuck.'

'I never have no complaint! I—'

'You don't have to prove anything to me, Mrs Mariella. Everything just *fine*.'

'*My name is not Mariella!*'

'Hush. I never mean to upset you. If you want to make a contribution for more paint you can leave the coin right there on the paint can.'

Before Anise could say another word, Mixie pulled open a pink door and went into the house, slamming it behind her. Anise stood staring, aware of her jaw hanging open. She could hear the other woman's laughter, carolling through the windows.

Oh no, you did not just slam a rass door in my face.

'Mixie!' She wrenched the door open and ducked inside. '*Mixie!* If you don't come back, I *swear I going call up the radio and tell them you paint up Intiasar factory!*'

Laughter, somewhere tinkling.

Anise snapped her mouth shut, the sound of her own voice harsh in her ears.

Three ceiling fans undulated in the rafters.

She had never been inside a whorehouse.

There was no vulgar erotic art or women exposing themselves, only new bamboo chairs and large, plump blue cushions. Everything so very clean. Newly waxed floors. She could smell the shine.

She heard scuffling somewhere to her left, and the creak of stairs.

'*Mixie?*'

The scuffling abated. She listened to the fans whistling. Where were the other women? Did they have the day off for holiday gallivanting? Maybe they only worked at night.

The next room looked more like she'd imagined: eight velvety chaises longues, clustered around three large and intricate changing screens. Through the windows, she could see the quivering Dukuyaie hills. A thin red stream poured down one of the rises, snaking its way around trees; a river turned red with bauxite? She fingered a screen. The artist had worked in purples and blues: fish in trees, birds lolling underground, winged lizards. She guessed the women hid behind them, and were presented like confectionery, to be chosen.

She missed sex.

There had been three serious men, and a few others, before Tan-Tan. She *was* a good lover, whatever Mixie said: enthused, appreciative, even skilled. Her healing hands helped slow the grind, helped eager men who popped too fast. She'd liked the layered negotiation of sex, from the very beginning. It wasn't just pleasurable, or intimate; it was *interesting*.

She missed her husband's body. The longer she did without it, the less she could imagine doing something with it.

Snapping at Mixie was ridiculous. This sudden need to prove she felt all these things and could do all these things surprised her.

You had just the right number of man before bitterness full up your spine.

Four serious men, if she counted Xavier Laurence Redchoose.

No, no, she couldn't count *him*.

She stood abruptly, hesitated, then slipped behind a screen. She rested her chin on the top of the frame, peeping out at the expectant chaise longue. She slid a finger down the side. Thought of men watching her. Tan-Tan, watching her.

Xavier, watching her.

Such a name on the lips. Slow: *Zaaaay-vee-er.*

She twirled, crouched down, popped her head up and over, smiled at an imaginary, admiring audience, waved. She teetered on the wrong foot, smelled herself as she lifted her arm. Of course, she would never. Sell her body. Who could name that price?

She pushed out her bottom lip and sighed.

Was Tan-Tan punishing her? What man refused a woman's body, laid out and waiting?

Bastard.

Stop it.

Why you not angry?

Did all whores sleep this mellow? Like children put to nap? There was something prim about this whorehouse. Which man could grab or snatch or fuck raw in here?

Anise kicked off her sandals and rotated her ankle from behind the screen. She stuck one arm out and waggled it.

Greetings, macaenus.

She'd tried to be patient. A man was not a woman. But she'd finally asked Tan-Tan straight. Standing at the door of the room where he weaved, needles and cloth in soft bundles around them. *I mean, what we doing, Tan-Tan? You vex I say no? You feel bad? You feel sad? You . . . don't want me no more? Because I can't take this for too long.* His eyes had been limitless, looking up at her calmly from his loom. The three minutes in which he said nothing at all, just looked through the back of her head, were so like forever that she'd cried out, and crept away shivering.

After that, asking would be begging. And in this *life*, she was not begging a man for sex, again.

She examined herself in one of the mirrors. Thirty-seven and she didn't look bad. Her skin was clear and healthy, a little swollen below the eyes.

So you don't think he cheating on you.

How the hell I supposed to know?

But what you think?

It's possible.

And if he a dog, you want to sleep with a dog?

No, if he really a dog, I gone.

She pulled a face at her reflection, stuck her tongue out. Let Mixie come in now, and see her playing like a little girl, nah? She turned away from the mirror and surveyed the stairs and landing above her. Stepped forward. Heard a *thunk!* sound as something hit the floor.

She glanced down and saw her own vulva rolling at her feet.

Oh Jesus have mercy.

Somewhere, past the shock, she was amused at invoking her father's lone god.

Oh lord lord have meeeercy.

Her entire pum-pum had come loose: like a heavy battery falling out when the tiny locking device is retracted. Compact, self-contained. No blood, no mess. Just a chunk of her, lying there, rocking slowly.

Anise screamed. Then when nothing happened, she stopped screaming. She bent closer, shaking her head wildly.

'Oh my gods – oh my gods – oh my *gods*.'

The vulva stared up at her, like a meaty bit of cake. Yes, that was it: someone had sliced into her pelvis and scooped out the whole thing. She might cup it all in a handful. There were *freckles*. She hadn't known that about herself.

Oh my gods. Do something, anything.

The swirls of hair, the openings and curls – at this angle it made an odd kind of face.

My pum-pum laughing at me.

Check to make sure you not dead.

What?

Just check.

She took her pulse, slapped her cheek, pulled her hair, pinched herself, trod on her own foot. Most of it hurt.

So you not dead, then?

No, fool!

She dared not feel between her empty thighs – the prospect of a gaping hole was horrifying. Sharp, broken pelvic bones, dangling fallopian tubes; would she be able to touch her own intestines? She swallowed spittle, trying to stay calm. She had to do something, but what?

You don't name healer? Heal something!

The voice in her head was quite hysterical.

Even if she could put it back, would it ever be the same again?

Oh lord, have mercy. Who know what could happen to a pum-pum, out in the world on its own?

Anise took a deep breath, grabbed the vulva, parted her knees, crouched and shoved it back. There was a kind of *voom* noise, as if a void had been blocked. The entrance to the universe, perhaps. It tickled. She giggled ridiculously.

No pain.

She rose out of the crouch, slow, slow, hitched her robe up, and looked down. The pum-pum lacked character and detail from this angle. Lovers had the better view. She placed a hand over it. Cors flooded her hips, making them tremble.

Take time, take time!

Warily, she stood upright and parted her legs. Shook her hips, waiting.

The vulva seemed firm.

She jiggled: it might dangle if it came half free, like a child with a full nappy. Horrifying. She jumped up and down. Hopped from one foot to another.

Everything seemed secure. Reattached, the pum-pum throbbed invitingly.

Somewhere, someone began to scream. Anise jumped, startled.

Thunk.

Rassssssclaaaht.

Her pum-pum lay on the shining board floor again, rocking back and forth.

She bent to pick it up, wavered, then shoved it deep into the pocket of her skirts.

The screaming was coming from above her, filling the whole watermelon house and threatening the walls. She ran for the stairs, hesitated, then took them two at a time, clutching the soft contents of her pocket jostling against her hip, only vaguely aware of Mixie running from the opposite direction, too late to avoid their inevitable collision on the landing.

Both women teetered, Mixie near-falling; Anise grabbed her arms and they recovered, gulping breath. Mixie had a tendency to sore throats, perhaps, and she'd had bad acne during adolescence.

Mixie yanked her arm away. The wailing continued.

'What *happen*?' Anise said.

Mixie glared. 'I don't know, but my pum-pum just fall out.' She paused, as if she expected Anise to shatter at the news. 'I did try ram it back, but it go sideways twice. What is your *cors*, lady? I never damn well ask you. You bring bad vibes into my house?'

'*Me*? It don't have nothing to do with me. I'm a healer.'

The screaming increased in volume and urgency.

Anise plucked at Mixie's sleeve. 'Where are the other . . . *women*? If it happen to us, it could be everybody.'

'Yours fall out as well?' Mixie couldn't have sounded more satisfied.

The screaming paused for a millisecond then crescendoed, like a slapped child taking a shocked breath before the roar. Mixie sucked her teeth and strode over to a closed door. Anise followed, her back straightening and determined. Her hands were silver to the wrists, like she'd been dipped, or painted.

12

It took three minutes for Dandu and Sonteine to exchange happy pleasantries and seven more to sneak into the attic. Dirt-streaked and smiling, they found it stiflingly hot and cluttered but just the right place for holding hands and thinking about this Great Big Thing they were going to do tomorrow.

Get. Married.

After some time of handholding, Dandu nuzzled Sonteine's neck. Giggling and squirming, she settled down between the old lamps and the wine barrels, sighing contentedly as he opened her robe. They were happy with this part: his mouth alternating between her nipples, him looking up to see if his tongue pleased her; rocking against her until he had to roll away, not wanting to stain her clothing. *You can do it, Dandu*, she'd said two months ago, in such a small voice, on a day when the foreplay was particularly agonising. *It hurt you so much.* But he shook his head; it horrified him, to take what she wasn't ready to give. He would be more than these other men.

And who knew what to do, anyway?

He looked down at her: those swollen lips, eyes soft and trusting, smiling a little smile that would be mockery on other women but love on her. She was rocking against *him* today, pushing her groin into his thigh. That was new. He looked at her dark, shining body, beyond her wondrously familiar breasts. He felt an urgent need for something more, in this eleventh hour. Could he touch her in other ways she liked? Some small proof that he could satisfy her? If she could just let him reassure himself.

He licked oil. He kissed oil.

Her eyes flew wide.

He dipped his tongue into her navel; heard her hips lock. He couldn't look up at her face, because the fear there would make everything much more difficult. He'd seen it before. It had cost him erections and come back in his nightmares: the panic on that dear face when anything threatened going too far.

Oh, trust me Sonte, he prayed.

He slid his tongue down her quivering stomach. It seemed to both of them that the wind stopped outside, and crickets ceased chirping and the nearby mountain held its breath.

With one sudden, fluid, gentle motion – he would remember it all his life – Dandu lifted Sonteine's ankles and spread her wide.

Sonteine clapped her hands over her face. It was nothing like the obeah woman's examinations or the violence of others. But he was looking *into* her, and she couldn't watch him doing it. All she could think of was how bare she felt, and did she smell bad, she was so wet, and was he disappointed at how she looked, and would it hurt?

Dandu kissed her stomach, hovering. He was waiting. For her permission.

Slowly, slowly, she let her breath out, in one shuddering, shaky heave. He waited, lips on her stomach. She took one long breath and another and then, because he wasn't doing anything scary and all she could feel was his comforting hands, not the fingers of a mad somebody, but calm and confident, she told herself everything was fine.

The moment he felt her relax, Dandu slipped his tongue inside her.

Sonteine grabbed his head and pushed her hips so high and hard against his face and moved up and down against the bridge of his nose so fast, it hurt his neck and took all he had to stay there until she stopped moving, gasping and near tears from the intensity of her feelings.

They pulled apart, like sticking plaster, shocked.

Sonteine's heartbeat hurt her chest. She propped herself up on her elbows. She felt soft all over, and tremendously exposed, but happy as well. She wanted him to come closer and hold her.

'Dandu?'

He gazed up from between her knees. He looked horrified.

'Sonte . . . is . . . it supposed to do . . . that?'

★

This was why his father had made him swear to respect her. *Don't force or frighten her, Dandu. Treat her like a lady. Is my friend child.* But how could he have guessed his disobedience would have such disastrous penalty? He'd never heard tell of such a thing. After all, her bosom was still intact after months of play.

'Oh, we shouldn't have,' moaned Sonteine. 'Look at what I gone and done now, oh gods . . .'

Such a pretty, soft thing, nestled between a pile of papers and a broken lamp from the days his mother collected them. He reached out to stroke the pum-pum, hesitantly.

Well. He wouldn't let her down.

'I going stay with you forever, you know that, right?'

'But . . . but . . . what we going do about *children*?' wailed Sonteine, sounding not unlike her mother. She hadn't taken her eyes off the pum-pum since it came free.

'There is plenty of children around.' He wasn't sure what he was saying, but something had to be said. 'We going find one.'

He tried to soothe her. She insisted he keep it; she couldn't bear taking it with her, the thought made her teeth chatter. What if she dropped it outta road? What if someone stole it? What safe place could she store it, with her ridiculously prying mother, and all the over-cleaning in her house? There was a maid that was a *spy*, she was sure of it.

Dandu held her hands and made her recite the names of flowers until she calmed down. He promised to keep the pum-pum in a safe place. They would keep the terrible secret between them. They could take it out and look at it if they wanted and think of a different life they could have had. He didn't say it, but his mind was working: perhaps if he could find someone to help, to examine the precious thing, they might fix it. But who could be trusted with the pum-pum of the Governor's daughter?

They stole down from the attic and he sent her back through the window, because time was getting on, and if they were found up there with the pum-pum out-o, it would make everything so much worse.

He should have known he couldn't handle this sex business. It was a sin and a shame, his abject ignorance.

'Gods, Mamma going to know,' moaned Sonteine as she climbed over the windowsill. She was cupping her skirts into her pelvis, like she was holding things together. 'She *always* know when I do something stupid.'

Dandu snorted and kissed her goodbye. He was not fond of Mamma Intiasar.

After Sonteine was gone, he wrapped the pum-pum in a piece of bed sheet and went down by the river for a walk, and to look at it carefully. The river was his best thinking place. The sound of liquid trickling past had always calmed him, but it didn't work this time. His stomach churned acid. He hoped upon hope that Sonteine wouldn't leave him once she had a chance to think about it. He had never heard anything in this world as rich, as complex and as pleasing as the sound of Sonteine moaning when he put his tongue inside her and made her pum-pum fall out.

Crouched under a tree, Dandu unwrapped the cotton to peek again. Such a pretty thing. He turned it into the light, admiring it, hardly believing it was there. The pum-pum, slippery and young, tumbled out of his hands and into the river, where despite his desperate attempts to retrieve it, it was carried away by the current.

★

Sonteine paced through Pretty Town, biting her lips. Her pum-pum was so often frightened and tightened that when it slipped from its moorings and away from the rest of her body, she had felt momentarily relieved, as if someone had cured her of a chronic pain. But now, with every step forward, her decision to leave it behind felt wrong. She should be all *together*, like everybody else. She'd been too rash.

Was it her mad quaking that caused the falling? She'd never felt anything like it. None of the good girls talked about things like that, although there were whispers, of course, about the pleasures of lovemaking. But, not *that*. She shivered; half pleased, mostly worried. Was it Dandu's fault for opening her up? For putting his tongue inside her? Was it hers?

She looked up to the skyline as she crossed underneath the Torn Poem. She often looked at Mas' Xavier's restaurant, especially when she felt stressed or worried. Ever since she was three years old and first heard about the macaenus. She imagined the Torn Poem as a castle of delights, a delectable ending to a myth told at bedtime. Xavier Redchoose was like a single, precious wish, granted to all of them. What could be more special, more luxurious, than a man born to cook just for your individual appetite? He gave you what you needed, and that wasn't just food: it was inspiration. Everybody said Xavier's cooking lingered: you could pursue your dreams with renewed fervour, see yourself in a different light; believe in the unachievable. He was the very *best* of macaenus, she relied on it.

For a long time, she'd hoped for the courage it would take to make love. And she'd become convinced that the act would be entirely possible after Xavier Redchoose fed her.

But even *she* didn't expect macaenus food to put a misbehaving pum-pum back.

★

Hah Genevieve Okeiliah Nathan pulled off her old, cracked earphones and nodded at her engineer. He cued up an hour of music as she got to her feet, stretching her stiff spine, rotating her neck. She waved. He waved back. She let herself out of the booth and walked around the squat radio station, with its massive antennae threatening to crack the roof.

He was waiting in her tiny private room, sitting against the wall. His hairline was starting to thin off his fine, high forehead and it made her feel affectionate.

She sat down on the floor beside him and leaned in, so they were nose to nose. His heavy arm lay in her lap. She was thinking about asking him to move it when her pum-pum rolled down her leg and fell between them, like a brown sea sponge.

The smell of salt.

Io struggled to his feet and yanked Hah up beside him. They stood looking down at the pum-pum, fetchingly displayed against the white board floor.

'What the rass,' said Hah.

'You alright?' asked Io.

'Well, no.'

Io picked it up. They examined it together. Plump in the right places, creased and glistening.

'Is like a sculpture,' said Hah.

'No, juicier than that. Fresh soursop.' Io nudged her. 'It's alive. Here, hold it.'

She slapped his shoulder lightly, skittered backward. '*You* hold it!'

'You afraid of your own pum-pum?'

'No!'

'Then hold it!'

'I'm afraid!'

They laughed until their stomachs hurt. It didn't occur to either of them there might be a problem with reattachment. Io sat between her legs. Hah drew up her robe. Io gently pressed the pum-pum back into her body and crawled in closer to be sure the edges were neat.

'Io?' said Hah.

'Yes?' His lips twitched.

'I think since you down there already, you should stay.'

'Well, since I down here,' said Io. 'Already.'

In Dukuyaie all the doors in a certain part of that island locked themselves, causing four accidents, seventeen children to cry until they fell asleep and one man to contemplate his sister-in-law's cleavage. When he tried to seize her breast, she boxed him. One of his teeth fell out and rolled under the bed, where it rotted into a sweet pulp in less than a minute.

13

Xavier marched down Carenage beach, cursing at the top of his voice. The sky felt closer, radiating massive, irreconcilable energy. Damp sand clung to his ankles.

You know him, you know him.

Who the rass had the nerve, the courage, the *gall* to sing about him on the radio? To call him *impotent*? And why? Surely no one would object if he went and kicked in the radio station door and demanded Puppa Gyallis give him the singer, the musicians and the songwriter. Before he slapped *him*, too.

Man who soft. You don't want no man who soft.

That damn song was going to be in his head all day.

He reached a small cove, sheltered by tangled overgrowth, and sat down, panting. He'd left the pick-up jetty far behind on the other side of the bay and there was nothing but manchioneal bushes and sea grapes over here. The waves rolled in faster, spitting and jagged, the sand littered with broken blue-and-white sea urchin shells. He remembered the moth and grappled for the red pouch, his stomach plunging, but it was still around his neck, just hanging askew. He tucked it back under his tunic, shamed at anyone seeing it.

They'd probably write another rass song about *that*.

Behind him, someone coughed.

The teenager who'd turned off the radio stood less than five feet away, long gleaming black plait sloping over his shoulder, bare-chested. His pants were creased with grease and salt water.

Indigent.

The boy looked up, unblinking, and Xavier was startled. There were no whites in his eyes. He'd heard that could happen to the indigent over time, but surely this one was too young. It was oddly beautiful.

'Why you following me, boy?'

'You even *know* the man who singing that song about your penis?'

'*No*,' Xavier growled.

The indigent beamed. It was such an infectious, complete expression that Xavier surprised himself by smiling back. The merriment gave the boy a kind of gravitas. Hard earned, that smile.

'I am not sure what I think about people making art out of mischief,' said the boy. 'I am trying to decide. There are many things to consider.'

'I know how I feel about somebody making a *fool* out of me.'

'You feel foolish?' The boy spat a strand of long, dark hair out of his mouth. 'But you are not impotent. Maybe the song is a metaphor.'

'For *what*?'

'You never know. People is a complicated something. So is art.' He spoke with the confidence of the young, who thought everything they said was new.

'I think in this kind of song, there is not so much complication,' snapped Xavier.

'People can be so very simple in a complicated way.'

He didn't know how to respond to the boy's open, curious face. Had his mother taught him no manners at all?

'How you think any of this is your *business*? What you name, anyway?'

'Romanza. You might as well talk to me, Xavier Redchoose.

Vex-up by yourself is not a good thing. You know there is a special kind of bullfrog in the bush? He swell up when he vex.'

'*What?*'

'You remind me of that bullfrog. If another man-bullfrog take his woman, he swell. If he don't stop sulk, he burst.' For the first time, Romanza looked gloomy.

'You calling me a *bullfrog*?'

'I used to try to talk them out of it, but one of them did burst while I was talking to it and I couldn't get the smell off for a week.'

'*Romanza*. You not even give me a family name to prove you come from somewhere.'

Romanza shrugged. 'Where I *am* seems more important.'

Don't underestimate them, was what Des'ree said about the indigent. She'd done walkround in the Dead Islands once or twice, but nary a one had come out to cook in her presence. It made her furious.

'Anyway,' said Romanza. 'I think that song is a good start to a day.' He coughed and spat into the sand. 'You can think of anything *worse* going happen to you today than a man on the radio sing-say your dicky don't work? Betterment *must* come.'

Xavier began to laugh. His own brother not trusting him to meet some mystery woman, the fisher-boy's moth, this ridiculous walkround, as if he was some guaranteed breeder of young, privileged women. If things didn't pick up, he might as well just lie here and let life burst him like a bullfrog, yes.

Romanza grinned.

'See it there. Improvement already.'

Xavier laughed harder. He bent forward and found he couldn't stop laughing. Romanza pounded him on the back. He gasped for air, ribs aflame.

'Breathe. You think I want people walk-and-talk, say I kill you? These rass people don't like no indigent already.'

Tears streamed down Xavier's cheeks. 'Stop. *Talking* – !'

The boy fell silent and pounded him. It did feel good to laugh. Perhaps it wasn't the most dignified idea, to go kicking in some radio station's front door. A final giggle slid off the side of his mouth and fell into the sand, foaming. They watched it for a while.

Maybe he'd swim over to Dukuyaie. Walk around the artists' section. Ingredients were generally good among creative people.

Io had left so abruptly. He touched the red string around his neck.

Romanza coughed into his closed fist. 'Are you alright?'

'Yes.'

The boy flinched and hissed. 'Lie, man.'

'You have cors to know a lie?' Now *that* was a fascinating and unfortunate idea.

'Yes.'

He should have guessed. People with mental cors had a different attitude to life.

'But people lie all the time, without even thinking about it.'

'Yes, I *know* that.' Romanza looked decidedly grumpy.

'It hurt bad?'

'Depend on the lie and the day. Some is a quick burn, some make my belly run.'

'You ever vomit?' He felt a little cruel, but he could ask awkward questions too.

'Once or twice. When the lie expensive. When it hurt the person to tell it.'

'Ah.'

Romanza's face lit up. 'Anyway. I know you have a special meal to find, so I gone.'

Xavier sucked his teeth and picked up his satchel. The notebook rustled. 'Total fuckery, is what.'

The boy's black eyes seemed even deeper. 'Why is it fuckery?'

'Is all distraction tactics for the election. Intiasar worried, and everybody just out for freeness and *holiday*—' He snapped his mouth shut. He was right. But what did he expect this thin, wild thing to know about political games? It was time to get over his own rass self and do it.

'You never meet her, then.' Romanza spoke mildly.

'Sonteine Intiasar? Have *you*?'

'No.' Romanza gazed into the water.

What was he doing in Pretty Town in the middle of the day, anyway? Indigent generally stayed in the bush.

'She a good woman,' said Romanza.

'How you know?'

'I don't.'

He was in no mood for riddles. Romanza waved at a small girl inching out past the shoreline. Children were taught to swim from birth, but this one had the look of adventure, like she might take chances. He walked to the surf's edge.

'Don't go any further, little one.'

The child paused, wriggling; she looked at Xavier, then back at the horizon.

Xavier held up a single finger, the one that always convinced Chse to mind. 'Your mother wouldn't love it.'

The girl sucked her teeth and paddled back to the shallows, bottom lip drooping. He liked her defiance: the fat scowl and the bits of seaweed in her hair. Nya would have written about her, maybe. In her pieces of paper all over the place or in one of his notebooks.

'She won't go back out.' Romanza coughed. 'I hear Sonteine Intiasar is very intelligent. Devout. Very respectful of macaenus food.'

Why did he care?

'How old are you, Romanza?'

'Nineteen.'

'You look younger.'

He remembered himself at that age: certain everything began and ended with Des'ree, electrically conscious of her other aco- lytes falling away, like dead flowers. He was the only one she invited to her bed more than once.

Are you macaenus, Xavier? With your special hands?

Romanza walked over to a bush that looked like the other bushes, pulled something free and came back, paring his prize with a moon-sharp knife. 'Something I want you to taste.' He finished stripping the large thorn, revealing light purple flesh.

Xavier took the thorn and rubbed it between his fingers. It was strange to see a plant he didn't recognise. He sniffed, then put it on his tongue. Started at the icy cold.

'Good, nah? You can walk many miles with only a few.'

Xavier rolled the thorn flesh around his mouth. Something citric, pure and light, varnishing the back of his throat. Familiar. He pulled the notebook out.

'Like grapefruit,' Romanza said.

Yes. But beyond that was a faint, dissipating perfume he couldn't name. He closed his eyes, trying to separate taste and smell.

Lying on his stomach in his ama's back garden. A waning afternoon. Lining up bugs for battle, under her bushes . . .

'Rose,' he breathed.

'*Yes!* I could never work that out.'

Xavier scribbled. *Cold roses through the heat. Grapefruit and rough sand.* What was that feeling? *Hot afternoons, children out of school, running towards the shade trees. Relief.* Yes. A simple feeling: relief from heat. *River water. A pallet in a shaded room, cool under your back.* He underlined several words, palms throbbing. *A reduction but dish must be cold.*

Yes, this might be right for Intiasar's girl-child.

Romanza handed him another thorn and he sucked again. The same shock ice and that meandering perfume. *White flowers and grit on the plate. Hydrangea?* He licked his stained mouth, hardly hearing Romanza saying he'd find something else. A single, perfect spoon of purple thorn ice, to end the meal. The ice would steady the bride's nerves, cool her blushes; slow her new husband.

He wrote the word *innocent*, then hesitated. Intiasar had probably done his best to keep his child unsullied merchandise. But the girl, who knew what she really was? She might be stupid and goat-eyed, using her body like a weapon. She might be brighter than him.

The next page of the notebook was filled with Nya's handwriting; lost in thought, he sketched a hydrangea on the page, then absently used his thumb to blur the lines. A good woman, Romanza said. But what did an indigent know of high-hill people? They were all the same. Bullies. Des'ree used to come back from their parties late at night, drunk. Sometimes he went with her as second chef. Men paid to gulp water until their bellies exploded, a healer hired to put them back together again; he'd once seen a boy eat money until he vomited. *How you can be part of that*, he'd railed at Des'ree. *You better learn to grin-up with these people*, she'd snapped. *You think they believe you special?* They had come to his ascension ceremony, though. So many rich people in his new home, sidling close. He imagined them deboning him, eating pieces of his face and sucking the gristle. *You must come to see us, dear Xavier. To our luncheon, to our best house. Meet my niece and my daughter.* All this, with Nya standing beside him. How was he to *feed* this kind of person? They were empty.

Better he spend his time asking why two people talking to him about *starvation*, this morning.

Romanza was on his knees, digging in the sand.

Xavier tapped the notebook with his pencil, slowly, then faster as a delicious idea occurred to him. He could cook Sonteine Intiasar an *indigent* wedding feast.

Intiasar said he wanted food of the people. What better than food from the ones judged the lowest, the dirtiest? The ones who had no money and needed none. The noblest, who knew animal music. A meal from the ones who didn't vote and shunned houses. The smile hurt his mouth. Food from the sun children.

Yes, yes. It was the perfect answer to everything.

If he could just get them to talk to him. Even the moth pedlars had shuffled away as fast as possible, once business was done.

He began to pick purple thorns from the bush, scratching his hands occasionally, filling his satchel. Romanza came back and helped. The bag bulged.

'I couldn't find the herb I did want to show you,' said Romanza. 'Ah, well.'

'You can find it somewhere else?'

'Dead Islands, if the sun is right.'

'Come, nah. Show me things.'

Romanza looked surprised, then pleased. 'You would come bush?'

Xavier grinned. 'That depends if you think Sonteine *Intiasar* might like the bush.'

Dawning amusement on the boy's face.

'Oh, I think so. But probably not so much, her daddy.'

Xavier hooked the thorny satchel on his back. They began to walk down the beach. The adventurous girl-child was still sitting on the sand, humming and dripping silt on her robe. Xavier thought of Olivianna and her pink lungs and the travesty of her belly. He waved and the moth pouch shifted on his chest.

The child waved back. She was singing *she don't want no soft man, cast all soft man into the tree.*

Romanza glanced at him.

Xavier shrugged. 'What might a soft man find up a tree?'

'Plenty,' grinned Romanza.

He could see the Torn Poem from here, with its safe red roof.

They walked towards the sand dunes and the islands of the Dead.

✱

He'd thought of taking moth after Nya died, of course he did. He'd stopped for her and now she wasn't there anymore. He'd heard tell of underground tunnels in the Dead Islands, woven with insects, but he doubted it – there wasn't the demand. Moth was expensive, precise work: a small but lucrative business. The moth pedlar brought his product in ostentatious boxes, with menus. Sphinx moths, dry and muscled from flying thirty miles an hour. Sister moths, using the moon and the stars to navigate. Yellow Precipice moths were good with adami tea: they were born without mouths and never ate. The moth pedlar made up these names, to fire the imagination and the pocket, he knew that. But he appreciated the time.

Clean, the pedlar said, pulling the ribbons off. *Very clean, this moth.*

He could have remembered the man's name if he chose, and sought him out, but he had never taken a moth into the Torn Poem.

Only Anise had ever asked him questions, his head in her lap, lying on the floor inside her little yellow house.

When you did start, Xav?

I don't know.

He did know, in pieces; but he was ashamed to think about it. Her kind face was wide and worried. His mouth bled onto her silver hands.

I . . . Faltering. I've always done it.

When is the earliest you remember?

He thought of lying under his ama's rose bushes with a moth in his pocket, but it was nothing new, not even then. Meeting Nya, he had some in his school satchel. His second night in Des'ree's house, she'd found one among his belongings, some cheap and pilfering breed. She'd laughed. *You need a pouch, for a start*, she said. *I will get you one.* They'd sit in Des'ree's garden at night, menus in hand, him choosing for them both, she stroking her breasts in the dark. She seemed to have an unlimited budget for moth. Wild Indigo Duskies. Hairstreak moth. Glassy Wings. She packed Sunrise Revenge moths and Red Melters in his luggage on the day he left her house. *A goodbye present*, she said.

Ten years old, maybe, he said.

Oh, Xavier, said Anise.

He'd loved the sound of his name on her lips. Imagined it leaving a fleshy residue, like an oyster. He knew how old he was, and where and when. But he had only fragments of the memory, and there were days when he doubted them.

*

It was only when Io got a job, left home and began to send back the greatest portion of his pay entirely unbidden, that the unemployed Pewter was shamed into shift work, hoisting midnight lobster pots and trapping crabs, coming home with his handsome tail soaked and fishy. The crabs made him angry. Xavier didn't know why.

He was ten and his mother took him to the rum bars.

Her favourite place had a corrugated iron roof, propped up by raw boards, and three weeping chairs. The bartender slopped out ladles of cheap banana liquor that gripped the teeth. A man snored in the corner.

Treiya shoved a sharp-lipped cup at Xavier's mouth. *Swallow it, nah. My macaenus.* She only talked with this bare ambition when she was drunk. *We going to be* rich, *all 'sake of you. My beautiful boy.* He moved his head away and the alcohol slopped down his tunic. Abruptly, she abandoned the struggle and sat upright, her seat bowed under her bantam weight. She wore expensive blue sandals with many straps, and while her robe was still clean, she'd lost her thigh cuff back in another bar. She'd hitched her robe up on both sides, crammed into her underwear, making her hips lumpy. Her breasts swayed; he wanted to cover his eyes: against her and evenings like this one. He could see her mouth moving wordlessly, counting. Was ten minutes a respectable time between one drink and the next? Was seven?

The shoes were a gift from Pewter, who bought her things so she wouldn't look like a crab man's wife.

They sat in the gaunt rum bar, two blue lights shining from the back board. Treiya paid for drinks. The man in the corner flopped forward from the waist, his knuckles bathed in the dirt floor. He snored lightly, almost a whistle. The bartender offered a plate of razor clams. Treiya snatched it: she hadn't eaten all day. The night sky was purple. The bartender was silent; Xavier was silent; the prone man whistled; his mother drank and ate clams. He could see the pores in her face and the movement of her throat. There was a rich, stale smell in the air. She pulled the clam shells apart and dropped them on the floor, gripping Xavier's arm when she was finished, and shoving him out. He looked up at her, hoping they were done for the night.

What you looking at? she snapped. Her breath was bad. Soon they would be back in the kitchen, she scrubbing at his liquor-stinking tunic, telling him she sorry, telling him Papa don't like the smell.

Xavier glanced back at the bar. The sleeping man raised his head through the blue light. The boy found himself staring into the man's shockingly familiar face as if it were a mirror.

Dust covered his heart.

The man who looked just like him belched.

Xavier stared behind him for as long as he could as she dragged him away through the moonlight. He could still see the man in his mind, blinking, giggling, blue the colour of the dirt ground beneath him, blue light from the bar pouring off the corrugated roof, the rum bottles, his skin. Rich blue, radiating through the darkness, like a heaving sea.

Hey, Mamma, the blue man called after them. *Give me your shoes.*

★

179

It was just done raining the night he stole back to the bar. The air was fresh and new, even inside that horrid tavern where the blue man was wide awake and dancing around a woman.

Xavier hovered at the entrance, watching the man's furious wrists and two long front teeth, the woman protesting, the barkeep yelling. He watched the man staggering heel to toe to heel, a chanting rodent: *Catch the queen – where the queen – who going get the queen –* waving his arms. *Never* seen *a woman look so wicked.*

In his adulthood he could only remember chunks of the blue man: liquid fingers, ankles that barely held him up, those dark rodent teeth set back and gaping. His real father, finally abandoning the irritated woman, staggering up the dark road, pissing three times in one lurching journey: spewing his guts in quaking shadows.

He was ashamed, following on, thinking, *are you me?* but of course he was. They were identical in a way that would make old ladies blush, remembering the superstition: there was only one way to make a child favour you this much. Your mother had sex in her bottom and the seed trickled into her womb from behind. If you wanted a child the father couldn't deny, that's what you did. And yet his mother and the blue man hadn't looked twice at each other. Maybe they didn't remember making him. He tried not to think of them in mutual, sweating stupor, Treiya an orifice.

Two drunks, rutting.

He trailed the blue man into the Dead Islands. Wah, he took long. Sniffing, scratching his muzzle, retching, spitting, squatting to shit, cutting his bare toes on glass and bleeding, cursing.

Xavier looked at his feet and followed the noise.

Finally, the blue man seemed to recognise a patch of bush: flung himself down, dug beneath it for a large dirty bag, drank noisily from something. To Xavier's astonishment, he uncovered the waiting coals of a fire, slowly washed his hands in a thin, dark river and began to cook.

He worked with an exquisite mound of peppers: yellow, red, green, purple, black, orange in the firelight. He broke them open, dragging out the seeds, set some to bake, sliced others thinly, fried them with onions, oil, wild leeks from bags he pulled out of his serrated clothing, salting the heads and shells of five large crayfish he knelt and caught from the river. He added the crayfish meat at the end, slurping the broth, crunching the shells and heads as if all were equal and as gloriously edible as the rest.

Xavier's stomach grumbled so loudly he was afraid the blue man might hear it. The man, the food, seemed to cast gilded light into the sky. When he was done eating, the blue man covered the fire and lay down. The night was quiet. Xavier thought he should leave. He contemplated stealing a pepper.

The blue man began to cry.

The man might as well have masturbated, for all the horror Xavier felt. He didn't know grown-ups could cry themselves to sleep. He crouched. If he moved, his new father might wake up and cry again. An hour passed. His stomach moaned. He became aware of a peculiar liberation, beyond his fear and disgust: out here alone, knowing his family must be looking for him. Everything, so still. Hands, scrabbling: anything in the dirt: a leaf, a berry? So hungry. Desperate, he crept forward to the pot. One finger, two. Taste exploding on his tongue. Scraping with his whole palm. He wondered if he'd ever tasted food at all. Peppers, so sweet with the onion and garlic and fish and delicate, dark wings; he couldn't have expected the frothy antennae, tickling the back of the throat: o!

The taste of silk.

It was so long ago, and he a child: half swooning, the moon above him leering and monstrous, the bush a snarling animal, he couldn't imagine what kind.

He screamed.

In front of him, the blue man's body was melting.

He backed away as blue liquid streamed towards his bare feet, mouth smeared with crayfish and moth, head pounding with disbelief. What was real? Could he trust his eyes? Around him, moonlit forms rustled. Someone clasped his shoulder. He could hear the hiss of the indigent men. Silver eyes and the blades of slender knives. Faces yawned in and out, elongated and old; their skin smelled of unpasteurised milk.

Boy, where your people?

He fell, crawled backward, moth hallucinations obscuring the kindness on the indigent's face. They all had crayfish heads and he was sure they'd come to drink the remains of the blue man.

Go home, said the indigent. *Here is not for you.*

He ran away as fast as he could, running on air, high, falling twice, gashing his arm on a sharp and bilious tree root. These things had happened, but he only had the crack of crayfish backs; the unalterable fact of his mother's cuckoldry; the fresh rain covering the moon; his stinging tongue; a hunger that never went away.

14

Anise squinted through the dim room. She could make out two things: a thin woman quietly crocheting by the window, and a screaming lump in the middle of the floor. The lump had tremendous vocal range, despite being buried under a mound of blankets, rugs and mosquito netting. The noise reminded her of those flamboyant old women hired to wail over the body at funerals. She wanted to stick her fingers in her ears.

The crocheting woman looked like a sunflower: her extremely long and golden neck was topped with shaggy golden-brown hair. Anise stared. She must have a very particular cardiovascular system, not to faint every time she looked down.

The golden woman pushed her hair away from her face, undisturbed by the hullabaloo. The yarn in her lap danced and knotted, her fingers moving smoothly.

Mixie plopped down next to the screaming pile and prodded it. 'What happen to you, Rhita?' The howling swelled. 'I don't have any time for this foolishness. Not today!'

The screamer flung the blankets back and glowered at Mixie. Uncovered, she was a small, expensive-looking woman, her cheeks, the backs of her hands, one half of her nose and both feet covered in glossy red-brown fur. Her blue and yellow robe went fetchingly with heavy pearl jewellery. An older, flatter-chested Mixie.

'Her pum-pum fall out,' observed the long-throated woman.

Rhita clutched her head. 'Lyla Anastasia *Establishment*! Don't you use that vulgar-*vulgar* word! You don't see I'm dying?'

'You not dying,' said Lyla.

Two sisters! Anise moved further into the room. It was overcast; this part of the house didn't get much sun, and the curtains were thick.

'Look what I get, coming to visit this blasted whorehouse yet again, 'sake of family! Trevor always telling me I going to catch something!'

'I ask you to come?' Mixie snapped.

'You are my *baby sister*! And now look! Trevor going accuse me of infamy! What kind of woman – what kind of woman *things* fall out?'

Anise bit the inside of her cheek. Her own vulva felt hotter in her pocket.

'Well, clearly you not anything special, since is all of we it happen to,' said Mixie.

'I am very special to my *husband*! Not because *you* don't married!'

Mixie's face puffed up. 'I look like I need any rass husband?'

'You need somebody to keep your backside quiet!'

Lyla's crochet frothed down her knees. Anise wondered what she was making. 'And you?' she asked. 'Are you – ?'

'Just fine,' said Lyla.

'Wah, you put it back?' said Mixie. 'I couldn't get the right angle.'

Lyla ignored the question. 'Look like is only woman crotches drop. I don't hear no man bawling out for him hood. Anybody turn on the radio to check?'

Rhita flung a piece of white netting over her head and face. It made her look like a lugubrious bride. 'What about meeeeee?' she wailed.

Mixie clucked her tongue. 'Gods, Rhita. It not so bad. I going help you put it back.'

'You can't fix your own, but I must trust you with mine? Trevor—'

Lyla sucked her teeth loudly. 'When last Trevor come to your bed? Once, twice a year? Man like that have three mistress and wifey know but don't *want* to know. Pair-and-a-spare kinda man.'

Anise winced. Did they never do business with *single* men?

'You just miserable with the whorishness!' shrieked Rhita. 'My husband still have interest in *me*!'

Lyla held the crochet out in front of her. It looked like a dress. 'What you need it for, anyway? Mine fall down at my foot, laugh-laughing. So I laugh-laugh with it and I fling it through the window.'

Rhita stopped muttering. They all stared.

'You did what?' said Anise.

It was true. As she sat looking at her newly independent vulva, it occurred to Lyla that it had long been a nuisance. According to all reports, it was a remarkable specimen: men blubbering and whining for it, jealous women. Plump and easily moistened; full of dedicated musculature. She was known in the house for making men bawl out in pleasure and many chose her over younger stock because of her internal discipline. But eventually the time for all that would pass. What would it be then but a husk, reminding her of bygone fumbles? No, she was happy to dispense with it. She'd patted it like a dog and tossed it through the window. Hopefully the wind would carry it away, but she didn't really mind.

Anise thought the courage to do such a thing was revelatory; nevertheless, she must be mad, throwing away healthy body parts.

'Inevitable,' sniffed Rhita. 'If you abuse a body, eventually you lose respect for it.'

'So you done with the whoring, my girl.' Mixie sounded disappointed. 'You know that is your cors you fling out, though.'

'Nobody don't know what meaning this dropping have,' said Anise. 'You might yet need it.'

'Hello.' Lyla smiled pleasantly. 'You talking to me about my underneath again, but nobody never introduce you.'

'This is Um-Mariella,' said Mixie. 'She looking for her husband.'

'Mixie, I already said—'

'Well, Ummariella, *I* think it is best to say goodbye to things that no longer serve you.' Lyla spoke cheerfully. She reached for a ball of muted pink yarn on the floor beside her chair.

Mixie jerked her thumb at Anise. 'She say she a healer. So she might put Rhita's crotches back, for a start.'

'Oh, healer nah.' Rhita looked comforted.

'My name is Anise Latibeaudearre, married Joseph, daughter of Pauline,' said Anise. 'And I *think* I can help, although I don't have no training in pum-pum reattachment.'

'Well, you is the best chance we have,' said Mixie. She rubbed her upper arms, as if she was cold.

'What you do with yours?' Lyla asked Mixie.

'Downstairs in the refrigerator, my dear.'

They all rocked at that, even Rhita.

'But you rass mad, gyal.' Lyla laughed well: hard and unselfconscious. It felt good to be with women.

'Make sense to me. Is raw meat!' said Mixie.

That was a sobering thought.

'Mind somebody think is pork and fry it up,' said Lyla. 'Your own drop, healer?'

'The pum-pum in my pocket right now is *definitely* lobster.'

They laughed again. Mixie's magnificent breasts rolled under her man-tunic. Anise raised her hands, wiggling the fingers slowly. Points of burnished light sizzled between them, like the tiniest galaxy.

'Who first?'

Lyla said *ooh!* and dropped her crochet.

'Not *me!*' Rhita scrabbled backward, voice rising to a shriek. 'Oh no, I couldn't do that, I not going to be first, I don't know her like *that* – !'

Lyla laid the crochet aside and stood up. She had the expression of a woman who'd played a million games of catch. 'You know *us*.'

'Yes!' Mixie advanced on her sister. 'Come, healer! Do your thing!'

★

Ingrid had avoided serious love; she would make no man a widower she said, and so she broke their hearts instead. Until she met Biyohn. He took a precious thirteen months of her life convincing her he was man enough to stand by her death bed, born as he was, attached to his brother by the lobes of their ears and the fused fingers of one hand. Cors for patience, what else, the conjoined brothers joked. When the obeah women tried to take them apart, they found they shared the same blood and could not be separated without dying.

Biyohn understood mortality, so Ingrid took a chance.

She held the love light in her palms: offered it for the day, for the hour, for the moment. Emptied her precious seconds into him. When Biyohn left her for a married bitch who insisted her husband accept her lovers with no complaint but never took any himself, Ingrid was undone. She invited Anise and Biyohn's brother to a dance, where the brother wound his hips to the drum and bass with them all night and called his twin a fool to his face, keeping him there until early hours so Ingrid could look ineffably beautiful and strong and unaffected for as long as she could bear it.

On the way home and tipsy on too much butterfly, Ingrid took Anise to the sea grape tree where she'd buried the remains of Anise's daughters and scraped at the sand and cried.

Anise looked at the tree and thought of running or protesting or slapping her old friend, and did none of those things, just sat under the moon while Ingrid told her everything Biyohn had said about her smooth and perfect elbows, her soft belly, and the robes she chose. He'd seemed to find every reason to guide her by the waist through crowds; pinning her hem when someone trod and tore it, his fingers brushing her ankles. He'd brought her lemonade and his fears on a hot day: of not being a good man; of standing in his brother's shadow, literally, never escaping, and the days that he hated him more than any other human. How strange it was to see the fused siblings give each other privacy at the most intimate times, Biyohn's fingers and penis inside her, his brother's eyes opened wide and not-seeing.

It aroused me, Ingrid said, drunk and raging. She'd masturbated, she said, thinking of the wide eyes of the brother. Anise watched the small secret climb into the sky and get hitched in the sea grape tree. Her head was very light, sitting in this place where her children were buried.

She never spoke about that night to her friend, who either had no memory of the event or maintained a solid, shamed silence. Anise never went back to the tree and knew she never would. The burial spot was of no use to her. Who knew how many tides had washed the sea grape tree roots and pulled her daughters out to sea? They were all around her, in every part of the air and they couldn't be washed away.

✳

Anise sat back on her heels, puzzled. She'd gone from hopeful to downright vex and sweaty in less than an hour and there wasn't one happy sister in the room anymore. She'd helped obeah women in the birthing room and given out a thousand poultices for menstrual cramp, so she had seen more women's bodies than most – but she'd never worked with such an *odd* phenomenon. There should never be sharp *edges* between a woman's thighs.

Bubbles bounced in the air between them all.

Rhita was being surprisingly brave but it was maddening to work – to *be* – without her *own* pum-pum. Anise feared her liver slivering free. An annoying draught kept going through her, like teeth on edge. But Rhita had tried to put hers back too fast and now it was stuck, and you really couldn't leave somebody like that.

'Why it taking you so long to fix it?' snapped Mixie. She'd been patient for a time, stroking Rhita's head and murmuring encouragement, but ten minutes ago she'd thrown her hands in the air, lit a pipe and begun to pace, smoking and flexing her left arm, as if nursing an old wound.

Anise sighed and dipped between Rhita's legs again, twiddling, pulling as gently as she could. Her fingers slipped between labia and thigh. Rhita whimpered.

'I know this is difficult,' murmured Anise. 'Sorry.'

Lyla popped a bubble above her ear. Mixie tripped mid-stride, cursed, then carried on pacing.

Anise exchanged a glance with Lyla, who patted Rhita's hip.

'You alright?' Lyla asked Mixie quietly.

Mixie sucked her teeth.

Anise's hands were sticky and her lower back hurt. She reached back and pushed energy into the aching muscles. Rhita smelled sweet, almost like vanilla. She'd retracted all the hair on her body, leaving her every surface clear as glass. Anise could see her own reflection, the wooden beams, see Lyla's eyes and snaky throat, all looming back at her from the glassy skin.

She straightened up again.

Rhita shifted hopefully. 'You fix it – *ow!* Raaaass*claaaht!*'

'We might have to call someone else.'

'Who we calling? A *real* healer?' Mixie was rubbing frantically now: her temples, that left arm, her forehead. The pipe lay smouldering on the ground.

'Watch yourself and that pipe,' said Rhita. She sounded tired.

Anise applied a bubble to the back of her aching hands. This wasn't about technique; the more she worked, the more this pum-pum falling felt heavy and significant. Perhaps she shouldn't *try* to fix them; was she overstepping her bounds? An obeah woman would know what this meant in its proper context, would know history, more spells than she did, bring the force of the collective to the task: their sole purpose was to curate magic.

Another thing you can't cure, she thought. 'Somebody can turn on the radio? I really need to know if this happen to anybody else.'

Lyla snorted. 'You think the fools who run them places care about woman?'

'Maybe that woman host will bring it up?'

'I doubt it. *She* not a fool.'

Mixie trod on the hot pipe and began to hop around the room, swearing violently.

'Mind you do yourself damage,' murmured Lyla.

'Me? Not you throw away your owna pum-pum? Take your own advice.'

'Cho,' sniffed Lyla. 'The body is very adaptable.'

Anise wondered if she regretted it, just a little bit.

Rhita propped herself up. 'Don't I tell you, mind the pipe?'

'*Everybody shut up!*' Mixie threw the pipe against the wall, where it shattered. They stared at her. 'I want the *whole lot* of you *out* of my place!'

'You want me to drop my intestine out on the street?' Rhita howled. 'I not leaving here until Miss Anise make sure I alright!'

'You always was selfish about everything!'

'I glad to be selfish, rather than sell my body to any hurry-come-up man with two coin!'

'Judgemental *bitch*. Nobody wouldn't buy from *you*.'

'Who the rass you think you talking to?'

'You, twist-eye, jealous, grudgeful little bitch.'

Quick as she could, Anise reached in, twisted and pushed. There was a rewarding click.

'Ooooow!' bawled Rhita. 'How you handle me so rough? I – oh.'

They held a collective breath.

'You alright?' asked Lyla.

Rhita moved her hips slowly. 'Wait. I soon tell you.'

And just like that, she was furry again.

Anise grinned. An anticlockwise twist and a confident push: all in one movement, that was it. Gods, let her be quicker with Mixie. Not to mention her own self. If she really had to ask, Lyla might help her.

Not sure what you fixing your own for, if nobody don't want it.

'That feel fine to me.' Rhita bared a gap between her front teeth, a feature many Popisho men found attractive. 'Aahh, yes, boy. Pain gone. Look like you work it out.'

Anise sighed and nodded. 'Mixie, you can go get yours?'

'I want everyone in here to leave, *now!*' snapped Mixie querulously.

Lyla was standing by the window, pressing her nose against the glass.

'You looking for what you fling away?' Anise asked.

'No.' Lyla's eyes flickered over the pacing, furious Mixie.

Rhita picked up a blanket and folded it. 'Mixie, why you so miserable?'

Mixie pointed at Anise. 'I want *her* out, and I want the whole of you out.'

'What, just dry, so? Is only she-one in here offering to fix back your *place of business.*'

'I can handle my *own* things!'

Lyla raised her voice for the first time, neck weaving. 'Not *again!*' They were silent. 'Mixie, I don't see why you need to hold everything in your belly. You behave like nobody can help you.' Anise decided Lyla's neck was quite the loveliest cors she'd ever seen. 'We probably don't have much time,' said Lyla. 'So you better let them know what going on in here today.'

Anise stared at Mixie, who was shaking. She spoke gently.

'What is the matter?'

'Nothing.' Mixie's voice was faint. 'I just need you to leave. Please, why you staying so *long*?'

'I wish you would let in the breeze,' said Lyla. 'It not going to make a difference when them come.'

'Difference to what?' asked Rhita. 'Who?'

'You don't have to be alone.' Lyla's voice was mild. 'None of them girls couldn't stay, Mixie? I wouldn't let not *one* of them back in here to make no money again.'

'Is *me* tell them to leave! You think I going let them mash-up, 'sake of me?'

Lyla hugged a blanket to her chest. 'I am *here*, Mixie.'

'Me, too,' said Anise.

She knew the rising force of a storm when she saw it.

✳

Anise was used to veneration. Even when she walked far from her workspace with nothing to identify her cors and the men called out and waggled their tongues, one of them would eventually catch her demeanour, like a smell. *Wait! Give some respect to the lady, you don't see is a healer?* And Pastor Lati child, to boot.

But who considered the life of a whore?

For two weeks, Mixie has been saying no, no, no to Governor Intiasar and the men he sends to negotiate. No, she don't care every other whorehouse doing it, she will not let no man in here for free, sliding, pulling, tugging their wedding rings off their hands, like that mean anything at all. No, not even for the Governor and his wedding antics – he a rich man and he can pay well for these girls who work hard. *Never has there been a slave in Popisho*, Mixie says. *We should be proud of that.*

They were coming anyway, they said, even if they had to strip the pink off the walls and burn it. *Put a glass by the door for the wedding rings*, that's what Nelly Agnes and her blue-hatted sister had been talking about, Nelly's lip all curled up at the mention of women like this.

And who considered the life of a whore?

Intiasar, he wrote a letter. Mixie had it.

Do it because I said so.

Across Popisho, Mixie's whores sit and wait for news. They scan the horizon, strain their ears for shouting. They hold their breath and their foreheads. Some want to go back and stand with Mixielyn Sharon Establishment the Second, but she said no, she said if they try to help, she will never dance with them again, or eat butterflies after shift; she will spit at their feet, they will never get another coin from her purse.

Others are too frightened to offer, but they think of her.

The four women left in the watermelon house look at each other and are surprised to see they agree. It shouldn't surprise them. Even the quietest woman in Popisho feels inside herself the potential for virago.

'Damn disgusting and out of order,' said Rhita. 'I don't see no charity inside here. This family only have *expensive* underneath.'

Anise was aware of her entire body: the backs of her calves tight, her nipples scraping against cotton.

'Let them come,' she said. She headed for the stairs.

'What you doing?' asked Mixie. She looked both terrified and relieved.

'Trust me.' She still had Ingrid's teaching. She knew how to begin.

It took her no more than a few minutes to find Lyla's abandoned pum-pum, springy and soft under a crocus plant below the window. The spell would be small; it was only her seventh; Ingrid said to use them sparingly. This spell might complete Lyla's crochet dress or weave a plait or cut a piece of a lawn crisp with a machete. It wouldn't hold back swarms or armies.

It would hardly fill a jar or your belly if you ate it, nor could it clean a whole house, if asked. But it might be enough.

She walked upstairs, cradling her small prize. Her own vulva cooled against her hip. Might it eventually lose heat and die?

'I am afraid, Teacher.' She spoke out loud. The walls rippled in the heat, impassive. She imagined Ingrid's merriment: *two-three pum-pum more than enough for this!* She wouldn't have been scared.

Ingrid had beaten the sheets with her fists and called out in a kind of wordless triumph as she died.

Anise's chest hitched.

The women followed her instructions as quickly as they could. Rhita and Lyla scrubbed the veranda floor, drying it on their hands and knees, sprinkling salt crystals and green pepper flakes. Each woman removed her thigh cuff. They nestled together in Anise's hands: red, yellow, brown leather, gold inlay.

Mixie and Lyla dragged the heavy dining table out into the front yard and set chairs around it. It would be helpful if they could get the men to sit down; it was harder to attack once you'd sat down in somebody place. Anise took white yarn from Lyla's basket and strung it from the eaves, like a washing line. She hung the pum-pums from it, side by side, facing outwards. Her own and Mixie's. She turned Lyla's upside down and tapped it. Three red ants scurried out. She fastened it next to the other two. It would have to be enough.

They reminded her of masks.

How might her father and husband feel, watching her prepare to face men? She didn't know. There was no time to ask them, and it troubled her that she wasn't sure.

Did a macaenus have the time to consider the life of a whore?

He would, surely. The thing she remembered most about Xavier was his kindness.

His beautiful, tired hands.

The sisters joined her on the veranda. Lyla wore the just-finished crocheted frock: like a fisher's net, weaving around her long, bare throat, long bare waist, down to long bare ankles; orange twine, pink and peach, inlaid with glistening shells. Her skin was moist, her sunflower head, brilliant. Curve-bellied. You might lick her in the sunshine.

Lyla looked up at the swaying line of glorious flesh; she reached up to stroke her contribution and smiled at Anise.

'Maybe is a good thing to say goodbye in a more *useful* fashion.'

Mixie sat down on the veranda wall. Her chest looked shrunken. Rhita put an arm around her. 'I would offer to string up my own, but it fix back tight-tight, like nothing never happen.'

Mixie nodded.

'Hopefully the same for all of us when we done.' Anise tried to speak lightly.

'If they don't rip them down,' said Mixie.

Surely no man would harm a healer.

What a stupid thing to think. You not important. Man hold down child and granny and you know the amount of bad-lucky woman you meet every week: broke heart, broke face, spirit in the mud. The whole of them come to you for healing, so don't go on like you don't know. When man behave bad them take it seri-ous, like is a work of art, and the government don't care.

She couldn't listen to her fear, or she would run.

She focused on Lyla's amazing frock. It was as if the woman was still weaving, her fingers in motion. She didn't seem to need her pum-pum to feel her own power. She didn't seem to need anything. Could she be just as self-contained as Lyla, and wear pretty frocks?

'See them coming, there,' said Mixie.

Yes, they were. Dark and smiling men, slipping through the gate.

The women held hands.

15

Romanza watched Xavier, sitting at the front of the long, smooth canoe, scooping double handfuls of sea water and pouring it over his head. Droplets nestled in his dreadlocks like translucent insects. He was pleased to see the macaenus looking so relaxed.

He could hardly believe he was taking Xavier Redchoose to the Dead Islands, to neck-back! He had it all planned out. First, they would go to the Jehjeh Gardens in the west for herbs and fruit the macaenus probably never heard of, then to meet *real* people, cooking on the bare ground. He'd never expected to buck-up the macaenus on walkround today; you always *wanted* to see him, of course, in that way you wanted to see something rare and fascinating, but you never thought it would happen. He was relieved at his luck; who could have known his father made Xavier so angry he was liable to throw up his hands and serve Sonteine a cup of sea water? Break her heart!

That wasn't going to happen in here, today. He knew he could inspire Xavier into cooking something spectacular, walking out the Dead Islands, and breathing right. Cooking an indigent feast was a master stroke. His sister would love it; Intiasar would be furious. And so *much* could be learned. And taught. Which, as Pilar always said, was just another way of learning. *Macaenus come!* Yes indeed, the indigent were ready for *this* macaenus, for this quiet, earnest, angry man. Pilar said they'd never taken to Des'ree. Too loud.

And maybe by the end of the day a little something might just be revealed and painted up all-about, in orange. Some whirling cook-man truth. You never knew when *that* kind of thing might arise.

The canoe was manned by two older indigent men. As soon as he and Xavier crested the dune on Carenage beach, the vessel had slipped around the headland, as if it had been waiting. There were so many things Romanza loved about the indigent; this uncanny ability to be in the right place at the right time was just extra style. Their instinct for each other was unparalleled.

Sunshine beat a pattern on their backs. The ocean seemed light green, the seabed empty and rippled.

He knew one of the oarsmen well. Berel, son of Art had three granddaughters and a wife with a cylindrical body and her eyes on her back and he was staring at Xavier as he rowed, his brow brilliant with sweat. Xavier turned to meet the stare. Romanza watched the two men hover in tension. Eventually Berel looked down and bent back to his task. His arms were threaded with veins under the black, sand-encrusted skin. Wah. It was some man, to outstare an indigent elder.

Xavier Redchoose was an entirely impressive somebody, and all the more because he didn't seem to know it. So handsome of course, but something else that felt substantial in the bone. You heard about him all your life, about *all* the macaenus and their kind, but it was only in person you could appreciate the sweep of this body, the weight that suited him, those kind and worried eyes. He was ethereal and grounded at the same time, and it was strange to see. Like when you woke up in the morning to a ghost loping through the trees and accepted that this was the way some people were meant to spend their time.

Romanza had taken the third set of oars for a time, but soon gave up, sweating and grinning. *Not so easy, baba!* Berel teased, slapping him on the shoulder. He'd resumed starboard, and trailed his hand through the water, creating a foamy wake. Xavier was doing the same thing, one huge hand breaking the water.

Romanza thought about the so-few lies the macaenus told, and the biggest lie, looped around his neck. Moth eater, thinking no one would notice.

Whoo-oo, said the oars through the lime water. Romanza coughed.

According to his father's municipal records, nobody lived in the ninety-nine tiny cays that made up the Dead Islands. In practice, everybody knew hundreds of indigent were scattered there on any given one-sky day, although most *were* uninhabited: stale, unyielding rock, toilets for petulant birds and pockets of undiscovered strangeness where no one dared go. Uncle Leo kept his warehouse on the largest cay, where the off-island ships slipped in for the toys, and the most ordinary-looking Popisho citizens were hired to be sure there was no chance of foreigners sighting magic.

Berel began to sing in time with the oar strokes, and the second man joined him. A common funeral dirge.

start a journey
oh my gods
start a journey
my brother gone down the road
you know that he
start a journey

'Which soup your people eat on Temple days, Romanza?' called Xavier.

One of the oarsmen broke song to call out pumpkin, and they all laughed. Red bean people were said to be hot-tempered and pig-tailed, just like the recipe, while pumpkin soup lovers had delicacy of spirit and thought too much.

'Pumpkin deep, like meat,' Romanza nodded. 'If you get the right one, it season food like blood and fat.'

Xavier turned away from the water to look at him.

'Yeah man, but red bean is subtle. Years I trying to cook my Auntie Yaya's red bean soup. I ask her, I watch her do it, but all she do is 'quint her eye and show me a clenched hand for measurement.'

'And you know is not even a hand, so they lie!' said Romanza.

They all shook their heads at the vagaries of woman cooks who pretend to share tips.

The oarsmen sang on.

flying with birds
oh my gods
flying with birds
my sister gone down the road
you know she gone
flying with birds

'And you like pudding,' said Xavier.

Ah, that macaenus instinct he'd heard so much about.

'My mother make the best pudding. Bread pudding! Cornmeal pudding! Vanilla. Sweet potato. Edges crispy, soft centre.'

He let himself feel sadness. He missed her. He missed having a mongoose. He'd left a yard full of tame ones at the family compound. They'd converged on him, whining and snuffling, that time he went back to visit his mother, a few months after he left. He'd torn his hand climbing a rock face and the wound was going septic. He'd wanted pudding and to forgive her. She looked faint when he walked into the house. He held his damaged hand out, palm up, wordless.

You still my little boy. She sounded frightened but happy. *You know I never could do the right thing by you.*

She bandaged him. He wouldn't go there again. It made her tremble.

'I going make you pudding, when you come and eat from me,' said Xavier.

'And when would that be?' Romanza smiled. 'You don't come cooking out here.'

'Sometimes my invitations get brought back by relatives, say their cousin walking bush years now and nobody don't know them anymore.' Xavier paused. 'You wouldn't come Torn Poem if I ask you?'

'I don't know,' murmured Romanza.

He didn't, truly. The idea of sitting inside, of being fed in that way . . . it had been too long, now. Roofs, they were too high, too flat, pretending to be skies. It might be too strange.

He wondered if *he* had become strange.

Xavier lowered his voice. 'How long you living out here?'

'I was sixteen.'

'Young.'

'Mmm.'

Romanza coughed and shifted.

'You eat poison, Romanza?'

'Eat some just this morning.'

Xavier looked fascinated. 'It good?'

'Not so much good, as interesting.' *Like moth*, he thought.

'What it taste like?'

'Rice.'

Xavier chuckled. '*All* poison taste like rice?'

'Some of them. And it sting your mouth. Like macca bush.'

'Then why not just eat macca?'

'We do. But the effect of a different but similar ingredient is not the same, macaenus, you know that.'

The oarsman who wasn't Berel glanced up at the word, then dipped his head when Romanza shot him a look. He didn't want anyone to fawn over Xavier; the man was so clearly private.

Xavier nodded at the oarsman. 'Is alright, brother. Don't mind, Romanza just protecting me.'

Romanza winced, faintly embarrassed. Perhaps he was being presumptive.

'Romanza, can you *tell* a lie?'

He shrugged. 'For sure.'

'Well, now. I assumed you was a truth-teller as well.'

'Most people assume it. But it would be a harder life if I couldn't lie.'

Xavier seemed to consider this.

'It helps me forgive a lot of the lies, knowing I need them myself.'

'Tell me why the indigent eat poison.'

He was amused. How could a macaenus not know?

'Same reason we do everything else. To show the land we love it. Accept all of it.'

Xavier nodded.

'And how many different kinds?'

'Three hundred and seventeen ways to poison yourself and dead, last time I check.'

'*What?* Taino was the seventh macaenus, and he had the widest knowledge of poisons and coagulants. He only identified thirty-three poisonous plants in the whole of Popisho.'

'Then you have some ways to go.' Romanza grinned. 'You want to know more?'

'Tell me!'

Romanza talked for a while: about the preparation of poison, more complex than people imagined, with much grinding, roasting and burying in hot earth and careful measuring necessary. The indigent ate a live, mostly raw diet, but the rejection of meat was a myth and the consumption of fermented and malodorous things was central. Xavier wrote fast in his little notebook: a prickly fruit called a stinking toe, that smelled like the gods had cursed it; a complicated feasting ritual involving carrion, claws and horns, but only if the animal had died naturally – of old age, or other animals attacking. Ritual was important to the point of impracticality, he explained, delighted to be giving Xavier so much that was new: the intricate carving of large quantities of fruit and vegetables; a ceremony involving jubilant regurgitation to honour parrot mating practices.

Xavier slapped his thighs delightedly. 'But you sound like a cook-man!'

'I not too dusty.' The praise felt good. 'But indigent can be very contrary. One born-day feast, some friends served nothing else but so-so plantain. Fried, boiled, mashed with pepper, salted, with tamarind to make plantain cakes, green-roasted, crisp-chipped, and plantain soup topped with avocado. All because the man we was celebrating *hated* plantain.'

All four men hooted over the ocean tide.

The oarsmen had stopped singing; the canoe was slowing, anchor falling through the warm, diaphanous water. There was a soft thud as it trailed the sand floor and caught. They drifted. The sun on the water felt almost hypnotic.

'Why we anchoring?' asked Xavier.

Romanza climbed to his feet. In the distance he could see twisted skeletal trees and bushes he knew would be scarlet, but that was still some way off.

Perfect.

He walked up the canoe, swaying, and talking low with the oarsmen, listening to the water. Here was where concentration was absolutely necessary. He crouched as the oarsmen examined the ocean surface. Put his hand in the warm ocean again and thought of Pilar: his hair, his erection against his belly, his hard mouth, the love.

'What we doing?' asked Xavier. He looked a little worried.

Romanza patted his shoulder.

This was going to be so much *fun*.

16

Xavier inched up the anchored vessel carefully; he'd toppled more than a few whole-tree canoes in his time. The oarsmen adjusted to the rocking, like pieces of song that belonged together.

'Why we stop?'

'We walking,' said Romanza.

'What that mean?'

He was enjoying Romanza. The boy was mountain-thin: stripped to the bone. Not nearly as renk as he'd first seemed. He had knowledge, and he was thoughtful. It was surprising to take so much pleasure in his energy and merriment. To hear Des'ree tell it, the indigent were habitually sullen and close-mouthed, but Romanza had an imagination.

Eventually, he'd put his notebook back into the satchel with the ice-thorns, and just listened to Romanza speak and the men sing, melting into the space and the silences, when they came. The heat, making him sleepy. The moth pouch swinging, near forgotten.

Now, the warm sea stretched before them, their canoe like a single brown seed pod, floating in the expanse. There was nothing to walk on and nowhere to walk to.

'Come,' the boy said and stepped out of the canoe into the ocean.

Except that he didn't step into it. He stepped out *onto* it, as if it were a wet floor.

Xavier stared.

Romanza was walking on water.

Flip-clap, his bare feet. *Flip-slap-clap* and that *grin*.

The oarsmen looked on.

'Is more cors, again?'

Romanza trotted sideways on the ocean, as if making room.

'Come join me.'

'How?'

'Don't think about it.' The boy beckoned.

Xavier put his hand to his throat. He must protect the pouch, but they'd all recognise it for what it was if he removed it in front of them. Why had he laced the rass thing around his neck, so boasty?

'Why we not taking the canoe in?'

'This is the best way,' said Romanza. 'Don't dive or jump in, mind. Keep your sandals on and just step out.'

The canoe quivered.

Xavier turned his back, closing his fist over the pouch and tugging it out from under his neckline as fast as he could, slipping it into his satchel. He opened his mouth to remark casually about removing jewellery and then shut it, remembering Romanza would know the lie. He pulled his dreadlocks on top of his head and knotted the satchel strap around his forehead. Romanza watched him, bright-eyed.

Now for impossibilities.

'You sure?'

'Come!'

Xavier winced and put one experimental foot out of the boat, hovering. Romanza slopped back and forth on top of the sea, lifted a heel clear, hopped and landed. It really was spectacular to watch. 'Come, nah!'

Xavier cleared his throat. This was ridiculous.

'Gods, Xavier. *Do* it!'

Xavier pinched his nose and stepped out of the boat. His right foot hit a nobbled, sturdy, wet surface. He squinted, chuckled and understood, half in and half out of the canoe.

It would have been a pretty cors, but Romanza wasn't doing anything more than standing on top of a blue coral reef, its surface a mere quarter inch under the blue waves, and so virtually invisible. He'd never seen a uniform bank of single-colour coral before.

'Trickster!'

Romanza laughed. The oarsmen watched, dark staring eyes amused.

Xavier completed the movement out of the boat and onto the rough facade. Standing high above the sea floor, looking out at acres of shimmering liquid, he felt disoriented, as if he'd fallen into a piece of the sky.

'You like it?' asked Romanza.

Xavier breathed through his nose. He was tiptoeing.

'I don't know.'

'Stand strong. Try to feel good.'

Gingerly, he lowered himself onto his heels, letting the reef take his weight. Coral could be hellish sharp, like the crooked teeth of an enormous sea beast.

Romanza waved the oarsmen goodbye. As they pulled off, Xavier's head weaved; he fought the impulse to beg them back. There was a visceral, frightening sense of nothing to hold on to.

'We going walk the reef over to land?'

'For some time, yes.' Romanza looked puffed with pride.

'And then?'

'Reef run out.'

'But you said we not swimming.'

'Trust me, you not going to get wet if you follow me.'

'I going beat you if you soak my bag, boy.'

'Come. Time passing! A man needs the sea.' Romanza lowered his voice. '*You* need the sea, Xavier.'

'Do I?'

He straightened his back and looked out. The water loomed, ocean and horizon crushed into each other. For a moment he had the impression of nothing else at all, anywhere. The world had come to an end. Water, fire, earth, air: you were a fool if you underestimated any of it. And was this what heaven felt like?

He teetered, disorientation increasing. If he wet up the moth, he could get another moth. Yes, he was still thinking of the moth. If he wet it up, he could get more, but no, he wanted this one. Something about the fisher-boy's penance, the extent of his mistake, letting Nya's body wander off alone, it all made this moth even more splendid. This was the one he had been called to contend with. It belonged to him, for better or worse.

'Come!' said Romanza, and turned his back, and began to walk.

Xavier followed. He didn't know which to watch most, his feet or the pinprick Dead Island trees in the distance, praying they'd close on them fast.

Crabs and shrimps, pastel pink and white, scuttled out of the coral to peer at them, disappearing as quickly as they came. Occasionally a petrel swooped down, picking jetsam off the rich expanse, glaring at the men, so far out here.

Splish-splash.

Like a child, learning to walk. Under his feet, the blue ledge. How deep did the reef go? His mother's bedroom had been littered with white coral and sea urchin shells after Pewter passed

209

on. She liked to have the sea around her. And curtains a lovely colour blue. Io dyed them fresh for her when he visited.

Romanza hummed.

> *my brother go down to the sea*
> *o children*
> *he come to end a journey*
> *my brother wash away*

'Look!'

He looked down: saw a cluster of light yellow sea anemones, waving like friends; sea cucumbers; three red-and-white-striped fish, darting, flashing, lifting themselves free of the water, sucking in the air. He stared harder. Tiny legs stuck out of their hindquarters. Little red faces turned up, fluttering eyelashes, fish with eyelashes! Two of the fish fled across the coral, thin legs glittering. They might have been holding their skirts above their knees. The men's laughter cracked the horizon, running a thin golden light across it, and the reef felt stronger.

'Runner fish. They so close to the sun, they turn amphibious,' explained Romanza. 'I like those fish.'

'Me, too.'

'You ever see a mackerel smile?'

'No . . .'

Romanza waved east. 'You can find another stretch of this high coral over by the west side of Dukuyaie. The girls swim out and take off their clothes and bathe under the moon. They been doing it since the gods were boys. I never see a mackerel smile until I see them over there, smiling at woman bare belly-bottom.' Romanza stretched, palms up towards the cloudless sky. 'I hear some places in the world prettier than Popisho, but I can't believe it.'

'No,' said Xavier. How could there be?

Romanza began to turn in slow circles, arms outstretched, head back, eyes closed. Xavier remembered turning circles in the garden this morning. The boy reminded him of himself. He felt vain, self-conscious.

'What you doing?'

'*Feeling* it.' Romanza revolved. 'Hush.'

He had no intention of dizzying himself more.

'We have places to go . . .'

The boy stopped, pulling air into his lungs. He coughed. 'You spitting in the Governor's eye with this feast.'

Xavier hesitated. 'Yes.'

Romanza began to pick his way across the coral again. 'Good.'

'I thought you was rooting for the bride.'

'You ever cook bad, yet?'

'No.'

'Then. All I can do is help.' He paused. 'I don't like the man. That is not rare.'

They moved on for a while, in the blue quiet. He'd never known the indigent to want anything but privacy. Maybe Romanza *did* know Sonteine Intiasar. But how could they ever have met?

'Romanza, a child come to my place this morning, malnourished, belly swell. One of your people. You ever see that before?'

'Little-little. Is a bad season for some fruits.' Romanza pondered. 'There are some who don't care for themselves in the bush. They get old, or they have problems in the head. Some of them is out here for that reason. But a child?' He looked troubled. 'We help each other as we can. Everybody know if you don't pay attention you can find yourself slim-down, quick. Sometime the same food don't give the same nutrition. But is not common.'

'I ask her mother come talk to me.'

'That won't happen. I notice you saying *your people*, like is not all of we people.'

'I never mean it.'

'Ow, to rass.'

'Sorry. I mean I never think before I talk.'

Romanza coughed. 'I know you think we different from you. Is true.'

Slop-splash. He was becoming used to this.

'Why you think a woman might feel *worried* before her wedding?' asked Romanza. His voice was low and thoughtful.

'What I know about young girls and weddings?' So there *was* a connection between them.

'You was married.'

'That don't mean I know anything.'

What *did* he think, of women on the brink of such a thing? The night before her wedding he'd watched Anise rubbing geranium oil into her skin, sitting on the edge of an orange cushion, knees together, feet west and east, tummy pouched out, like a child playing rag-doll. She said she was happy. Had Nya been happy, dancing with him at their wedding? They'd made a sight: neither of them very good at it. Was Sonteine Intiasar happy? You hoped they were. What else could you do?

Romanza put out a warning hand. 'Stop a minute. Reef done.'

'What that mean?'

'Just pay attention now.'

Romanza stepped off the coral reef and onto something else, dark and woolly under the water. It looked to be just the size of his foot. Xavier strained to see. Whatever it was, held him. An outcrop of stone? Romanza took a second step forward and pointed at the place he'd been.

'Step on that.'

Xavier hesitated. Felt like an old blind woman he'd once seen, faltering through Pretty Town, hissing: *A step is there, a step is there?* He'd wanted to pick her up and whirl her around until she giggled.

''Fraid like a puss!' crowed Romanza. '*Come*, macaenus!'

Xavier blew air through his nose and stepped out. Whatever it was, boulder or tree trunk, it held him. Just right for two large feet.

Romanza jumped to the next shadow.

'Faster! Walk where I walk!'

They jumped: another and another, all flat and accommodating shadows, just below the surface. A grown-up version of stones through a river. It was like being young again. He felt gleeful.

'A secret path! All the indigent know it?'

'Is not a path, nor is it secret. The route going change tomorrow.'

'I don't understand.'

'Things change.' Romanza walked backward a few steps, feet barely wet. He waited, then went forward again. 'Put your foot right *here*.'

Xavier peered. Something different about this one.

'Is seaweed. I going sink.'

'Wait. *Wait*. You lose the moment. Stop. Yes. *Now*.'

Tentatively, Xavier stepped onto what appeared to be a huge mound of sea kelp. He exhaled sharply. The kelp held.

'Now where?'

'I stepping off this, you step on.'

'This going to take forever.'

'How you mean? We nearly reach.'

He was right. He could see a sparse beach and the details of what looked like a vine forest.

Long-cut draw sweat, short-cut draw blood, so the saying went.

'You walking the way you should walk,' said Romanza. 'Swimming is unnecessary.'

'I like swimming. Just not today. What you meant, when you said things change?'

'They always changing. Just people don't pay attention. Put your foot here.'

Xavier frowned. 'You saying there are enough surfaces, in different places, in the water, to make it so anyone can walk across?'

'Yes.'

'So, is a path. But if things are constantly shifting, how you can guarantee the path?'

'I told you, I not following any path. I following what is here in the moment, ready to take me. Some of the rocks will be here for a long time, yes. The coral reef going be there for many years. But some of the . . . *things* you stepping on, they gone forever, the minute after you step. They just passing through. So it don't make no sense looking for them again. The seaweed you just use, it pass and gone now – you just take a ride for a little while. And if it pass you by again it might not ready for you.' Romanza paused, thinking. 'The skill is *trusting*, that makes you step right.'

Xavier's knees wobbled. 'This is all *chance*?'

'Step *here*.'

'Romanza, *what am I stepping on?*'

Romanza hummed.

Xavier began to curse, very long and slow.

'Step here.'

'I don't believe you have me walking on water *by chance!*'

'You don't like the walking? Wait, don't step, it gone. Alright, come. Step here.'

If he didn't look down, he could pretend he was back on the coral reef, not balancing on some fortuitous log passing in the waves. 'It gone, *what* gone? Gods, you be glad I *can* swim.' He checked the satchel was secure on his head. One wrong step and a plunge was inevitable. He would have to kick up, strong, to make sure his head didn't submerge.

'You not understanding me – step here. Is not chance. Is trust.'

'But what if nothing passing when you need it?'

'Something is always passing.'

'Even if I accept that and believe that your *trusting* is always enough to let you see something every time it come along – because you so attached to the earth and the *sky*, because you name indigent – I *still* don't see how you sure the lucky thing going to hold your weight. Not to mention mine.'

'Look at me.' Quite suddenly, Romanza dashed forward along the surface of the water, ten feet and then back again, rocking madly, left foot, right foot, plait flapping, shaking his torso and arms, a delighted spasm. Just the way a cat dashed around when it lived inside a house. It was one of the strangest things Xavier had ever seen.

The boy stopped, panting.

'But you don't even seem like you looking for anything.'

'I *not* looking for anything. The only reason we doing it the *looking* way is because *you* have to look because you don't know the skill.'

'So you saying if you do that running again, right now, it would be a whole new set of things holding you?'

'Probably.'

'But Romanza, that don't make no *sense*. You mean you never been delayed? You never drop? You never get stuck in the middle of the ocean waiting for something to come by?'

'Of course. Every time I stop trusting and pay too much attention. Step there. Oh, wait. It gone. Now, step. Right. No, *right*.'

Xavier stalled, one foot in the air, bobbing, cursing, and put his foot back where it had been. 'This is pure foolishness. I going swim. Then I going kill you.'

'You don't see we making progress? Tell me, you worry about your next breath, the one you take after this one?'

'Only if it don't come.'

'And don't it come, every time?'

'Well . . . yes.'

'And you never think about it nor pay *attention*. Gentle, here. This going make you feel better.'

They stepped forward and stood together on a larger surface: smooth and white, rippling in the water. The pale facade was slippery, and it took some concentration to stay upright.

'Tighten your stomach and bend your knees a little,' said Romanza.

Xavier half-crouched. 'What is it?' He'd asked this question far too many times for one day.

A huge eye rolled lazily, right next to his little toe. Stern intelligence. A mercenary tail. He felt the tremor of the creature moving forward in his ankles and tail bone.

He began to swear again, slowly and carefully, under his breath.

'You have me walking on a raaaaaaasssss stingray? Boy, when I get out of this ocean I *really* going kill you.'

'Him? He don't care.'

'He don't *care*?'

'He might not like you in the water next to him. But this is fine. See how good he is? We can go far on him.'

The stingray jerked and Romanza was jolted. He stepped one foot off the animal and into the sea but was no more than ankle deep before something else seemed to hold him up and he righted himself, like a strange aquatic cat. The black eyes danced.

'See? But it take time to learn.'

What did it matter how? They were doing it, the sea beast moving steadily. The sky hustled closer, full of gusting, clear white clouds. He could feel the ray accelerate, silence stretched to a needlepoint, wind picking up. They stood, grinning like fools. He felt delicate: felt the softness of his skin, no barrier to an attack; how quickly knees could be broken, neck cracked, belly pierced. To be alive was a gamble, a bizarre miracle. He pulled the satchel off his head and shook his 'locks out.

'Yes!' yelled Romanza. His plait whipped against his cheeks in the wind. 'Oh *yes*!'

'My stepfather loved stingrays,' said Xavier. 'He took my mother out to admire them. And seahorses, he liked them as well.' He was talking faster than usual, for no reason he could understand. 'They had a good time together. He was a *good* man.'

Pewter had loved the austere beauty of the rays; hadn't thought anything that lived in water should be killed. How had he known that about the man, yet never sympathised with his resistance to fishery?

The creature's back flowed under their feet.

'My daddy took me gambling when I was young,' said Romanza cheerfully. 'I told him when people were lying.' He pulled a face. 'He never see it as cheating. Just using his advantage. The lies made the cards jump.'

'Young like how young?'

'Six and so.'

Romanza sighed. Xavier thought that if they weren't right here, right now, he wouldn't have been able to hear that sound.

Above them, a seagull bounced and called. A huge shoal of black and golden fish looped around the stingray, a surge of violent choreography.

He'd heard there were certain parts of the Dead Islands – not everywhere, but some places – where you knew you nearly reach because the water turned black and the fish turned white and the spray on the edge of the waves was white and the seaweed was black and the closer you got, the sky turned and the clouds were black and the very sky was white and the arms reaching out to help you onto land were white and the sand was white and the children, why, all you could see were white teeth and white gums and white dresses and black legs and white orange trees that squeezed white orange juice and white wild piglets with black ears or vice versa and occasionally, when you thought you'd go quite mad, a flash of silver, or purple, or one of the indigent looking at you with their sharp cheekbones and uncompromising eyes in pink or orange or black.

Xavier looked down and sucked in his breath. The water was black and the fish were white.

'I miss my father,' said Romanza. He coughed.

Everything, changing. Colours seeping out of the world.

'Dead?'

'No.' The word seemed enough.

Oh Lord, said a passing petrel. That was what it sounded like.

Romanza rubbed his mouth. 'He don't like anything that I am.'

'And what is – ?'

'The light will be strange here for a while,' said Romanza. 'Prepare your eyes. Blink twice *hard*.'

'I already see the change in the wat—'

'*Now*.'

Blink.

'We reach.'

Blink.

And they had.

Startled, Xavier slipped *braps*, fell off the stingray and sank into black water up to his waist. Romanza stepped lightly off the fish, onto a log and then onto the snow-white shore. A pirouette and call for encore would have been appropriate; the smile was back.

Xavier blinked again. He felt the flicker of the stingray against him as it made its unhurried way back into deep sea. He waded through the strange black water, up to the edge of the surf, head still light and full of sky laughter, shielding his eyes against the white brilliance of the land.

Romanza stopped abruptly. Xavier crashed into him and would have fallen if not for Romanza's deceptively strong hand, shooting out and steadying him. They teetered, the boy's plait splashed against them both.

The sound of coughing.

Xavier rubbed his eyes furiously, willing them to adjust to the monochrome. The boy was down on his knees.

'Romanza?'

The coughs were coming faster, heavy, hard, barking sounds. Romanza looked up, wiping his mouth on his bare arm.

'I—' Coughing. 'I—'

So sharp, the coughs shook his entire body.

'I-I – *can't*—'

His arm was covered with grey earth and wah, the black liquid pouring out of his mouth.

*

Fathers and fathers. It was he who told Pewter about the blue man. Why did he tell him? They'd had an ordinary life, even the hard times had been ordinary: running with the other boys on the streets after school; fed and watered by anybody with a hot oven; crack you over the head if you don't answer quick enough or dare kiss your teeth at an adult; watching the old men fan themselves in the shade, leaping up to *whack!* dominoes down onto the play table; wash yourself before bed and mind your crotches don't smell and no one ever missed the family evening meal. Why did he tell him? After all, the blue man was gone, and no one ever need know.

He went home that dreadful night and everything looked ordinary, but it wasn't. Pewter was his father and also his father was melted in the Dead Islands. His mother wanted him to be macaenus, but he didn't want that; it was too much, too big. He was only ten years old. And why did he feel as if someone had singed him all over, and why did the ceiling of the house yawn like a gummy mouth?

You sick with fever, scolded Treiya. *How you mean to be walking street all night, like a pheasant?*

He'd never had a problem Pewter couldn't fix. A broken thumb or a bully at school; the rules for stick-chase; a squeaky door; an otaheite apple tree that stopped bearing. Perhaps Pewter knew something he didn't know about seeing a man with an identical face. Was he delaying the fixing of this particular puzzle by not telling?

If he didn't do something then he might be responsible for everything.

Pap?

Yes, Xav.

Nothing.

Alright.

Pap?

Yes, Xav.

Mamma take me to the rum bar every night you gone.

Pewter looked up from where he was mending an old crib. He was the kind of man who got an idea into his head and pursued it regardless of logic and he had decided that one day his boys would need a crib for their wives.

Xavier spoke on, sweating.

I see a man there, look just like me, he blue.

Pewter nodded and began to clean his tail thoughtfully with his tongue.

Pap? He look just like me—

Go away now, Xavier.

Children know what is real. And little boys can frighten men. Xavier waited for his father to bring the ordinary back. He was quite convinced he would. All he needed was patience.

★

He was sitting at the kitchen table practising reading on the day Pewter made a decision. What happened took most of the morning to begin. Pewter's tail twitched. Treiya began to spit frequently, as if something nasty was in her throat, first through the window, and then as the day went on, into her closed fist, which she wiped on her skirts.

At 2.08 p.m., they broke into a terrible argument, both speaking at the same time, in the same moment, mid-sentence, as if a silent quarrel had been happening all along and had only now become sound. Pewter made fists and hit himself for emphasis: *Mind I fling you out with these two hands, this place is mine!* Treiya pulled Xavier close so he was trapped in the raging breath between them. *You worthless*, she screamed. *These boys worship you, but you is a worthless, good-for-nothing reprobate. You stink. Your feet stink and your mouth stink. You ugly. You poor. You can't do anything. My son will save me!*

I build this place, bawled Pewter, and Xavier wondered when he would call her a drunken whore.

Yes, the mother said. *You build this stinking place, but how many times you turn from me? Never touch me or embrace me? I hope something tear down this house and we dead in here so you can see that you never do* nothing *in this world good yet!*

At three minutes past three, sunshine roaring, his father began to beat and beat his mother, arms stretched high up and back over his shoulder, like he was throwing rock-stone, striking out like a hysterical child. Xavier tried to get in between them but was shoved away by both adults, by Pewter's swollen, lashing tail. Io could have stopped the fight, he was strong, but he was far away. What good was any kind of cors if it couldn't help you protect your mother and be a man?

You can't even beat good, said Treiya, sobbing and scurrying. *You can't even beat good.*

Look at me how you used to look at me! yelled Pewter, and Xavier thought, when will you tell her the real reason you hitting her? *Look at me like you used to*, Pewter whimpered, creased on the floor like an oleander blossom.

The next two hours were the worst. Not because Treiya's right eye was swollen like a naseberry going black with juice, not because the beating made her bones move strangely under her skin, nor because Pewter's ear had a chunk missing where his mother bit back. Not because he himself had a splintered bone in his third toe, left foot, where Treiya trod heavily to avoid a blow, but because the beating had stopped.

Please and thank you, said Mr and Mrs Redchoose.

Pewter gently pushed a bead of sweat from his mother's eye. When she went to bathe, he scrubbed her bruised back and helped her into a fresh robe. He patted Xavier's head when he passed, shrinking, for the outhouse. Treiya said she wanted hibiscus for the table, *go cut some, nah Xavier*. Pewter commented loudly on the quality of the dinner and how he glad Xavier take a little break from the stove, let him taste his wife's hand once in a while.

After dinner, they swung together in a hammock, where, according to his mother, Pewter had once tried to force her – and because Xavier didn't know what rape meant, his dread grew, because what had Pewter tried to force her to do and would he do it now, again, as they swayed?

Don't worry, said Treiya. *Wipe you nose. And take some bizzi tea. I can see your lungs still a little heavy.*

Why had the fighting stopped? Why had his father not mentioned the blue man? Could they not see each other's battered bodies? How could Pewter forgive the things Treiya said? How could Treiya forgive being made a human pudding? Press her skin, you'd leave dents.

Married people, holding hands in the hammock: *please and thank you.*

When neighbours asked, Treiya said she reached for a heavy fruit jar on a high shelf and it fell into her eye and Pewter hung his plait over his bloody ear. And when it was time to go to Temple or play stickball or teach domino, Pewter shook his head.

You know why, Xavier.

Their deformed, angry faces stayed with him.

By the time his stepfather died in a putt-putt accident, just after his nineteenth birthday, he'd felt nothing but relief.

17

Ah, it begins softly. Anise looks up at the blue and red butter-flies, dancing above the whorehouse.

Kurru-kurru-koo-koo, sang a ground dove.

Koo-koo, its mate.

They stood in line on the veranda, holding hands, the dark mahogany table and chairs set out in the yard. Anise was between Mixie and Rhita, Lyla furthest away from her, toes pointed outwards, shoulders strong. Rhita's fur seemed thicker.

'Don't let go of each other,' Anise warned.

'Yes,' said Lyla.

Rhita nodded.

Mixie's hand felt hot and sweaty. Anise wondered vaguely what her cors was; her sisters' magic was so physically evident. She felt Mixie stiffen, watching the four men walking into the garden.

'Greetings, Miss Mixie.'

His voice made Anise want to run. He was squat and muscular, leaning sideways on a walking cane. The cane seemed more for style than support. Its head was as heavy and glossy as his face. The men behind him looked clean and rich and they were smiling far too much, elbowing each other, pointing at the swaying genitalia above the women's heads.

'I ask you how you do, Mixie,' said the man with the cane.

Mixie sniffed. 'You never actually said that, Archie Howard.'

'You very rude, girl.'

She didn't answer.

Archie seemed to consider something, then change his mind. He indicated the men behind him.

'Before the avalanche of husband come down on your place today, I bring three early *special* guests from Governor Intiasar. As discussed.' He showed his teeth. 'I have also brought a fine urn, where the men can leave their rings. I know you going make them feel welcome. Even though' – his eyes swept the women and settled on the twitching Rhita – 'I expected *different* stock.'

'What you trying to say?' Rhita squeaked. Her fur was on end, making her puffy.

'*Shh*,' said Mixie. She was watching Archie like you'd watch a wasp nest. She began the introductions, formal, like Anise had instructed. 'This is my sister, Rhita, a well-known elder—'

'What?' said Rhita. 'What she call me?'

Anise nudged her quiet.

'I *know* Rhita,' said Archie. 'What the hell is going on here?'

'She will not be *stock* for anybody. On the far end is my second sister, Lyla. She is retired from the business.'

'Since when?' Archie looked amused.

'Today,' Lyla smiled calmly. The shells on her dress sparkled and shone in the sunlight. 'Congratulate me.'

'You are the best whore I *know*,' snapped Archie. He didn't look so amused now. 'We done settle this thing.'

You know he fuck both of them, at some point, said the little voice. *To make it so personal.*

And if he did, so what?

'The final woman you see is Anise Joseph, a . . . a spiritual advisor.'

'Don't look like *nobody* working here, today,' said the man directly behind Archie. He looked no less than seventy, with a happy kind of moustache and thin, flabby calves.

Archie balanced his cane against his knee so he could clap his hands. It was a neat and elegant motion.

'Yes, very clever, Mixie. Now please bring the gentlemen up into the house and show them the other girls.' The other men rustled; one looked bored. '*Now.*'

Mixie's voice wavered. 'Nobody else not here.'

'What?'

'What I tell you?' said the old man with the moustache. 'See it there.'

The youngest man stepped out of line. He was light brown and clean-shaven, quite handsome, stabbing the air above them with all fifteen fingers on his left hand.

'I want to know what kind of whorehouse have pum-pum string out in the air. What I supposed to do? Pick and smell before I sample?'

'That could be interesting.'

Anise started. She'd forgotten the face, but she knew that phrase. That voice.

Brother Pedrino Blowsnaught.

He'd fixed the roof of their church, eaten parishioner's cake and brought her rare thick-bound books of native myths. She was thirteen. Her mother told her to call him Uncle, but her lips weren't happy about it when she said so. He was as sweaty and fawning as she remembered him, his body too close to her mother's, whispering how her church dress looked so . . .

'. . . *interesting.*' Blowsnaught fiddled the waist-string of his black cotton pants. He'd gained weight and it suited him.

'Greetings, Anise Latibeaudearre.' A thick smile. 'I see you continuing your mother's good works amongst the needy and the downtrodden. My, how you look like her, now you grown.'

She could have killed him, talking about her mother in that voice.

The old man cupped one hand behind an ear. 'What she said?' He had sad dog eyes to go with the merry moustache. 'Only one Latibeaudearre I know, and that is the big Christian pastor down in Battisient. What business pastor family have here?'

Archie turned his cane in the grass. 'Everything is *fine*, Mas' Collins, I assure you.'

The handsome, many-fingered man shrugged. 'I don't think this is interesting at all. Archie, I don't have long, today. I only come because Intiasar boasting about best free crotches in Popisho. If this going to be a thing, I going leave you to it.'

'Mas' Garson, there is no problem here.' A dove shuffled across the yard. Archie kicked out at it and stumbled. Rhita sniggered. His face darkened. 'All you have to do is pick one of the other women.'

'No other woman not *here*,' said Mixie. Her voice was more confident. 'I not playing, Archie.'

Without any warning or sound, Archie darted towards the veranda steps. Mixie stumbled backward, dropping Anise's hand. Anise braced herself. She could feel her own strong arm, involuntary and unbidden, palm wide, flung out into the blue air.

Archie Howard bounced off the protective spell that Anise had wrapped around the house. He flew more than fifteen feet into the air and landed bam-splat on his backside in the dirt. The pum-pums ricocheted madly. Everything came to a quivering halt as the men and women stared at each other, shocked.

'Well see there now, is a set *spell* we dealing with now,' groaned Mas' Collins. 'What a prekeh.'

228

Blowsnaught leapt forward to help Archie, but the shorter man shoved him away, face purple. He hoisted himself upright, panting.

All fire and damnation coming now, thought Anise. Archie Howard had the look of a man whose shame-tree was tall, the kind who saw even compromise as failure. She wondered how much beating the spell could take. She grappled for Mixie's hand, panting slightly, but the younger woman pulled away. She was crowing. 'Yes, to raaaaassss! You see that, Archie? Not one of you coming in here for no *freeness*!'

'Quiet your mouth,' said Archie.

Anise could barely hear him, that horrible voice so low and even. But Mixie didn't seem afraid anymore. She was practically dancing.

'I even offer cut-price, but all you want is *your* way. So is no way!' She took up her defensive stance between the women again, clutching hands, re-knitting the line, spreading her arms out, jerking Anise and Rhita's shoulders upwards with the motion. 'Come, nah. Try force me.'

'Mixie,' murmured Lyla. 'Take time.'

Archie moved back towards the house and the spell, cane extended. His eyes did not leave Mixie's face. The other men bunched behind him. They seemed such ordinary men, such as would come to Anise for stomach aches and leave behind puny secrets.

Archie pointed his cane at her.

'Which *spiritual advisor* stand for slackness?'

She felt anger rise in her throat. Was it not Popisho in this yard, too?

'The lady said no, and you don't *care*? I curse *your* slackness. Archie, son of which woman? Your mother shame, today.'

'Understand something.' Archie spoke deliberately, and he was smiling. 'I would fuck my own mother quicker than it going to take me to break your spell, and I going do *that* fast.'

Her rage came in splendid colours. 'Rapist,' she spat. She heard Old Man Collins gasp. 'Kiss my *backside*.'

'I coming for you first,' said Archie. '*You* first. Then you pay *me* for the privilege!' Oh, he was serious. How long would the spell hold?

'Who the *rass* you think you threatening?' said Mixie. 'She a guest in my house!'

'I coming for you, too, bitch. Just wait for me.'

Garson stepped forward, Blowsnaught on his heels. 'Archie, *Archie*! You really don't have to hot up your nerves on our account.'

'Yes,' squeaked Mas' Collins. 'Gone too far now, we have a church girl calling me a rapist? I am a pillar in this community, man. I never come to hold down nobody. Intiasar assure me a good time was to be had.'

'Then leave,' Archie snapped. He moved even closer, cane jabbing for the spell again. 'I going break this rass spell and mash up this place and if is me-one have to do it, oh well.'

'Mash up what, man? Don't be a fool. This is turning into fun.' Garson clasped his huge hands in a begging gesture. 'Miss Mixie, is so you name? Don't listen to Archie. You made your point and now I want you more.' He pointed at the swaying vulvas. 'Just show me which of them belong to you and I happy to negotiate a healthy price.'

'Garson, I promise you a free service today,' growled Archie.

Garson inched closer to the veranda steps. 'Well, it look like you was wrong. Mixie girl, how much?'

Mixie purred. 'Name a price, I take down mine, just for

you. *My* own, you all understand that? *I can do what I want with it.*' She licked her lips. 'Whatever *you* want with it, Mas' Garson.'

'I starting the bid at fifty coin.'

Mixie blew Garson kisses. 'Not one under seventy-five.'

Anise stared, confused. She could hear Rhita muttering angrily. Could Mixie truly lie down with any of these fools? They were still holding hands. 'You don't have to *talk* to him, Mixie,' she hissed. 'We can just stand here until they tired.'

'And then what?' Mixie pushed her breasts out.

'Seventy,' said Garson.

'It gone up to ninety, boy.'

Anise looked at Lyla, desperately. The sunflower woman shook her head, face pitying, voice gentle.

'What you think we *do*, sis?'

'Once a whore, always.' Rhita looked furious. She dropped her sister's hand and pulled at Anise. 'Mixie, kindly hold off one second, so decent people can leave. Come, Anise. How we get out of here?'

'Eighty-five,' said Garson.

'One hundred and twenty.'

'We don't.' Anise lowered her voice and gestured at the waiting men. Mas' Collins was shifting toe to toe, Archie watching Mixie and Garson. He might have been a statue. Blowsnaught's eyes were fixed on her. 'You want to go out to *them*?'

'Sold,' said Garson.

'Mixie!' snapped Rhita. 'Don't you *dare*.'

Mixie reached one long, graceful arm towards the white cotton thread above them, her fingers hovering and teasing. A chorus of distress from the other women. Archie's lips moved soundlessly. His eyes were enormous. Garson put his cheek against the spell, stroking the thin slice of magic between them. Mixie stroked her swaying pum-pum.

'No, Mixie!' Anise yelled. *'Don't do it!'*

'No,' Archie whispered. 'Don't.'

'It's *mine*,' said Mixie.

Shoooooop, said the force field. Mixie pulled her pum-pum – and Garson – towards her, swift and right. Through the force field he came, nearly tripping, practically on top of her.

The remaining genitalia bobbed gently. Anise felt the spell tremble back into place, like a waning ocean. Diluted, but still holding.

Mixie slithered into Garson's lap. He stuffed his face into her labia.

'No,' said Archie. He put a flat palm against the spell and pushed. The veranda shuddered under Anise's feet.

Garson pulled Mixie's skirt up over her hips. He reached between her thighs and shoved. She groaned, her laughter like sobbing. Anise closed her eyes, unable to watch. She could hear Rhita pulling at her, complaining and angry, Lyla yelling, could feel Archie, walking the length of the veranda now, bashing his stick against the spell. She opened her eyes, nauseated.

Blowsnaught followed behind Archie, grinning. Her stomach boiled. The veranda rocked. Mas' Collins was heading back towards the property gate, shaking his head.

Send somebody, she thought. *If you so outraged, help us.*

Archie's stick crashed up and down. *Stop, stop!* She fought the queasiness, pushed handfuls of energy into her belly and chest.

'Come, Anise,' said Rhita. Her voice was thick. 'I not *watching* this!'

'The whole thing will come down if we leave!'

'I want to negotiate a price too,' called Blowsnaught. 'One

232

thousand, clean.' There was a heavy change purse swaying in his hand, and he was smiling at the two remaining pum-pums, plunging through the air.

'Nobody else not *working* here today!' She sounded too rattled. But Blowsnaught was not looking at her.

She whirled, knowing before she saw.

Lyla's dress might have been on fire, so bright was she: breath lit, long-waisted, neck weaving, whole body trembling and open and pointed at Blowsnaught.

Oh, Lyla. You said you done.

It *was* her cors.

Mixie raised her head. Garson gnawed at her throat, squeezing one exposed breast. Her face was gleeful, watching Lyla burn. She laughed again, punching a fist in the air. Anise wondered how she could have thought it grieving, this sound so like a horn and jubilant.

'*Yes*, Lyla! I know you coulda never give it up!'

Lyla: reaching up-up-up, teasing, simmering fingers, up towards the roof and the hanging pums. Was this the victory they'd wanted all along? Money and plenty of it? Was it the only way they knew how to win?

Shoooop, said the set spell and the pum-pums danced.

The spell thinned like a spider's web around them.

Lyla hauled Blowsnaught into her resplendent arms, his sweaty tunic against her pretty crochet fire dress.

'*Come*, Anise,' urged Rhita. 'Take your property down and don't watch anymore.' But she couldn't hear Rhita clearly; couldn't *see* Archie or what he was doing, now that Blowsnaught was there, his stink, his body blocking her sight, set spell glimmering and rippling around them, obscuring her senses further. Mixie was turning on the radio, blaring a popular dancehall tune,

233

undulating against Garson's handsome body. Blowsnaught, putting his hands around Lyla's waist, she offering her pum-pum, the one with the cors, the one the gods gave her, but he was shaking his head, eyes on the white thread above them, reaching up with massive hands, to the only one left.

'I don't want that, I want *this*.'

Hers.

Lyla reached upwards with him.

Horrified, Anise leapt forward.

They flung themselves into the air, all three: a tangle.

Shoooop, last vulva down and the spell crackled into nothing. Anise buckled with stomach cramps. Heard Lyla yelling: '*Catch, Anise!*' Looked up just in time to see the woman throwing her pum-pum at her, realised she *must* catch it despite the griping sickness, grabbing through the air, praying, scrabbling, nearly losing her slippery grip, yanking the precious thing towards her chest.

Chaos. Blowsnaught and Lyla were yelling at each other. Mixie wrapped her long legs around the sweating Garson's waist, his terrible thrusts, her eyes fixed on Archie's face.

So you really fix that pum-pum back, Mixie. When needs must.

Archie bellowing. Archie thundering.

Even if Anise could have moved fast enough, what might she have done to stop Archie from picking up the rough-hewn mahogany table and raising it above his head?

Nothing at all. Watch cors.

'Oh Jesus,' said Garson, his handsome teeth lost in Mixie's hair. 'Oh, *yes*.'

'No!' screamed Mixie. 'Archie! *Archie!*'

Archie tore the table in half and threw it at the veranda.

Blowsnaught's head-back took a corner as it landed. He stumbled off the veranda and fell unconscious, into the yard. Archie began to pound the walls and veranda floor with the other half of the table. Tears were pouring down his cheeks, splinters and shards flying, fists bleeding.

Mixie dismounted Garson.

'Archie, stop it, *stop!*'

'I told you I didn't like it, Mixie. I told you, I didn't like it, and you wouldn't listen. *I told you I didn't like it . . . !*'

The music on the radio stopped.

'*Stop hurting yourself!*'

Archie halted, shuddering.

Anise cradled her pum-pum. Lyla's knees seemed to come undone; she sat down heavily on the floor. Rhita crouched over them all, like a mother animal.

The radio was the only sound, along with the breathing.

'This is an important notice from the office of Governor Intiasar. With immediate effect, there is a twenty-four-hour ban on sexual intercourse. It is illegal, punishable by life imprisonment, to indulge in carnal activity of any kind, repeat, any kind, until 2.10 p.m., tomorrow afternoon.'

18

Sonteine's hands slipped on the oars. She paused for breath, sweat on her top lip. She couldn't remember the last time she'd rowed herself, and the lack of practice showed. Mid-afternoon and she *still* felt basted in oil, like a side of meat, gummy and furious. She rubbed her hands in her hair, along the soles of her feet, the front of her robe and then plunged them into the ocean. The canoe rocked to the side. She was in the middle of the most frustrating experience of her entire *life*.

Her mother had been hot on her as soon as she walked back into the house; there was no right way to lie about something this important. *Where were you in that Horrible Moment?* demanded her mother and she was frozen because at first she thought they were talking about the maid in the dark kitchen-corner business. It was only when Mrs Intiasar tried to lift her hem that she realised she wasn't the only one who'd had an accident – and that none of it was Dandu's fault. Her mother said the maid cleaning the gazebo squeaked *eep!* when hers fell out, and that the young wife one-door-down who was sitting with her in the garden taking lemonade said *bloodfire. She'd* had more presence of mind than anyone around her. Shot straight up to the house, calling for someone to find Sonteine, flinging her own . . . *situation* into her purse for safekeeping. Then she'd remembered her one-child wasn't home.

I am not your one-child, Mamma. Don't be ridiculous.

Her mother ignored this. Where *is your – it –* that*?*

So then she did have to tell. Her mother screwed her eyes very tight and held her head in her hands in a way that Sonteine thought ever so melodramatic, but she was used to her mother getting everything wrong. Imagine if she'd acted so dramatically when she didn't get what *she* wanted, which was a *reasonable* mother.

The Governor have to hear about this! Her mother had an irritating way of referring to her husband and the father of her children by his title.

You mean Pap?

You know you very out of order, Sonteine Ignoble?

Mamma went pounding at her father's office door, which was the one thing her generally sanguine father could *not* abide. At first, he said he really didn't need to *hear* all this woman business, but when more was explained, he strode out of the office literally struggling for breath.

In the midst of the yelling, Sonteine had given as good as she got – after all, it was *she* who climbed into Dandu's bedroom, and *she* who let him look between her legs and how was it *his* fault that the blasted thing have to fall out right that minute, especially now she knew it wasn't just her it happen to?

Tell that boy you coming back to get your jewel! her father bellowed. Despite her clear explanation that she felt best with Dandu keeping it and that calling it a jewel was stupid, her father looked like he was contemplating a stroke. She felt sorry for him, so she stalked over to the phone, feeling self-righteous.

Until Dandu told her about the river. His teeth were chattering.

You lost it?

She could feel her mother fluttering spasmodically, like a hen before death.

Suh-slipped, stuttered Dandu.

237

So now I going kill you, said Sonteine.

The Governor's first idea after *that* revelation was typical. He wanted to send out very many men, beating bushes and lifting up stones and invading houses.

Sonteine glared. *Review this, Papa. You going to send out hundreds of men to look for my* pum-pum? *What make you think that is a good idea?*

Which ended *that* stupid matter.

How you could trust a crebbeh with something so precious, yelled her father. He got very angry indeed when he couldn't solve things with money. She'd seen the safe in his office: stuffed with coins it was, and he never seemed to run out. There were neat bags stacked on the shelf, the perfect size for a bribe.

He is not *a crebbeh*, she yelled back, even though she had never been angrier with a human being than she was with Dandu right now. *He going to be my* husband *tomorrow and if you and Mamma want any grandchildren you better try come up with something fast because I don't. Have. A. Pum-pum!*

Then she locked herself in her room and called Dandu back and asked him what he really was thinking, taking her underneath for a walk like it was a bunch of rassclaaht *bananas*.

The immediate problem, as her parents saw it, was to prevent . . . *besmirchment*. If no one could have sex, and no one knew *why* they couldn't have sex, then it followed that no one would take the chance and have sex with her jewel if they found it. By the time she'd spoken – more like screamed – at Dandu for the second time and hung up, she could hear the sex ban being announced from the radio in the house next door.

. . . illegal, punishable by life imprisonment, to indulge in

carnal activity of any kind, repeat, any kind, until 2.10 p.m.,
tomorrow afternoon.

Sonteine held her head like her mother had. Really, she had the most *stupid* parents. Fear before common sense. A government command with no explanation did nothing but set up a mystery and what was more human than trying to solve one of those?

And now this radio woman, calling the house. She didn't trust *her*. Mamma said it was good for Pap to go on the radio and just say everything was fine and talk to this lady about embroidery and children and how sad he was to see his one baby-girl fly away to be a big woman on her own and tell people the colour of the wedding decorations. But she had been listening to Hah for months now, and that was *not* a woman to be played with. She wasn't what Pap was used to, taking his money bags down to the radio station with him and chatting about the weather then leaving them there. All the radio hosts – even Puppa Gyallis! – were nice to politicians. Miss Hah might not be so nice. And Papa could not calm himself when challenged.

If any man, in the whole of this archipelago, touch my daughter pum-pum, I going cut him balls off and make him eat what left.

Please gods, he wouldn't swear like that on live radio and tell everybody what was lost in a river.

She rowed just as fast as she could: past trees, beaches and peasant houses, pink and orange and lime, like large, colourful sweets hanging in the bush. A man standing next to a yellow house made a rude gesture at her. Sonteine was tempted to get up and throw one of the oars at him, but then she would only have one oar and that would make her as stupid as everyone else today.

She scratched her shoulder. Her wings itched when she was upset. What was this world coming to when a woman had to go out searching for her own pum-pum? Men could not be trusted to do anything but look pretty.

She set her back to it.

Papa was a *little* bit right to be protective. Part of her body was in jeopardy, after all. She hadn't told him where she was going, but on a calm day she thought he would have approved. People said her father had overseas ways and a delivery boy's cors: for speed, and what kind of inferior magic was that? They didn't *know*. He was a spiritual man. A deep-feeling man. And he liked that she had her own mind. She wasn't sure what she would do when she found her pum-pum. How she might make peace with the fear, what shape it would be in, or whether Dandu would like it after it came back from its adventures. She wasn't even sure she wanted Dandu to see it again, ever, having been so gut-wrenchingly *careless*. But *she* wanted it. The longer it was gone, the more she felt wrong. It belonged to her and she should be in charge of it.

If anyone knew where a pum-pum had run to, it was the Obeah Fatidique, so that's where she was going.

Dukuyaie creaked in the distance, its silken shore green and lemon.

★

There had never been a radio conversation like it in Popisho before, no, not in the whole of history. And eventually everybody agreed that no one but a woman could have accomplished it.

'Good afternoon, ladies and gentlemen. We are lucky this late afternoon to welcome our Governor, the Honourable Bertrand Intiasar. Good afternoon, Mr Governor.'

'Please call me Bertie, Miss Hah. All the pretty girls do.'

'I prefer giving you due respect, Mr Governor. Thank you for keeping our appointment. There is so much to talk ab—'

Intiasar interrupted. 'It was no problem, Hah. I left a late lunch with my lovely wife to come here for you. My *wife* does call me Bertie. Is she who said I should spend some time talking to the first woman radio host ever in Popisho.'

Hah coughed.

'The subject of discussion is, for many of my callers, a matter of urgency. An hour ago, you put out a statement to all radio stations in Popisho. A complete ban on sexual intercourse, for twenty-four hours. This ordinance makes lovemaking a crime, Mr Governor. My first question is: why?'

There was a pause as the entire island tried to recover from the *directness* of that renk-and-out-of-orderness.

Eventually the Governor responded, his voice deep and even.

'My, Miss Hah. Such incisive questioning. Well. This is a missive sent out in partnership with the Council of Health.'

Another pause. The Governor appeared to be finished.

'And . . . ?' said Hah.

Anyone in the archipelago who wasn't listening began to listen.

'And', to rass! And!

'With great respect, Miss Hah, in the last few months, an environment of unnecessary *questioning* has come about. A lack of *trust* in the wisdom and experience of government. *And* I have never been treated so rudely.'

'Governor, surely you could not expect to legislate *lovemaking*, without context or reason. Do you and the good Council really think people will accept this?'

'Of course.' Intiasar spoke coolly.

'On what basis?'

'Young lady, it is only one day. Eight hours of that, most people going sleep. I cannot imagine which animal can't hold strong for that short amount of time. I will answer intelligent and respectful questions, but I will not be browbeaten. Do I have to remind you that I am a guest on your show?'

'You are, sir, and we are pleased to have you here. Let me put something else to you. A series of calls have come in this afternoon, and we decided not to air them. We were concerned as to their veracity, and then about their potential to cause public outcry. We wanted more information, more than rumour and panic. We are now in a position to put this to you: are you aware that approximately three hours ago, all adult Popisho females suffered a genital accident?'

'Wha-what – what – ?'

'Their pum-pums fell off.'

Stone cold silence.

'Are you aware of this matter, Governor?'

'I don't know anything about it.'

'Is that so?'

'Yes.' Firmly.

'So you have not been in contact with your daughter or wife this afternoon?'

'I told you, my wife had luncheon with me.'

'And she has suffered no injury?'

'*I think that question is entirely impertinent and stupid.*'

'Excuse me. But the larger question is a fair one, considering so many women seem to have had this experience. Dukuyaie, Battisient, even people from the *Dead Islands* call us this afternoon, Mr Governor. The timing of the Council's ban could not be more suspect.'

'That is hardly empirical evidence.'

'I agree. But it is anecdotal evidence. And widespread.'

'Strange things ordinary in Popisho, Miss Hah. Come, now.'

'True-true. But gods laugh if you ignore them. And none of us not stupid. Clearly there is a connection between these genital incidents and the ban. Why not just put out a clear and sensible explanation confirming this?'

'You are sitting there, presuming to tell *me* about what is sensible?'

'Yes, sir. What is the Council of Health doing about this incident? Are they checking that vulvas are being refitted without damage? Do they know whether they will fall again? What are they doing to ensure women's safety?'

'*Safety?*' Intiasar was shrill. 'You is one of them kind of woman who speak like is only woman walk this world. What evidence do I have that any of this is happening?'

'We counted calls from 367 men and women this morning, and they telling us this happen to all their friends and family. Every female working here has suffered the same fate, and each call seemed to represent at least two others. This is why we making this public: for that woman who don't ask no question yet or for men who are worried about women they care for. If this was penises breaking off, I cannot help but think the matter would be treated more urgently.'

Three beats of silence, then a sharp intake of breath. An unmistakeable scuffling sound.

For years after the interview, people speculated about those few seconds. Some said Governor Intiasar whipped out his manhood as proof of its safety. Or that he grabbed some part of Hah's anatomy. But everyone agreed that the moment was not a good one, and that Hah handled whatever it was like the strongest kind of Popisho woman.

She managed not to laugh at the fool.

'*Governor.* The men calling here are doing it because they concerned about the women they love. Mothers and sisters and friends. What are *you* doing to reassure these men and women?'

'The sex ban allows us to assess the situation.'

'It allows you to assess the situation you just said you knew nothing about?'

'Well . . . I am speaking in theory, given the Council's decision.'

'So you signed off on a missive from them without knowing anything about the matter? But you are the head of the Council.'

'I object to your fresh and rude questions, young lady! How would you feel if I asked you about the state of your pum-pum?'

The smallest of pauses. Intiasar seemed to press some kind of advantage.

'You don't think your public deserve to know if Miss Hah suffering problems, too?'

She answered smoothly.

'My pum-pum fell off at half past eleven, Mr Governor, yes. At the same time as everyone else, and now I am well. The matter is an easy one to fix, if you know how. We are consulting obeah women, despite your Council refusing to give us permission to interview the head of the Obeah Fatidique. Council don't do anything without the Fatidique, but the obeah women said they had no warning of this sex ban. So now we interviewing you, sir. Such things must be discussed openly for the good of Popisho. Especially when you are required by law to call election soon. What are you and the Council of Health doing to address the concerns of thousands of voters?'

'Everything we can.'

'Give me an example.'

'We are monitoring—'

'So the sex ban *is* connected to the detachable pum-pums? The ban *helps* our women?'

'We – we – well—'

'Is there some evidence that intercourse going to cause problems in the future? For man or woman? That it might cause infection or recurrence of problems? People all-calling me about Miss Pretty competition going on tonight, ask me if is best we cancel. Who want to walk on that stage, afraid their pum-pum going to fall off again in front of the whole of Popisho?'

'My dear lady. You are overstating everything. Cors *ever* in Popisho – you said it yourself! In this life I couldn't tell you how much fool-fool madness I see in our wonderful country, and I know is the same for you. How you could be stirring up trouble when man disappear, reappear, have eye roll down him face, child swim under water two hours, like fish, and other child come out of coney belly? And a thousand other cors? This is precisely why we didn't speak of this matter directly. Right now, you making people panic. This station don't have no social conscience.'

'But when has an event ever been so widespread and simultaneous?'

'All the *time*, young woman. Look to history! You said you care about our people, but you are, right in this minute, scaring the rass out of them. How responsible is that?'

'I would appreciate an honest answer to even one of my questions, Mr Governor.'

'Who the rass you think you talking to, *gyal*?'

A collective gasp across the islands. Oh, the gyal moment. The moment a man abandons any hope, any dreams of sweetness, when he put a certain kind of stone on the table.

'Sir, you are our most senior public servant. I asked you why you issued the sex ban. What you and the Council of Health are doing to address the concerns of voters. Why I can't interview the Fatidique. Why they not standing with you. In what way the sex ban helps our women. I asked if you are concerned that sexual intercourse could cause problems in the future. All in an election year. I still don't know the answer to any of these questions. *Bertie.*'

Crowing, across the beaches and rum bars. Men beat tables and each other's backs and women bent over at the waist from laughing. Men scuttered over to them, hands on hips and heads.

'You alright, baby? Nothing not falling?'

'Mash him *up*, Miss Hah!'

'Fresh and rude man, calling her gyal. Call him Bertie, yes!'

'Him not answering one question good. And then him asking her about her pum-pum. You ever hear such a thing?'

'Ladies and gentlemen, I am afraid that island Governor, Bertrand Intiasar, has left my studio. So. The sex ban is still in operation, and we have no answers. But listen me, now. I not waiting on no Fatidique. I looking for women to share wisdom. We throwing it wide open. Call and tell me if your own did fall out and how you fix it. Nobody don't call me and tell me this conversation is slackness. This is too important . . .'

End of interview.

★

In Pretty Town, a corpulent and very beautiful grandmother came in from a strangely heavy breeze to rest in her hammock. She barely stirred as a tiny mongoose crept through the folds of her labia and into her womb, where it found what smelled so good: a sugary, blood-enriched lining. The mongoose ate its fill, inadvertently killing the grandmother, and when the dead woman sat up and her soul crept out onto the bed sheet, the mongoose ate that, too.

19

Xavier stood on veranda steps, looked out at the rain dripping off the fruit trees, moisture swept by the wind across flat red earth. They'd run right out of the monochromatic patch on the Dead Island beach, but the thick clouds rolling over the mountains were still grey and black on the blue.

He let the raindrops spatter off the zinc roof and onto his hands. The water acted like a balm for the fear he could still feel in his flesh.

Panting, running, pounding throat, the boy slung over his shoulder, like a sack. Romanza's eyes rolling up in their sockets, his body diminished. Indigent coming, it seemed from nowhere, to shout instructions: *Go obeah woman, three mile from here! You will see her place!* Several women running beside him as long as they could, urging him on, telling him messages were being sent before him. Was it mud on his heels, or was Romanza coughing blood over his shoulder? Black and brackish: he couldn't tell for certain, but he knew the smell of blood. A small building looming, the only one he could see for miles, surely that was it? Indigent running out of the house to help him through the sudden and determined rain, and finally, finally kneeling on the ground, putting Romanza down, chest wheezing, afraid, the boy very still; agony as he was helped to his feet by several hands, snapping, *No, I'm fine, help him!*

Nothing good ever came of the Dead Islands, nothing, nothing. But he could have wept in gratitude for them all, seeming to know what they were doing and what was best.

He fall and lick him head? He eat something? Somebody hit him? He have any set spell on him? He have sugar in him blood? I don't know. I don't know.

He didn't know anything useful, not even Romanza's family name. He hovered at the boy's forehead, saw crimson blink in, staining the boy's chin. He licked his thumb to clean the dried blood just before a stretcher was brought. A fat obeah woman pushed him away from the door with a kind but authoritative motion. *Let go*, she said. She had a round face and small, earnest hands. He was left on the muddy veranda, ceaseless rain trickling down the walls of the house like sweat.

Xavier ran his hands up and down his damp face. There was tobacco in a bowl on the wet table and he could smell it, harsh and sweet. Everything would be *fine*. Not like Nya. He'd had the chance to act this time. He wasn't too late.

The thought of another death on this day was insufferable.

He stepped out into the rain, distracting himself by identifying plants: two hog plum bushes and several kinds of mango trees. The hot, wet air smelled of spice. He looked up at pale orange pawpaw trees, fingered a pile of freshly picked green coconuts, pineapple plants, a black sapote tree. Examined a tangled vine he didn't recognise, heavy with clandestine gold-green vegetables. A small, musical pond, swelled by the downpour. He stooped to examine a limestone statue of a woman's face. Romanza's blood stained his satchel. If the boy died, who would he tell? How could he find that gambling father or the mother who made good pudding?

Beyond the property there was nothing but flat red clay for as far as he could see. Running, he'd splashed through shallow, sparkling rivers the circumference of his ankle, but nothing more. It was as if this small house and lush garden had been scooped from elsewhere by a giant hand and plopped down on the edge of the world.

He shivered; thought of sweet peppers and crayfish. Blue man, pouring over river stones.

So quiet. Somebody had to come and tell him something.

He dipped into his bag for the red pouch and slowly laced it around his neck again, leather strap caressing his skin, tracing the gathered edges, dipping two fingers inside, barely touching the insect. He brought his fingers up to his nose. The smell was like earth and seed and something else that reminded him of being afraid. He held his hand out and stared as the rusty flecks from its wings washed away. Nearly seven hours since the fisher-boy left it for him.

Anise told him to turn inside, when the hunger came. To speak gently to himself; to know that some part of him needed attention.

He was a fool, to be under this thing again.

He was sure she had long forgotten him and his troubles. An acquaintance knew the Latibeaudearre family, and he'd asked after her for a while, after the last goodbye. Casual-like. The acquaintance only ever used adjectives to describe Miss Anise. The modest house she'd bought with her handsome husband was pretty. She seemed happy. Devout. Respectable. Calm. None of it sounded like the person who had walked with him in the hills and believed in him so ferociously. Eventually he'd stopped asking. The family acquaintance said she felt useless, sad, offended to no longer be of service.

The rain was easing.

He looked up at the sound of rustling. A woman stood at the garden gate, searching through the compost heap. Her body made him think of a figure-eight rye bread: he imagined a crisp, sour plait under her clothes. He squinted. She wasn't scavenging the heap, rather she was putting leaves *into* it: pulling them off the guava trees overhanging the fence. It seemed such an odd thing to do.

The woman leaned back, mouth open, and drank rainwater. Her lower jaw yawned, wide, too wide, teeth scabrous, then the entire lower jaw broke free, falling down her chest and onto the ground.

She turned to stare at him.

Xavier pushed the heel of his hand into his mouth. He began to walk towards her. Surely not. Surely not here. Not now. He fought sudden, furious nausea.

Surely not Nya.

He fingered his tunic, tacky with Romanza's drying blood. The back of his neck, sticky. He walked closer to the rotting thing. She tore at the guava trees again. She was wearing raindrops on her broken face, on her ears, hair and arms, like crystals. He couldn't breathe, as he reached the gate, staring hard.

No, not Nya.

He felt thudding, raw relief. A wind chime tinkled on the veranda. The ghost twisted what remained of her decaying neck and face like an owl, 360 degrees. Xavier swallowed. Who was she here for? Who needed to see her? Who needed to help her? Should *he* do it?

The ghost belched.

One thing at a time, or it would all whirl out of control.

'Xavier.'

He turned around.

Romanza was standing on the veranda, dwarfed in a clean tunic two sizes too big. It made him look younger, as did the

251

solemn expression on his face. Xavier's throat hurt. He didn't know what to say.

'Leave the ghost alone,' called Romanza. 'We let them walk free, here.'

He couldn't bear to argue. Looking back at the broken woman stopped him from rushing the veranda, from pawing the boy in a ridiculous manner. *You good, boy? You hurt? Because I was 'fraid.* He tried to joke. 'That obeah woman coming to tell me why I nearly break my back running through the bush with you?'

Behind him, the ghost chuckled and hissed. They watched her slink off across the flat expanse, one shoulder higher than the other, a scribble against the oily earth.

No, not Nya.

'Greetings, macaenus.'

Emerging from the house was the same obeah woman who had pushed him back at the door. She was fatter than she'd seemed before, and very short. He had an ephemeral impression of her shoulders disappearing, as if she was not a solid thing at all but existed somewhere as air. She laid her head affectionately on Romanza's shoulder, patted his hand, then straightened, her indigent gaze on Xavier as he came up the steps. Her dark pink eyes were bright and round, like a good octopus. She wore a heavy purple headwrap and the eye make-up of the Fatidique: thick, black, feline strokes, a white streak inside the bottom lid. Romanza smiled and hugged her into his side. The boy needed a hug, anyone could see that.

How quickly one could learn to care.

'Teacher,' Xavier said, for want of anything else.

She patted her large stomach gently. 'Most call me Cannon-ball, after the plant.' She gestured to a glutinous round fruit vine he hadn't recognised. 'It is a nickname from my family. It was their intention to shame me, and they are still irritated it hasn't worked.' She looked up at him, a small smile playing on her lips. 'You see the young man is well?'

'Is he?' She was such a neat and compact woman. He felt himself twitch. A curse on anyone who said he was *soft*.

'Tell him how you are feeling, Romanza,' said Cannonball.

'Better, macaenus. Much better.'

'That's good. That's good.'

Xavier sat down heavily on the steps, gesturing for Romanza to take the single rattan seat. Cannonball patted Romanza, who sat down. He looked tired, and pale.

Cannonball's pink eyes flared yellow, like the burst of a match.

'Romanza would like for you to know what is happening, yes, Romanza?' The boy nodded and she smiled. 'Macaenus, I understand what happened looked very frightening. Romanza said it was painful. But he is not dying.'

She had a soothing voice.

'His lungs are clear of any infection or injury, but the throat was laced with small, deep wounds and old scar tissue, all of which I have healed. We don't know *what* is irritating the throat and making Romanza cough for months, but I don't think it is life-threatening, whatever it is. Romanza has been taking larger and larger amounts of unripe ackee fruit, which is, as you know, highly poisonous. Ackee *is* a cough suppressant in the short term, but it also inflames the throat and the wounds being created by the coughing can't heal. So we had a cycle.' More stroking of her stomach. Xavier wondered how soft it was. 'You agree, Romanza? No more poison, until we know the cause.'

Romanza nodded.

Xavier frowned. 'What of the vomiting . . . blood?'

'Several blood vessels finally burst from the strain, but it was never anything more than that.'

'He lost consciousness.'

'Ackee lowers the blood pressure. Given the amount he's been taking, I am surprised he has not fainted before.'

Xavier felt ridiculous: at his own running and panic.

'Treating symptoms alone, as you know, is stupid. We must find the root. I think you should come back to me, Romanza, to check for curses, complications of magic and maladies of the mind. I am also concerned that you're slightly malnourished. Dehydrated. If you do not return for regular treatment, this may get worse.'

There was a sudden burst of sunshine. The rain slid to a halt. Xavier wanted to lay his head on a woman's breast and sigh.

'It is ironic that this young man needs good *feeding*, given he is friend to the macaenus.' Xavier winced. Cannonball flapped her hand. 'Come now. I mean it in jest.'

He thought of Oliviana, and if her mother would come. Of Chse and the way her ribcage and limbs suggested she'd grow tall. Io's obeah woman said her elongating bones were already like steel and her skin was remarkably malleable; he imagined her stretching those arms between Soin and Pluie, a human bridge, could it be done? *It tickles, Uncle*, was what she would say. She'd love Romanza – she'd always wanted a big brother.

Cannonball reached up to touch the wind chime above her head. 'I will leave you to talk. Stay, as long as you like. But come and see me before you depart, o macaenus.'

And then she was gone, oil on water.

The men hesitated. The boy's sudden vulnerability, the carrying, it was an intimacy between them; Xavier wasn't sure what should come next, or how to behave.

'So, you good,' he said.

'Well, not really.'

'You said so.'

'I not in no pain. She heal me for now. But we don't know the cause.'

'No. Well.' He plunged forward. 'I will pay for everything.'

Romanza smiled faintly. 'She don't want money, macaenus.'

'I think she will.'

'She don't charge indigent. She is one of us.'

'That don't mean she won't appreciate it from me.'

'You too concerned with money.'

'Nobody has ever said that to me before.'

'I like being first.'

Such mischief. What was it like, to be free?

'Boy, you know you rude?'

'Always. But you don't think I am. You think I'm just fine.'

Just fine, Xavier. Nothing wrong with you. That was what Anise had said.

Xavier stepped back out into the garden. He twisted two pawpaws off the tree and laid a handful of ripe brown tamarind pods on the veranda table. He chose a green coconut from the pile he'd noticed before and used a machete propped against the tree to chop into the husk, turning the nut around in one hand until he reached the liquid, applying the tip of the machete to make a hole at the top. He passed the coconut to Romanza, who drank deeply.

Xavier cut a coconut for himself and swigged it. He began to crack tamarinds, pulling out the pod flesh, adding sugar and black pepper from his palms. Romanza watched him curiously. He passed one of the treated tamarinds to the boy, took back the empty coconut and chopped it in half, slicing a flat, thin piece of the husk so Romanza could scoop out the gelatinous white flesh.

Romanza ate slowly, as if he expected to be in pain, bits of coconut jelly, nodding at the taste of the makeshift tamarind sweets. Xavier sliced the pawpaw in half, emptying the tiny black seeds over the veranda wall. Sometimes he added roasted sesame to pawpaw or watermelon chunks, but this fruit was so sweet and good they needed nothing else. No fee-fee, faw-faw.

'Did you ever have a dog?' Romanza's face was tacky with fruit.

'My stepfather said we couldn't afford animals we couldn't eat.'

Romanza spat a tamarind seed into the air.

'Your family was poor.'

'Just normal. Although there were hard times.'

'You have brothers or sisters?'

'One brother.' He paused again. 'Who is your family?'

Romanza rubbed his chest gently.

'I don't want to talk of it.'

They were too similar, in some ways. 'You can't stay nowhere until you feel better?'

'I feel better. And I stay somewhere.'

'Inside, where people can take care of you.'

'You know my kind can only take so much inside, macaenus.'

'Cannonball said you need to come back.'

'I going come back.' Romanza sucked a sweet and sighed contentedly. 'Fruit and sweetie, though, macaenus? I expected more from your hand. Maybe you can't really cook at all.'

'That's what you needed for your throat. If you really let yourself *feel*, you'd know—'

'Oh gods, he swelling up like a *bullfrog*.'

They grinned at each other. It was raining again and the rain looked white, like splattering paint. There were no flowers in this garden.

'How you *know* I love sweetie from when I was young and coconut water?'

Xavier shrugged. 'Because I know.'

'*I* never recall. Until now.'

'Yes.'

The wind chime tinkled on the still-black veranda and as Romanza turned away, Xavier could have sworn there were black tears smudging the boy's face, like ink.

'I soon come,' said Xavier and stepped into Cannonball's house.

✳

He missed Entaly most of all after the testing was done. On her twenty-sixth birthday he took a walk and filled a basket with edible flowers: pumpkin blossoms and marigold, lavender and orange bloom, mixed through with sage and bits of mint – each petal examined for wrinkles, each stalk for rot – and sent a girl to deliver. He waited, pacing, fingers black from Scissor moth antennae. He liked to think of his old friend's pleasure, uncovering the details of the gift. Surely she'd come to terms with her disappointment. He needed a friend. Perhaps she did, too.

The girl returned with the untouched flower basket and a letter.

Entaly wrote to say she'd woken up thinking of him. She said she didn't want the flowers. What she wanted for her birthday was for him to stop taking moth. It was, she wrote, time for him to change.

As soon as he realised what he was reading – and it only took the first few lines, as such letters tended to have a particular energy of their own and this one was throbbing slowly in the late afternoon light – he'd held it at arm's length, eyes flitting across the paper, hardly allowing the words to form sentences. *Care. Love. Should.* He couldn't breathe, could barely control the speed at which the meaning crashed in on him. Such a long and rehearsed letter. They'd never spoken of his addiction. She must have been thinking this way for a while. She wrote as if the moth had made him stupid, saying things he'd told himself a thousand times. In every paragraph, she said she loved him. Told him of his weight on her head, and how frightened she was that he'd die.

Did he have to be responsible for her pain as well?

There had been no revelation. The letter, if anything, made him worse. He felt more evil and stupid and sorry and guilty than before. Ate moths until the inside of his mouth burned and his eyes were bloodshot, his ankles paper, neighbours frightened to see him in the yard.

Now he turn macaenus, it mad him?

He hadn't needed friends to tell him the moth made him thin and haunted, that his raw joints creaked and his nose ran. He'd woken from nightmares knowing it, clawing the pouch. He might have sent the same letter to his mother; after all, he had promised himself to speak to her before the drink killed her. Knowing what little effect it would have had, ah, it made him hold his head.

Let me be, he thought.

He knew a happily married healer who said he didn't understand his rum-head patients but couldn't let a woman pass without seeking her frock-tail. A neighbour who took care of her children with great love and attention but flew into a spitting rage if they backchatted her; a man who lectured his daughter about honey-bush smoking, but ate too much food when he was ill, or frightened, or sad. Another friend, a kind woman, who *had* to have the last word: he'd seen her screaming into people's faces for it. Io couldn't bear a lover's abandonment, even if it killed him to walk away first. Moue had never been without a man, not since she was a teenager, and wore it like something to be proud of, and when he asked her one day, *now what would you do if you found yourself alone*, she said she was sure the chickens needed feeding.

What we need to soothe ourselves.

He never replied to the letter, but he saw Entaly in Pretty Town weeks later. She stepped to him, anxious and tearful, and he walked around her and away. If he stayed, he risked howling, pounding the earth and losing what little control he had left. He didn't want to scream at her, because it was love she'd offered, love she was beating him with, love, love, love—

＊

Cannonball kept a large refrigerator in her examination room, and floor cushions. She met him by the door, smiling and o, those rippling shoulders, gesturing for him to sit. Xavier shook his head, but she pressed him down firmly. When he was settled – long legs stretched out in front of him, part of him sure she was amused by his discomfort – she perched on an embroidered cushion. Her breasts rested gently on the rise of her stomach and he thought she was quite perfect.

'Is there something further you need to tell me about Romanza?' he asked.

'Romanza must mean a great deal to you, if you're willing to interrupt the hunt. Is he your acolyte?'

'Hunt?'

'Walkround been on the radio all week.' Cannonball adjusted her robes, and for a moment he thought she might show him her cuff, except obeah women didn't play those games. 'There are three competitions to win your *own* special wedding feast. They don't say you will be cooking, but they do imply it, like people don't know you are strict in these matters.' She looked affronted. 'You've been seen in the Battisient hills, where you slaughtered fourteen pigs with your bare hands then paid hundreds for them, and in Dukuyaie, where you attempted to seduce someone's wife, who drove you off with a curse.'

Perhaps the gods were trying to show him something with this delay. An indigent feast *would* enrage Intiasar. Perhaps he should be obedient: gather some pleasant food, let the charade play out. Except Sonteine Intiasar was in his sights now. He had to feed her *properly*. Despite everything.

'The young man need to eat a ram-goat head,' said Cannonball, as if she could hear his thoughts. 'Soup would be traditional.'

Mannish water was its name: made from goat head, tripe and the feet. One of macaenus Plantenitthy's recipes. They said Plantenitthy often sat in Lukia's town centre with a vat of mannish water, giving it away to giggling girls for their sweethearts. It was best reheated in an old pot, slurped hand to hand, man to man, late at night, with the background crash of a bowls tournament. It was a good idea, but he wasn't thinking about the groom. What pleased Sonteine Intiasar would please Dandu Brenteninton. Somehow he knew that, and if he was wrong, that was the way it *should* be.

'May I suggest not too much pepper, as the stinging sensation in the mouth, while potentially erotic, actually decreases—'

'I know *pepper*.'

'Yes, of course.' Cannonball looked embarrassed, and he was alarmed at the idea of embarrassing her. She grappled to rise from the low cushion. Guiltily, he moved to help, but she waved him away.

'Was there something else you wanted, Teacher? Can I pay you for Romanza's care?'

She took a white package from the refrigerator. It was the size and shape of a medium potato. She moved it hand to hand, almost caressing it, an expectant look on her face.

'Macaenus. There is a . . . *ditty* being played with great regularity and sung on the streets with no small enthusiasm. Many people think it discusses your . . . ahm . . . *talents*. Or lack of them.'

'I heard it.'

'Women have called the radio to discuss these . . . allegations, and some have been cut off, as they are quite . . . hysterical. They say you are *wonderful* and they know from experience.'

She looked entirely gleeful.

'*What?*'

'Others are saying your quest is not for food, but that you are searching to cure your impotence. I wonder which is true.'

'*Enough.*' He'd thought to seek her counsel, to ask if she'd seen any starvation among the indigent, but she was insubstantial; a gossip. What kind of obeah woman was this? Too young, out here hiding in the Dead Islands, too far from the Fatidique.

Cannonball looked crestfallen. 'Most men would want to know the details of their character defamation.' She looked at the ground and squeezed the little package in her hand. 'I just want to *help*.'

'I don't need any help.'

Cannonball tapped her chin, her pink eyes anguished.

'No, no. Macaenus. I have wanted to speak to you for a *very* long time. You don't remember me, do you?'

'I don't—'

'Why should you? I was one of the first, one among *many*, and you were busy in the kitchen. But I hoped . . . well, we all hope . . . you will *see* us.' She bit her lip. Whatever her problem, he thought, she should have more control than this. 'I can still see *you*, through the kitchen window. Like a *possessed* man. It was astounding to watch you work, this mad, sure thing. And I knew immediately. I have treated so much of it.' Her voice rose. 'I thought they were all weak, then I saw you. You had recently ascended, not two years before, but it was still on you, like oil.'

'What are you talking about?'

'But you hurt me, macaenus. The waiter came: "Tonight, for you," he said, "Xavier Redchoose sends traditional fare. Pumpkin soup. Salted cod, cooked down with Scotch bonnet pepper and onion. Sweet tomatoes, he grow them with he own hand. He also send dumplings, to scoop up the gravy. A tureen of jimbilin juice, you see the colour? The haunch of a coney, slightly blooded, do not fear, he knows it will please your palate. Corn, one fat ear, running with butter; a handful of tender green beans, dried in lime – eat them last." I was offended. I thought: plain, peasant food.

'I had a beautiful man with me: long-backed and large-chested, and I, well, I was not obeah, then. There was no chance of his attention until I promised to take him to your Torn Poem.

262

The name, even that conjures fantasy. The man's face when he saw my meal! He thought you were mocking me. I wanted fanciness. I saw it on other people's tables.

'But then we tasted! Ahhh. He licked his fingers, licked his wrist where there was a stray drop. I couldn't look at him: he suddenly seemed dull. For here—' All the time she had been grasping the air with her hands, in an impassioned effort to express herself. 'Here was not just *food*, but an *experience*. It was *all* of Popisho, the smells and textures, it was – it was – all our *love* and our losses and our beauty, struggles, history, our childhoods . . . it was perfect, it was perfect for *me*. I know what it is to sit and miss home. I don't understand how you could have known . . .' Her voice began to die away. 'Well now. I have made a fool of myself. I am sorry.'

He was mildly horrified. He *avoided* the kind of people who waited for him after service, sending Io to escort them out. How many times could you say *thank you, I glad you enjoyed my hand*? Why say it, when he'd already worked so hard to send them what they needed? None of it was about seeing him. He saw *them*. Let them eat and go, and think on digestion, and memory, if anything at all. But Cannonball's chin was trembling. She was overcome. Her knees, were they shaking, as she picked up the potato-sized package?

'I have here what you need.' She was beseeching, no, this wasn't good at all. 'I have *waited* to be the one to give it to you.'

Xavier got to his feet; it was best to do that now. She didn't seem to notice, her eyes on her gift, hand outstretched. Reluctantly Xavier took the item offered. He squeezed it gently. The package was light, like dough, or something fatty. He sniffed it.

'I know you trying to help me, Teacher. But again: the song is a lie. I am not impotent.'

She clasped her empty hands. 'This is not for your *penis.*'

The package moved violently against his cheek, changing shape and texture, as if he was holding nothing at all, yet it writhed hot before he threw it back at her, cursing and realising.

'*Ghost heel!*'

He'd heard about this abomination. *You ever eat ghost heel, Teacher?* Martin and Sisie, giggling in front of Des'ree. She, snapping. *Of course I eat it. Now get out of my sight.* What could have been so powerful it made Des'ree nervous?

Cannonball gulped, snatched the squirming thing from the floor and cradled it. She seemed near to tears.

'Macaenus. I give you with the greatest respect, the *greatest.*'

'You must be mad if you think I eating *that!*'

'But macaenus, o gods, I beg you, listen – !'

No, no, no. The heel of a ghost, he may as well eat Nya.

'I am not a *cannibal.*'

'Is not *cannibalism.* Is the greatest, greatest form of spirit worship. You take the dead inside you . . .'

'*No!*'

'Macaenus, every obeah woman in our nation knows this as the highest form of ritual. Nothing more powerful than cooking with it. Is a *profound* tasting experience. You *cannot* be macaenus without tasting this. Barnabas and Plantennithy before you, Jean Sean Belgha, Baio, your own beloved Des'ree.'

'*I don't care!*'

Like eating Nya! His brain screamed.

'How painful is the hunger?'

'I don't know what you're talking about.'

'Macaenus. I can *see* it on you.' Her belly was quivering, magnificent. 'You might be blessed by all the gods, but that will *not* save you from dying in the middle of the street from moth.'

264

He moved across the room, and away from her, skin hot, voice low and suddenly shamed, but for what? He was innocent. He was not eating anything wrong.

'You are *years* behind, Cannonball. I *stop* with that. I wasn't even taking it when you came to the restaurant.'

Her sadness seemed gone, like the sun under cloud. Her smile made the room colder.

'I heard you stopped. But no one does, however long they think they are free. This is my area of expertise, macaenus. My life's work. The moth eater is *always* moved to begin again. I hoped, because you are macaenus, that you had some *quality* that might make it different. I even thought of studying you, if you would let me. But I could smell the hunger on you, then, just like any normal somebody. It was on you then, and it is worse today. A long time, you have had this companion on your journey.'

He felt like a little boy again, could almost smell rum on her breath; might she dance like his real father, wear strappy blue sandals under her robe?

His mouth was watering. He wiped it.

Cannonball shook her head. 'Wah! Look, nah! I talk just a little and your tongue awash!'

'Be *quiet*.' He could not recall speaking to a woman so. Much less, obeah.

'The eaters I have known describe it as a kind of unrelenting sea in the mind. The sea cannot be controlled, you *must* fall again, eventually. The indigent' – she stopped and chuckled wryly, as if remembering someone she used to love – '*we* know. We stay close to an eater. We *accept* ghosts, we accept the rot, we accept the death-smell, we *hang* the moth until it is ready, macaenus!' She stepped forward; repulsed, Xavier shuffled backward. 'Why you think Romanza cleaves to you? He smells

265

it, too. The fool that helped you stop should have told you all this. But maybe they did just want their money.'

'I said *shut up*.' Anise had been the kindest, the best.

Cannonball unwrapped the ghost heel and held it out, naked and twitching. It looked like old soap gone slimy. 'In my dreams, I am the one who gives this to you, a culinary *tour de force*. A *cure*. It saves you. You take it into your kitchen and cook for me.' She sighed, an ecstatic, repulsive sound. 'The heel is holy. You lucky we meet today, macaenus.'

'I told you. I stop with it.' He sounded thin and weak.

Eleven years, seventy-two days and nearly eight hours ago. With his face in Anise's lap, he had stopped.

See the dirty moth eater, there!

Cannonball had such pretty dimples when she smiled hard.

'But, macaenus. You have one around your neck right now.'

She was close to him, hands on his waist, light and sweet-smelling, palms up, insectoid, like every obeah woman. He didn't know when she had moved. He reached down to push her away; his fingers fell through air. He stumbled.

'Oh, Xavier.' Her voice was musical, imploring. 'You *must* take one, today.' Her breath was aromatic against his cheek, one stubby finger plucking the moth pouch free, slithering out from under his tunic, hanging between them. 'Let me tell you a secret.' She leaned further in and he let her, for a second, even welcomed her: 'Heel is *better* than moth.'

If you see her ghost, kill it, Xavier. That was what his mother-in-law said. *Promise me.* But Nya was not coming back for saving; she was gone. And he was here. And he was hungry.

Who feeds us, he'd once asked Des'ree.

The ghost heel twirled and writhed when he picked it up. Shame almost made him sag.

Cannonball rocked back, her pink eyes wide, hands patting her breasts. Spittle down her chin.

✱

He remembered Anise meeting him at the front door of her yellow house late at night, grabbing him as he lurched towards her. He could feel her heels sliding with his weight as he struggled to stay upright. They tottered to the middle of the room, where he sank to his knees, surrounded by her lamps. In the night and her presence, they were like living, lunar creatures.

He fell, dragging one with him. Heard tinkling glass and felt shards in his palms.

What is it? Anise said.

He lay on the floor, curled on his side. It was easiest and safest. He didn't want to break anything else. She crouched over him, clearing glass, hands flickering back and forth.

Don't cut yourself, he mumbled.

He'd thrown away all the moth in the house, banned the indigent with his beribboned boxes, braced himself to do without it. Ever since the old obeah woman folded him up and said she had no love spell. Three days lying in a position much like this, clutching the floorboards. When he dragged himself to the toilet this morning he'd defecated blood, coughed blood, blood in his nostrils, bright red eyes. Blood caked his sandals.

He couldn't do it alone. He opened his mouth. Anise would surely see the raw roof and the bloated tongue. Her face was grey. Or was it silver?

What is the last kind of moth you take?

What it matter?

Tell me.

Banana moth. He laughed. *I ate it slooowly.* No more than eating sweets. Subdued yellow wings, marked with brown lines, like a child's crayon drawings.

He reached out for Anise's face, but she was on the other side of the room, picking up things, mixing things.

She came back to his elbow and asked him if he could sit up. It took three tries. She made him suck a small, cold sponge; fed him spoons of an acid liquid; rubbed cold oil into his back, temples, scalp. Everything cold, even her hands. He put his face into her hair, and it was cold there, too. She sang and lit a fire, burned incense, asked him for his day-god. He laughed. The god that ruled over his day of birth was Kinteet, god of marriage; depicted in statues, eating his own bottom lip.

She fed the fire blessing papers in his name, asking Kinteet for guidance.

You doing so well, she said.

He opened his mouth to ask her if she was mad and vomited into her lap. She put a salt crystal on the back of his tongue to calm the nausea and humiliation.

Hours became days, shuttered in with her. Tinctures, unguents, the changing of the weather, she over him with a clean cloth, helping him piss, a constant fog of silver around them.

I see you, Xavier, she murmured it over and over again. *You just* fine.

Yes, she was mad. Perhaps that was necessary.

When he could stand, she took him into the hills, to walk and sweat.

Your wedding, he said. *You should be planning. I am so sorry. I still have three weeks. Plenty of time.*

Anise—

268

Is my cors to help you, Xavier.

Was this between them no more than her job, her destiny? Regardless, he had nothing to offer her. The hills were green, and she seemed to know everywhere that was cold.

And I see you doing your very best.

Best? He found himself raging at her in Entaly's voice. *I not doing my best! I still want it, look at me. Disgusting.* He choked on his own words and began to curse.

Keep walking, she said, and walked on and upwards, him gasping for breath behind her. *Look at the hills and the plants.*

They walked every day. The roof of his mouth healed. He began to talk. He described the forest and the mountains like she wasn't there beside him, seeing it too. The honey-whisky-coloured leaves. The shapes of clouds. He talked about his garden. The hibiscus looked like it had been bleached in tea and the lemons kept bearing all year and how the sound of his mother's voice had been so beautiful, singing in the kitchen, splintering the sides of her mouth. Did Anise notice how pomegranates were shrinking? One ponganat, as the children called them, used to feed three boys for the afternoon, big as a watermelon, but now . . .

He wept.

Anise listened. That sacred gaze. Deep listening; deep attention.

His second time, he told her, how good it had been, at Big Cousin Nester's house, who kept her moth under her bed. He and Io were there for supper, and she busy in the back: him, like a dog, sniffing-sniffing. Once you took the silk, it called to you, from other people's hiding places. He confessed a whole childhood of thieving, his face in his hands, Anise's cool thumb in the back of his neck.

You were a child.

No excuse! I knew better.

No. A child, Xavier.

And when they were done walking out the hills, he found he could pick up a moth between his thumb and forefinger and not be insane anymore.

You fix me?

There was never anything wrong with you. My Xavier.

Mine.

20

Anise watched the men flee after the radio announcement, stumbling and cursing, angry but afraid, as if the whorehouse might by its very nature amplify the mysterious sex ban. Garson pulled up his pants; Blowsnaught skittered after him, winded and bloodied, bowing at Anise as if she might, as the owner of a now-forbidden pum-pum, detonate.

Mixie and Archie crouched, knotted together on the veranda floor.

Archie used his fists to wipe his tears, pulled Mixie to her feet, and spat in her face.

The women went *uuuuh!* as if he'd gut-punched them. Lyla lunged forward, but Rhita moved just as fast, locking her arms around her sister's waist and pulling her away. They tussled silently, viciously, elder sister restraining younger, Archie bracing his big-headed walking stick above his head. It would have been a death blow, no doubt.

Mixie fell to her knees, scrubbing her face with both sleeves.

Archie stalked out of the property, head up, gaze straight, skirting one half of the ripped, heavy table that lay in the yard, the other hitched in a custard apple tree.

Anise grabbed Mixie. The younger woman had wrapped her arms around her head, a cowed sculpture. Her eyes were screwed shut; if she opened them to see the shame it might scalp her. Bubbles dived around them, like miniature birds, or butterflies.

Anise guided Mixie back into the house. Laid her down on a velvet chaise longue, murmuring. She trickled energy from the crown of Mixie's head, across her face, watching her mouth moving soundlessly. She healed a small cut on the back of the woman's thigh, soothing, rocking. Singing. She checked that Mixie's pum-pum was truly, safely back between her thighs, trying not to think of Garson's shuddering body, her touch light and fingers whispering, a benediction.

Still, the eyes so tight shut.

Her own vulva quivered in her pocket. How basic her terror had been, watching it tossed about and threatened by dirty fingers. It was time to put it back where it belonged. She felt its absence like a foreboding, like the dark horizon that heart patients feel before their first attack.

Bubbles. Mixie giggled sleepily, dozing.

Eventually Rhita came in to swap places with Anise, squeezing her forearms in gratitude, curling around her sister's body, nestling and stroking.

They had been as brave as they could be.

Ingrid would have shrugged and reminded her of the dying women they'd known: running households, husbands, children and veritable empires, with only the occasional tremor on their surfaces.

★

Anise went back to the decimated veranda steps and Lyla, who was examining the potholes in the veranda tiling and sniffing the odour of men.

'For a moment there I did really think you was going to use *my* crotches to fuck Blowsnaught,' said Anise.

'I would never.' Lyla began to pick up broken pieces of peachy tile. 'But there wasn't no time to warn you.' She flinched as the tile grazed her palm, blood rushing to the surface of the skin, sucked it, waving away Anise's concern. 'I got caught up in the whole of it, but when I realise what he actually *want* . . .' She shook her head. 'That man was trying to find a whole new way to rape you. I didn't think anything could surprise me anymore.'

Yes, that was what had happened. Anise applied a bubble to the back of her own neck.

'You need to take that serious, healer – when somebody bring violence to you. Don't push it down. Sit with it. Tell people who will hear you.'

Right now, Anise couldn't think of a better witness than Lyla, but she didn't say so. They were quiet for a while, stacking the tile bits in a heap.

Lyla plucked at a small hole in the weft of her glorious dress. Anise thought of her on fire, the warm small of her back. Her magic pum-pum was perched on the veranda wall, a gathering of dark flesh and hair. Lyla paused in front of it, shaking her head.

'Lyla. When you got caught up. You seemed so . . .'

'What?'

She searched for a word. 'Wanton?'

'I does get like that.' Lyla picked up the vulva, turning it over in her hands.

'You going throw it out again?' She was absolutely sure that discarding it was wrong.

'I going bury it under some rock.' Lyla put it down. 'I getting a new life.'

'But you were so . . .'

Lyla smiled. 'What more, again?'

'Irresistible?'

Lyla stroked the thin gold chain on her neck, her tongue between her teeth. 'You flirting with me, Anise Joseph?'

Anise grinned. 'See? You can't help it.'

'All the more reason to make sure it gone this time.'

'Maybe if you did just have sex with someone you love . . . ?'

'Is not a matter of *love*,' snapped Lyla. She crossed her arms. 'What *you* know?'

Anise hesitated, stung. 'I don't know how to *talk* to you.'

'Why you have to talk to me any special way? Just talk like you talk to anybody *else*.'

'I don't *understand* why you throwing away something so important.'

'But I never *asked* for your understanding. The pums is not important to *me*. I tell you already, you just don't like my answer. It feel good to *me* that it gone. I am going to have a new life. I don't have to feel like *you*. I don't have to be like you. And just because we different, that don't mean I wrong, *either*.'

'But, Lyla! You were *glowing* when he pulled it down!'

Lyla's mouth twitched. 'Yes, I *know*! I can be a *complex* whore, Anise. Gods, leave me nah!'

They scooped up shattered tile, giggling.

'*Anyway*,' said Lyla, 'you know how man behave when they get this quality kind of love? Them try to do *impossible* things.' She snorted. 'Believe me, I can do without the trouble.'

'I am never going to agree with you.' Anise picked a bubble from the back of her leg, rubbed it between her hands and applied it to her temples.

Was Tan-Tan somewhere doing impossible things for a mystery woman? She wanted to feel his arms around her, something different from today's bastards, smashing, grabbing, entitled.

Who tell you he not that kind of man?

Gods, he was never that kind.

She knew women who insisted you could tame a man only

274

so long and no more. But she didn't believe that, it didn't have to be true. Some men, surely, knew how to control themselves? Like Xavier.

Is not any kind of control when a man don't want you.

Thinking on blasted Xavier Redchoose just made her feel worse.

If you told Xavier Redchoose that a man step to you with violence, he stone-cold kill him, y'know.

'You alright?' asked Lyla.

'Mmm-hmmm.'

He don't even remember me.

How you mean? You give him back his life!

Lyla looked like she might ask again, but Rhita came out of the house. She sat down in the single intact rocking chair.

'She still sleeping. I think she know that she and Archie done, this time.'

The sisters sighed.

'Archie was always an idiot,' said Rhita.

'Well, that's not so true,' said Lyla. 'Him was actually alright up to a point.'

'Really? Which point was that?'

'Mixie was whoring when she met him. He love her same way.'

'That don't make me think any more of him. A good man asks his woman to be *better*.'

'He was her client?' asked Anise.

'No,' said Lyla. 'They met at him friend house or something. She tell him plain in the first hour, she was a whore. They would have celebrate ten years next month. Me and him used to be friends. Sit down right here and drink rum, plenty night. Then our mother did dead few years aback and that's how Mixie buy the place from the woman who was retiring.'

'*Amplifying* the sin,' said Rhita. 'Mamma wanted you *out* of it.'

Lyla ignored her. 'Archie help her set us up good. Is him interview all the new girls and make sure them get health checks, make sure the clients know how to behave. But he was getting a little funny, last year. Just as we start make big money, he grumbling about whores and whoring.' Her mouth set. 'He said some disgusting things about women. I couldn't believe that was my friend. Mixie start lie down with less man to appease him, but that wasn't his problem, even if *he* say so. What he *really* never like is her independence.'

'So she left him?' said Anise.

'Dash him out, yes. She never like how he was treating her girls. For weeks he come caterwauling at her window. She throw water on him and pretend like she wasn't hurting. Then he come a few days ago, say he partnered up with Intiasar for the wedding celebration, how we can go *up* a level with business. Mixie was excited, joking about how when we *government approved* all the clients going to be rich. I think he did hope it could get her back.'

'I don't get it.'

'Archie never mention Intiasar say that the *publicity generated* supposed to be enough for us. They probably right about that, but I know Mixie. She *don't* do things for free. She was always strict on that. She never care that other whorehouse doing same thing today. And Archie never want to look bad.' Her neck trembled. 'I never even get a *lick* on that bastard.'

'Bastard,' Rhita grunted.

Mixie slid onto the veranda, looking sheepish. She sat down in her hammock and regarded the mess.

'Backside,' she said. 'He mash it bad.'

They all nodded.

A fat wild coney with a pretty snout trotted through the yard, then posed, ears cocked, under a sapodilla tree. Lyla and Rhita caught passing green butterflies and chewed thoughtfully. The coney pulled off one of the green sapodillas and ate it, looking pleased with itself.

'So Governor make jucky-jucky illegal,' Mixie said.

Lyla nodded. 'That man really don't like whore.'

'I don't *understand* him,' said Rhita. 'First he expecting free-ness for he married friend, then he put out sex ban?'

Mixie gave Anise a yellow butterfly. A good breed, young and tart on the wings.

'Butterfly plentiful in this yard,' said Mixie. 'Crunchy wings.' She hooked a passing orange-and-red-striped butterfly with her index finger and popped it into her mouth. It was such a delicate motion that they all stopped to admire her.

'You always so classy with that butterfly, even when you get drunk on it,' teased Lyla.

'I think the sex ban must be because *everybody* crotches fall out,' said Rhita. 'Mixie. You should tell Orange Man about what happen here today. How Intiasar send man to rape us off. That would mash up the stupid wedding.'

'I wouldn't know how to find him, my dear.'

'So you're *not* the Orange Man?' asked Anise.

Mixie grinned. 'No mam. I am merely a helper.'

'And you just torture me and wouldn't tell me.' It made sense, though. One man could only do so much, but if he had an obliging collective behind him, he could accomplish what Orange Man did. She'd assumed cors, but perhaps it was simply community.

'Some months back,' said Mixie, 'Orange Man leave us a letter in the custard apple tree, say if we inclined, he would be delighted.

277

And if we thief the paint from the factory, more to the better.' The mahogany half-table trembled in the tree. 'He leave messages when he need me. I never see him yet, although sometimes I stay up late to watch. I don't always have time to be creeping around, but I real proud of that factory paint-up, though.'

'It really is good.'

They smiled at each other.

'I think maybe him is one of our regular customer,' said Lyla.

'I think Orange Man have a little more perspicacity than *that*,' said Rhita.

'I wonder if Orange Man know if Miss Pretty contest still keeping tonight, 'sake of everything happening with woman right about now,' said Mixie. 'I usually pick up two, three new girl every year when we go.'

'Them couldn't put that off, people will rise up,' said Lyla. 'We need to get the table out of that custard apple tree.'

Rhita squinted. 'Lasso it with a rope and pull it down.'

'Won't that just make it fall on top of you?' The butterfly froth on Anise's tongue made her twitch. Delicious.

'Depends on the length of the rope.'

'So you do this before?'

Rhita rolled her eyes. 'Oh *yes*, many times.'

'Throw rocks at it,' said Mixie.

'No man, it too big for that.' Lyla gazed at the tree.

'*Big* rocks.'

The afternoon was hot and getting hotter. Lyla went off and came back with an icy jug of carrot juice, a bunch of pepper grapes, an avocado as big as Anise's head, and some cornbread. They ate hungrily.

'We could wait for a hurricane.'

'Or a person who tall.'

Rhita giggled. 'Think laterally, ladies. It have to come down? It could stay.'

'And lick some fool in him head? I don't have no insurance in here.'

'*Kick* the tree,' said Lyla. They all laughed some more.

'We need a obeah woman with a chicken and a candle.'

'No obeah woman not coming out for *this* foolishness,' said Mixie. 'You run out of set spell, Anise?'

'You already mash up one of my spell. But I set your rass tree on fire, if you like.'

Mixie stuck her tongue out at her.

Rhita waved her hand. '*I* know, I know! All we need is some large branches to brace the table, then one of us can climb up and dislodge it and the rest of us here can slowly lower it to the ground.'

'And you're sure that will work?'

'Well, I can see it in my head.'

'Dynamite,' said Lyla solemnly.

'Someone *could* climb up and push it down,' said Anise. 'We would just have to keep clear.'

'Like who, so?'

'Blasted Archie need to fix it and give you back a new table,' grumbled Lyla. 'I don't like how a man just get to come in here, break up things, fling people table in a tree and go about his business.'

Mixie burst into tears.

'Gods,' muttered Rhita. She sat down in the hammock and began to swing her sister back and forth violently. 'Hush, hush, hush, hush.'

'He never going to forgive me,' said Mixie. 'Stop, Rhita, that *hurts*.'

'Forgive *you*?' Lyla rolled her eyes. 'The man spit in your *face*.'

'You have to get rid of him,' said Rhita firmly.

'Him luh-huh-*love* me.'

'Him have to take the love and lick you in your head with it?'

Anise laced her fingers together. Too long since a man held them gently; put his tongue to these palms, took the time to touch these wrists. She bit her nail; ripped the cuticle, healed it. Her cors was running low.

'Don't push her so hard,' she said. 'This is not a simple thing.'

'Is my *fault*,' said Mixie.

'Is not your fault. Violence can look like passion,' said Anise. 'Passion is compelling.'

Mixie peered at her. 'It *is* my fault.'

'But why?'

'I said it.' Mixie faltered. 'And he spit.' She stared forward.

Anise stroked her hand.

Mixie curved herself into a small shape and peered at them. 'I never *said* it before.' They waited. 'But he was upset because I was fucking Garson in front of him. All these years I never *said* it and he always want me to.'

'Said what, though?' Rhita looked puzzled. Lyla hushed her.

'I never said it to *any* man.'

Anise's hands hummed; skin humming.

'Lay up in the bed with me all these years, and he *begging* me to say it. Say he can be OK with me and the clients, if I can just *say* it. Take all his worries away. But is my last thing *left*, and I'm thinking there is no *money* for that, what is the price for that?' She was fighting tears, but she also seemed confused, chopping the air with a single hand, punctuating her explanation. 'And I couldn't think of a price for it, and so I never.

Because if I tell him, what else I *have*? That is the *last* thing I have and he can't get it for *free*! But he *crying* and we here and you all making so much *noise*. So I just *said* it.' She pointed to the broken floor. Bewildered. 'Right there. *Iloveyou.*' The words sounded foreign and ripe in her mouth, as if she were speaking some dead language.

'And *that's* when he . . . *spat* . . .' Lyla sucked her breath in.

They all leaned back and contemplated the secret, fizzing like a hot newborn, entangled in the weft of Mixie's white hammock. Anise tried to pick it up, but her head was too full and soft: three butterfly was quite enough on a day like this.

The secret whirred away from her, like an unidentifiable insect, turning over and over in the boiling sunshine. When it brushed past the custard apple tree, the half-table came crashing down so hard that the neighbours came over that evening to ask if everything was just fine and dandy.

'Is just now you come?' Mixie asked them. 'You don't see a man spit in my face today?'

★

Secrets. No one knew that the sound of Xavier Redchoose had stayed with her for years. Once or twice she swore she heard that chuckle and looked up thinking: *well, you finally going to see him again*, but Xavier wasn't there, it was someone else and that was just fine, probably for the better.

Well, it had to be, didn't it, you a married woman.

She knew where to find him of course, everyone did, but it was out of the question. So tall: she thought of him as bumping into ceilings, although she'd never seen him do it. He had to duck to enter her house. She imagined him leaving trails of his hair on her ceiling, and the faint odour of his smile. He'd walked like a big shy animal, one foot in a circle of grace and the other skittish. So kind! He'd showed her how to boil, beat, bake; told her the history of herbs and about the insides of things. She was a bad student. She didn't remember burning or curdling anything, but the food was wrong, and she could see his puzzlement. He asked her to crack the joints of a chicken carcass so she could connect with the bird, but the chicken fat made her retch.

Gods, you bad at this, he said, his brow creased, and nudged her with his elbow.

Secret smiles.

She hadn't eaten properly until Xavier showed her how. He took the class outside and sat them on the grass and told them they ate too fast. The day was murky, the sun sitting in a cloud soup.

Our ancestors ate slow, and that is how macaenus are taught to eat. Slow and—

Long? piped up one female student, smoothing her hair. The night before, she'd confided her intention to have a macaenus baby by the end of that year.

Xavier smiled at her as if she'd said something clever.

Yes, and with concentration. I going teach you.

The woman preened. Anise wanted to slap her.

Xavier indicated a tray loaded with their day's work. She felt miserable, looking at her chicken skewers, dressed in too much garlic and pepper, rubbery and salty.

First, greet the food.

Tittering and muttering from the students, but she saw how important this was to him.

Smell it. He took a breath. *Imagine where it came from. The men and women who laboured to bring it to you. The animal that gave its life for your nourishment.*

He said to let the food sit on the tongue for as long as they could bear, then roll it around the mouth. Chew slowly, keeping the teeth close together, so the taste stayed on the tongue.

Block your ears so you can hear yourself eating. Think again of where the food came from. Give thanks.

Why? asked one man.

Xavier looked surprised. Considered. *To see what happens to you.*

He would say no more. He asked them to do it for one meal a day and she had tried. She'd wanted to please him. She was sure he was wise and correct. Certainly her bowels were clearer and more regular, her skin more glowing than usual. But her mind wandered. Ingrid had always complained about her lack of concentration.

You been meditating since you was five, *Ingrid.*

Well, that is true.

She could hear the su-su; she wasn't stupid. She, an engaged woman, spending all those late-night hours with a macaenus! Everybody know them is ram-goats! But she'd decided Xavier needed company – someone with whom there was no o macaenus this and that.

Eat, he said, when it was plain even he couldn't teach her. *Cooking don't matter if you know how to eat.*

But what the rass, Xavier. I should know how.

Why waste time on something if you don't love it?

Something heavy in his voice with that, and she tried not to think on it. It was their penultimate night and she was definitely, finally going to tell him about Tan-Tan, because after all, wouldn't that make everything clear between them?

Lord, girl, you never want it to be clear.

When Xavier had asked about her family and food, she told him about the trays and packages left at the church door at Easter and Christmas, and her scornful family picking through them. Most of it was repackaged and sent to the indigent, which was quite right, but she still remembered the departure of a sumptuous coconut cake, sent off to the bellies of potential Christians. She'd wanted a piece of that cake.

You know indigent don't eat cake, right?

But . . . Papa sent them everything!

I guarantee they not eating no sugar, unless is fresh cane. He'd shifted closer to her, the night air warm and perfumed around them. *So what you think of the eating-slow thing?*

She giggled, closed her eyes and opened her mouth, like a baby bird, parodying him, never expecting the gentle hand under her chin. She stayed very still as he tilted her face up. Her mind worked a million miles a minute; if she moved, she'd fall over.

I going to kiss a macaenus.

He didn't kiss her. He fed her whole prawns, poached in lime shavings and thyme. A roasted purple onion, sweet as fruit. Oranges he fetched from the refrigerator; the cold flesh, then the peel, doused in rum and set on fire, charred and bitter. Soft grilled cloves of garlic. She realised how quickly she still chewed and gulped; discovered she didn't like aubergine when she slowed to taste it. He made her open her eyes to greet a yam salad, to finger the textures and the colours like a child. She could almost feel the food rolling down her throat: a sensation so delicious it was alarming.

It was only when he used his thumb to push her robe a single, brimming inch away from her collarbone that she stopped what was happening at the edge of itself.

Xavier.

He looked into her face.

Everybody knew about macaenus. All whores. Big appetites in everything. The women joked after class: *how big you think he is?* The threat of that excess troubled her. What profit her, this madman, hacking at meat and singing out orders in the kitchen, popping guineps open, sucking them ferociously? Taste, adjust, pass, squeeze, using his hands like a spice rack. The women tittered at his happy groaning over the stove. What profit her, this hot thing from deep in the earth and from up in the air, inching closer?

Is so they stay, people said. *'Sake of the god-blessing.*

He attracted sycophants like flies. She knew that kind of person: so many teeth, pulling at her father's raiment. *Pastor Latibeaudearre, a word, a word with you* . . . There seemed a haze of something unpleasant around them, and around her father in their company: the set of his cheeks, as if he scorned and pitied them in equal measure. Mamma Lati, comforting the disappointed as he turned back to the pulpit and the incense, drenched in his robes. She didn't want that in her life. The *obsequiousness.*

Up off the chair she was, away from Xavier and his gentle touch and delicious food, thanking him for his time, as if they were strangers, trying not to see the confusion – maybe even hurt? – in his face. She couldn't hurt a man blessed by the gods, surely. And she wouldn't be one of his devotees. If she bowed to him a single time, she would be lost, and never find her way back.

He would eat her, slowly.

Wouldn't it sweet you, to see him, after all this time? See if he still tall?

Of course he still tall.

When she had heard his wife died, and the rumours that she did it to her own self, Anise had taken her altar onto the veranda and spent a whole evening praying with the cicadas, for his sadness.

If she wanted her body all whole again, it was just so she could find a little corner and think all-softly on Xavier Redchoose.

Romanza stood in Cannonball's back yard, eyes closed. Head up. Sniffing through the raindrops.

He'd smelled the sweet tremor in the earth as soon as they stepped off that stingray onto the black-and-white beach, but he'd thought it came from him. He'd mixed it up with the sweetness of the blood in his throat, the same taste as the cough he'd been coughing for weeks, the blood and smell rising and rising and then it had been too late to think of anything at all.

He felt embarrassed to have been so dependent on the macaenus. Scooped up into his arms. What had he looked like, helpless, a child who couldn't take care of himself? And *crying* over a tamarind ball!

Now that the bleeding had stopped, he could tell that he wasn't the source of the sweet oddness. He could feel a quiver in the house wall, see it in a poor-me-one bird's furious brown wings and on the surfaces of puddles left by the rain. The smell was getting stronger.

Was this what Pilar had warned him about? And could it actually be what he thought it was?

He barely recalled stories from school, there had been so many, but he did remember the teacher telling his class the tale of the emancipated.

A long time ago, she said, in 1838 to be exact, 203 emancipated slaves had sailed here from very far away, arriving in all the beautiful shades of black that were possible. Their leader, a man who called himself Papa Indigo, presented the indigenous people of the archipelago with a piece of paper called a deed, gifted to him by the white father who had enslaved him then been forced to free him. Papa Indigo said the land belonged to him, now. The islands had been in his father's family for a very long time, even though no one had ever actually been here, ascording-to-how it was so far away from anything civilised.

The red and original people handed the paper back. Such a thing was not possible, they explained, as the earth didn't belong to anybody except itself, and it didn't even have a name. The emancipated retorted that after centuries of bad people and very bad experiences, it was time for *them* to prosper. Fights broke out, said the teacher. The emancipated were few, and they had absolutely no magic, but they had new weapons, new diseases, an inordinate faith in a singular god, and an enormous resolve, which seemed to be a by-product of surviving all the bad experiences.

We not going back, said Papa Indigo. *Slavery days done.*

People on both sides did more bad things, although everybody agreed, years later after the peace was won, that the emancipated started it all by shooting off a man's arm then getting vex when it grew back like a lizard's tail.

Eventually, when civil war had raged for far too many years to be sensible, the earth and the sky, whipped up into vexation by the always-mischievous gods, took action. Together they produced a furious and very sudden hurricane, which came down on everybody at 3.07 p.m. one clear-sky day. And what a storm, with sweet rain and raging red wind! Former enemies took refuge together for three whole weeks while it danced outside, ripping up the land so nobody could have it. Very different people were forced to listen to each other, and to work to survive.

Some people even made babies, said the teacher, and the class giggled.

When the hurricane was done, everyone agreed that the whole war had been a foolishness – a veritable poppy show, was the phrase the emancipated used. And they should know, after hundreds of years of slavery, which was the ultimate in ridiculousness.

And that was beginning of you, the smiling teacher said to the rapt children. *Out of many, come one.*

Six-year-old Romanza had been quite happy with the story until another child put up his hand and asked what they should do if a sweet hurricane came back. He'd expected the teacher to say it was all so long ago, and not to worry, but instead she said it was a *very* good question, because sweet hurricanes were real and the obeah women said there would be more. Ordinary hurricanes were dangerous enough, but a sweet hurricane meant the world was going wrong. Still, the most important thing to remember was to take shelter and trust that you were absolutely in the right company. That was what sweet hurricanes were for: to teach you something.

Romanza jiggled in his seat. The teacher asked if he wanted to say something. He did, but there were too many ideas in his head. What if he was locked in with the boy who used to be his best friend, who punched him in the face because he said he liked the lavender flowers best? What if he was locked in with his mother's best friend Mamma Bryer who smelled like stale fish and wanted to put mustard plasters on him to build fortitude? And later, when the children were talking under the schoolyard trees, one boy said *he* never want to lock in with his father at-all-at-all, and he put his head down low when he said it. Romanza felt a lurch in his belly when the boy's father came to pick him up in the afternoons, because what could possibly be so bad?

When he went home and told his father these things, Intiasar took him to a stickball match and then they sat by the ocean and his father cracked corny jokes and Romanza laughed until his nose near fell off.

The teacher said that seventy-six people had died, mostly the emancipated, because their houses were broken down bad-bad. The next day at school, the class did a little skit and recited the names of the dead at the end. Each child had to read five names, but Romanza got six, which was quite hard.

'Linden Prosperity Hughes, musician from Tuku died,' Romanza murmured. 'David Wilson, builder from Dukuyaie died. Kaye-annie Francis Tuberose, forewoman from Dukuyaie died. Cecilie Annemaria Seabell, wife and mother from Battisient died. Isaac Breymar Mason . . .'

He didn't remember what Isaac Mason did for a living, or the name of the last one and he wished he could.

If this wasn't sweet hurricane, he didn't know what it was. He needed Pilar's counsel and the touch of his hand.

He paced the wet veranda, eating the last of the tamarind balls, for comfort. Maybe he should tell Xavier about the sweet-smelling tremors; he would know who to talk to about it. Or Cannonball: she wasn't high in the Fatidique, but all obeah women had its ear. At least ask if they could *smell* it. Why was no one saying anything?

Perhaps he should just do what he'd been doing with everything else that was important: bring it to the people.

CAN YOU SMELL IT, TOO?

Yes, that would do. But there was also Sonteine's wedding

to think about, and he needed to help Xavier with that. He couldn't be off stealing paint right now.

His throat hurt. He coughed. His spittle tasted like sugar. He almost expected a crunch between his teeth. He hawked and spat.

There was a bang from inside the house. The front door flew open. Xavier strode onto the veranda, Cannonball on his heels. He looked furious. Her hair was in mad disarray, her chin quivering. They were both weirdly silent. Romanza called out.

'Xavier, what – ?'

Xavier flung a white package onto the ground. He did it with a nasty flourish, staring into the obeah woman's face.

Cannonball planted herself firmly in her doorway and crossed her arms.

Xavier brought his foot up high and stomped on the thing. It burst, like a raw bladder, splattering across the drenched veranda. Xavier stomped again, grinding down until there was nothing left but a thick patch, like glue. White paint. Sperm. What *was* that?

'*Xavier?*' yelled Romanza.

Cannonball began rippling in the breeze. Not just her hair, but her shoulders and belly, her head shaking back and forth. The rain, swept by the wind across the porch, flew through her. Romanza moved closer, concerned. It was melting her feet. Why live in such a rainy place, when you could melt like sugar?

'Romanza, I need to leave here,' snapped Xavier.

'By all means, macaenus,' said Cannonball. 'Please step off my property as *soon* as you are ready.'

'Where?' said Romanza. He'd thought of trying to make peace; saw now it was impossible.

'Dukuyaie.'

Romanza tried to catch Cannonball's eye, but she was only

looking steadily at Xavier, as if she hated and loved him in equal measure. Dukuyaie. Had Xavier given up the idea of using indigent food?

'I show you the fastest—' he began, but Xavier was already through the garden and pushing at the gate, his shoulders shaking; why was everything *shaking*? Romanza trotted after him, letting rain soak his hair, glancing back at the obeah woman's house. Cannonball was lying on the veranda floor.

She was licking the veranda floor.

Romanza whipped his head back to Xavier, gesticulating to show him, but he was too far up ahead already. What in all the gods had *happened* between them?

He trotted harder, caught up and matched the older man's stride, trudged next to him. Xavier was silent and hunched.

'Why we – ?'

'Just *show* me.'

'You can run?'

Xavier glared. 'Can *you*?'

'Come, nah.'

They set off. The bush spread before them, black and red and white, scraggly and thinning, like an old man's beard. The wind blew hard, filling their ears. Romanza could feel his hair sticking to his forehead and cheeks. His muscles unset. His sphincter relaxed. His chest hurt, but he ignored that. He wished Xavier would untether too; prayed for the man's shoulders to fall, for his arms to flow. Surely you couldn't stay angry when you ran across the Dead Islands.

To onlookers they might have been a smudge; they were moving faster than running. The horizon was purple. Crunching, grey earth. Matching footsteps. Same pace, same tread.

Breathing, steady.

Easy.

They flew, for a while.

'Cannonball say something about me?' asked Romanza.

'What?'

'Anything about my *sickness*?'

They were soaked to the bone.

'Everything with you is as she said.'

Well, that wasn't a lie.

'So why you mad?'

Silence.

They reached the hill top, bent double. Below them, a long beach, wind swirling in the sandbanks, filling the sea-line with gold dust. Romanza spotted two black canoes, tethered under cannonball trees. One burst free and spun along the shore; a ladder; someone's big-faced clock.

Xavier tripped in the sand, scrambled to keep his balance, fell heavily, his weight on one ankle, grunting painfully. Purple thorns scattered out of his satchel, followed by a shiny notebook, which burst open, pages flailing, pushed along by the wind. They reached for it at the same time, crashing foreheads.

Xavier reeled back, swearing loudly, grasping head and ankle. The notebook rolled into a pool of water.

Romanza rubbed his forehead, which hurt like hell. He scooped up the notebook. It didn't look so bad. The cover was strong.

Xavier snatched the book. '*Look!*' He waved it around, flicked through the pages, clearly agonised. '*Look*, Romanza!'

'Is not so bad—'

Xavier hopped about on one foot. He hugged the wet notebook to his chest. '*Ruined!* I knew it!'

'But Xav, it's not ruined—'

'Since when me and you is the same size? *I tell you to call me Xav?*'

Mortified.

'I—'

'Man, this is my *wife* things. You understand? My *wife*. This blasted place trying to mad me? That bitch back there must think I won't take her backside to the Fatidique. And where the *hell* is a boat? I going to have to hop-hop down this damn sand dune like a fucking *chi-chi* man!'

Romanza felt his chest might break open.

'*What* you just said?'

Xavier stuffed the notebook down the front of his pants.

'My *ankle*, boy, I—'

'Chi-chi man? You mean bottom feeder?' Rage, boiling through the wind. 'Pilar always warn me, can't trust *none* of you! Why the hell you think we live a-bush, eh? Men like you and my *father*!' His whole face hurt, but he couldn't stop yelling. 'Playing cards, he have to win! Election, he have to *win*! Both of you cut from the same *stinking* cloth. *He* want you to do walkround. *You* don't want to do walkround. *Selfish!* Anybody ask *Sonteine* what she want?'

'*You are Intiasar's son?*'

Romanza's head cleared. The man was taller than him. Bigger than him. Abruptly, frighteningly so.

'You – I – you—'

Xavier repeated himself, enunciating carefully.

'Are. You. His. Son?'

What to say? All his fight was dried up, as suddenly as it had come.

Move. He apt to kill you right now.

Romanza Intiasar backed away from Xavier Redchoose.

Watched as Xavier staggered down the dune, falling to his knees, rising again and falling.

✳

Mrs Intiasar's maids often masturbated her in the morning. It wasn't something she discussed with anybody, least of all the maids. In fact, she hardly thought about it.

The Governor frequently left his hammock and joined her on the pallet to talk – he valued her opinion on society, politicking and what robe he should wear to so-and-so engagement – but sex was mercifully rare. She assumed he took mistresses and visited whores, which was just fine with her. She'd given him the two children he wanted and that had been hard enough. These days she thought of that green pallet in the middle of the room as a peaceful place, a kind of oasis between them.

She didn't like to see the maid's faces during the task; it was too distracting. It was hard to find faithful staff; domestics were like cheese or milk, with expiration dates. When they spoiled, her old houseboy Salmonie fired them. He was a true stalwart; he'd worked for her father, a former Governor, until he died.

This present girl was eager to keep her job, it seemed; she had taken to seizing her, in unexpected venues, as if they shared some great passion. Mrs Intiasar had had to push her away several times. If she kept on like this, Salmonie would have to be called in. There was enough to be worrying about.

The impending election announcement was making her husband fractious, stamping through the house and holding meetings on the back veranda, complaining about hidden enemies, even though he knew she didn't approve of politics after supper. Her mother had enjoyed the debate and the drama of a political house until all hours; not she. She'd told Bertrand when they were courting, if he wanted a happy home, he was to ensure her children never woke up to the sound of plotting.

She'd chosen her husband well, despite his vulgar cors. Speed. If you'd told her she would marry *that* when she was a young girl, she would have been appalled. Such sacrifices! But he was a good man, for her purposes.

After the debacle of a radio interview, she went to see him in his study, sure he would need a back rub and a chance to swear. She found him counting more coins than she had ever seen. He tried to order her out, but she shut her mouth and sat beside him, contemplating the sacks. A man on his own, hurriedly counting money, was never up to any good. The other radio stations would need even more money now, to discredit that dirty Hah gyal.

The Governor paused, waiting on her censure. She looked back. This was what you did, to prosper. He needn't feel bad for playing that game.

Ah well, Mamma, he said, and took out a little knife. *I am just one mango man, after all.* She watched him cut away strips of his skin, pieces of hair, then slice deeper into the forearm, so he could bleed onto the money. She helped him bind the wound and looked away as he straddled the sacks for the final part, groaning when he was done. A bribe, sealed with all his bodily fluids. She hadn't heard that sound for a long time. He smiled at her faintly.

They should have known they were in serious problems when the Fatidique refused to set spell against Pony Brady three months ago. They'd set one for every other rival: in the last decade they'd moved the air and earth for the Governor and his money. When Pony start come-up, come-up, making it clear he intended to stand against Bertrand in the election, Intiasar swore he was the Orange Man – that blasted orange graffiti even reach the side of their house last season! But rumour had it that the Fatidique leadership was changing, and the favour was refused. *Refused!* The Governor come back to the yard so vex, the maids and the mongoose-them alike had to hide in the crawl space under the house.

It turned out they needn't have worried about Pony. Strangled by his own nastiness, all over the walls of Popisho early this morning. So Pony was no Orange Man, but she could have told Bertrand *that*. Pony didn't have the balls for anything else but troubling people's girl-children.

These bitches who used to jump obeah circle and ride the gods with Bertrand by their side, they were disgraceful. Disloyal. It suited the Governor to seem nothing more than a businessman, but she had watched him in that obeah circle, eyes rolling, naked, talking to the gods, clasping hands with the Fatidique, deep in the drumbeat. It was his love of their traditions that made her marry him. Not very many people knew he could sing a whole year's worth of Temple songs, and he'd learned them out of love and faith.

Mrs Intiasar sipped the cold chocolate at her elbow, spat and glared. That blasted maid might rub pum-pum good, but she never know how to make chocolate. Too much pepper. She set the small blue mug on her vanity board and hissed at it. The mug disappeared, with an audible popping sound. She hissed again and the spoon was gone, too. When she was a child, she'd imagined another reality, a kind of ethereal warehouse on the way to heaven, packed with all the things she'd ever made disappear.

It was almost strange she'd never tried to disappear a whole person.

✻

A mile out from the Dead Islands, a certain kind of man, the kind excited by sorrow, catches a ghost-who-used-to-be-a-woman by the arms. He takes her away from the beach and the hot air. When he lays her down, he is distracted by the sweet stink filling up his whole house: jasmine and lemon balm, angel's trumpet and kiss-me-quick, the extra-sweet nectar from pink hibiscus flowers and climbing oleander. But he soon forgets, because the creamy texture of her heel is like goose liver and the taste of her tears is exquisite and people always saying you should put ghosts out of their misery.

Xavier stood in the neat yard, looking at the house. Above him, cream buildings melted into the hillside, a smooth road snaking through them like a dark belt. He flinched as a putt-putt zoomed past, slicing the quiet. It felt as if he'd been standing here for a long time, the moth pouch humming deep in his satchel, seeing the same image in his head. The same image chugging underneath everything the whole of this one-sky day.

Dip the first two fingers into your pouch. Throw the head back, like a bird drinking water. That simultaneous crunch and inhalation. Throat, quivering and iridescent. It took your ears, your throat, your nose, your eyes.

Gone, he'd be gone.

Why you think Romanza cleaves to you? He smells it, too.

So Romanza Intiasar got his beauty from his mother's side, then.

He'd let the boy inspire him, and if he'd stayed with him one minute more, he might have beaten the beauty off him.

Both of you cut from the same stinking cloth.

Romanza might be angry now, but boys were always angry with their fathers; who knew when he might next sit with Intiasar over wine and speak of the macaenus? *How vex you make him, Pap, all day he let you mad him.*

Pink grapefruit and ortaniques littered the earth. Cashews dried on a plastic sheet near a large open-air altar, flanked with goddess statues, five feet high, its coral brick warm in the late afternoon sunshine. Three long, thin orange-and-black cats posed like striped stick insects, grooming themselves. One began to purr loudly then stopped, as if embarrassed.

Most people believed Intiasar's son had gone foreign years ago, like his father before him, part adventurer, part traitor. But all it would take to bring him down was this one fine son: flagrant, indigent, lying with men. *Bad blood*, they'd say. *Curse from the gods*. Nobody would vote for a man who had lost control of his boy-child.

He could see Intiasar's colouring on Romanza now, the same playful twist of the lips.

The old trees in the yard stared at him, rustling their sticky, tie-dyed leaves. *You have a moth*, they seemed to say, *so close to your mouth*.

He'd washed his sandals in the angry sea, but he still imagined he could feel the ghost heel's glutinous remains. It had squirmed in his hand before he flung it down, like a slug under salt. Writhed as he mashed it underfoot, popping like a fetid eyeball. He thought of the ghost in Cannonball's yard, how small and helpless and ugly it had been. Cannonball was just like any pedlar. *I have plenty heel*, she'd whispered. She might as well have said it was—

Clean.

A cat pawed the empty air and licked its backside.

On impulse, Xavier knelt in front of the cats and the altar and placed ten fingers on the edge of it. Looked up at the statue of Eheh, goddess of surprises.

He offered her blank eyes a prayer for the soul of the person whose heel he'd destroyed.

A flock of olive parakeets fluffed themselves in a coconut tree.

The image: two-finger dip, head flung back.

He had to knock on the front door, now.

Dozens of thin, silver-white plaits fell down her shoulders. The style suited her very well. She'd shrunk; or perhaps he'd grown in the minutes it took her to open the door, his fingers dangling, biting his bottom lip like a schoolboy. She carried a heavy ruby monocle and an orange cotton shawl and began her examination of his body at the groin, glancing at his feet, then up to his face. When she saw it was him, she put a hand to her cheek and grinned.

'Hello, Des'ree,' he said.

Des'ree stepped backward, shooting out a hand and pulling him into a large, old-fashioned receiving hall. She slipped the satchel off his shoulder, stood on her tiptoes and kissed the corner of his mouth, chuckling. Her lips were warm. It seemed the most natural thing, and he was amazed at her ease and his spasm of pleasure.

Des'ree glanced at the ceiling. 'House.'

The hall bulged, elongated and spat out a perfectly formed coat rack. Des'ree slung his satchel on a hook. His satchel holding moth. He wondered if it might shake and quiver. She pulled her shawl off, revealing yards of gleaming neck and shoulder. Her skin was soft and unblemished.

'Well. Xavier Laurence Redchoose. You like what you see?'

He shifted uneasily.

'You look good.'

'I know that. I was enquiring if how good I look pleases *you*.'

She reached up to stroke his cheek; he let her touch him. She smiled and nodded; seemed satisfied by something she saw or felt. Her teeth were white and strong.

'Xavier Redchoose, to rass. Come sit with me, nah.'

He hesitated as she turned away.

Most of his ascension day had gone well. Children danced; there were skits and speeches and tears and music. Sweet. Merry. Nya wore a dotted robe that made her look like a butterfly, and he wanted to stroke her hair. Des'ree danced. Io and his wife were still together back then, and they kissed in a corner after a hushed argument. The cheerful crowd applauded when Intiasar got up on stage. He seemed a little tipsy and everyone thought that was fabulous.

The Governor said congratulations. He said it was a special day. He raised his glass. He said he was very *happy* that Popisho was sure and secure once more. Bright and right. He liked to rhyme. *You know how I mean, gentlemen. And ladies I sure you feel this too, if you honest. We back to basics.*

Xavier sat seething. The implication was clear: they had a male macaenus once more and a solid, married man at that.

Des'ree snorted, got up and left. The crowd murmured. Xavier rose to follow her. To let his master-teacher leave alone would be the most grievous disrespect, and anyway, he agreed with her. Which was when he felt Nya's nails in his arm. He looked down; she was glaring at him. He sank back into his seat, confused, then realised the problem. He couldn't leave his wife to follow a woman who'd once been his lover. Everyone knew.

He wrong, Nya, he whispered. *Come with me.* But her face was dull with anger and Intiasar was calling him to come on stage, and the invited guests were applauding and around them the crowd began to chant his name, and something else, he realised, which made him joyous and sick at the same time. The cheering was not just coming from his property, or the beach below it, but bouncing from house to house, bouncing across the hills, across the whole of Popisho, the entire archipelago, like some primordial chorus.

Xavier, Xavier, Xavier!

His head had ached for three months afterwards. It was people's hunger inside his skull, yowling and wordless. It took tremendous concentration to make food out of their feelings: to understand through his pounding head and his anxiety that the woman on the corner table would need meat to rip and suck; that the man beside her would be comforted by tiny, elegant edifices; that a third would benefit from spice and hot liquid. His first cook quit in days, and the second, and the third. Perhaps it was the smell of his smouldering, worried hands that frightened them – burnt garlic, burnt sassafras, burnt salt – he'd never lost control of his cors before. Too often, he worked alone. He kept waiting for Des'ree to come back and help him. An afternoon would have been enough. An hour. A steadying hand, an acknowledgement. *This is normal*, she might have said. *It will pass.*

'Always so very thoughtful, Xav.'

Des'ree was standing watching him, her breasts still tender. He opened his mouth to reply; the staircase shifted itself in front of her small feet. She took his hand and squeezed.

He pulled it away, smiling too hard.

'You have a bandy house!' He was glad for the distraction.

'Is very useful.' She indicated the staircase. 'Come, nah.'

He hesitated again. 'Is a long time, Des'ree . . .'

She looked over one bare shoulder. He remembered that look.

'You here now.'

He watched her climb the stairs, skirts whispering against her thighs and rear. Followed on. How had she managed to make it so anybody listening would think *she* the wounded, waiting for the return of an intractable child? He was not here to pay penance.

He wasn't sure why he had come.

Eventually he had confided the headache, the sense of abandonment, to an obeah woman. She suggested he read the macaenus journals stored in the Fatidique Temple. He'd always meant to do it, so he began immediately. The diaries were his saving grace. Soroi wrote about the sudden onset of leg cramps; Baio of a vomiting sickness that plagued him until he learned how to cook fowl succulent inside a bladder; Jean Sean Belgha of new persistent allergies. All pains faded with time, as they fed their people and learned their duty.

Why had Des'ree never warned him? Her carelessness made him angry.

When Nya died, she'd sent no message.

The stairs murmured and breathed.

'All women should have a bandy house,' Des'ree was saying. 'Obeah women claim there's one in every district, but only the daydreamers and the writers notice.' She laughed, or was it the house? 'Mind how you go. It still getting used to you.'

They climbed.

He knew a little about bandy houses: they were adaptive, they moved like animals, learning your ways. Two rooms could become six in a trice then expand again as guests arrived; as quick as it took to walk in and out of a room thinking, now where is my clean underwear or where is my walking stick, the items appeared. They said old people shouldn't live in bandy houses, what with balconies moving and studies changing into conservatories.

He imagined the house cupboards were throats, swallowing

his bloodied bag off the coat rack, corners chewing the notebook like teeth.

Des'ree chuckled again. It *was* her, surely?

On the second floor, they stopped to admire a three-foot-long, nineteenth-century quill on the wall, its wooden hide worm-holed with age; brilliant-coloured masks carved out of stone, iron, wood, inlaid with human hair ringlets. Des'ree stroked a huge black boulder crouched on the landing, burnished as glass.

'A sculptor down Soin give it to me. He comes to visit it. Say he waiting for the art inside to reveal itself.'

Xavier put his hand on the smooth surface of the stone, inches from hers. Des'ree moved her fingers away.

'Maybe he just looking pum-pum,' she said. 'He can get some if he brave enough to ask.'

The stone bulged up at Xavier, making him jump.

'Don't be jealous, Xav. The house get agitated if it feel any bad thing towards me. House!'

The boulder subsided.

'I not jealous.' He managed to keep his voice even.

That shoulder-look from her, again. She walked across the landing, haunches see-sawing against her dress. Same Des'ree: not listening or waiting for an answer.

What had she been doing in all these years of silence? He remembered lifting her onto his shoulders so she could dust the eaves of her restaurant, her thighs sweating against his temples. Once she'd challenged her acolytes to make four dishes in twenty minutes, using the same ingredient, and Martin beat him because Des'ree kept putting her hand under the countertop and stroking the sensitive spot between his testicles.

He was developing an erection. He paused on the stair, surprised, a little shaken.

On the fourth floor, she guided him into a cool day room filled with soft couches, white orchids on the sill and an artificial rock pool, where platinum-coloured fish blipped and flitted. A glass of orange juice slipped out of the floor. A bowl of yellow apples gleamed on the sideboard.

She sat down, smoothing the flat of her hand along the couch and slipping her bare feet into the pool. 'Sit anywhere.'

A steaming mug swelled out of the couch beside her. He picked it up and perched next to her, shifting his body to conceal his penis, sniffing the perfectly brewed adami tea. He could leave now and head for the nearest drinking house, wave his penis around, to the tune of that stupid song. Did she still take moth?

Des'ree made a soft sound and the couch lengthened itself by several feet to accommodate his height.

'This really is a good bandy house,' he said.

'Yes. It help with the beard.'

'Beard?'

'My boys all discovering they dicky at the same time, so I get a beard. I think is all the man-vibes filling up the house.'

'Des'ree, what are you *talking* about?'

'I might have to fling them out when they get older. They not turning me into no man.'

'Which boys?'

She clucked her tongue. 'You never know I breed?'

He stared, not knowing how to feel. 'But you—'

'Yes, I know I'm too old. And I know I say I never want any child. But there you go. Life! Six fine boys.'

'*Six* pregnancies?'

'I look mad, to you? Just one.'

She was pregnant for fourteen months she said, and the obeah women not one piece of use, 'sake as how they'd never dealt

306

with a pregnant macaenus before and never know what was normal. She didn't know who the father was but there were several candidates. Of course, it was a shock. But like most things that were new she'd eventually found it fascinating.

'Never see so much rass obeah woman crowd up my place and worried! Trying to order me around. *Me!* I tell them to flash their tail out of here.' Her eyes sparkled. 'When time come, it never hurt, but you would have to travel *far* to smell anything like it. One cord, thick as my wrist, and all of them string out, like grapes! Six afterbirth, too. What a drama.'

'You gave birth alone?'

'Well, the cats helped.'

Sometimes he forgot her cors was speaking to cats.

'Why you never – ?' He stopped himself.

'Just like grapes,' Des'ree mused. 'Why I never what?'

He shrugged.

Call for me.

She'd not needed an obeah woman to look for her children's magic: she knew it when they began beating time in the womb. When her wrists and her teeth couldn't contain the trickling sound, she took her belly to the nearest music master, who taught the embryos old-time ditties, hymns, musical riddles and the dirty lyrics of the dancehall. People called them the Choir. These days, she rented them out. It got them out of the house and made old ladies happy.

'You taught your children dancehall slackness before they *born*? Des'ree!'

'Everybody see them as one,' she smiled. 'My poor boys. Anthony, Cyrus and Robert. George and Gideon. Patrick De Bernard-Mas.'

'How old are they?'

'Eight.'

He suddenly felt foolish and ungrateful. Six babies was a reason to abandon your acolyte, surely? Especially when that acolyte was macaenus? Old enough to run his own restaurant, his own life? To please his own wife? Hadn't she taught him everything she knew in this world, and what more did he want? And yet, the age of the boys . . . she could still have sent message. If she cared enough. He gulped adami in an effort to clear his head. Was the bandy house working on his mind, so his very thoughts pleased her? Surely it was not a good place for children, a house this responsive to her moods and needs?

He knew her moods.

He put his head back against the sofa. His inappropriate penis threatened to tear through something. She'd taken her feet out of the fishpond and was half reclined, eyes hooded, watching him. He wanted to strum her mouth with his thumb.

'I thought they was singing on the radio that your dicky is no longer a thing of fury?' She pointed at his crotch. 'Clearly, that is a lie.'

The first time she called him to her bed he'd been soaked with worry. He was used to Nya; to the arpeggio of young girls. She would show him something coarse, he was sure: break him into pieces. But she was sitting by her window, looking out at the evening, waving at days-work maids taking the long road down the hill, eating soft apples. *You talk*, she'd said.

His ears were hot at the memory.

Des'ree stood up, stretched full-length and walked across the room, towards a pallet pushing its way through the floor as if she'd commanded it, pulling her robe over her head as she went, back and buttocks bared and gleaming.

'Come and lie down with me, baby.'

He tried to ease the tightness between his eyes. She still used her sexuality as everything: a bargaining chip, an anecdote, a battering ram, love. What made her so irresistible? It wasn't her face or thighs; he'd never been a man to compartmentalise a body; all parts of women seemed to have everything to do with the rest, like a recipe. Perhaps it was her unrelenting ease. She'd insisted he learn fast what pleased her. No hiding in the dark or innocence. *Pay attention*, she said. *Attention is everything in this life.* Her body was not perfect; she expected him to like it as it was. She was bleeding that first time and shrugged when he discovered it. *What of it? I'm female.*

He learned; he got good. Orgasms so long, he sat back on his heels to watch her, writhing in the evening light like an ordinary miracle.

'I can't see you from here,' Des'ree called softly. 'You can come closer.'

Around her, board floors began to sprout bright grass. She brushed her hands over the moisture, breasts flat, dark nipples hard. He hadn't known he liked it best with dew soaking his knees and thighs, but the house knew, and that was because she knew.

'How long until your children – ?'

'Long enough.'

He sank down beside her. The grass thickened. She watched him, rubbing her fingers through her pubic hair. Something fell out of the rafters into her lap. She picked up the earrings, fashioned of cream bone and red coral. Old native things.

'Thank you.'

'I didn't—'

'The house gave me because you're thinking nice things. They are very beautiful.' She kissed his forehead. 'Nearly as beautiful as you. My Xavier.'

He groaned. He might do her damage, bite her too hard, find himself unable to wait.

She put her hand on his chest.

'You know I can.'

'Can what?'

Her face was serious. 'Take. You.'

He sank his face into her shoulder. He should have broken all his bad habits, by now. He should have laid Nya to rest. He should have stopped wanting to suck moth antennae from under his fingernails. He should have stopped thinking about Anise. He rubbed his thumbs across Des'ree's belly to distract himself.

It occurred to him that he kept women in his pockets, so he could take them out again.

The erection made his hipbones ache; the pressure squeezed against the back of his head. He wanted to rub against her, but she held herself away, teasing him as she pulled his tunic over his head, remarking happily on his stomach and arms and skin.

He pulled off his pants. Eating her, eating moth, it was the same thing. Something that couldn't be stopped once it started. Did she still take it? He couldn't tell.

Des'ree pulled him on top of her, sharp and hot under his hesitant hands. She smelled of bamboo and sweat, tasted of something sour, but not unpleasant, like sweetsop – and he was grateful and soon enough, not even that, as she took one finger and stretched liquid from the tip of his erection to the tip of her tongue, and the ability to think was stripped away from him completely.

'Mm,' she said, and he gasped for breath at the small, aroused sound.

She put a perfect, soft mouth over his penis and swallowed, sliding down to the root. Her favourite thing was to use her mouth. The tongue spiralled around him, and he could feel her smiling. *Is always better to smile when you eat something*, she used to say. She stopped sucking and straddled him, lifted up to slide him inside her, a slight hiss of amusement as she missed, tried again, pulling him up past the wrong places then sinking down as if the last time was yesterday. She was wet enough but drier than he remembered. He looked at the orchids on the sill to stop himself breaking inside her; pressed his thumb just above her clitoris, adjusted her slightly so she could rub against him.

'So *good*,' groaned Des'ree.

Sweat shone across her shoulder blades; her stomach muscles trembled. The skin on her stomach folded and creased. Sweat crept up her forearms and disappeared into her armpits and her hairline; shaking her head was like salt spray, a lovely, tranquil smile on her face. She rose and fell over him; he embedded her neck with something like rosemary, made the tiny hairs on her nipples sweet. He put pepper inside her, just long enough for her to feel the sting, and she gasped at the old trick, clasping his hands, raising them to the ceiling, leaning against them so she could wind her hips in low, fluid circles. Sex with her was science. Cream and sugar. Measurement. Then into the heat.

'I missed you,' she whispered.

He panted; she put her arms around his neck, whimpering. He held her hips, moved her body faster.

He didn't believe her.

He came to himself some time later, testicles soft, thighs wet, his mouth leaking onto her breast, her arms cradling his head. He had forgotten her ribcage, the way she sleepily repositioned herself after orgasm, her breathing. He felt himself plunged back into the texture and smell of who they'd been, as if he were young again. The sour anxiety in the pit of his stomach. The old vigilance. It took all he had not to bolt.

Her raging. Her nastiness. Once, after she'd screamed at Persemony for ten minutes, the girl protested. Des'ree called her mother a whore. Persemony clicked her fingers, and the pot of marmalade bubbling on the stove slammed into Des'ree's chest, splattering her robe and bare neck with burning hot Soin oranges. They stood, all of them, staring, shocked. Des'ree pulled the hot fabric away from her skin, ignoring the pain. She cupped the trembling, furious Persemony's face in one burnt hand. *You*, she said, *will never be more glorious than you are right in this moment.* That night, all food was cooked in Persemony's honour.

He began to inch off her dozing body. Des'ree protested softly, the light turning her elbows and knees and the shadow below her chin purple. He drew further away, grass prickling. The floor had sprouted red physalis fruit. Did he require such pretty fripperies for sex, or was that for her? Her smell filled the room.

When she'd announced him her successor, all he could think was that he'd be alone with her now. The excitement of it, the despair of it. He was determined to do his best. He'd loved her. But no, he'd been mistaken. *So when you moving out*, she said. He was shocked, heartbroken, relieved. The thought of being in her *way* – she who had wrapped herself around his body – was too much to bear. He was gone before nightfall. Sitting in his mother's house, feeling tiny but too tall for the pallet, like he'd survived a long, exquisite storm.

Des'ree opened her eyes and touched his shoulder. He fought to control his breathing.

'Xavier?'

If he said it wrong, pieces of them might shatter.

'Baby, what happen?'

He dug his fingers into the grass.

'What?'

'Why did you have to make us so *frightened*?'

'What are you talking about?'

'You know Entaly try to kill herself, twice?'

Des'ree sat up. Her face was calm.

'Yes,' she said.

'Everybody know Sisie is a drunk.'

'I know.'

Her face: composed, unreadable.

He thought of Romanza and what it was to care for somebody.

'I don't know what happen to Martin,' he said. 'Granted, I hear he have family. Nine child, last time I hear. Nine mothers.'

'That would not be unknown.'

'He couldn't stay long enough with not *one* woman, Des'ree? Not even long enough to breed her *twice*? And the worst one is Dominique. You hear what he did four years ago?'

'You going to tell me, I am sure.'

Her face, so still.

'He throw away his eye.'

She inhaled sharply and he was glad to finally hurt her.

'I visit him after. He said the eye made a cracking sound when it come out, like an egg out of its shell. He was sitting alone. Even after he blinded himself, it was only me bother to go and see him.'

A silk robe glimmered through the floor and she wrapped herself inside it, hooking it at the cleavage. The hair on her dark arms was red-brown. Behind her, through the window, the late afternoon sun.

313

'And where is Persemony?' Her voice was singsong and gentle. 'My pretty, pretty Persemony. Tell me, Xav.'

He looked at the floor, growing physalis.

'Nobody don't know.'

She shook her head.

'Like your wife, eh? I was sad to hear how she ended.'

He didn't know if that was true. His throat felt battered and he still wanted moth moth moth. Dip and fall back. Smooth fire.

'Then why you never come to her funeral?'

'You were so *angry* with me, Xavier.'

Her delicate frame, the nimbus of silver above her head, he was frightened anew. Not by her power, like when he was Romanza's age, but at the sight of that power trickling out of her: the inevitability of her passing. He could see her as dust on the floor, lost between coconut shards and pimento.

'Your fault, Des'ree.'

She turned her face away. Spoke softly.

'And why is it my fault?'

'We were young. We trusted you. We . . . *adored* you. You were everything to us, and you made it so we couldn't see anything else but you. You set us against each other. You paraded our affair, even though it hurt them. Don't you – can't you *see* – ?'

'That was so *long* ago.' She turned and put her arms out for him. 'Look at how you twist up, man. Come and see me, nah? I straighten you.'

She would not say sorry; it was beyond her. He got up, pulling on his faded, twisted pants, and began to search for his sandals in the grass. It had been wrong to come here, stupid to let her see him struggling. She'd already taught him how to cook and not to trust a soul in this world.

'You take so long to reach, and now you going?' Her face

was sad. She moved closer, but he jerked away, annoyed to find himself electrified and swelling again.

'Don't *touch* me.' He *could* say it.

Light, insidious fingers on his penis.

'*Stop.*' He took her hand and bent the wrist away from him.

She gasped, more in surprise than pain. 'Who you think you handling so?'

He dropped her hand and walked towards the door, but house, she said, and the door handle melted and streaked down the wood.

'Let me out.'

'Who you think you *talking* to?'

'Open the rass door.'

'No!' Hands on hips, and how could he have thought her old? Breasts heaved; head up, sparkling, she was drowning in light. Imperious, scalding. 'Don't think because I give you little pum-pum in here today, you don't owe me respect, Xavier Redchoose.' She held up a hand as he protested. 'Yes, *respect*!'

He had an aching need to urinate; could feel it twisting his groin. But he wasn't frightened anymore.

'You in my house. You just climb out of my raaassclaaht bed. For the rest of your born days, I am going to be your master-teacher.'

'You don't deserve the title.'

Her face warped. 'Who else you have?'

He stared at her. 'Move out of my way.'

'Make me.'

'Des'ree.' He was talking carefully, now, the care of a man about to lose himself. 'Get out of my way.'

'No.'

'*Move!*'

'*No!*'

He caved his fist into the wall above her head. Des'ree flinched. The house moaned and the walls moved closer. She looked alarmed.

'Oh, Xavier. The house will *hurt* you.'

'Fuck the house.' He turned away, swearing, groaning, the pain in his hand registering. She followed him.

'You telling me all these things I do: Entaly, Sisie, Dominique. And what is the matter with *you*, boy? Tell me that, too.'

'Go away.' He clenched his fists.

'Xavier, the house will hurt you if you touch me.'

How could she think it? 'I would never hurt you.'

'You just grab me up like a dog!'

He felt hot shame. She seized his face, her nails digging in.

'Is what I do to you, Xavier?'

'Get away from me!'

'What do you say I did to *your* life?'

He screamed it. '*I married the wrong woman!*'

She sank back.

'And what that have to do with me?'

The anger made him stutter.

'She was j-just *like* you. Controlling and pushing and pulling and never the same twice and I couldn't – I couldn't – get a *hold* of anything – I know I was a bad husband—' He was gasping for breath. 'I – know she was *sad* . . . I tried – I just – !'

She put her arms around him. He tried to push her away, but she wouldn't let him free. They teetered, struggling. He should have been able to pick her off him, like a mosquito. He pushed again, harder this time, but her fingers were locked behind his neck. Glazed eyes, blinking up at him, blunt mouth, long, thin eyelashes – all buried in puffiness. Too much milk and

316

not enough fish oil – she should know better. Her eyes rolled upwards. She lolled in his arms.

'Des'ree?'

She was asleep. The smell of something tremendously sweet. His eyes felt like blinking, granite things, his mouth slack.

'Des . . .'

He fought, but there were dreams coming up through the cracks of him, furling around his calves, nudging elbows and temples. Thin green tendrils twisted around their bodies, binding them together: waist, wrists, ankles, between Des'ree's legs and lacing her throat.

Red fruit dreams.

23

Lyla sent Anise up to her bedroom for privacy and to put back her pum-pum.

'Call me if you need me, though,' Lyla twinkled.

Anise stroked the mosquito net hanging in the room, thinking again of the absurdity of walking around with her own vulva in hand like a bunch of flowers. How was everyone else managing? Tomorrow would be a busy day at work.

She felt the pum-pum's weight. Why was she hesitating?

She thought of her cheek on Tan-Tan's knee this morning. There were so few memories of her pregnancies and her dying children and she was forgetting them. He should be helping her to remember. He must have memories she didn't have. She *wanted* them.

His silence was unforgivable.

Don't trust anyone who keep telling you what's wrong with you, Ingrid often said. She'd talked faster and faster in the days before she died, like she wanted to remember everything she'd ever thought and leave it with her friend.

Because she couldn't think of anything else to do, Anise sat down on the shiny whorehouse floor, put her pum-pum on the pallet and looked at it, hard-hard.

Still brown and warm and nice.

Hesitantly, she used one finger to stroke the very top of the mons, surprised at its fatty, downy fullness – unfamiliar, despite a life of touching herself. She used to masturbate at teenaged sleepovers at Bonamie's house, right after her cousin fell asleep; the idea of doing it at home was embarrassing. One night after her aunt came in to out the lamp, she and Bonamie had confessed to each other. She couldn't remember who'd had the courage first.

You do it?

Yes.

Me too.

And she'd felt reassuringly normal.

But obviously she wasn't normal. There was a problem, somewhere. She just had to look as close as she could bear.

Healer.

Her vulva was surprisingly hot to the touch and damp, like a piece of aromatic sod. She pressed lightly around the outer labia and above the pubic mound, checking for tears or damage. It was strange to touch a piece of her body so intimately yet feel nothing at all. She could trace pubic bones through the skin, they met just there, part of the hip girdle. She moved her hips carefully. The painlessness was so *odd*, given that bones were broken.

Labia parted as she probed, giving her a pleasurable shock at the colour of her insides. Red or pink, she couldn't decide. Below that, her anus, a twinkling brown-pink thing itself. She drew back, amused at her own reservations, then leaned forward again. It was just part of a body. She smoothed the curly, dark hair trickling down and around the aperture, letting her embarrassment die away. She smelled fine, just fine.

She took a deep breath and used the first two fingers of both hands to part the outer lips so she could study the colour more closely. The hood of her plump clitoris peeled back with the movement: an infinitesimal motion that made her jump.

She bent closer, fascinated.

A few years before she died, Ingrid said people in foreign had *finally* worked out that the clitoris was subterranean.

She rubbed her finger just above the hood, feeling for the rubbery, movable rod under the skin. It reminded her of chicken cartilage, the shaft connected to the bone by a suspensory ligament. *Our obeah women have known for centuries,* Ingrid said. *Imagine a wishbone, and think of bulbs that fill with hot blood, and muscle pulled tight across all of it, building tension and spasming like the stars. This is a gift only for women, only for pleasure.*

She imagined the entirety of the clitoris, hot red flesh under the skin, thrumming and bubbling. She spread her labia further, both sets of lips protecting the vestibule, the delicate area between them. She liked that word for this part of the body. A chamber. A channel, opening into another place. A waiting room. Vestibule: it was also the name for the central cavity of the inner ear and for the space between the cheeks and the teeth. There was a vestibule inside the heart.

Beyond that, a tiny, winding road. She imagined herself grooved, her fingers sliding along soft patterns carved inside her by the gods and time. She almost expected a croaking lizard to poke its head out of her . . .

Vagina. Dare she peek?

Fingertips dampened. She could *see* the remains of her hymen! Tiny pieces of crinkled tissue: the corona. The wet walls wrapped around her careful, exploring fingers. She giggled. She had never considered how truly magical this flesh was, producing liquid if tickled. She pushed her fingers deeper. There was a small silver crackle as her cors exerted itself, inspired perhaps by her fingers' location. The more aroused you were, the further the mouth of the womb pulled back. *Tell the man to go slow or you not lying down with him*: she charged money to teach women this. To teach them holy no's.

Daughters. Leaking through *here* and out of her.

She swallowed spittle.

Keep on, keep on.

She couldn't see or feel any evidence of disease. No bruising or infection. Nothing bent or broken. None of the noises or smells she could feel on other people: no cancer, no sexually transmitted disease, nothing airborne or feverish.

There was nothing *wrong* with her. Nothing to tell her why they died.

It was just so.

Anise reared back and opened her mouth. The sound that came out wasn't the scream she expected, but the belching noise before vomiting. She cried. Tears trickled down her wrist. Her chest convulsed. If she could just concentrate, she could throw herself to the mercy of gods. Jai would help her be free.

What the gods do for you? You love them all your life and what it bring you? How it save you?

She pulled off a bangle and scraped it down her left arm as hard as she could. A welt bloomed.

Breathe, breathe.

She scraped again, but the images came anyway. Tan-Tan bent over someone else's bulbous belly, his cheek resting on it; Tan-Tan's fingers, shooting patches of warmth down the back of another woman's legs to soothe the pain, like he'd done for her, four times, so many *times*! Her mouth shook. She leaned forward, holding her head, nails in her scalp, spittle down her chin. Further: forehead to the floor, arms wrapped around her belly, she let herself wail.

She had cried before, over the years. In corners. In the time it took to spread a new table for the next massage. Two, four, seven tears on the steps up to work, beaming wide at anyone who called out morning. A tear behind the fridge door in the time it took to open and close it, Tan-Tan complaining: *Gods, Anise, why you burning out my electricity?* She'd even let a few free in her father's church, creeping in, late one night, no one to see, standing in front of his pulpit, finally kneeling, just in case . . .

Anise moaned.

Give them back to me, oh pleasepleaseplease.

Just in case what happened to her children was a punishment from her father's jealous, solitary god.

Thou shalt have no other god but Me . . .

It was more than she could stand, these memories of hidden, timid crying.

'What am I going to do?' she asked the walls. 'What am I going to *do*?'

A single black-and-white butterfly crouched on the ceiling.

She cried for a long time, until she thought that madness must be next, but it didn't come. She didn't hallucinate, nor did her mind splinter. She wanted to break. If she was a hundred pieces, she wouldn't have to feel.

You have to feel it.

She covered the vulva with her hand.

What had Mixie said?

Mine.

Anise crouched, as if giving birth; a finger slipped into syrup; she gasped and grasped again; pushed it back into place.

Twist, click.

A shower of silver, up her thighs and into her back.

She fell to her knees, sob-laughing. She didn't hear the knock

322

on the door, was only conscious of sound in the moment it came. A woman, asking questions, calling her name, but she couldn't speak, and eventually there was silence. She was only aware of lying on her side, eyes wide, seeing nothing but the physalis, snatching her into dreaming and whirling.

24

Romanza walked through the Bend Down fish market. It was near-empty in the late afternoon, the sellers hanging on for chat and gossip more than anything else, finishing the pack-up, offering cut-price deals. Around him, scales glittered: mackerel, tuna, leaper, snapper, sea snake. Sometimes squid, male seahorses – best when pregnant – and fresh grey crabs with pink bellies. He liked this part of the market: never a frozen fish, milky eyeball or flesh that didn't snap back under the light pressure of his little finger.

Pretty Town was stinking-sweet, now.

He could feel the fishermen staring at him, and the weight of the Torn Poem's roof, glittering above them all on the cliff. He stooped to look at a gold-flecked sea snake; still so fresh it would slide off the bone in Xavier's skillet. Should he buy it, take it up to there to help make peace?

He didn't have any money. And it wasn't for *him* to seek exoneration.

So many gods they had, for curry and cloud formations; a god for the disappointment you have on the first birthday that no one makes a party, yes, that very moment, a whole *god*; gods for fast-moving insects; but no gods for men who loved themselves. It was why Pilar said he never believe in none of them, never support no god, no goddess, no man in the sky with or without beard, black, red, blue, gold or white. *Only this earth you can trust*, he said. Digging his hands into the clay. *Family spit in your eye, friend gone, but this is here.* It was the only thing he knew to make Pilar angry.

Chi-chi man.

It had slipped out of Xavier's mouth so easily. He'd felt reduced: young and disappointed. They were words sharpened by the emancipated, by their Christian churches: the rage of their slave-past made them hungry for crucifixion. He had never painted on the churches of the Lord; he wanted to burn them to the ground. And he'd thought better of this macaenus.

'What you *want*?' snapped the sea-snake stall owner.

Romanza looked up, letting the hot indigent stare do its work. The stall owner dragged his eyes away.

Romanza skirted around another man, splashing fresh water over his wares. It ran down the fish and puddled on the concrete. Salt had gathered in the cracks of the table. Like Xavier's hands. The vendor used his fist to pound a brown turtle's back, testing the freshness. You could hear it in the backbone.

Romanza was taken with a spasm of sweet coughing. It hurt. He wanted to eat poison and sit in a tree. Abruptly, he felt lonely; the market loomed. He took Cannonball's medicine out of his pocket and scooped water from the concrete to wash it down.

He had to go away now, from these people. Another fisherman glared at him. He looked back, trying to be brave. At the heart of his anger had always been bewilderment.

It is something cruel deep within them, said Pilar. *They don't even know.*

Romanza left the market and found a quiet side street, facing Carenage beach. He leaned against the brick wall of a haberdashery, eyes closed, breathing. The cough was dry, and not as painful as before, but it would surely get worse again, as long as the sweetness in the air kept on tickling his throat. He would have to find another obeah woman; the idea of Cannonball made him nervous, now. It was a great shame; he'd appreciated her healthy, fat rippling body and her clear concern for him.

WHAT'S YOUR ALTERNATIVE?

Dry and peeling letters on the wall. He scratched at the orange paint. Cheap, locally made stuff.

Sonteine would be cute tomorrow. Happy. Sweating across her top lip, which happened when she was excited and nervous. Her wedding frock was orange, to match her personality. He painted in orange because of her.

He'd decided to go see her walk down the Temple steps tomorrow, after the blessing, crowd waiting, yelling: *kiss, kiss, kiss, kiss!* Pap wouldn't spot him, there would be too many people. He wasn't even sure his father would recognise him anymore. He had to go; whatever careless muck Xavier Redchoose was now *bound* to serve for that wedding feast was his fault.

Sonteine would never appreciate no chi-chi man jibes, which is why he could never tell her.

The loneliness nudged at him; he pushed himself forward. The door of the haberdashery opened in a burst of frangipani and the smell of roses; a bell tinkled. A woman glared out at him, hair powdery and thin-hipped. She was armed with a long, thick walking stick.

'Move from in front of my shop!'

Romanza frowned.

'I never mean—'

'I said, move!'

He spread his hands. 'Gods, Mamma. I not doing anyth—'

'Take your dirty, stinking, infected rass away from my place, *indigent!*'

He was confused.

'Infected?'

'I have two girls in here! You not putting your filthy hands on them, make them lose their pum-pum!'

'*What?*'

'You want me to call my husband? He beat-you-kill-you!'

Romanza backed away. People said the indigent were strange, that you had to be careful if you crossed them, that they were moth pedlars and beggars, and some of them were. But he had not heard this kind of prejudice.

'Mamma, who trouble you?' The man who limped up wore a soft red tunic and a benign expression. He had careful eyes and didn't look like he missed much.

'This nasty, dirty, stinking, thieving indigent bastard!'

That was enough. 'Old *lady* – !' Romanza snapped.

The red tunic man put a hand on his shoulder. Romanza shrugged it off, but he put it back, fingers slightly gripping. 'Take time, Mamma. He going right now.' He lowered his voice. 'Is better you leave. Go back in the bush.'

'Who the rass *you* is? Nobody don't have a right to tell me where to go!'

'Brother. Too many people hot-up right now, with the sex ban and the rumours,' muttered the man. He didn't look angry; he looked concerned. 'Mind how you go, don't look at any woman. People liable to hurt you.'

'Leave and don't come back!' yelled the woman.

'Gods, lady. Come see to *me*. I am the customer in need!' Red Tunic strolled over to the protesting woman. Romanza tried to calm himself.

Pilar, Pilar, Pilar.

'Nasty indigent, look how he *stink*!'

'Mamma, Mamma. Be *easy*.' The tall man shot him a last look, ushering the aggressive woman back inside her shop, gentle hand steering her elbow. 'Come sell me five tin of that paint up there, or you can give me a six-tin-for-five price. I need to paint my fence.'

Romanza jerked. The lie tore around the shop siding, adding small cracks to the brickwork and killing three spiders. He pulled his elbows into his chest, fists tight, feeling the impact in his tailbone. He leaned against the wall again, panting, letting the toxins leave his body, little puffs of air out of his mouth. Thoughts, darting and diving, like fireflies.

After some time, the tall man exited, weighed down with paint tins. He saw Romanza, leaning, swallowing.

'But you still here?'

Romanza looked at the tins. The man placed three of them on the ground.

'I want to know what that woman is talking about. What infection she mean?'

'Sometimes I forget indigent don't listen to the radio. You don't know Governor Intiasar call a sex ban today?'

'*No.*'

'Everybody think is because of what did happen with the women, earlier.'

'What happen?'

'Noon today, braps! All the woman's underneath out on the floor, and people chasing them around like is mus-mus!' He laughed. 'First the stories was funny. Somebody mistake one for squid and fry it up with pepper and lime! Man hiding their wife own. Then things change.' Here his face became stern. 'Rumour saying is the indigent, spreading infection and that cause it.'

'But we hardly *come* to town.'

'Is a very stupid thing. Bad vibes on the street. Rumour that when Intiasar announce his election campaign tonight, some-body going try kill him. All this talking about alternative. People thinking bad alternative.' He looked at Romanza carefully. 'People have a way to get crazy when change come. But it will pass. What we need is someone willing to get up and challenge Intiasar. Good people will listen if somebody decent make an argument against him.'

'*You* look like you could get up and say those things.'

The man chuckled. 'I have a little girl to take care of, my friend. But I glad to know I would get one vote.'

'Indigents can't vote.'

The man nodded. 'Yes, indeed.'

Romanza continued looking at him.

The Red Tunic man smiled.

'That long look. What you see?'

'Paint.'

They looked at the cans at their feet.

'Doing a job in my yard.'

Romanza groaned.

'Beg you, don't say that lie again.'

The man remained silent, rocking slightly on his heels.

'You not doing no yard job.'

The man took off his tunic and thrust it at Romanza. He was left standing in a white, sweat-stained undershirt.

'Put on that. It harder for them to see you indigent, with a good tunic.'

Romanza thought of refusing, then nodded and pulled it over his head. It smelled pleasantly of the man and chervil and ginger.

'What you using the paint for?'

329

'What cors you have?'

'You not going tell me?'

'What cors?'

'I know when you lie,' snapped Romanza.

'Truly?'

'Yes.'

'Alright. But that don't entitle you to my business.'

That was true. But he didn't care.

'You is the alternative?'

The man smiled.

'*Are* you?'

'Why should I talk to you?'

'Because I . . . *paint* too.'

They stared. Romanza could hear his heartbeat in his ears.

The man's face split with a grin. 'Well, now.' He rubbed his chin, picked up a can and tested its weight absentmindedly. The paint can turned from white to orange. 'I always thought I would meet *you*,' he whispered.

Hairs up on the back of his neck. Romanza breathed in the chervil from the borrowed tunic. He was suddenly, ridiculously excited.

The man picked up all six tins of paint and began to limp away. Romanza thought that his limp did not diminish his power, which came from his eyes and the kindness in his skin.

'Wait!' he yelled. 'What you name? What if we need to . . . ?' He didn't know what. '*Something?*'

The man pointed up the cliff and towards the restaurant. 'You can find me at the Torn Poem. My name is Io. Son of Pewter.' He hoisted a tin of paint high in the air, like a surrogate fist. 'Don't look so worried, Orange Man. You smell that sweet in the air?'

Romanza felt a thrill. The truth was being painted all about by Xavier's *brother*; what could be better than that? 'Yes I do. *Yes!*'

'Only good things can come from such sweet air.'

Romanza turned for home, beaming so hard, his cheeks hurt.

He might have been cruelly satisfied if he'd stayed eleven more minutes, long enough to see the old lady through the window of the haberdashery, slumping and snoring where she fell. Her head will be sore when she wakes, with the physalis bleeding red into the windowpane.

★

The obeah women come for Sonteine, right through the yellow walls. Everybody's heard of this trick, but it's rare to actually see. One moment she is alone at the door of the Fatidique Temple, calling out and making echoes, and in the next she's inside, and the women are *shoooop*-slithering through the walls, fluttering around her, like a shoal of golden fish. Outstretched arms, but not touching. Smiling, even though their mouths are serious, and their eyes are serious. She's never been examined so minutely. They have the full measure of her in seconds, they see she is frightened to be here, see Dandu's thumb print on her left hip where he gripped when her pum-pum fell; see everything she's ever been or ever will be.

The smallest obeah woman put a hand on Sonteine's head. Her body flopped. The itch in her back, the emptiness between her legs, the fear, all gone. Sonteine laughed but no sound came out. The obeah women laughed in the same moment she did, as if they were yellow pieces of her, in a mirror. The woman touching her head had yellow eyes; they all had yellow eyes. Sonteine put one hand to her cheek. They put their hands on their cheeks.

She wiggled her toes.

Wiggle-wiggle, the obeah women.

Wrinkled her nose.

That, too.

But she couldn't forget her purpose here.

'Something ran away with my pum-pum.'

Yellow eyes, all around her.

'We couldn't tell you where to find it.'

'Why? I know you know.'

She did; she was them. Then she should know. She shook her head.

A woman with sharp pink horns spoke.

'You can get what you want without it.'

It was not a reprimand, but Sonteine sucked her teeth scornfully, so they all did it. This was why she didn't like obeah women. Always speaking in riddles. Why couldn't they be plain? In the middle of their teeth-sucking, they took her hands, which meant perhaps she'd taken her own hands?

The yellow room filled with obeah light and strangeness.

25

Xavier dreams that Nya returns, her eyes filling her skull, eyelids gone, sockets stretched into her forehead, mouth and nose horribly vestigial. Returns to him wrapped in funeral binding, a shuffling parcel, peeping around the door. He clenches his teeth, holds out his arms for her dead, soft body, but her bandages are unravelling, spiralling out of her pores and scalp, out from under her tongue and from the depths of her black oesophagus, all billowing in some supernatural wind which threatens to snatch them both off their feet. Struggling, shielding his eyes, he looks out at the milky sun and sees that the muslin bandages are tethered to the ocean.

The waves are dragging Nya Redchoose out into the depths, where his mother's family once made its livelihood.

Horrified, driven by self-preservation, he tries to drop her. Nya's huge eyes pour water; her rum arms wrap around him, nails in the back of his neck, and he cannot tell in this moment the difference between her smell and his mother's smell.

You can put me down now, boy. It gone bad, already.

Then let me go, Mamma!

Her fingers, tightening, muslin pulling at her skin and organs. In the distance, whales beat the sea. The water is an inferno, scalding the horizon.

Her blood, sprinkling the sand like cloves.

★

He woke, half screaming, into Des'ree's terrified face. She was crying and scrabbling up his body, like a ladder to an exit, breaking tendrils and scattering red fruit.

'Xav – *Xav* – !'

He grabbed her, pinning her arms to her sides, pulling her into his chest. She thrashed, bony and indistinguishable.

'What – just – what – ?'

'Shhh.'

'Don't *leave* me – !'

'No, no. Shhh. Bad dreams.' Her wet cheek, against his own; he rocked her, felt useful to her, then troubled by the feeling. She was wheezing.

'The *boys* – the physalis stifling them – !'

He held her tighter, his heart thumping in his ears. The room stank of the fruit.

'Cyrus, he was – and Dean – I couldn't stop my Robert, my *Robert!* – that bastard physalis, choking them – !'

'*Shhh.*'

'You think something happen to them for true-true?'

'No, no . . .' he muttered. *For true-true?* A child's phrase. Her breath smelled like iron, as if her gums were bleeding. His whole body felt stiff from arching, from, what? Screaming? His throat hurt.

Des'ree cried a little more. They napped again, no longer inside the dreams, but exhausted by them. He examined the broken fruit smearing her throat, eyes half closed, thinking of his mother's funeral: of relatives chanting over the body, asking her spirit for forgiveness, forgiving her themselves. It took a long time and everyone in the room. He'd become convinced he was the only one keeping her spirit there, touching the bound body again and again with his fingertips, as was the rite, saying the words: *I release you, Mamma*, back itching, like everybody was waiting on him. Only a moment of true clemency was needed. Could he not find one, to help her body rest?

Finally it came: a spiral of black smoke rising from her remains, her soul dissolving and soaring. He was afraid to breathe, lest he delay her place in heaven any longer.

Would the blue man be waiting for her?

He imagined Nya's ghost finding him here, crouched in Des'ree's arms; her contempt at his weakness.

I know you would find your way back to this old bitch.

Nya could be vicious.

Physalis trickled down the walls and onto the floor, *pa-pa-pa-pa*, filling the room. He became aware of how deep they were in fruit: Des'ree was covered to the waist. He pushed physalis off her face and heavy eyes, unlaced vines from around his collarbones and throat, shuddering. If they stayed here long enough, the fruit would drown them. He felt drugged.

Pa-pa-pa-pa.

'What is going *on*?' Des'ree's voice was weak, and new.

'I don't know.' He made himself sit up, propped his back against the wall and pulled her up beside him. She was too thin. The house seemed to respond to her movement, and the pattering sound dispersed. 'Maybe the bandy house gone bad?'

'I never fight anybody in here, maybe it don't like it.'

He was sorry, for disturbing her equilibrium, her home. For coming and not getting what he needed and not knowing what that was.

She brushed physalis off her breasts and arms and lay back against him. 'I felt like I was going to *die* if I never sleep. Just sudden, so. Did you?'

'Yes, it come on quick.'

'I dreamt the physalis choked all the children, *everybody* own. Can't remember last time I had a nightmare so *tangible*.'

'No, you don't have many dreams.'

'You remember that?'

He stroked her back.

'What you did dream?' she asked.

'Nya.' He cleared his throat. The dread had returned, the prickle on the back of his neck, that expectation of her peering around a corner. A damp hand on his elbow. He was out, and he would be late back home at this rate.

Des'ree patted him. 'Bad?'

'Vivid dream, yes.'

'You never really used to tell me about your feelings. Family and so.'

'I told you things.'

'Not anything more than minimum.'

He considered that. 'No.'

'You never trust me?'

'No.'

Her voice was muffled against his chest. 'I was trying to be exciting. Mysterious. I didn't want you all bored.'

'You were those things.'

She traced his eyebrows with a single finger. He thought of Anise. Was she well? Did she have bad dreams?

'Any acolyte come to you, yet?' Des'ree asked.

'Not yet. I guess they'll start soon.'

She bit her lip. 'You need to be better than I was.'

How could he be better? How could he be worse?

'I was *so young*. Plantenitthy had his heart attack before I could – *feel*—' She searched for words. 'The Fatidique wasn't even sure I was his successor.'

'How you mean? Everybody know Plantenitthy name you.'

'He only took four acolytes. Pissing-tail fools, the lot of them, and no challenge for him. I loved him, he was the gentlest, sweetest man. Afraid of everything. He died of a broken heart, I don't care what anybody says. We were alone and he said it: *You is macaenus. Forever and always.*' She snuggled closer. 'But he never told the Fatidique. And there was no reason to believe me.'

He moved restlessly under her. He hadn't know her ascension was so tenuous.

'The Fatidique read his journals for some kind of answer, but there was only one relevant entry. *Des'ree is weak, but she will grow into it.*' Her laughter was a bad sound. 'His journals were an *everlasting* love letter to the same-said woman who never loved him. It made me so *impatient*. Live *life.*'

Four more years of training, she'd been due. Many said her womb would spoil the meat.

'I didn't know he had journals. They not on record.'

'I think the Fatidique kept them back. My status was already problematic.'

'So how they decide in the end?'

'They found me in an old Temple song. Some tiny half-sentence. *Des'ree rises*, or some such.' She grunted. 'He was right – I had to get stronger.'

Rumour had it she'd put her period in the soup of a man she'd overheard chatting badness on Plantenitthy in her restaurant. *You have my blood in your food, boy*, she said, when he stopped her to remark on the quality of the meal. When the man said he'd rather have that than food from a fat fool who ate himself into a heart attack, Des'ree spat into her palm, slapped him in the face and threw him out; after all, only the very stupid ignored the nuances of adiposity.

337

'You keep a journal, Des'ree?'

'Of course. Badly. You get them to read after you choose your acolytes.' He stroked her. 'I knew it was you, day one, when you come.' She paused. 'You say I frighten you. But you did frighten me, too.'

'I was *sixteen*, Des'ree. And then we were all *nineteen*. And you were not *well.*'

She mouthed words he couldn't catch. He could not decide what he felt about her. But he was glad to be saying these things, and he couldn't comfort her anymore.

'Des'ree, I have to move.'

'Yes, yes, of course.'

He stood up, cold, trying not to shiver. She wrapped her arms around her knees. The house warmed.

'Xavier.'

'Mm.'

'I sorry.' She sniffed.

And there it was.

'I am *sorry*, Xavier.'

He muttered something unintelligible, heart rattling. He wanted her to say more, to say it again, to say nothing else, ever. He wanted to stay and to leave immediately. He wanted to sit at altar, or climb a tree, have her stand underneath and chant it. Find Dominique and chant it. Hold Sisie's head. It wasn't enough, now he heard it, but what was she supposed to do?

Des'ree sighed.

'I tried to get them back together once,' he said.

She grimaced. 'What they said to you?'

'They were . . . magnanimous.'

'I thought you and Entaly might have something, one day.'

'Something like what?'

338

'I don't *know*.' Her mood was changing, and it made him nervous. She trailed her fingers through the physalis. 'I have to get somebody to check this house for malfunction.' The physalis huddled into corners of the room and vanished. 'Maybe that you could be a comfort to each other.' She sucked her teeth. 'But Nya was going to have her way, don't it? I should have *told* you not to marry her. You really can't blame that on me. She was such a sour gyal.'

'Des'ree. She still *walking*.' It was more than he could stand.

She bit her lip. 'Still? How she don't come to you yet?'

He shrugged, weary.

'Is only Nya could get you to stop with the moth, so what I know about anything?'

He was surprised that she, of all people, couldn't see the new hunger on him.

'You give it up?' he asked.

'Please.' She snorted. 'In a minute. Easy things.'

'But you took a *lot*, Des'ree.'

'Of course. You too. But we not ordinary.'

No, she couldn't see it. He would accept her sorries and her blindness.

Something occurred to him.

'Plantenitthy ghost must have walked, too. He seek out the woman he loved?'

Her cleavage looked tattered. 'He died in the kitchen. I caught him before he made it out the house.'

'And you did it – you what – *did* you . . . ?'

Des'ree put her hands on her hips. 'I took his heel.'

He stared. She was astonishing.

'You hungry?' asked Des'ree.

Most people expected blood and chopping from her, but he knew, at heart, she was a baker. Her kitchen had always enjoyed that precision. The scrubbed-down, measured care of a pastry cook; her anger when they worked like pigs. Not so, now.

Provisions hung from her kitchen ceiling and teetered in piles. Scarlet dragon fruit, sliced on the diagonal, for their theatrical, creamy centres; dried plums in small barrels; fingered citrons and their golden shoots – each one as big as his fist; jackfruit and bunches of mint. Someone had spilled fat vanilla pods and furry tamarinds on the floor, along with a child's slingshot. In the larder, big stone jars of sugar and cocoa beans; handprints in the shredded coconut. A mound of small, worn sandals in her ice room, piled next to slabs of rich, fatty butter. Unrefined, dark sugar crunching under their feet. An abandoned tower of empty boxes, obviously built by little boy hands. Ants.

The remains of several breakfasts: tomato skins, dried egg, bread ends, fruit peel, all strewn across a long, heavy table. Clothing, taken off and dropped. Xavier couldn't conceal his surprise. In her sacred kitchen, where she'd growled at him for a single blood splatter?

'The bandy house don't tidy down here?'

'I know where everything is.'

He sat at the table and she bustled around, pushing chaos aside, laying crockery, bringing him a good red wine and the morning's bread, yeasty and delicious in his mouth; coney sausage she'd slaughtered and cured; sliced, pickled artichokes from her garden. He was starving, and it was just what he needed, crunch and earth, the care of her hands, a sense of her wrestling things into the light, a meticulous savagery.

Des'ree snapped on the radio, to an all-music station. The song playing was indigenous: a skeletal drum and no words. He watched her fingers on the food; she moved differently than he remembered. Slower. There was less finesse. The sausage was sharp, sweet, hot, impeccably balanced, but she'd hacked the artichokes; her knives needed sharpening. Again, he was surprised.

'You want me to sharpen your blades?'

'No.' She grinned. 'They are exactly as I like them.'

'That *can't* be true.'

'It must be. If I wanted them sharper, the house would do it.'

'The house nearly just killed us with physalis.'

She nodded. 'It is a worry. But nothing like that never happen in ten years.' She put a slice of goat's cheese in front of him, coated in black pepper and ground dried sour cherries. He dipped a finger into the cheese and put it on his tongue.

Dip, swallow. 'That's good.' He wondered if his moth was lonely, hanging from the coat rack. Mad moth thoughts.

'How is *your* cooking?' Des'ree asked.

'Fine.'

'You going to feed everybody in time?'

'Let a few more years pass, I'll know.' Now that Nya was gone, the kitchen was a more peaceful place, his work better, his goal easier. He hated that it was true. He stared at the heavy kitchen doors, open to the cat-speckled yard, slow-creaking. Nya's ghost could slip in here now and tell him he was a bastard for thinking it.

Had Des'ree *really* had the strength to rip Plantenitthy's dead-walking body apart? There was no way to talk of such things. What would he ask for? Her technique? The particular nature of her fortitude? If it made her sick? If she'd needed comfort afterwards? If Plantenitthy's corpse fought her? Did ghosts fight?

'You'll feed everybody. Except for indigent, eh?' She chuckled and passed more sausage over, in the exact moment he wanted more. 'You could always go out in the bush and find them. I did try.'

He surprised himself by opening his mouth and telling her what Romanza had shared, about carrion and poison. He'd expected himself to hold it all up in his chest, or to lord it over her, letting out tit-bits, but he had forgotten how pleasant it was to tell her things. How intelligent she was. She leaned on the table, listening carefully – she *could* listen! – then interrupting excitedly. Had he recipes? What proportion of poison and for how long? Was the cooking ritualised or just survival? Were the indigent more communal eaters than they'd ever thought? She clapped her hands.

'So you *have* been walking bush! And they telling you things they never told me. That is so *good*.' He was confused; he'd expected her to be jealous. 'You did always love walkround.'

'No, I *never*, Des'ree.' Now he was irritated. 'You think I did love watching you steal people recipe?'

She looked comically puzzled. 'You think Miss Lou and Mistress Joyce never know I was taking their things? Come now.'

'What you mean?'

'Sometimes I despair for you, my Xavier. They leave out the things for me to take them. And when they see it on the menu, they come and squeeze my hand!'

He swallowed.

'How you expect me to know that?'

'Everybody *else* did. Gods, you so *serious*! How Nya did manage with you?'

'She obviously didn't,' he snapped.

342

She got up from the table. He watched her slice into a mighty pudding, big as a putt-putt wheel.

'What you cooking for Intiasar's breeding feast?'

He shrugged. She slid the pudding onto a plate and in front of him, two spoons in her hand. The smell was amazing. Romanza would have loved it; she would have loved Romanza. He could see them, cackling and cooking with poison. He felt a rush of affection. At the boy's black tears, and his talk of indignant frogs. He should have stayed on the beach. Controlled himself. Listened.

'You not doing it, are you?'

'I never said that.'

She handed him a spoon, amusement all over her. 'I *know* you not doing it. I been wondering all day how you handling it. You don't know how to work politricks yet?'

'*You* are the one walked out on Intiasar's speech on my ascension day! Talk to *me* about diplomacy!'

'Did I?' She looked pleased. He couldn't believe she didn't remember. 'Do the Governor a favour, Xav. You can use him later.' She narrowed her eyes. 'You can't, can you? You never could compromise. I was always trying to get you to bend. But you *are* macaenus. Bending is not in our nature.'

He had no idea *what* he was going to do about *any* stinking Intiasar.

'The whole country think you doing it.' Her voice shook with mirth. 'When you going tell them you not? You *really* want to shame Intiasar? That man bound to get unconscionably vex if you try mash up him daughter wedding.'

'He'll recover.'

Des'ree pushed the pudding plate closer. 'Eat this.' She put up her hand as he protested. 'I *said*.'

He picked up the spoon.

A caramel crust, aromatic with cinnamon, and he thought he knew what the pudding was, but the taste had only just begun. On through soft pumpkin, the crunch of smoked almonds. The sweetness of the caramel played against the earthiness of the rest; the smoke lingered. Just when he thought it was done, a deep burst of something citric. It was remarkable; it brought him back into his own body.

She sat, beaming as he groaned in appreciation. 'Is not too much?'

'It's astonishing.'

She picked up her spoon; they ate together, talking through it, like when she taught him, except this was a conversation between equals. The crunch, then earthy sweetness; subtle nuttiness, that perfect orangey endnote. Every time it hit, he wanted to grin at the audacity. The playfulness. She seemed genuinely interested in his opinion. He watched her. He could imagine her, merry with her children. Did they look like her?

'The boys have made you musical.'

She was pleased. 'You always knew what to say.'

'Tell me about them.'

He'd never seen *this* smile on her before. 'I think Cyrus set to be a lawman. Sell a jackass its own tail. I don't know about George or Anthony yet, they going find their way. Anthony swims and runs very well. Maybe George just want to be a father. Can you imagine? Eight-year-old boy, and something in him so loving. Patrick vex before he leave here, today! They gone to sing for a couple down in Lukia, married seventy-three years. Patrick don't like the singing. He do it because his brothers like his company. I only send him because I require him to mind what his mamma say, but I not going make him do it too much longer. Who else? Robert! That little boy going sing 'til he heart burst. Gideon might even be a cook.'

Joyful, that was what she was. He squinted.

'You ever think about what you would have done if you wasn't macaenus?' she asked.

'Not really, no.' He licked his thumb and scraped the pudding plate for crumbs. 'It's what we are.'

'Is something you going think of in your retirement. Trust me. Could you have been happy in your garden, tending your beautiful flowers, not a cook-man at all?'

He pondered. 'I can't imagine it.'

'Will you try?'

'Why?'

'Maybe thinking about what *else* you are will help you when your acolytes come.'

'I need help?'

'You will.'

Two of the striped cats pranced into the kitchen. One had a large rat in his mouth, its tail drooped. Des'ree hissed. The cat with the rat left. The cat without a rat jumped on the table and wound between them, purring. Des'ree purred back.

'I don't really feel like a macaenus anymore,' she said.

'This pudding . . .'

'That's cooking, not being responsible for making every last rass in this archipelago *happy*.'

He didn't believe it. She relished the power. This was just another idea, another mood change. 'You know what is the most *irritating* thing about you? You going forget you said this, next week, when I bring it up again!'

She laughed. '*That's* the most irritating thing about me?'

He tried to stop his own laughter – 'No!' – but she was laughing so freely, he had to join in.

Outside, cats watched them lean against each other.

Des'ree slid closer, circling his shoulders with her arms. Her face was still and peaceful. It was good to remember there had been times when he was happy in her company. Time had magnified his dread.

They sat listening to each other breathe.

'So you going to come back and let me irritate you again?' she asked.

He didn't know.

'Xavier?'

'Hm?'

'You afraid for my children? You think I not taking care of them?'

He looked down at her. 'Yes.'

She nodded. 'I been looking at myself, you know. These years. I learning things, I hope. I have people helping me.'

'Alright.'

'Xavier.'

'Hm?'

'Do the wedding thing. It will make you feel good.'

He groaned.

'You know how many people calling in to the radio to say they want to see you, how it gladden them heart, how they never know if you was going to ever walk with them again, how they afraid Nya passing kill your spirit?'

'Io said it would happen that way.'

'How you really going to ruin a young girl's wedding? Sonteine is a nice young woman, lacking in the usual entitlement of those high-hill fools. And Dandu is good for her. Quiet and steady. You should meet them. She so *excited*. Keep coming over here, asking me what I think you going cook?'

He was surprised at the affection in her face.

'You know Sonteine? You know her brother?'

'Dandu live just over here-so, he and Leo my neighbours, so I see Sonte all the time. I don't know the brother, though. Funny you ask that, I did forget Intiasar did have two child—'

He meant to tell her everything, then, in a rush: of Romanza's broken face on the beach, and was he right to have left him there, and now what, was *this* what a son felt like? And moth, always moth: *seems I not strong like you.* Bow his head and ask his master-teacher all these things. But Des'ree had stopped talking and stopped listening and she was raising a silencing finger and staring through her kitchen window.

Xavier shot to his feet, just in time to see the man creeping through her yard, scattering cats like chickens.

He could have sworn the house heaved and spat him out, tripping, Des'ree just behind, reaching out to steady him, clutching her grey robe. Her yard was piled full of physalis and the man they'd seen through the window was lifting a long box onto her altar.

'Greetings,' said Xavier, brightly. 'What you have there?'

The man jumped, cowered. Indigent.

'You have a delivery?'

'Yes, see it here.'

'I take it from you.'

The man hesitated, hands hovering above the package.

'Is a *special* delivery.'

'Special is good.' Xavier smiled, but remained alert. Gift-givers in a macaenus yard couldn't always be trusted.

'For me?' Des'ree stepped forward, pulling her diaphanous clothing tighter. The man's unblinking gaze rested on her throat and barely covered belly.

347

'Well?' Des'ree smiled encouragingly and stretched out her hand, palm upwards.

The man clutched the box closer, backed away and bumped into the altar. The statue of Eheh teetered; the cats fled. Xavier leapt forward but was too late. The goddess crashed to the ground. He could hear Des'ree behind him, protesting the heresy.

The indigent dropped the box and fled, heels scuffing orange dust behind him. The box lolled in the dirt, broken open, packing straw sifting into Des'ree's cashew fruit.

She sank to her knees beside the statue, cradling it in her lap. The fall had cracked the back of Eheh's head. A single clay ear lay in the dust. She picked it up gently. Xavier helped her drag the goddess upwards and lean her against the altar. Des'ree placed the ear beside its owner.

'Blasted indigent. If you take her inside, the house will mend her.'

Xavier hoisted the statue through the large kitchen door and returned for the ear. Above his head, the eaves rippled, as if boiling. Des'ree was prising open the box.

'Well, now,' she said.

The indigent had brought her three puppets: intricate and cotton-soft. A girl, a mother and an ama, stitched with great care into red and white robes and gilt slippers. The grandmother: each eyelash glued on individually, ten perfect toes. A perfect pink tongue in the girl's mouth; a sparkle, a shimmer, in the mother's eye?

'Look! She has a cuff!' Des'ree lifted the hand-embroidered robe. She touched the toys with reverence. 'Who send them?'

'Some nervous admirer,' said Xavier.

'No, no. Look! The box says Int/Bren. Is from *Intiasar*. Why would he send me a gift? Or maybe is Leo?' She searched through the detritus, flourished an invoice. 'But this is boxed for export. You know how long since I see one of Leo's toys? I did have one of those wooden acrobat lizards when I was six. He climbed up and down his little wooden tree, and his scales changed colour. Everything that Leo made, was like he put cors in there, some of us.' She beamed, a puppet on each arm.

'The puppets are lovely,' Xavier said, gently. 'I have to go.' He wasn't sure what he was going to do next.

Des'ree waggled the puppets.

'Go over to Dandu. He just next door. You will love him.'

'Des'ree . . .'

'Be *nice*, nah.'

'I *am* nice.'

'I think you should go. I going bathe. Have to look good tonight.'

'For what?'

'I'm judging Miss Pretty International.'

'The beauty contest?'

She shook the girl puppet at him, then reached out to clasp his arms. Her face was serious.

'I know that I have caused terrible things to happen.'

He waited.

'No excuse, Xavier. I know it.'

He drew back. She was bare.

'You could find your acolytes, Des'ree. Tell them sorry, too. Is not me, alone.'

'Eh.' She let out a puff of air. 'Would it be enough?'

'No. Do you want me to help find them?'

'Perhaps.' She drew fingernails across her ragged mouth. 'Perhaps. I don't know, today, but I will think on it. I will. Remember something.'

349

'And what is that?'

She bent close.

'I make you, Xavier Redchoose, macaenus-standing, and macaenus for all time.'

The words that had begun their separation. That original benediction.

Darkness was settling onto the Dukuyaie hills. Des'ree began to light the lamps in her yard. As if she knew the humming was due, and heard the sound of feet, tramping in unison, before anyone else.

'Them boys coming now,' she said.

'Mamma!'

'Mamma!'

'Mamma!'

'*Mamma-o!*'

'Mamma!'

'Deh-zerrrr-ray!'

Des'ree beamed all over her face, deftly lighting the last oil lamp.

Six boys came pouring into the yard. They were not in formation, as one might have imagined from the perfectly timed stamping and the melodious singing voices, alto and contralto pouring into each other, pouring back out again, into his throat and ears. They were a rag-tag bunch, moving around and gesticulating at each other with elbows and toes, singing almost absentmindedly.

Oh ha ha
Where are you?
Oh ha ha

Who are you?
Oh ha ha
What are you?
What are you?
What are you?

And Des'ree was calling out with such love.

'Robie, you come back in with that same sore nose? You lose your 'kerchief? Gideon, I did ask you get me some of Miss Jane good soap, what, Cyrus never remind you?'

Oh ha ha
What are you?

One shoving another, playfully, singing; two more dangling freshly caught lizard and raising them for their mother to see and singing; another examining the puppets, number six grabbing the smiling Des'ree around the waist, she leaning down, scooping him close, the boy singing and keeping his feet in time as he pinched her cheek. All as if song was breathing and nothing to be thought about at all.

Oh ha ha
Who are you?
Oh ha ha
Know yourself

Brap, brap! A final ground-drumming, a group pirouette that appeared to have nothing to do with anything but the joys of the world, and the entire Choir began to talk to their mother at the same time. She seemed able to talk back all at the same

351

time too, gathering them closer to her hips, like multicoloured skirts.

'You did what? Really? The old man pay you? You bring mango? Well, didn't I tell you: bring mango? Oh, you *did* bring the mango? Good! Don't *thump* him. You never hear me? Now which rude boy in here calling me De-zuh-ray like we is the same size? Of course I have food, what you think? You alright? I said, don't thump.'

He turned away; this was private. He needed his satchel from the bandy coat rack and he would be gone.

'Oh *you* did dream too? You lie! What, *all* of you? Was it a bad dream? Piglet? You know I not taking any pig in this house. Cyrus dream him girlfriend? Well, that sound good to me. Cyrus, what you said, you never dream no dirty girl? How you going scorn a girl, when your mother is a girl? Gideon, I need you to do something for me. No, I don't want no more fruit, you don't see the yard full up of physalis? Yes, darling, the mango is fine. I going cook with them physalis for weeks. Oh, I never know they don't eat good, thank you. So we going to have to sweep them up. No, I not letting the house do it, we have to do *some* things!'

Yes, she was a master-teacher.

He felt a tug on his tunic sleeve. One small boy, teeth blazing white, almost dwarfed by the satchel in his arms. A face just like his mother's, sniffling. Xavier took the bag and smiled as hard as he could. If he snuck the moth up and into his mouth right now, the child would think nothing of it. But the high would snap his back straight; the taste would set him trembling. He might fall down.

'Hello.'

'You are the o macaenus?'

'Yes.'

'More than Mamma?'

'Not more. A little less.'

The boy stared at him. 'You feeling sad?'

Xavier contemplated how to answer a child like this. Just like Romanza.

'Yes.'

'My name is Gideon. You can have a mango if you like.'

A fat one, perfectly ripe, blushed red on the green.

'Thank you, Gideon, son of Des'ree.'

He looked back at her to say goodbye, but she was being whirled away, wining her waist, silver plaits, back into the house, brandishing the puppets at them, her voice nearly drowned out with the chatter.

'Mamma! Mamma! Somebody bring the puppet for us?'

'No! My own! All for *meeee!*'

A chorus of appalled protest. The house was lighting up. What noise!

'Mamma said I must take you over to Dandu garden,' said Gideon.

Blasted stubborn woman.

'You don't have to do that.'

'Mamma said I should take you, and if you said no, take you.'

Xavier slipped the mango into his satchel and pulled the pouch out. The string snagged on something inside and he yanked harder. It wouldn't come free. The little boy watched curiously, rubbing one bare foot against the back of his calf, toe-nail making white lines on the dry skin. The smell of onions and ginger and green peppers. Xavier peered through the window. Des'ree at her stove. He would never get to her, through them. And that was right and proper.

The pouch string snapped; Xavier clutched the little bag in his fist.

'What is *that*?' asked Gideon.

'Nothing,' said Xavier, and threw the pouch away from all of them, down into the Lukia valley, so hard and far, his arm hurt.

26

Anise dreams she is a tree: standing on her hands, fingers stretching into the soil, making roots; cuticles sucking moisture from the earth; cold water rushing through her veins, replacing the blood. She gasps as the liquid thickens and turns into sap, bathing her uterus, dripping into her ovaries. The sap blends, hardens, changes: her ovaries fill with precious stones.

She dreams of giving birth to emeralds, Ingrid lacing them around her neck and fastening them in her ears. They dance, whirling under a sparkling, young moon. She can feel the dream ebbing away; reaches out as if she might delay its departure, stay where she is calm and joyful, Ingrid waggling her fingers at storm clouds, shouting. But she can hear noise coming from outside, on the road, near the factory, pulling her into reality. Music, a whole caravan of people passing and jollificating.

Her head pounded. Groggily awake, now. She wanted to go out and pull the revellers apart: kick, scratch, gouge anyone in her way. She could put her thumbs into eye sockets and tear the bone. Just so they could all shut up, shut up, shut *up*.

Heal.

The crowd cheered, as if it could hear her thoughts.

She began to distribute healing across herself, moving like a convalescent. She'd broken one of her fingers, she didn't know when or how: the smallest seam. She cleared the mucus in her nose and throat. She was running very low on energy. An Ingrid massage was what she needed.

She hadn't tried to cure Ingrid. Her friend wouldn't have let her, anyway. Neither of them was infallible and to try and then fail, o, that boulder would have been too heavy. Ingrid hadn't told her when *she* would die; that, too, would have been impossible to bear. It was hard enough to know when a friend was dying, to be two days before the losing, to be one day; twelve hours; three. One.

Magic went only so far and no more.

Around her, the room stank. The lumpy welt on her arm troubled her, where she had scraped herself deliberately. She was not usually self-destructive.

Anise sat up, slowly adjusting to the dimmed light. Physalis was heaped to the roof, as if the gods had found a hole and poured it in.

Lyla lay on top of a huge scarlet mound of fruit, snoring, arms and legs flung out, like a theatrical performer. Anise smiled weakly.

'Lyla?'

'Hm?'

'Lyla, o! Wake up!'

'No, girl.'

'How you mean? *Wake up!*'

Lyla sat bolt upright, as if someone had applied a flame. She looked around at the red madness. 'What you do?'

'Is not *me*. I don't know.'

'You alright, though? We did hear you crying.'

She didn't know what to say to that.

They stared at the room together. The fruit blocked the door; it was pouring off the balcony to the garden below, a pattering stream. The smell was overwhelming. Lyla coughed.

'How we going to get *out* of here?' said Anise.

Lyla stumbled to her feet, and promptly fell down again. Her neck looked shorter with the irritation. 'Why today so *extra* Popisho?' She knelt clumsily, then pushed her way to the balcony, using knees and arms to scythe through the sticky fruit. 'What a *nastiness.*' She reached the balcony, stuck her head over and yelled.

'Mixie, oy!'

'Oooh-ooh!' in return.

'You and Rhita alright?'

'Yeah, man. In the garden. House full up of this stupid fruit, though. What happen? Healer dead?'

Anise rolled her eyes. *Such* a bitch. 'I am *right* here, Hot Crotches!'

'Facety same way, healer! Listen me! Lyla?'

'Yes, man.'

'Rhita gone to go get Trevor to help. So much fruit we can't get inside, and you probably can't come down. You try?'

'We can't get to the door, much less out!'

Silence.

'Mixie?'

'What?'

'We can't get to the *door.*'

'I heard you.'

'Then why you never say nothing?'

'Don't I tell you already that help is coming? I don't want to waste my breath bawling out my business.'

'Mixie!'

'What?'

'You know you on my last nerve?'

'Probably.'

'Tell us when you know something.'

Silence.

'Mixie, rassclaaht, *man*. Answer people, nah!'

'*Alright*.'

Their voices set Anise's teeth on edge. Down to her bones hurt. She needed to calm her nervous system: to run or swim – no, it was too late for that – she needed that massage, or to sleep long. Applying and reapplying weak cors to her own self was like pissing and drinking it. No real sustenance.

She began to take long, even breaths, in through the nose, out through the mouth, enough to make a candle flame tremble, trying to ignore the physalis smell. Who knew it could be this sickly sweet?

Lyla waded back in. 'Oh well, we stuck and I starving. I guess we eat physalis until they come.' She unwrapped a plump fruit and sucked it, spat it out. 'Rass. Don't eat that.'

'What?'

'Don't taste like physalis at *all*.'

Anise nibbled. It was like eating mushy nothing.

Lyla sat down as best she could, a curious golden angle, legs wide-spread. 'Why you was crying?'

Anise sighed. 'Married things.'

Lyla seemed to hesitate. 'You look tired.'

'Cors low.'

'What you need?'

'Quiet. Touch.'

'You need a hug?' Lyla looked alarmed at the very idea.

Anise smiled painfully. 'Is alright.'

'I will do it, you know. No charge.'

They laughed together, gently.

'The pum-pum alright?' asked Lyla.

Anise nodded and closed her eyes. 'Just let me breathe a while, Lyla.'

In. Out. The day darkened. She could hear roosters in the hills, and croaking lizards, their cries bouncing like an auditory illusion. Lyla cleared her throat.

Breath. In. Out.

'So your husband work in the factory over so.'

'Yes.' Could she not be still?

'How he look?'

'Lyla, I just need—'

'Tell me, Anise.'

She opened her eyes, confused. Lyla's edges were blurred and warm.

'Short.' How odd it was the first thing to say. Panting slightly. 'A little taller than me. Broad. Big . . . arms.' Anise stopped, abruptly aware of what was happening.

Lyla looked at her, steadily. Anise swallowed.

'Good . . . *skin* for a man. Um. He has a small scar, on his . . . left cheek.'

'And?'

'He is . . .' She coughed, uncharacteristically embarrassed. Lyla looked straight ahead. 'Thick. Down . . . below.' Were they *doing* this? 'Seven inches, maybe. He . . . um . . . like . . . you to . . .'

Lyla raised a finger. 'They hardly the same when they come here.'

A beat.

'He have a ring in him lip?'

Anise let her breath out. 'Clink against the—'

'– drinking glass,' said Lyla.

'– drinking glass,' said Anise.

Mmmmm-hm. Just like that, you know.

They listened to people singing on the street.

'Long time you know him, Lyla?'

'A year or so.'

She cough-laughed. She'd been trying to convince the woman who was sleeping with her husband to *keep* her most excellent, her prize-winning, her most magical pum-pum.

No wonder he run you.

'And how . . . often . . . ?'

'You don't need to know anything more. I promise you.'

'Oh, I do.'

'Wives always want to know. I promise you, it not going serve you.'

'He come here regular, Lyla?'

'Yes.'

So, in the end, the old butterfly neighbour had been wrong. No pregnant drama, no public shame. Tan-Tan was just a regular whoremonger. A liar of the ordinary kind, like so many worthless men on the road. And she knew most women around her would think it just the way of penises. But she wasn't staying for *that*. Not she. Not Pastor Lati child.

Cheat on you just so, for a grind; buy it, when he could get it at home? Is not like he fall in love, to rass.

It brought an odd kind of relief, knowing she was going to live without the sound of him. He would not be there to tell her about the latest news in town; nor would she have to move his shoes out of the way when she came downstairs in the morning. There would be no need to make fresh June-plum juice, or to come home from work to check on him before she went out again. He would not sit with her in the evenings and point out the colours in the darkening sky. Her dreams would not be punctuated by the whirr of his loom. No tapping on the bedroom door when she slept late, the sound of his voice – *Anise-oh*. Gentle. And would he miss her, the particular smells and sounds that she made?

'I don't *want* him, you know,' said Lyla.

'No?'

'Not even a little.'

Anise flexed her hands. Sparkling lights flared across her knuckles in the darkening room, ebbing, sputtering dead. She shook her head.

'So he want *you*, Lyla?'

She'd assumed wrong again, my, she was all kinds of wrong, today.

Lyla looked discomfited for the first time since they'd met.

'I told you, already: men try to do impossible things. But I going to have a *new* life, sis and I not taking no man with me. Pum-pum disposal guarantee *that*.'

She wouldn't have expected to hear Lyla so stressed.

Her eyelids fluttered. She slid her fingers into her groin, checked her ears and middle toes: anywhere there might be stores of silver. Her head spun. She was going to faint. She just needed *rest*. Something. Xavier's fingers in her mouth and oh, his *smell*. She would never forget *that* in all her born days. *That* would fill her up. Lyla was speaking languorously, but she found she couldn't hear her, anymore. She still liked Lyla, and perhaps that was the strangest thing that had happened all day.

Needed. *Touch*. Anybody. She began to crawl across the fruit.

Lyla watched her coming, wary.

Her feet were like cotton wool; lips swollen. It didn't really matter who: anybody, even a woman who was fucking her husband.

Her hands on Lyla's wrists, thighs, belly.

So drowsy.

Lyla slid her fingers on top of hers. Belly. Soft and golden under that splendid frock.

In. Out. Breath.

Life.

Oh my gods.

Sweep-swoop of a strong infant heart. One hundred and ten beats per minute. Mouth, still-webbed feet, taste buds beginning to work. Kidneys. Asleep in good liquid, pulsing, rolling lazily.

Pure, new-child energy.

Her ears felt hot, like this morning, her tongue huge. Energy roared through her. If it didn't hurt so very much, she might have celebrated long and loud with her new friend.

'How . . . *how* you planning to get *that* out, Lyla? Without a p-pum-pum?'

Anise began to crawl backward, sliding through fruit, on her backside.

Get away. Yes.

'Anise, what are you . . . *doing* – ?'

She felt Lyla pulling at her foot. Everything was fruit-blocked, but no matter. She *had* to leave. Tan-Tan, he must be so very *happy*, a chance to bring another child, so why he sloping round the house like a ghost? Must be guilt, nah.

Sliding backward. Just needed to be by *herself*.

'Get *through*,' Anise slurred.

Lyla, calling out to her.

No, no, no, she wasn't dealing with any more of this foolish-ness. Done, now.

'*Anise!*'

Anise Latibeaudearre-married-Joseph pushed herself through the bank of physalis head first, and into the wall of the water-melon house.

She had a fleeting impression of stalks and scent, then a tremendous silence. A snarl of her robe caught – on what? – and threatened to pull her back into the room. She unravelled it slowly, remembering the smooth skin of limes in her hands this morning.

Thoughts and feelings scattered around her, like rain on the roof.

Everything had stopped.

Years later, she'd compare the experience to early childhood, when she'd lost herself an hour at a time, staring into the black centre of a candle. Nobody told her how – the meditation was instinctive, comforting, but it made her father fractious.

Get up and do something nah, child.

Nah child nah child nah child.

His words popped and disintegrated in the air. All words meant the same thing. Nothing was more important than anything else. Her appendix was the same as orchids and her memories belonged to everyone. She would have remarked out loud at the smallness and the enormity of it all, except she'd stopped breathing and speech was the same as sadness.

Awe, wonder, fear, despair, all here, all gone. No more than a moment. Forever.

Breathing and breathing and breathing.

Sogood sogood

nothing and everything

Anise Latibeaudearre walked through the fruit and the wall of the whorehouse, into the dusk air on the factory road. Nine indigent men stood shouting instructions at each other and hauling a mighty box between them, a large white INT/BREN label stuck to its wooden side. Three were singing; ah, it was *them* who had been outside all this time, making so much noise.

She stared, the breath in her mouth and her body hot and bizarre.

Her left sandal was gone, so she kicked off the other one and turned to look at Mixie's house: perhaps she'd simply torn through? But no: the wall was perfectly intact. She could hear Lyla crying out, and Mixie yelling back. The air around her shimmered, warm and sweet.

Look at you, boasty, doing even more magical and necessary things.

'Hey,' she called to the indigent. '*Hey!*'

They didn't look up, just yelled and puffed. She wanted to tell them they were the same as each other and the same as the box, and that a mere thought would move it for them. She wanted to explain that she could walk through walls now and that meant also through the back of their skulls, in the time it took to stand here and admire the dust around her feet.

She shook her head at the size of her thoughts.

'*Hey!*'

The men finally looked up and the odd feeling of everything-ness began to fade.

'A pregnant woman inside there, she need you.'

She left them, running towards the whorehouse garden and calling out; she walked towards the sea.

★

The Dukuyaie beachfront was enormous and empty. She tied hip knots in her robe, examining the dark, purple-rimmed clouds, felt vague and unformed as she entered the ocean, mindlessly moving her limbs through the soft, oily water. She liked the swim between here and Battisient: the water was shallow and less saline than in other places.

I feel so good.

Ordinarily she'd be cleaning out the secrets at dusk, rearranging her stock, counting the day's takings, looking through the window for last-minute clients, chatting to passers-by, trying to avoid the nastier elements of su-su. She turned on her back and floated, thin white robe billowing under her chin, feeling the water everywhere. She could see the mountains where she'd walked with Xavier, stopping to show him cracked crab shells and bright yellow beetles mating. He had thought her wise. She'd felt wise. But she hadn't known she *was* the lavender fissures in those shells, or that she was inside that thrashing moment of insect life. She'd just walked through a solid mass. Ingrid said that kind of thing was easy to learn; Anise hadn't considered its complexity. She wasn't sure she would have been able to do it except today.

She kicked out as seaweed entangled her ankle. A salty wave smacked her in the face, and she gulped, spluttered, laughed, spat, sniffed and began to swim again. She might have been moving through perfume. This calm acceptance would leave her soon, she felt that – she was still an ordinary person, she had not transformed into the black centre of a candle. But could she hold on a while longer, to this hope that everything was good? That so much more was possible? Even if she was never a mother and never knew why?

She took another face of brine and giggled under the darkening sky. It seemed outrageous to feel happy, but she was.

27

Anise wasn't home, so Tan-Tan headed for her workspace. Sometimes he went there when he knew she was away. He liked to be among her things and look at the bright walls and cushions; to think of her sitting on top of him, impaled, warming him with her kisses. Especially when he'd behaved badly. And there had been those times, oh yes. He was no perfect man. But he kept his promises. His daddy said a man who couldn't keep a promise wasn't shit on your sandal, and he was right.

His wife, he thought, had an uncanny ability to make a man forget where he was in the world, to draw him into another state of consciousness. Before they stopped having sex, their morning love had made him drift through the factory, until the boss-man shouted at him. Was it that very dreaminess which birthed those odd, watery nothings, and made Anise so unhappy?

He wasn't sure what the future held, but he knew he'd been fair in his part. All he had to do was keep his body away from his wife, and he'd done that to the letter. She said she didn't want no more baby, and he heard her when she said it.

It had taken everything she *had* to tell him no, and some small part of him admired her for it.

So when she put on perfume and ran her hands over him, he knew he had to be the stronger one. A woman could try to prevent pregnancy – watch the moon or cover up a hood-stand with anything she liked – but everybody knew there were no guarantees. One slip became a slide and he was not, in this life, going to watch his wife's face break apart again. Or have her vex with him, say *he* take advantage of her weakness. Anise had never had any self-control in matters of love. There was no *point* in some long womany talk-talking about the matter. It only caused arguments. If abstinence was necessary – and they agreed it was – what was the point of any further ifs, ands or buts? There would be time for sex with his still-pretty wife when they were older. He'd heard a woman's middle-age was a splendid time for love.

When tempted, he concentrated on that damn board in the floor, stinking with baby liquid. And like most men, he had other, much less complicated options.

But then Lyla go and get pregnant and that changed it all.

At first Lyla was nothing more than a beautiful woman he saw on the beach and wanted, that strange weaving neck poked above the waves like a periscope or a rainbow heron, she day-dreaming and floating, he distracted by her soft golden muscles, she cutting her eyes at him when he called out to her.

Boy, go away unless you got money.

He'd never really watched the whorehouse before; never seen or gave a damn about a whore. Now it was all he could do to stop his gazing while at work, knowing she was across there with his baby, his *chance*. There was something about Lyla that promised happiness. He couldn't put his finger on it. *Don't take it serious,* she said, *is my pum-pum distracting you*, but there it was: happiness, despite her smooth, closed whore's way. Could their child be a whole thing, squealing, suckling its mother's breast? He'd almost convinced himself the fault of the dead babies was his own. *What a man like that good for, eh?* That's what they said about him.

Keep machete in the bedroom corner, machete dull.

Lyla intended to leave the whoring, she said so, and so he

would leave Anise. It was time to accept that a dog did not expect to live with a hummingbird.

In the meantime, for a little while longer, he could let himself into his wife's space, and smell her things, and sit and think of good times.

*

Tan-Tan pushed open the door to Anise's workspace and stood, puzzled at the shattered glass and broken shelving. Disembowelled cushions, cracked bottles and what was that . . . *stench*?

He glared, unable to believe his eyes.

Someone had defecated in the middle of her day room. Where she was *kind* and talked to so many people who didn't deserve her time. The rage so disabled Tan-Tan that when a head-bandaged Pedrino Blowsnaught came out of the adjoining room, pulling up his pants and flourishing a hammer, he didn't try to kill him as quickly as he might have done.

Blowsnaught stared at him like a frightened rat, then tried to dive out of the window. Unfortunately for him, it was a small window and fear hadn't shaved inches off his hips. Tan-Tan recovered his wits and dragged him back into the room, roaring.

'You – you shit in my wife's place? Man, you come here and *shit*?'

Blowsnaught began to babble.

'She set spell on me!' It was remarkable he managed to talk at all, given Tan-Tan was punching him after every syllable. He doubled over, hacking and pleading. 'A *big* spell! It wasn't deserved! Not at all! I was only there because Intiasar said free-ness, man! Don't hit me!'

Tan-Tan paused in his punching to change fists. He was

ambidextrous and efficient that way. *If* Anise had set a spell on this nasty fool, it was for good reason, that he knew.

'Stop, I beg you! I am a good man! Ask anybody!'

Tan-Tan regarded the fool closely. There was something familiar in his affect.

'You did *want* her! You don't think I can see it? You hurt my wife? *Where she is?*'

He began a fresh hitting. Blood dribbled out of Blowsnaught's broken mouth.

'I never said nothing bad to her! I never touch!'

'How you mean, never touch, like that is something? She a married woman, you *fool*!'

The older man managed to pull free and scramble backward. Tan-Tan strolled after him and picked him up by the neck, where he dangled, screeching. He carried him towards the brown lump still steaming in the middle of the room.

'You look like a dog to me! You know how they train dog?'

Blowsnaught obviously did. He began to shriek even louder.

Tan-Tan knelt beside the mess and took a firmer hold of the squirming man's neck.

'*No-no-no-no-!*'

'You stinking dirty bitch-dog! You come into my wife place and desecrate it? You know how she love this place? You know how she pick out every single rass piece of furniture? With love? With her own hand? A woman ever love you yet? Stinking dirty bitch-dog! I going to train you in here today!'

Then a curious thing happened.

Blowsnaught felt the grip on his neck-back ease, and the grinding forward motion halt. Then Tan-Tan dropped him. It happened so quickly he nearly fell into his own shit anyway. He gazed at Tan-Tan's still body. Heart attack? It hadn't killed him if so, with the clean breath and chest of a remarkably healthy goat-kid.

Just asleep.

Blowsnaught grimaced. To think of pretty Anise, lying under this beast. He got to his feet and kicked the younger man in the gut, hard.

'Ow, ow, rassss!'

He hopped around, then collapsed, fingers trailing in Tan-Tan's groin.

If you'd looked through the window, on your way to late Temple, you might have thought them lovers. Since as how they were strewn with scarlet physalis, like confetti and like Temple bells and love.

★

Sonteine lay on the dry, golden floor, arms outspread, knees up. Her body felt heavy and peculiar. She had woken out of a dream in which she was flying. Her wings were transparent, and she'd rolled in the sky, delighting in the heavy support of the air, using the thick muscles in her back. Below her, Popisho was like ants.

'Hello,' said her mother. She was lying on her back in the same position, facing the opposite direction, arms outstretched, the top of her head inches away from Sonteine's. They were both naked. The walls suited her mother's dark brown skin and her short black hair.

'Hello,' said Sonteine. She couldn't keep her eyes open and didn't understand why their nakedness didn't matter. 'Hello,' she said, again, and they dozed in the gold-coloured shadows.

A month or two went by. To pass the time, she told her mother about the flying dream. She had the wings of a dragonfly. Folding them was as simple as crossing your arms, melting them back into her shoulder blades and down her waist. Then wah, one flicker and they were out again. Like slipping a knife free or winking at a pretty man, 'except I don't ever do that, Mamma.' This was why she held her back so straight – bending the wings inside hurt – and why she was compelled to roll over and over in water, the closest thing to open air. But the most interesting and wonderful thing was her mouth. It could elongate, like a proboscis, could reach the very centre of the wings between her shoulder blades, and groom them.

'Cors, so late,' murmured Mrs Intiasar. 'What a thing. You not supposed to be able to do that.'

'I *know*!' said Sonteine. She would have clapped her hands, if she could. Her mother didn't sound angry at all.

The months rolled on. She found she couldn't stop speaking. About the men who'd frightened her, and how Dandu didn't, although she couldn't understand how he'd fit inside her, because she could still only think of her body like an eye, and his body as a stick or a stone. She was astonished how the smoky walls helped her to speak her most intimate self. And astonished by her mother, listening. She was used to Mamma Inti misunderstanding, interrupting, yelling, used to editing herself and knotting herself tight. She'd learned to do without a mother. But this thing, this wedding night, felt like a mother's job. Could she not do this one thing?

'Please, Mamma,' she said. 'I don't know how to be.'

A few years passed.

Her mother began to talk about hog plums. Did Sonteine remember the best way to eat them, cold out of the stream? You nibbled a hole in the top and sucked out the juice. Then you sucked out the seed and popped the empty skin onto the end of your tongue and waggled it up and down before eating the rest, did she remember?

Sonteine giggled.

Her mother talked about being young; of sitting on a low wooden bench with her best friend, Shasa, two Battisient girls in the rain and the bench had a roof so they didn't get wet. The plum harvest was coming in and the farmers walked past with cedar wagons pulled by goats. The wagons were filled with fruit; yellow, red, blush and blue, wet from the day's storm, and the rich scent filled the streets and made the sides of her mouth ache. The men flicked the goats, to make them kick their heels and remember who was boss. The girls watched the men and the goats and Mrs Intiasar, whose name was Nesrine then, said juice was really all hog plums were good for, but Shasa said *her* mother soaked the skins in rum with raisins and cloves for cake at blessing times.

As the men rolled by, Shasa took her chin in her hand and kissed her. It was the third time they'd kissed, and she didn't yet know where to put her tongue, but Shasa was patient. She was impressed by the softness of her friend's mouth. They smiled against each other's cheeks and sat in the wet air holding hands. The plums were like tumbling gemstones, bouncing in the back of the wagons. She thought the men might call out or beat them, but nothing happened. The men's eyes were like the goats' eyes and the plums, red and blue and yellow and that day was what she thought about when she lay down to make babies.

Today, when all the women's belongings fell out, she'd examined her own. Nestled in the soft hair, a tiny red plum, wet from the rain.

Sonteine wanted to ask her mother why she didn't stay kissing Shasa, but it was a stupid question because everybody knew why. Certain men didn't like that and what men didn't like had to be kept indoors and never became law, even though the women did most of the work and obeah women were in charge of the magic. The thought so tired her she let silence lie down on her like a blanket.

Nine years passed. Sonteine thought about Dandu. She felt very sorry for him, because she knew he'd search and strain his ears, and questions with no answers were the hardest kind. Who would wear her wedding dress that had taken so long to make and who would eat the wonderful food the macaenus prepared? Perhaps Romanza would come and take the meal to the indigent. Her father: could he win an election without women in the house, or would he retire? Perhaps he'd go overseas again, because he was quite a sorrowful man and she was sure he had his own plum-kind-of secrets.

She was cheered to think of all the people that would miss her.

They aged. She felt her ribs and wrinkles and lines in her face. Their skin lost its spring and bounce, turning to paper. Slackness infected her muscles, even the ones she used to smile. When she touched the top of her mother's head, the texture of her hair had changed and Mrs Intiasar said she was sure it was all white, or perhaps there was nothing there at all by now, and do you know where we are, Sonte?

'No, Mamma.'

They spoke back and forth, listening in turns; spoke of everything they'd ever thought of, or felt, or seen, or heard. Sonteine was surprised to find that her mother never ran out of things to share, and Nesrine Intiasar was surprised at the same thing.

After nearly ninety-four years, when they were little more than skin and eyes, and so linked that there was nothing left to say, but simply joy to feel at knowing and being known, the obeah women poured through the walls and said wake up and go home. And Sonteine found herself alone, clothed, and as young as she'd ever been. And the obeah women mimicked her smiling.

*

There were fewer problems with the Popisho pum-pums than you might have expected. One hundred and twenty-four problems, to be exact.

The first pum-pum that caused a problem belonged to an eighty-three-year-old woman who lost it on the Pluie high street. A candle-maker picked it up and took it back to the lady, who screamed and said she'd never looked down there and wasn't going to start now. The candle-maker took it home, built it a small hutch in his front room and surrounded it with peanuts, oranges and fennel seed.

The second pum-pum rolled up to the head of a teacher-woman's bed. The man she was sleeping beside burst it between his palms and watched it bleed. When the woman woke up and realised what he'd done, she poured hot oil into his ear, killing him.

Problem pum-pums numbers three to 117 belonged to women who needed professional healers to help reattach them, but the rest of the female population managed themselves, or with the help of intimates.

Pum-pums 118 and 119 belonged to a couple who played with them all morning, inadvertently mixing them up. Slotting them back, they realised their mistake, but it was too late to take them out again and so these two women who loved each other were linked together in a more profound way than they'd ever thought possible and treated their genitals with even more reverence than before.

Pum-pum 120 was given as a present to a young married man by his equally young wife, who loved her husband but didn't like having sex with him. He took to walking around with it in his lunch can, or sometimes in his pocket, and he tried to think about his wife every time he used it. Two were stolen: one by a little boy who saw the owner lose it and couldn't make himself run down the road yelling, *Miss, Miss, you drop your crotches*; the other, problem pum-pum 122, was taken by a certain well-meaning but inexperienced young man about to be married and accidentally dropped into the Pineapple River round the back of Leo Brenteninton yard, but you never heard me tell you so.

Only thirteen men attempted to have sexual intercourse with free-range pum-pums, although 1,462 men, if questioned the night before, would have said that they might, if given the opportunity. Each man who tried to commit this entire act of fuckery found himself overcome with depression, painful acne and arthritis. Five of these men committed to lifelong celibacy.

The too-embarrassed boy gave the pum-pum to his mother, who purchased an advertisement on the radio, and several women came forward to claim it. The correct owner took it home after a hair, shade and smell match.

The pum-pum dropped in the Pineapple River was found upstream, trapped between two rocks and a cold-water trout, by a woman who decided she was tired of living in a small town on the chilly outskirts of Battisient forest, where Governor Intiasar did not care about water or medicine or the importance of school resources. She sold the pum-pum for a vast sum of money, to an obeah woman who gave it to another woman who was born with a mirror between her legs instead of genitals. A cursory examination revealed that the pum-pum still had its hymen, which actually meant very little at all, as all kinds of women, of all ages, have bits and pieces of their hymens left but very few of us know that. When the obeah woman examined the Pineapple River pum-pum she *did* think it might have belonged to a woman suffering from vaginismus. The mirror-crotches woman said she found Pum-Pum 122 just juicy enough for *her* life, and the obeah woman was pleased.

Sonteine Intiasar left the golden Fatidique Temple and tripped over pum-pum number 123, which was sitting outside, next to a grunting coney. Delighted at her luck, and mistaking it for her own, she brushed away a single red ant, crouched under the pale white sky and popped it where it should be, which was when the experiences of a prostitute's lifetime rushed into her bloodstream, causing her wings to rip out of her back so suddenly she had to sit down, lest she vomit and faint. When she finally stood up, it was with the facial expression of a woman whose purpose had become clear.

Lyla had given her number 123 to a passing coney, you see, and laughed when he trotted off with it hanging from his mouth.

★

Popisho dreams for one strange hour. Every woman, man and child under the clouded sun, shivering in the sweet wind spreading across the land. A hunting mosquito made a *strooops* sound and scurried away, convinced everyone was dead.

Except for the indigent. They stretch, and blink and look around themselves, watching the red fruit spread, bubbling up through cracks in the ground, sprouting in host trees, breeding from nowhere. They gather together in the Dead Island flats watching the toy warehouse, drawn by the violent trembling of its blue roof. Physalis brims out of its windows and pours down the walls, spewing juice. They know it as the fruit of the dead, picked for graves.

Romanza moved restlessly, hip-touching with Pilar. Time felt as if it was stretching thin, like something gummy between his fingers. Juice beat the warehouse windows and stained the earth red.

'What *is* it?' he asked.

Pilar rubbed his shoulder blades with one hand.

'I miss you.'

Romanza let pleasure run through him. More than once Pilar had assured him he never missed anyone, simply celebrated when they came back, which wasn't the same thing. He wanted to be missed.

Pilar gripped him around the waist, lifted him and kissed him on the lips.

Someone said: 'Well then, go on now,' in a warm voice.

The best place to be was here, with them. But it felt as if the factory had been shaking for more than a year. He let Pilar lower him to the ground.

'The day, is like it stretching into years. You feel it?'

'No,' said Pilar. 'But I do think sweet hurricane coming.'

He had been just about to say it.

'When?'

'Who knows? Days, weeks, today? But is clear to me. The earth is not bearing good things as it used to. The food is not the same.' He put a fierce hand on Romanza's throat. 'Even your chest is protesting, beloved.'

'That is why?'

'Yes, we due. The earth vex. Of course we would feel it first.'

'Why you never tell me this morning?'

'I never sure that it was the right thing to do.'

'And now?'

'Now, I am sure. I need your help and your love.'

Romanza felt thudding relief. The soil stank of ancient warning, and he wasn't alone. They could plan.

'No one going to shelter us, they think we passing disease, but we could get into churches and old houses if we start to organise now.'

Pilar smiled. 'You still young.'

'Don't chat foolishness, you and me nearly the same age! We can do it. Break into public buildings.' Romanza pointed at the quivering warehouse. 'That could hold two hundred! Put the children in there, anyone come to fling them out, is easier to protect.'

'That warehouse going to mash up any minute now, you don't see it shaking?'

'The factories, then.'

'Some will go inside when it start, yes.'

'Well . . . we can *organise* them!' He felt he might go mad. 'But we have to move.'

Pilar shook his head. The warehouse roof trembled, like a man with fever. 'What is the first thing we learn about sweet hurricane?'

'It brings lessons. People change.' His school days had meant so little, with the vinegary smell of halls and recitation. 'We all *know* that. Pilar! What happen to you?'

'I am *here*, Romanza.' He spoke like the hurricane had time to come and pass, and still he would be finishing this sentence. 'The first thing we learn is that it takes us by surprise.'

'What you mean?'

'Coney trapped with lizard. Mothers and daughters. Enemies. A man find himself in a house with his friend wife. The child is alone. Servant get lock in with master, and by the time they done, there are no masters.'

'But we *know* this one coming. This is our only chance to save ourselves!'

'We not *supposed* to know. See how they don't know in town?'

'Then why the physalis come? Don't it trying to warn us? Is a portent.'

Pilar put his hand on Romanza's cheek. 'It come to tell us goodbye.'

The horror made him cold. An older woman, naked to the waist, sat on the ground, teats swaying, throwing handfuls of fruit over her head. Others joined her, giggling and pushing, and the mourning dust streaked across their skin. No, it was unconscionable to let them die.

'If you don't tell them, I will,' said Romanza.

Pilar's voice was small. 'I beg you, let it come.'

'To kill us? How that *help* anything? Where is the meaning in that? They *hate* us! They not going to mourn us!'

'Not all of them hate us, just the loudest.' Pilar would not take his hand away. 'We are *here*, Zaza. We cannot die. But we may have to pass, for them to learn.'

'I've always trusted you, Pilar. Is you *teach* me. To water-walk. Everything. To love. But no, not this!'

'Why not? Death is an idea. You watch things die every day and you rejoice. The beast dies and his blood is dust. Millions of deaths, flowing around us. Everything is as it should be.'

He wanted to scream, at Pilar's quiet, at his faith. He wrenched himself away.

379

'Don't trust *me*, Zaza. Trust the earth.'

Children galloped past, sneezing, physalis piled around their calves. Romanza sank into the warm, wisp-covered fruit. He coughed; the warehouse convulsed. The doors burst open. Later, some said the fruit flew so high it filled the heavens with scent. The indigent scampered before the explosion.

'Beloved,' said Pilar. He was looking at Romanza but speaking to all of them.

'*Pilar.*' Begging, coughing; the juice might fill his lungs.

Pilar walked away, pushing through physalis, like swimming. He spoke to the crowd without raising his voice. 'We have work to do.'

A little girl hurtled up, with black curls and ears like a rabbit. 'A doll inside the warehouse with hair like mine. I can have it?'

'Of course,' said Pilar. 'But hurry, now.'

Romanza was glad for a last chance to fill his eyes with Pilar: walking into the toy warehouse with a firm step and a straight back.

He turned and began to run.

*

Everybody dreams: while physalis grow out of polished board floors and sprout on people's stairs, curling around sleeping bodies, stalks looping around cooking pots and choking the toilets, belching out onto the floor and popping open under sleeping heels, sleeping heads, sleeping buttocks, pubic hair, out of the flesh of dreaming knees. Each time a fruit bursts, it sprays juice into the air.

Meanwhile, the indigent hoist and pull; crack open boxes. This is a game, great fun. And justice, nah?

'South,' says Pilar, directing. 'Towards Pretty Town. And you take the high hills.'

A man says a shoal of water creatures will take him across to Pretty Town – 'Anybody want to come?' and there is clamouring and excitement.

They hoist boxes on their heads and strap them to their bodies and some simply take bundles; each no more than he or she can manage. So beautiful: your heart would hurt if you could see them.

The sweetness rose from the earth and shimmered in the air.

'Oh, Intiasar going to *shit* himself, today,' said somebody.

'Hurry,' murmured Pilar.

He took seven toys, small ones, for his back had never recovered from childhood.

✱

Across the Dead Islands, look and see! Look! A tall youth, breathing hard, arms pumping. Fast, fast. Watch him: handsome, running like his daddy-o.

✱

Tan-Tan dreams about his unborn son and how much it would hurt to watch Lyla wean him. He dreams of walking the night, rocking and singing the whimpering child to sleep. Of Lyla, coming out of the sea, trailing shells and a smile, for he still isn't sure in the heart of him, that she will ever love him. Dreams of Anise, forgiving him. She could: she is made like that.

He dreams of Blowsnaught – pig-dog! – waking before him, pushing through the physalis, dodging his own shit, passing a teenage couple playing catch with the fruit on the street. Dreams of the man's peremptory voice: 'Look here for me now, jump over to that window and call through, wake the man you see in there, tell him I sorry, yes?' and the footfalls of the youths towards his sleeping body. He dreams he can see them shoving and laughing, and that he can see himself, lying on the ground.

'Look how he spread out,' says one of the girls. 'Mister? Mister! The brother there said we must come and wake you, say he sorry, what he do you?'

Tan-Tan dreams himself snoring just before the dream ends. 'Why he not – why he . . . ?' asks the boy.

Tan-Tan Joseph died of a single red physalis: all it took to block his throat.

✳

In Battisient, the town crier ran through the streets and called out: only one hour until beauty contest start. 'Pretty-pretty girls,' he called. 'All good things come today!' Then his mouth filled with glimmering water and he couldn't say much of anything, anymore. People helped him to his feet when he fell down, leaking syrup from ears, nose, anus. He couldn't swallow the liquid quickly enough to breathe. A smart woman had an odd idea and threw him into the sea, and he swam out, restored.

Hundreds of Popisho citizens milled around the Grand Theatre, and up and down Carenage beach. Men winched torches into the trees, food stalls were set up and roasting had long begun. Children mingled excitedly. Where were the beauty queens, when would they come? There was rumour of something from overseas, some new treat from Intiasar. The children tripped over black insulated cables snaking up and down the sand and the men attending to the cables looked very important.

Old women busied themselves, sweeping up physalis and gossiping about their dreams.

'Old melons,' called a man, travelling the circumference of the Grand Theatre. 'Old melons and tomatoes.' Pronounced *tohmatiz*, like the elders. 'Twenty for a coin. Come give me your money.' He scolded a woman scowling at him. 'Sis, how you going to watch beauty contest without ammunition?'

'Is them things cause riot,' she sniffed.

'But is not *eggs*,' said the seller.

'Don't be so miserable,' said another woman. 'Nobody don't throw melon to *hurt* them. Only at the front of the stage.'

'Still,' said the first woman. 'Someone have to clean that. *We* live in Pretty Town. *You* don't have to clean it.'

The line into the Grand Theatre moved forward slowly.

Orange ribbons of graffiti growing on the walls, like fungus.

CHOOSE AN ALTERNATIVE

'Old melons,' called the man. 'Old melons, better than eggs.' He crushed physalis under his feet as he went. 'Don't buy no eggs.'

★

Governor Intiasar woke up, called someone to clean the fruit out of his office, then picked up the telephone when they were done. He made several calls, got up to check his office door was firmly closed and uncorked a good bottle of rum. It had been a trying day. And it wasn't done. Weddings and careless daughters and a radio interview that meant more blasted money to spend. And now nightmares, to rass. In the middle of the day.

Popisho was just too god-damned Popisho right about now.

He gulped at the bottle and waited for the burn to subside. His wife had called to say Sonteine was safe, and that was what he cared about the most. He didn't know exactly what mysterious female thing had happened, or who'd helped what and where, but the child said she had her wares back, firm and in place, and suffering no harm. So perhaps the sex ban had worked after all. He laughed out loud. Did no one yet *know* he was not to be trusted when he was in a bad mood? And wings, her mother said! Fill up the courtyard! Mrs Intiasar had sounded delighted. He couldn't wait to see them, right after the stupid beauty contest was over.

He'd believed Sonte when she was small and said cors going to be late, Pap. He trusted the word of his stubborn daughter, the same way he'd once trusted his son. She'd always been an independent child: determined and good-natured, despite her mother's obvious coldness. Filled up their place with friends. Even through all these years without magic.

Cors was a curse, anyway.

It wasn't really Sonteine's *sexual* indiscretion that had vexed him today; it was his own looming inability to fix things. But now all was well. If only everyone would *listen* to him. Had he not done his best for them?

He drank again. He'd dreamt rivers of money, running out of the windows of the warehouse, and from the engines of the export ships, into the sea.

People were just about palatable, when he had money. He poured white rum into his palm and patted it onto his neck and face. The problem was with *opinions*. What a quarrelsome,

384

loud people they were. That Hah woman was a prime example of unfortunate opinions, and he'd have to endure her again, this evening at the beauty contest.

After the election was over, the bribe to the radio stations would quietly change *her* life.

Woman radio host, indeed.

He sat very still for a time, biting his own tongue until he spat blood out onto the white anthurium under his window.

Pink mist rose off the hills and houses. In the three years he was overseas, he'd been feted in many countries. He saw cherry blossom trees in Korea and Cuban turquoise sea. Listened to lions roaring in a zoo in Romania. Drove through deserts, rode in aeroplanes, and looked at towering skyscrapers, covering so much space and land that he wondered how it was possible for the world to be so big and small at the same time. But he'd never seen the hills blush like here: every evening, at exactly forty-five minutes past eight.

So many precious things in this land, too many people. People were like butterflies. Zooting back and forth, streaks of colour and texture. Butterflies could only see in shades of red, green and gold: he liked that, and the proverbs of the old people. *Young butterfly never feel storm. True butterfly taste with them feet.*

And then there was moth.

He opened a drawer and slid out a box. Put his nose down to it. He'd never been a specialist in consumables; not for him, the fussiness of texture and pedigree. Who gave a damn, as long as a thing tasted good, felt good? But moth was something else. Conquest, that was what they tasted like. Before the cull five years ago, he hadn't ever taken more than a few butterfly with supper. But the moth rebellion had spawned tremendously interesting new varieties and one pink evening just like this, he'd reached out to a pile of the dead things, a present brought by some mewling landowner looking a tax rebate – just curiosity, mind you – and found himself . . . well, what to say?

All caught up and freshly inspired.

He hesitated, wondering if it was wise to take one now, so close to the evening's entertainments and responsibilities. A clear head was important. He balanced a bright green Lunar on his ring finger and licked off the scale dust. Save the thorax for last. One or two would be fine. Not like that damn self-indulgent macaenus boy. *He* knew how to manage his own destiny.

He'd proven he was more than a dirty-footed runner boy that was for sure. Awards and medals, women's adoration and easily acquired bodies. Men's jealousy, that was the sweetest part. If only he had some way to express the glory of what he'd been overseas. And the magnitude of his sacrifice. For Popisho! There had been too many questions, out in the wide world: about his background and how he ran *so* very fast. Where had he come from? What did they feed him back home? Yam and banana? Dasheen and coco? Where *was* home? He'd lied for a while; given other small nations the attention. Shared some of his green-black and gold cors.

But it really wouldn't do for people to find their way to Popisho, asking questions about magic.

Everything he did was for this place. People objected when he started selling the toys overseas, but look at them now, with their telephones and their electricity and blasted Xavier Redchoose, with his modern cook-pan and refrigerators.

'Make the god-thing easier, don't it, cook-man?'

The sound of his own voice startled him.

Look at him, running-running! What it good for?

They might think it worthless, but he still did the circumference of Packer Mountain five times every morning.

He'd had a good life until this bastard orange graffiti come up-come up, making it crazy. But that was fine, too. Eventually the man would have to reveal himself, and when he did, he would know what to do with him. He might even challenge him to a race.

See how far *he* could run in 9.58 seconds.

In the meantime, everybody jollificating with wedding plans, and even macaenus playing along like a coney with milk-teeth.

Bertrand Intiasar looked up and smiled at his oldest friend, tapping and coming through the door.

Leo spoke, repeated himself, then said it again.

Intiasar stared. He stuck his little finger into his left ear and scraped at the wax there, as if removing it would make a difference to this news.

Leo was taciturn, silent. He was soft and careless in a way that had always been financially useful. But his genius partner was neither a liar nor a joker.

'*What* you just said to me?'

Leo said it again.

'Somebody empty the toy warehouse.'

Intiasar exhaled through his nose.

'But the next shipment was in there.'

'Not anymore.' Leo spoke gently.

'But how – *how* is this possible? Where was security?'

'Sleep.'

'But who – ?'

'Look like the indigent do it. I have it on good account they didn't do no fruit-sleeping.' Leo cleared his throat. 'We don't know why.'

'That's –' he did some swift calculations in his head – 'that's over two million coin.'

'Is it?' Leo was looking at him carefully, but he was too busy trying to swallow the enormity of it all. In truth, it was closer to 3.7 million.

Absentmindedly, he offered the moth box. Leo shook his head.

Well now. He quite knew what to do. When people betrayed you, you crushed them, like butterflies.

'And someone is here to see you,' said Leo.

'You think I want any visitor?'

'I think you want to see your son.'

Intiasar took another moth, balanced it on his finger, his tongue, swallowed. Breathed.

'Romanza?'

'Is one son you have.'

He hadn't seen Romanza for years. Except once, when he was out running, he thought he did: in the distance, congregating with a few others, like beasts at the river.

'Berts,' said Leo. 'He waiting.'

One more of these moth, a little one, and he was done. He coughed on the antennae. His head swam. Leo's bottom lip waggled; a lizard outside became ten. Hallucinations. Bearable.

'Berts, man. Look how long since you see him. You not young, anymore.'

'You say indigent at my door?'

'Is *Zaza*—'

Intiasar stood up and adjusted his tunic. Moth dust and rum stains – he would have to change. Go to the contest, choose a winner, announce election to a rapturous crowd, go home. The moth might make the women look even more beautiful.

Sonteine was marrying tomorrow. Simple. Get business done.

'Tell him I said he's to run.'

'How you mean?'

'Just what I said. Tell him to run and find a yard to sleep in, tonight. Tell him not to make night catch him on the road. And don't look in nobody face.'

Leo hesitated, rocking back and forth.

'You—'

'What I said?'

'And the warehouse . . .'

'What I *said*, Leo?'

Outside, pink mist bled upwards, over the rooftops, tingeing the clouds. It made him think of being young and buying suck-suck, two for a centime. The suck-suck man, at the corner of the road, hacking ice with a machete, shaving it soft, spraying it with sugar syrup, eating his own ice and calling to the girls. The girls, calling back.

What you name, suck-suck man? What cors you have?

There were far too many indigent crawling on the road these days. It was best to cull vermin. Before it got too bad.

Oh yes, indeed.

28

Gideon seemed to know exactly where to find the dark-skinned young man they were looking for, sitting on the ground of a quiet, fronded courtyard, bowed over his own knees, cupping his ears as if he expected his head might fall off.

The grounds around them were some of the most sumptuous Xavier had ever seen, even in the growing dark. Labyrinthine. Towering old trees. This was generations of tending and planning and love and coin.

He couldn't believe he'd let go of the fisher-boy's moth. Into the good and healing Dukuyaie breeze. He could imagine it tumbling over and over itself, a tiny red-tipped toxin, up into the free air, lost to the mountains.

'O, Dandu,' said Gideon. 'You sleeping?'

The dark man shot upright, a distant, startled look in his grey eyes.

'Good evening!' he said.

The boy pointed at Xavier. 'Mamma said to bring *him* here.'

'If you are indisposed . . .' Xavier murmured.

The young man tapped his right ear. 'No, no! Please. You are welcome. I am Dandu Brenteninton, Leo's son.' He flicked the ear again, like an animal with an itch, and patted the boy's head. 'Which one *you* is? You sound like a Gideon.'

The boy giggled. '*That* is a macaenus, you know!'

Dandu raised an eyebrow. 'Is it now? But your mother is a macaenus, too.'

'She a girl. That is a *man* macaenus!'

390

'You know, I doubt it makes much of a difference at all. Thank you, Gideon.'

They watched the little boy run through the grounds.

'Macaenus. I wish my father was here to greet you, but he out dealing with the nuptials.'

Xavier smiled. How was he supposed to have this conversation, when all he felt was numb? His hand crept up to his collarbone, pushing at the skin, as if the pouch might still be dangling there. He blinked.

'Macaenus?'

He forced himself to speak. 'I apologise. I come without warning.'

Tap-tap of the ear. 'No, no. The apology is mine, please excuse the fidgeting.' His voice made Xavier think of chimes in Temple. 'I have a listening cors and I am a little *sensitive* this evening. It will pass any minute, now.'

'Listening – ?'

'I can hear several miles. But the point is not distance. It is, perhaps, depth. Layers of sound.' Dandu lowered his harpsichord voice. 'I have been writing a book about the sounds of the weather. The first chapter is about sunshine. I have been working on it for two years and I think I am nearly finished . . .' Tap, tap, his fingers. 'Sometimes I think I want to take Sonteine and go over the sea. I know that is not our way, but I would like to hear hot days in different places.'

It was a wonderful idea, sunshine sounds.

'Listen to me, talking about myself. I must thank you, from the bottom of my heart, o macaenus. Sonteine told me you run a strict and arbitrary dining list, and to be included, we so appreciate it.'

Did they, now.

391

'Sonteine wonders if she should eat your food with her fingers, or utensils. Whether you will come with the food, or send a server, and if it *is* you, will she be able to eat, from nerves. And what she should wear, as if her wedding gown won't be good enough.' Dandu smiled, gently. 'Please don't tell her I told you this, she is very proud. When she turned eighteen, she stayed up all night, hoping to be lucky enough to get her invitation to dine with you the next day. She says – how does she say it? – that macaenus is not about food, but the love good people have for each other.'

'Really,' mumbled Xavier.

'. . . so when we announced we were to be married, her father said he would come and beg your indulgence.'

Xavier snorted.

Dandu tapped his forehead. 'She will be very sorry to have missed you.' He grinned. 'I am not sorry. I do not know whether I could bear to watch her look at you with shining eyes.'

Dandu seemed so composed. The day before his own wedding Xavier couldn't catch his breath. Nobody had noticed. Perhaps he'd looked fine, too. Bougainvillea trees hustled and shee-shooed over them. What did Intiasar make of Dandu, this kind young man set to be his son-in-law? Was he a worthy replacement for Romanza? He seemed obliging enough. Romanza was not obliging. He was free and good, and he'd left him on a beach, hurting.

'Does love have a sound?' he asked.

Dandu smiled. 'Love is not a sound. It is a thing you do.'

It was helpful that he knew that.

'So you can't hear love?'

'Not so I could swear to it,' Dandu mused. 'Aha! Ears popped! That's better.' An elderly maid slipped into the courtyard with a tray of wine and water. 'This is Joisine,' said Dandu. 'Been with us forever. Like my mother, not true, Joisine?' The woman smiled and poured a good white wine. Xavier could see it was expensive. Appropriate. For him and his inappropriately stained tunic, and no shower after Des'ree's passion.

Well, now. He really couldn't contribute to *one* more piece of fuckery, today.

'Dandu. I really not sure I cooking that feast for you tomorrow night.'

Dandu's ears quivered. He might have grown whiskers and bared his teeth. 'But.' He smiled awkwardly. 'What of the radio competitions and the walkround? The stories? The ingredients you have already chosen?'

Xavier pointed at his bruised satchel, lying on the ground. 'That's it.'

Dandu raised his eyebrows. 'What is it?'

'A few rose-tasting thorns. There *is* a goat in my yard, marinating.' He tried to smile. 'I suppose I could make you a pot of mannish water.'

The young man started, visibly. 'You think I *need* such a thing?'

'I was joking.'

Dandu sat down and then stood up again. Joisine watched him, nervously.

'Pardon, macaenus. So you will *not* be cooking? Or you will be cooking . . . what? Goat? And . . . thorns?'

The fisher-boy's moth had been waiting on his decision all day: to take it or not take it. On balance, he'd thought he would take it. On this anniversary. The likelihood had been a kind of anchoring. Now he felt like the leaves, whirring in the dusk breeze, pulled off their trees, no moorings.

And Dandu looked like someone had punched him.

'I understand your disappointment,' Xavier said.

Dandu sat down, then bolted upwards again. 'You think I care about any rass *food*? That is the *least* of my *bumboclaaht* problems right now! I was so *close*, and really macaenus, is *you* come and interrupt *me*!'

Xavier stared. 'Close to what?'

Joisine placed a hand on Dandu's shoulder, but he didn't seem to notice. 'You think a man can be too nice?' The young man didn't wait for an answer. 'My girl cousins, my ama, all the maids in here, Joisine, you too, all telling me to give her *time*. So I sitting here, waiting and trying to *hear* her, so at least I know where she is and she alright. She make this little *tacka-tacka* sound on the floor when she walk, like a goat-kid. She say I not to call her no goat, but nothing don't sound like that in the world except Sonteine and a goat-child. And because of me, marriage over before it begin.' He glared again. 'You think sometimes a man can be too nice?'

'I—'

'Everything in me say: go find her. But all the women say hush, she going come back for her own wedding. You think I marrying a woman just because tomorrow is the *date* to married? Fire burn that and her daddy blasted election!' He put his hands on his hips. 'Well?'

'What is the question?' Xavier wanted to smile at the young man's *perfect* indignation but Dandu would surely lose the rest of his temper.

'You think sometimes a man can be too nice?' snapped Dandu.

'Surely.'

'Yes! I did know Sonteine was unfair, cursing me so. It was *slippery*.' He turned to the maid. 'Macaenus not cooking no blasted feast anymore, and you know what I think that mean,

Joisine? *I think that mean everything come to bump!* Tell Papa
I gone on the road to find my woman.'

'But Missa Dandu . . . you not supposed to move from here
before wedding, the gods will be offended . . .'

'Macaenus here know gods better than mere me and you! *You*
would do the same thing, don't it, macaenus?'

'I don't know the problem.'

'I lose it,' Dandu growled. 'There you go.'

'What?'

'Her private parts.'

'You do what?'

'Drop it in the river, gone.'

Xavier bit the inside of his cheeks to stop his laughter.

'You *lost* it? How did you find it?'

Dandu looked stricken. Joisine flapped her skirts.

'Don't upset yourself, Missa D—!'

'Somebody must have stolen it!' roared Dandu.

'Missa Danduuuu . . .'

'Joisine, I *begging* you go inside if this upsetting you! Because
I going find the man responsible and kill him!'

'Killing not really so useful . . .' said Xavier. Of all the conversations in the world to have, he could not have expected this
one. The melancholy maid scuttered back towards the house.

'I going,' Dandu said. 'Thank you, macaenus. For your *time*.'

'I think you need a plan.'

'You did have a plan when you leave your house this morning? Because it don't sound so.'

'Probably why *you* need one.'

Dandu scratched his ear, like a puppy with fleas. 'If you can't
even *cook* when that is what you *are*—'

He was just about to tell Dandu that he never *have* to be

there, and did he know that his father-in-law sending threats on a *child*, and to add a few choice and vulgar suggestions to boot, when they were interrupted by a very loud sound in the night air above them.

Something breaking through the treetops. Something fussing and cursing and joyous.

Taka-taka-taka.

Xavier would forever think of standing in that palatial garden, watching Dandu smile at Sonteine Intiasar flying towards them, over the trees.

She managed to land well, flat on her feet, breathless and beaming. There were pieces of bark in her hair and a scratch on her chin; her cheeks and robe were speckled with mud. She beat her billowing pink robe back down to her calves. The four huge wings on her back click-clacked, scraping against tree branches. They had deep black edges, as if someone had tried to smoke them, and eyelets like kohl-rimmed holes. Xavier had an impression of antiquity: they were artefacts, wrestled from some forgotten, elephantine building.

Dragonfly wings.

'Hair dirty, clothes dirty! And birds just looking at you like woman not supposed to be up here, move out of my rass way. I going to get pants, you hear? I don't care if Papa vex and call me a man.' Sonteine put her hands on her hips, lurched forward, righted herself and chuckled.

This was the girl he'd cursed all day? Xavier grinned. She was *magnificent*.

She had the same heart-shaped face as Romanza and matching shot-gold black hair, except hers was a sidereal froth on top of her head, with gold freckles to match. Where Romanza was thin and red, she was dark and strong: her shoulders broad for a

396

woman; small-hipped; an athlete's thighs. Her brother's smile. He felt a surge of affection.

Twisting her wings like a little girl showing off a new dress.

'You see them?' Sonteine glowed at Dandu. 'Them pretty, eh?'

Dandu disappeared around his fiancée, wings blocking him from view, calling out: 'A patch of blue is here, wait, purple and red stripes here! Sonte, can you feel this?'

Sonteine giggled and preened.

'How this feel?'

'Like mosquito biting me!' More giggling. 'Stop that!'

'And this?'

'Can't feel a thing.'

'But I bending it!'

'Don't bend nothing, fool!'

Dandu dipped back under the wings and tweaked her bottom. He put his arms around her waist and tried to pick her up.

'They're heavy,' he said. '*Substantial!*'

'Is not the wings,' she purred. 'Is the pum-pum.'

'*Shhh!*'

Sonteine slapped his hip. 'I find it and put it back, why you think I couldn't wait to come?'

'Gods, Sonte. Hush—'

She flapped, teetered and fell into his chest, struggled upright. 'I going behave myself. I know I not even supposed to be here. *Again!* So who come to visit?' She twinkled at Xavier.

He twinkled back. She was infectious. It occurred to him that perhaps he'd never seen a whole person before.

'Can I?' he asked.

Sonteine shrugged her shoulder. The top right wing poured forward, undulating between them. Xavier ran a cautious finger across the thickest vein. It reminded him of stiff fishing net, but Sonteine moved them as if they were liquid. The patterns created by the criss-crossed veins were gloriously convoluted: thousands of opaque squares, larger at the top, impossibly tiny down below, trailing in the deep grass. He squinted: the veins were flecked and sticky.

'They still bloody,' said Sonteine. 'Tear *right* through my robe.' Dandu fluttered worriedly, and she kissed him. 'You like my lovely cors?'

Some insects never grew wings, especially the females; others only grew them at particular times in their life cycle. The migratory phases of locusts. Polymorphic butterflies. Mating cycles.

'They are gorgeous,' Xavier said.

Sonteine nodded vigorously. 'What good taste, Mr Stranger. My name is Sonteine.'

'I know your brother.'

'Eh.' She was so bright-eyed and fluffy. '*You* seem to know everybody, but I don't know you.'

'O, Sonteine,' said Dandu. 'Shut up a minute.' He whispered into her ear.

Sonteine froze, quivering.

'You too *lie!*' The wings beat frantically, making enormous gusts of air, raising dust and stones and grass. Xavier and Dandu backed away, coughing. 'Dandu, I don't *believe* you! You have our macaenus standing in the yard like a puss' – her voice rose to a shriek – 'and you never *tell* me? Wait, macaenus! Oh my gods, *wait!*'

She stood very still, one eye closed, concentrating. The top right wing folded lengthways, then again, inched closer to her shoulder blade and sank into the flesh. Her torso bulged then smoothed, as if the wing had never been there. It would have been quite fitting to bow. Sonteine rotated the shoulder. There was something intimate about the transformation, like a woman dressing after love. He certainly should not be here; this was for them.

Sonteine leaned against Dandu and groaned. Her body began to swallow the second wing.

'It hurt?' he asked anxiously.

'No . . . just . . . *breathless* . . . not used to . . .' The wing-folding seemed an impediment to speech. Third wing: fold, sink, ripple. Hands on her waist, back curved, breathing deeply.

Fourth.

'So *beautiful*,' breathed Dandu.

Without the wings, Sonteine was an ordinary and happy-looking young woman. Hands out, head bowed, eyes lowered in deference.

'If I ever *know*, o macaenus. So *disrespectful* . . .'

That was quite enough of that. Xavier put his hands out for hers. He could feel the wings still rustling and locking inside her.

'Greetings, Sonteine Intiasar.'

She gulped.

'That is one *rass* cors you have.'

'Yes. But-but – macaenus. Why are you here *now*?'

She looked so very worried, but now she was in front of him, he knew *just* what to do about her feast.

★

He went to see Anise on the night before her wedding. Went to see her unmarried face one last time. He still fantasised about her, of walking the curve of the island rim with her, sand belching up pieces of throbbing moss and concave mauve shells. He imagined them naked together and standing on the beach, him oiling her from the soles of her feet, soaking her thighs in ginger oil, up to her throat and back down, spanning her waist and pouring oil on her fat, firm thighs. He imagined dressing her for her wedding: cuff, blue silks, earrings, anklets, sandals, stroking her scalp, asking, *you sure? You happy?* And *yes*, she would say, *yes, yes*, eyes distant, *yes, yes, all is well*, and then she'd turn him around and trace his spine with her tongue.

He had accepted the inevitable. He just wanted to see her face.

Anise had ushered him in. She was wearing a thin robe for bed. Her wedding dress hung over the door. She asked about his health, smiled when he said he felt good and needed no moth, placed his carefully wrapped wedding gift on her kitchen table, leaned forward, grabbed the back of his neck and began, clumsily, to kiss him.

He was astonished. How welcoming and demanding these lips were and why was his own mouth so still? Anise's hands were in his dreadlocks and she was taking his hands and putting them on her body: in the small of her back, where it seemed there was something jumping-jumping, and on her fragrant scalp. She was pulling him towards the pallet and her lap, where he'd vomited just weeks ago, and he was so shocked at her lust it took him some moments to actually hear what she was whispering.

Smell me, Xavier. Hurry up.

He shook his head, confused.

Eat me.

She ran her hands down his chest, pulling at the drawstring at his waist, cupping his hardening penis through cotton, both whimpering at the feel of that, her lips back and forth between his mouth and chest; frantic, like she didn't know how to begin.

No, he said, because he could still smell his vomit on her, and she needed a better man than he was.

She pushed away from him, eyes tangled, hair wild, one breast free, the nipple knotted. She looked so shocked he wanted to comfort her.

She dove forward again, sipped his mouth.

Stop. Stop. Stop. And now she did. Now she had to.

Her shame made him tremble.

Get out, she said.

All of that night, insomniac on Nya's pallet, he found Anise's secrets on his body. A handful of sweat, which he licked off his fingers; a gold-coloured snail that cracked as he rolled over; a prayer on paper under his armpit; brittle glass beads in one ear; dried saffron in his hair. Her secret feelings left marks at the edge of his mouth and freckles on his chest. He half expected Nya to draw back and say, *what's this?* to the secret desires Anise had left under his fingernails.

You done with the moth, said Nya. *I knew you could.* Except she didn't mean moth, she meant whatever else it was that might have gotten in her way.

Anise was the reason he'd wed with circles under his eyes, from lack of sleep and disappointment.

✳

Xavier peered into the black waves. He could just spot the wheeling white and blue lights over Pretty Town, the Grand Theatre in full swing. It was an easy swim. He ran his thumb

401

down his stubbled cheek. He wanted to bathe, shave and oil himself.

Would Anise mind him coming to see her? Did she remember him pushing her away from his body? If she minded, if she asked him to go, he would leave her be. But it had been a strange day, full of surprises and moments with sharp teeth. He'd seen how strong a healer had to be, stretching her back and leaning side to side to work out the kinks in her waist. Was she healthy and happy and safe? His head had been full of her, today of all days. It was still true that he'd never loved anyone like he had loved her, like Des'ree loved her children. Was that sad? He grinned; to skip around her body, admiring it, like Dandu at Sonteine's wings, that would be something.

He pushed his sandals into his satchel. Perhaps she would let him prepare the bush thorns in her kitchen. Peel them, pass them through a fine sieve, then through muslin. He would show her how to rub thorn juice between her palms, like a woman oiling her hair at night. Afterwards, she might lay him down for a massage: one, two, three, eight, ten of her silver fingers on his skin. She would feel the moth hunger on him, and how close he'd been to taking it. She would be proud of him, without saying a word.

I never, I never. Look at how close, but I never.

Seeing her face was necessary.

Around him, crickets sang hymns in the beach grass. His hands were grimy. He listened for signs of Nya for a while, just in case, wrapping the notebook in palm leaves from a nearby tree, knotting the satchel around his head. Perhaps she wasn't coming back to celebrate this anniversary. But he was going to return to the Torn Poem with this damn book intact, all the same.

402

He took the bag strap between his teeth. The salt air felt acid in his lungs as he waded into the surf; there was the smell of apples to it. He swam, strong strokes, head above water.

He wondered when Sonteine Intiasar would tell her daddy that macaenus come deliver his wedding feast early. How furious would Intiasar be? He found that he didn't care. It had been the right choice for Dandu and Sonteine. He knew by the way his hands had hummed, and the expression on Sonteine's face.

He smiled into the night air.

He intended to find Romanza in the bush. Take pudding in at least six flavours. Nothing as good as Des'ree's own, but everything the boy had said: *Bread pudding! Cornmeal pudding! Vanilla! Sweet potato!*

The sounds of the Pretty Town celebrations drew closer.

He swam on through the night sea, different from day sea, his head erect, protecting the satchel. Under the steely, flat surface of the water, chasms yawned beneath his thrashing feet, spewing new species: oil and scales mixing into nameless potions that baked in the moonlight and wrought cellular changes so minute only his ancestors would feel the effect.

Anise. Anise. Anise.

★

There were hundreds of people on Carenage beach, dancing and drinking up and down the long sandy strip. Coloured fires crackled, like hunched supernatural animals, flickering light across skin and faces and sand, so fast it made him blink.

Xavier trod water, sizing up the crowd and his best strategy. Most Pretty Town people knew him on sight, but much of this throng would be from other islands. He could rely on the pandemonium and the dark of back streets to act as cover as long as he got across the beach quickly. He looked up at the Torn Poem. Moue had lit blue lamps in the restaurant windows – it was their signal for good progress. He loved that woman. The embroidered goat would be fat with her herbs and juices and ready for the roasting; he'd bury it in his pit oven overnight, with cinnamon and allspice bark. He'd come to another decision: the goat was for family. Io, Chse and some of her little friends; Moue and her husband and their three children, Mamma Suth and Nya's father, perhaps Io's woman, if it was notice enough and his brother felt ready. Goat on its spit in the garden, so the children could help themselves with their hands. Fresh bread, roasted garden vegetables, Chse's favourite sweet things: tarts and cakes; ice cream with wonders inside. He should ask Moue what her children enjoyed.

Which direction was best?

Music, singing, laughter, flooding closer. His feet hit bottom. Fish flirted around his ankles. Go up the bank, under the sea grape trees. Or should he cut direct through the crowd and swagger?

Move, move. A singular, wavering man would draw attention.

'Macaenus?'

Water: splashing and churning. Xavier peered through the torchlight.

'*Macaenus?* Is you that?'

A pot-bellied man waved from the beach lip. Xavier groaned. Sander, the owner of his local rum bar. A kind, if obsequious neighbour. Sander was standing with a crowd of happy, noisy men, all of them peering over a bonfire and across the water at him.

'See him there! Look macaenus coming!'

Bumborassclaaht.

He considered turning back, but they were on him before he could swim away. It might have been as many as twenty, he couldn't tell, all wading into the waves cheering, like dressed for carnival, bright pink and blue paint smeared across their eyelids; images of snakes and suns across their wet chests; false eyelashes in silver and black; embroidered masks above pumping fists, singing. So much *noise!* Impossible to command them away, banging his back companionably, pulling him to shore, hoisting him into the air and onto a pair of strong shoulders.

'Man who hard!' the men sang. 'We defend all man who hard!'

Xavier swayed, wanting to clutch the skull below him for balance. What was this new fuckery? He yelled through the merry fray.

'Sander! What the rass is going on?'

'Macaenus! We been waiting to greet you! I have a man stationed on every beach and at your place!'

'*Why?*'

Sander cupped his hands around his mouth, but he couldn't hear the answer. A great many women were flocking towards them, adding to the clamour. In the distance, applause erupted over the Grand Theatre.

'Every man is with you!' Sander was yelling. 'Every man!'

'What?'

'Fuck that song! We don't believe a word!'

He groaned. Of course. How could the macaenus be allowed to return to the capital unsupported, with such disrespectful penile rumours abounding? Men like this would see it as a matter of principle.

'Man who hard! We defend man who hard!'

There was nothing to do but wait until they put him down. He gazed at the dancing girls.

Some of them were booing him.

He stared, astonished, as one brightly bedecked woman cut her eye and turned on her heel. Others were frowning and sucking teeth: he could see their lips moving. An older woman held his eye, flipped her robe up and touched her toes, exposing a bare, rippled backside and the quickest sight of a twinkling aperture.

Oh, the women were *vex*. What was happening? Des'ree once warned him it was *most* important for a male macaenus to keep women on his side.

Why?

You ever see a woman curse the gods?

Well, yes. Weekly.

So they look like they 'fraid of you?

'Man who hard! We defend man who hard!'

The men carrying him headed for the Torn Poem; that was a mercy. Cutting through carousers, passing street poets and magicians, children juggling fish, sellers and their wares. He felt battered and regretful of the women, but the men were hilarious: the one carrying him doing it so effortlessly, the rest pouring liquor down their throats and bodies. When he was younger, he'd wished to be this kind of man. Dog, knife, boat, house, woman: that was all they needed, and in that order.

Sander waved a bottle at him. He remembered the excellence of the man's cellar. He needed something special for the family lunch. Rum, Io was a man who appreciated rum.

'Sander! You have any good rum?'

Sander cupped a hand behind his ear.

'Rum!' screamed Xavier.

His voice cut through the crowd, and they chanted even louder.

'*Give him rum! Give him rum!*'

Up ran two agile men, clambering across the arms of the dancing crowd, clinging to each other's hair, feet balanced on mouth corners and ear lobes, like spiders. Before he could count to three or curse, they were standing *on* him, although he could barely feel them at all, balanced like acrobats, one per shoulder, feet clinging like marsupials. In the last few sweaty seconds before they did it, he made the mistake of opening his mouth to protest. Geysers of alcohol poured down from bottles, pitchers, mugs, handed up to the delicate, weightless men, streaming down his hair and into his face. Gasping, breathless, he tried to roar again. The man balancing single-footed on his right shoulder poured sugar rum straight down his throat.

And that was the start of it.

29

The sun took a breath and slipped below the waves; it was finally dark when Anise joined the line up to the Grand Theatre entrance, still squeezing the worst of the ocean out of her skirt.

She wasn't the only wet woman there, salty robes dripping, using their palms to flash-off eager, jostling men. Step too far from home and you were bound to buck-up sea, river or waterfall eventually. But she couldn't help feeling conscious of her dark nipples, exposed through her sheer white robe. She tweaked the material away from her flesh, hands crossing and uncrossing, and caught the eye of a dripping elder, watching her discomfort.

The older woman spread her heavy arms, cleavage long and squeaky with moisture, beaming scattered teeth.

'Is only breast, sis!'

Only breast, yes. She could walk through a wall, so who could question her, this day?

She let her arms dangle, felt simmering energy flowing into her wrists and fingers. Put her shoulders back. She was aerated. Her chin rose. If she could not relax here, where else?

The older woman applauded her then turned away, distracted by the clamouring, undulating, ripe crowd. A man in blue sang, his clear, lovely contralto reaching for the tin moon. Moths played above Anise's head; buzzing brown-and-white harmless things, scattered with olive spots. She lifted her hands up as if they might come to her.

Chattering children slid through the dust, fingers wagging, elbows wide, a parody of their mothers.

'Beauty contest! Beauty contest!'

'You can't be beautiful, you a *boy*!'

'I can be *beautiful*!'

She allowed herself to study them, these Popisho children. Everything they did was pronounced: chewing, walking, kicking. Elasticated, elongated things. How earnest they were! Red, black, all shades of brown, making miniature thunderstorms between their fingertips, blowing themselves into huge and circular shapes, speaking so loud they could be heard in the next island, speaking so softly the insects understood them, and in the case of one very dark-skinned boy, removing dripping red organs for his friends' amusement, including his oesophagus then, with particularly slithery aplomb, his entire backbone, which loop-de-looped through the earth like some bony snake before he seized it and swallowed it back into place.

Lyla and Tan-Tan, having a *child*. A boy. Strong, too. Or so it had felt, under her fingers. When had he planned on telling her? Soon? Never?

She could see the Torn Poem in the distance and lights blazing in the windows. Two, three, four of them: blue and white. Did Xavier light the lamps, or was he too grand for that? She imagined him stretching up, the shadow of his lightly muscled stomach against cotton. Pushing his sleeves up his arms. Shaking his 'locks out of the way. She was aroused by the memory, her reinstated pum-pum soft against her wet underwear. If he was to come upon her now, maybe she could smile, and ask him how he was, and hear his answer without worrying about what she was going to say next.

★

She had last seen him the night before her wedding, walking out through her door, her newly confessed love smeared across his mouth and arms and penis. After he was gone, she had lain down on the kitchen floor and looked up at a kaleidoscopic hummingbird hovering near her candle. She climbed on a chair wearing nothing but her wedding cuff and pulled stems and leaves and suckers out of the little trails Xavier had left on the ceiling. They sagged with overripe pineapples, dripping black and gold.

Xavier was the reason she'd wed with circles under her eyes, from lack of sleep and disappointment.

★

'Move up in the line nah, lady!' a child in a headwrap jerked her out of her memory. The child's father said she was not to be so damn out of order, talking to adults so. He pointed up at the dark cliff to the Torn Poem. 'If you too renk, you never going to eat macaenus food when you big.'

The child snorted indignantly.

Anise caught sight of a tall youth, slipping like an aquatic creature from one shadow to another. She liked spotting indigent, rustling through undergrowth, but this young man was not happy, nostrils quivering, head down. Beautiful hair.

Gone, like ink, before she could smile and make him feel better.

Her portion of the excited crowd finally passed through the gates and into the open-air Grand Theatre auditorium, its tall flaming lamps casting light on the high-shine limestone walls. Food and clothing stalls doing busy exchange; clink of coins and song; friends unfurling into each other's arms; something smelled like rotting blossom.

Anise found a corner and sat down to examine her surroundings. She felt quite self-consciously alone. She and Ingrid would be looking food by now, before the contest start, sucking shrimp heads.

The huge stage looked the same as it always had, the same thick pink curtain waiting to rise. But there were heavy-shoed men patrolling the perimeter, tracking back and forth. Higher perimeter gates, perhaps.

A ripple moved down the pink curtain, as if something breathed there.

'Nobody can't say Intiasar not spending money!'

'That is a distraction, man. I waiting on the alternative.'

'Months I hearing about rass alternative and I don't see the man reveal himself!'

'How you know is a man?'

'Only a man have time to be writing things all over.'

A burst of artificial light interrupted the musing. The crowd rumbled. The curtain began to peel back. Anise got to her feet as people rushed closer to the stage. She blinked.

Instead of the usual auditorium wall, a new contraption rose before them. Taller than her house, like the biggest painting canvas in the world! Security men ran around the screen, pulling intestinal black cables behind them. The air filled with crackling noises. People blocked their ears, the crowd chatter amplified with every electrical screech. Wide-eyed children clutched their mothers' skirt-knots and sucked their thumbs. The stage might have stretched across the moon. Strange apparatuses winched skywards, swinging above their heads.

The crowd gasped and pointed. They could see *themselves*, spreading across the thing.

Anise crouched. What cors was this? But even as the thought

rose, she knew it was no magic. Something entirely foreign threatened. She didn't want to see any part of her up there, stretched and wordless.

'Look, look!' someone yelled.

A woman was walking into the middle of the stage.

Anise's hand flew to her throat.

The woman stopped, still and alone. Behind her on the screen, her twenty-five-foot doppelgänger's eyes were downcast; they could see each hair of her eyebrows; the texture of her long patchwork robe in soft grey and blue; the pores in her face and the black and silver beading in her short, tight natural hair.

Slowly, the woman raised her head. She placed a single finger to her smiling mouth, waiting for their silence. Her lips were the same colour as her dark eyes. The crowd stared, open-mouthed, as she moved her left hand down to her hip, spiralling fingers, mischievous smile. Everyone knew the impending gesture, but to *see* such a moment, on this vast new apparatus, oh! it didn't seem possible.

Anise watched the falling wrist, breathless. Who *was* she?

The screen woman flicked up the skirt of her robe to show them a heavy, old-fashioned cuff, black and locked against her dimpled thigh.

She was not a foreign thing; she was one of them.

They roared their appreciation.

Anise flung her arms up, letting the sound envelop her. Drums began, echoing out across their bodies. Miss Pretty Gyal! How had she forgotten this excitement, or ever felt she was alone?

The black-cuffed woman began to dance across the stage, hands at hips, writhing her waist, bending forward, face cracked open like the sun, backside just fine.

'Dance just *like* that, sis!'

'*Shake out the coconut oil on them!*'

The woman took a bow and raised an appreciative fist.

'*Popisho!*'

Anise cheered back with everybody else.

'Welcome, welcome, welcome to the annual Pretty *Gyal* International Beauty Contest! I am Hah, daughter of Lus. And the pretty girls are *coming*!'

It was the woman from the radio. How wonderful.

'Hear me though, they could be pretty like *money*, nobody here winning tonight without . . . what?' Hah cupped a hand behind one ear. '*Lyrics!* Because all of we in Popisho . . . what?'

'. . . love argument!' chorused the crowd.

Hah leaned forward.

'What you say? All of we in Popisho . . . ?'

'*Love argument!*' yelled Anise.

'That's what I like to hear! We have eleven beautiful finalists, wearing the wonderful clothing of our islands. They going to show us frocks from designers in . . . north Dukuyaie!'

'Yes, girl! That's me!' Anise yelled as loud as she could.

The crowd around her grinned.

'Let me hear you cry out for . . . Dukuyaie west! Because I am a west fishing girl inside here tonight, people!'

'Yes, we see how you wet!' yelled a man in the audience, to general hilarity.

Hah rolled her eyes.

'You think I can't handle slackness, nah? Mind yourself! We also going to have designers showing from east and south Battisient' – more cheering – 'you know they bringing the *drama*, boy!' A group of women dressed in feathers and gold began to chant, 'Pretty Town-ooh-Pretty Town – !'

'Anybody going to take out they pum-pum, make we judge that?' It was the same joker.

Laughter and hissing from the women.

'Man, you don't see child in here?'

'Fling him out!'

Hah wagged her finger. 'You know is serious things you taking to make joke, boy!'

The man scowled. 'You the joke, Miss what you name? Hah, daughter of Lus? Is you telling big man to take Governor Intiasar *fuckery* sex ban serious!'

More hissing.

Hah smiled calmly. 'So you *not* taking it serious? Man who treat woman underneath like a joke *never* going please them when night time come!' She blew the heckler a kiss. 'You have things to *learn*, handsome! You want to be *my* acolyte?'

The man laughed appreciatively. She was so good.

'Enough politics in here tonight! We come for *fun*! Eleven must become two, so we need to start the cutting, and for that, we going to need *judges*! First on stage and here to do the job, we have businessman, philanthropist and pillar of the community, Jarrett Bartholomew *Garson*!'

Anise sucked her teeth hard. That same bastard who'd fucked Mixie and run, had he *paid*, in the end? Strolling onto the stage and waving like he was anybody special. The crowd cheered. Garson took his seat and flourished a pencil importantly. Behind him, onscreen, the pencil was near big as a tree. She wished he could see her, glaring at him.

'And we have someone *else* who know all about beauty.' Hah grinned slyly. 'Oh, oh, oh, *macaenus* . . . !'

The crowd exploded with excitement. Anise swallowed, heart thumping so hard, she hiccuped.

414

'Don't him dicky break?' a woman cried. Anise gave her such a poisonous look she ducked her head and moved on.

Hah fanned herself in mock faint and beckoned backstage.

'The one and only *Des'ree De Bernard-Mas!*'

Oh thank the gods.

You nearly piss yourself.

I never.

You did though.

Well, that's true. Anise grinned.

Eh-eh, said the voice. *What a way you mood get better.*

Des'ree came on to music and danced with Hah. She looked barely fifty, wearing a sleeveless carmine robe, her bare arms scattered with topaz jewellery.

Xavier's ex-lover, he'd told her all about Des'ree.

'I happy to see *every* kind of pretty gyal backstage waiting to come on,' Des'ree said. 'Big batty, dark skin, slave-hair, big foot, all of it.'

'Wah,' said somebody, scornfully. 'But you know is the light-skin, tall-hair girl going to win.'

Hah embraced Des'ree, the women whispering in each other's ears. Des'ree took her seat. Her arms blazed when she waved. She seemed to ignore Garson.

The most formidable woman he ever met, that was what Xavier said.

'And finally, that man you *all* been waiting to see and hear from, the man, they might say, of the hour, if not the whole *weekend*, that same man who run off my show today, left me-one there by myself—' The crowd roared with laughter and approval and Hah chuckled. 'I nearly bawl. But we going to *forgive* him for all of that, don't it, Popisho? We going welcome him . . . ready? *Bertie, oh!*'

415

Anise watched the mixed reaction as Governor Intiasar mounted the stage: some were up and cheering, but there was plenty hissing and stroopsing, and even people who threw things. Someone chanted, 'Goat, goat, goat, goat tax, goat, oh goat,' until a thick-chested man in heavy sandals came close. Which caused more hissing and clucking in the crowd.

Hah settled the Governor into his seat with exaggerated respect. Anise could see his lips pinching and his handsome facial hair on the screen. A blemish, it looked like an ingrown hair. This electrical screen was a stupid thing, Anise decided, and *very* exposing.

'You would never believe him try to tell her about her pum-pum today,' observed a young woman.

She'd forgotten how straight the Governor held his back and the sharpness of his jaw, as if he knew something normal people didn't. Her mother had called him a strong man on more than one occasion. Her mother would not have approved of Xavier, on his knees, or his moth tears.

'And now, finally, Popisho, we welcome the *queens!*'

Fanfare and more drums. The eleven contestants filed out, flashing eyes and waving to loud applause. You had to take a breath to let them all in. One large woman caught Anise's eye: glittering black skin, hair plastered close to her scalp like scarlet iron. She wore a man's lime-green suit. Popisho women never wore pants.

'Must be them slackers over in Dukuyaie sew such a thing!' said somebody.

'I suppose it keep her pum-pum safe.' The heckler was back.

Anise cut her eye at him and raised her voice.

'Yes ladies, you looking *good!*'

The heckler grinned.

416

'I see you, girl!' called Anise. 'Wear that pants!'

Other women joined in.

'Wear what make you feel good, girl!'

'Don't listen to any fool-fool man!'

The heckler leaned against a wall.

The debates began.

Hah announced the subject of each ten-minute round as the queens stepped forward in pairs, one then the other, delivering no more than five lines at a time. The skill of Miss Pretty lay in her speed. In her wit. Clarity. Point, counterpoint. For the love of argument.

And of course, she did have to pretty, *bad*.

Aiii, the crowd said, lifting their eyebrows, fingertips tingling in pleasure, touching shoulders. *Look at gods, this evening; what a piece-a body, hmmm!* Some contestants had come to stalk the stage and rage; others glided quietly, reasoning like pools of water, probing and pondering, flickering opulent fabrics. Others played: picked the words out of their mouths, picked jewellery and hats off themselves, admired it all and put them back again, shot the words out in clouds of acid jocularity.

Meat, skin, breath. Speech. Tongues. Eyes and bellies; pointed toes. Dip and fall back; come again. Hip-flick.

Anise watched Hah murmuring with the judges, Garson smirking, his hands too close to her body, the young host pretending not to notice. The Governor, more restrained, attentive, listening to Des'ree respectfully. *She* would know a sweet-mouthed swindler when she saw one, Anise thought.

Fast, faster, the women come and go. Anise closed her eyes so she could hear them even better.

This is what I see, the women say; this is what I think, feel, know, understand, wish. What I fear. Have learned. I am a witness. I am an auntie. I am a child. Here is my chest, the soles of my feet, my underneath. Anise remembers what Miss Pretty is for: opens her eyes to be with the women around her, sees the hugging and winking; mmmmm-*hm*, celebration; the grunts and nods; joins in with her own.

And sometimes the woman looking at you holds herself, her own shoulders, her breasts, she dances, touches her palm to her the bone of her pelvic girdle and pats her pum-pum.

Feeling part of something larger than yourself.

They watch Hah's light hand on moving shoulders, disqualifying candidates with a subtle tap – for hesitation; repetition; a superior idea skewering a chest bone; a lesser frock, crumpled, riding up, ripping. Queens: slipping regretfully off the stage and out of the fight.

Hah lingered near the redhead. Anise bit her lip, worried. There was something different about this suited woman, her fists clenched, hair gleaming. She was black-skinned as a good joke, surely it was time for such a woman to prevail? Shane her name was, older than the rest. Killing it.

Hah moved away from Shane and Anise breathed again.

The judges floated across the screen, examining stitching, finish, hot-pressing, hems, listening hard. Even Intiasar listened, it seemed to Anise, like he was hearing the Fatidique sing. The crowd listened, twisting faces, pointing to the sky in homage, clapping and stamping and flinging arms around each other. The heckler was still leaning against the wall, stroking his chin. He wore a blue boiler suit. Anise watched him cup his earlobe as Des'ree leaned forward to whisper in Garson's ear. The heckler sniggered.

'What?'

'Des'ree just tell Garson if he don't move back two feet with him dirty self, she going break all fifteen finger and pretend is the god-blood mad her, make she do it.'

Anise let him move closer.

'What a piece of pretty woman,' he said.

'Yes, they pretty, *bad*!' Two more queens were whisked away. She had a sore throat from yelling. And who could possibly choose between these last?

'Susmalis, Betti, Shane,' said the heckler. 'But I was talking you.'

'*Hush*,' said Anise.

Susmalis faltered. She had tiny light eyes and long eyelashes. The unforgiving screen showed the sweat at her temples, the delicate hairs on her upper lip you shouldn't be able to see at this distance. Evil.

Susmalis slumped. She wore a buttery robe, made in Duku-yaie, split at the sides to show off her strong legs. It was getting in her way.

'I don't *know*,' she said, again. 'Wait, nah.'

'Susmalis, you are . . . *out*!' cried Hah.

Now, these two. Standing, sweating, smiling at each other. The bigger, taller Betti, head to toe in scarlet moth-silk, making her final point. Swinging around so they can see the robe draped to her coccyx; see gleaming, ochre skin, fat and muscle.

Aaahh, breathed the crowd.

'*Yes, goodie!*' An ecstatic woman nearby was going hoarse. 'Show them the escoveich fish and okra *body*! The susumba, the cho-cho, the dasheen *upbringing*!'

Shane walked to the end of the stage and ripped open her lime jacket to reveal the bone-white corset cinching her surging waist. Stone buttons scattered.

'*Woiiii!* Boiled dumpling *body*! Boiled dumpling with the cornmeal in *iiiiiit!*'

Anise decided she would look *rass* good in that corset.

Behind Shane, Des'ree clapped and whistled. The heckler-man hooted.

And now all that was left was for the judges to go backstage and choose and come back and say who they chose.

Somebody would be vex; it was always the way.

★

Anise bought a yellow print robe while the crowd waited for the winning announcement; then she bought a handful of purple and yellow jewellery and a jaunty peach silk hat. She put on the hat. It was soft and floppy, and she loved it.

Nearby, a tired child whined; the mother slapped her. The little girl burst into tears.

Anise protested. 'Gods, sis, take *time*. What she want?'

The woman pointed at a cage of hummingbirds, manned by a whiskery merchant. 'She want one of that.' She rolled her eyes at the man. 'Let go the damn *bird*, I say. How you to sell bird, when they full up everywhere and free?'

They all three turned to stare at the bird seller.

He shrugged. 'A true.' He snapped open the cages. It was a good argument after all, and a woman had made it.

The hummingbirds lifted themselves into the air and the slapped child beamed, and nearly everyone in the Grand Theatre wondered about the sweet, cloying smell, but nobody commented on it.

It was only afterwards that everybody claimed it was them who said something first.

30

Romanza skirted his way across Pretty Town beach towards the Torn Poem, trotting against the Grand Theatre crowd. Mourning dust stained his pants up to the knees. He could smell frying onions, shrimp and popping fat. Curried goat and burning onion paste. Greasy-handed, happy people.

Final meals.

Before he left the Dead Islands he'd turned and looked back across the flat wasteland. Hundreds of indigent people, moving south, like a smooth, blue tributary through the twilight, boxes of toys under their armpits, on their shoulders, pushed before them, perched on heads. The image of Pilar's back and fingers, plucking him like an instrument. His chest hurt. Pilar was wrong, and so was his father.

Romanza moved faster through the crowd, muttering *excuse sis, sorry there*, coughing softly.

Uncle Leo had looked angry when he came back out to deliver his father's message. He'd watched them through the window and knew it wasn't going well. His father was thinner than he remembered, biceps flapping under his expensive clothing.

Go to my house, Zaza, said Leo. *Just for tonight.*

What was Uncle Leo worried about? Had he smelt it too, did he know the hurricane was on its way? He'd tried to ask questions, but Leo hugged him to his chest awkwardly, one-armed, murmuring sorries. How he should have come find him in the bush, way back when. His spirit told him to do so, but he hadn't listened to his own best judgement. Sonteine said he was well, he'd been reassured. *But look how you thin, boy! Grown up and handsome!*

No, Uncle Leo didn't know about hurricane, and he was running out of time.

We could talk, if you come by me, Zaza. I learning things. I trying to do better. But your father . . . he is not safe.

He should have come to Xavier first. How much time did he have? Would the macaenus even talk to him? Had he returned, yet? People would listen to a macaenus if *he* told them to shelter. Much more than any Governor. But a small piece of him had hoped his father would want to see him.

Would he have been able to step inside, with the roof bearing down?

A little girl sat on the steps up to the Torn Poem. She smiled, as if she recognised him.

'Did you see my friend, Olivianna?'

Romanza shook his head. 'Xavier inside?'

The child picked her nose and carefully wiped it on the front of her robe. 'But you must know her.' She patted her hips. 'She breathe out here and she have a eyes like you!'

'Little girl. You live here? You know the macaenus?'

'I am Chseline Rahtid Symphony Redchoose.' She clearly relished the sound of her own name; got up and tucked her arm into his, looping it several times. 'That macaenus is my uncle.' Her skin was cool, like brown snake in the bush.

Romanza grinned, despite everything.

'Is very important I find him.'

'I show you my papa, he can know.'

Io was standing at the back door of the restaurant. Those careful eyes on him, again. He wore a well-pressed blue tunic and trousers and his beard was newly trimmed. The brothers didn't look alike, but they had the same lurking power in their bodies.

This man would care. His graffiti proved his morality.

'Where is the macaenus?'

Io picked up the girl-child, who was plucking at his knees.

'I can go and find Olivianna?'

'Not now, baby girl. Go to Moue, while I talk to your new friend.'

Chse put her right thumb in her mouth, gagged and retched.

'How many times I tell you that you mustn't make your fingers long down your throat?'

Chse began to cry, more tired than upset. Her father cooed into her hair. Romanza thought of her long limbs, crumpled under a mad storm. It was more than he could bear.

'Where *Xavier*?'

'What you want with him?'

'Io.' A broad woman came to the door. 'If Chse ready, I take her to her mother house.' Io handed the girl over; she clung to the woman, one hand sweeping the floor. 'Goat still happy roasting, I be back for whenever macaenus reach.'

'We don't have much *time*,' snapped Romanza. 'He should be home by now.'

The woman shot him a look. The lines on each side of her mouth and on her forehead were so like his mother. 'Io. You don't have time for foolishness this evening.'

Io patted Chse and kissed her brow; the broad woman swept her away.

'What you want with Xavier Redchoose, Orange Man?'

He didn't have the time to say things nice.

'That smell isn't good. Sweet hurricane coming and I need to help the indigent shelter from it.'

Io crossed his arms. 'How you so sure?'

The man seemed amused, and it made him feel foolish and hysterical.

'My master-teacher tell me. I don't know when, but soon. If Xavier warn people, and everybody in town start shelter, the indigent might listen, too. We could . . . get people to go to the Dead Islands to help . . . or round them up . . . ?' He wavered. He wasn't sure how to accomplish any of it, but someone more powerful, older, must know. 'Nobody not going to listen to *me*.'

'Xavier is a man who walk by himself.'

'You never hear what I said? I know that. I know *him*.' How to explain to the man's brother what they'd shared in one day? His blood on Xavier's cheek, his wide, angry eyes on the beach before they parted. 'He . . . he would *want* you to listen to me.' Was that still true?

Io spoke gently. 'A whole heap of people think they know him, indigent.'

The top of his head might break open. 'How you could paint revolution all over the place, and not care about this? Hypocrite.'

Io's face darkened. 'If you can get Xavier to help you, that is on him, and you. But I have to leave here. I will tell him you came, if you leave a name.'

He meant it. He wasn't going to help. Romanza stood as tall as he could.

'My name is Romanza *Intiasar*! And you *owe* me something!'

Io raised his eyebrows, but he kept his voice even. 'Intiasar child? Eh. Now what do I owe *you*?'

'You *stole* from me! People trust my writings! You come and stand up on my back! That is not *your* reputation! People think is the same person!' He felt helplessness encircling him. 'You not any *alternative*! People going to *dead*. And you going to be the same kind of bastard as my father?' His voice trailed off. Pilar and now Io, both so certain he was wrong. Would Xavier be the same way?

Io leaned forward, searching his face.

'Romanza. That is your name? *Romanza.*'

His chest hurt so *bad*. That infernal stink. It was getting harder to breathe. He and Io should be able to understand each other. A better person would know how to do this.

'*Please*. We could die.'

'If that's what makes things change.' Io's mouth was right by his ear, and he sounded suddenly, immeasurably sad. 'Storm takes us by surprise, indigent. Let it *all* go.'

He knew what the smell was: his father's corruption, rotting the earth, infecting his lungs, spreading every time he looked up at one of those factory buildings, or heard him make another promise he would never keep.

You chose this, his father said, the day he left. *So take it. Eat it until your belly full. Don't come back.* But he'd expected the man to change. In time. Like the earth. Everything changed. To forgive his one-son. His name was Intiasar; he could go home anytime, surely?

The dark sky welled huge above them. Thousands of stars. Romanza slumped on the ground. Io crouched in front of him, a hand on his chest, on his temples. He thought of Sonteine, climbing the tree this morning, slipping and cursing.

Where *was* she? All the gods, where was his *mother*?

He was bleeding again.

In the distance, they could hear the sound of applause, rising from the Grand Theatre.

Romanza made himself get up and made himself run.

Sonteine and Dandu sit on a large water trough in his father's garden, their mouths close together. They are both trembling. Words tumble from her throat, Dandu's ears all a-vibrato. Small creatures sleep around them. They hold hands, swinging their legs.

A mango sits between them, blush on green.

She begins, picking it up and biting into it, using her teeth to peel a strip of green skin all the way down. The yellow juice drips onto her arm, her bent knee.

Dandu bends to lick it off.

They gasp, wrestle for the fruit, swap it between their mouths; he squeezes it, smears the juice down her cheek. They think of summer days and safety. He kisses her body, following the hard wings under her skin and down. She wets her fingers between her thighs, and he is light-headed when she gives him the same fingers to suck.

Cashew fruit pop open and rain onto the ground around them. Purple, scarlet, lemon and white blossom spiralling into her mad curls and making Dandu sneeze. Green fruit and vegetables swell and break open: guineps exploding in surges of juice; pears, aubergine, bright yellow tomatoes; showers of earth as new trees push through the soil, creaking, years before their time, force-ripened. He mumbles something into her jawline as she shakes her shoulders and the last fears tumble off them.

Their lips, wet.

They are no good together until the third try, when she tells him to slow down and he realises he *can* slow down, so much and so smoothly that she begs him to *please please oh gods please*

When they're done, she clutches him close, wraps her legs around his waist, so she can push off into air, so they can kiss in the sky, the mango seed below them bald and stripped in the damp and detonated garden.

✱

Hah walked to the left-hand side of the stage and slipped down, making her way towards a cluster of large tents. She entered one, rubbing the back of her neck and smiling.

Inside, Io waited for her in blue robes, an older man standing with him. The man was speaking passionately. He would have been handsome in his youth, before the jowls took hold.

'I know a bully when I see one, nah?' said the man. 'I know a bully, even though he charming, bad. And you been telling me for a while. So I done, now.'

✱

Governor Intiasar spoke to the two beauty queens separately. Shane spat on the ground and said no, despite her evident fear. He'd expected her to be defiant. Betti was more agreeable and he felt pleased. Her back was a thing of beauty.

He went through to the judges' tent next, taking a carafe of wine from a server. Garson was making jokes, trying to impress Des'ree. Some young cocks liked an old foot. Not that Des'ree was anywhere near old. She looked better than when she was young. Slave blood that was, bubbling up from the emancipated. She was a fascinating woman, despite her longstanding hatred of him.

Des'ree glanced up. He nodded. She raised a glass. She was conciliatory this evening.

'I think Shane,' said Des'ree. 'She is more articulate than Betti.'

'Ah, but we must take all elements *together*,' Intiasar smiled. 'I think Betti have everything to win.'

Perhaps he would coax Mrs Intiasar onto the pallet tonight. It had been too long. The promise of new sex always moved him to plan more.

If the young Betti left him any energy.

He drank, and argued pleasantly, and waited for news of the cull.

31

By the time they hoisted him up the cliff steps, Xavier was half drunk. He avoided alcohol as a rule, but Sander's rum was very pleasant indeed, blurring events in a most gratifying fashion.

The garden was as he'd left it this morning, which seemed like a decade ago: stuffed full of herbaceous goodness. He giggled. Most of the men who had paraded him there were left on the beach below, singing and drinking on. A haphazard game of stickball broke out. What a good thing they'd not *dared* to play games in his wild and wonderful garden, smelling of roasting goat. Was there a more trustworthy woman in this world than Moue? He should have married *her*; everybody, *anybody* better than Nya.

He hiccuped. Where *was* that dratted ghost? It was gone past *time* for her arrival.

'Come write in my book, Nya,' he muttered.

He could feel the man preparing to put him down. His face felt pleasantly warm, like handling meat on a fire on a cool day. Sticky with rum; his 'locks were soaked. Sander came to his elbow as he was lowered, gabbling: how important it had been to greet him on his return, so everybody knew he was a man to be reckoned with, not no soft man. Xavier tried to say that none of that was *important*, but his tongue was laced to the roof of his mouth.

Can't go to Anise like this, stinking of rum, no.

'Xavier?' Moue stood at the kitchen door, drying her hands on her apron. 'You alright?'

Sander genuflected. 'He fine, sis. He fine. Just a drink or two, you know. Or two.'

Moue's stony expression was the funniest thing Xavier had ever *seen*. She swooped forward, letting him lean against her. Sander grabbed the other side. Together, they frogmarched him into the dining room and manoeuvred him into a chair, where he contemplated the indistinct ceiling.

'He *drunk*,' Moue muttered. 'Sander, I going *kill* you.'

Xavier waved his hands in an effort to placate her but got another glare in return.

'Miss Nya said you should never, ever *drink*,' she hissed. ''Sake of your *mother*.'

Xavier waved a solemn finger. 'Well. Miss Nya is not *here*.'

'Macaenus!'

'She *not* here, is she?'

'*No!*'

Sander sat down next to Xavier, an imploring expression on his face. Xavier sat up as tall as he could. He felt as if his words were stuck, up near his wisdom teeth.

'Moue.' He dug his fingernails into the back of his hand. 'Beg you. Some cold water, some adami tea, very strong, sweet . . . hot . . . and some . . . *ice*.' How to run a garden, and how to sober up fast: those were the gifts his mother had passed on. She'd taught him how to quick-vomit the liquor around the back of the house before bed, but he didn't want to do that.

Moue shot them both a look of death.

'Sander need to go home to his *wife*.'

'But Miss Moue.' Sander wrung his hands. 'We here to talk of man things.'

'You mad? What is man things? I never see such a case of complaining, mewling *stupidity* in all my life. Cannot stop talking all day about a *song*. Insulting all the woman-them who dare to say that there is more to bedroom antics than *penis*. Xavier, you even *hear* this stupid song?'

'Once.' His head hurt. 'I was hoping to remain quiet and *dignified* about it.'

Moue glared at Sander. 'There, you see? If *your* cocky not working, sir, you have all my sympathies, but you need to take that home with you. Macaenus have *another* guest waiting for him.'

Xavier clutched the chair. 'Gods, who *now*?'

'You need to see this one.' Moue grabbed Sander by the arm. '*You* leave with me.'

Xavier sat in the quiet. He sniffed the familiar smell of the dining room: citrus and honeysuckle candles. The torn poem tree, bursting through the skylight. He rubbed the space between his eyebrows, alcohol gurgling inside his belly. Sober up. Take a long cold shower, scrub off the day. Then Anise. He was still going to see her. Her husband would have to vex if he got there late. It couldn't wait. It was the way the day *had* to end. Not no moth. That laugh of hers, instead.

Moue returned from the kitchen and set down the tray she carried, with a clatter. She walked around the room, flinging open all the windows. Air rushed in, making him gasp. It was always cooler up here on the cliff. A small teapot steamed; a large bucket of cracked ice, muslin, a big jug of water. She poured the tea, blowing hard on the surface before handing it over. He sipped. The bitter liquid made him snort. He dunked his face into the ice water, came up grappling for the muslin, dripping.

'Moue.'

'Yes, macaenus.'

'You can bring your child-them here tomorrow?'

'Well, why?' She was examining him minutely. Gestured for him to drink more tea. He obeyed. Dunked his face, wiped.

'We need to feed them the goat.'

'We do?'

'Yes!' He used the flat of his hand to drum the table. Was his head even a trifle clearer? 'And Io have a woman, you know. *She* have to come.'

She shook her head. 'What did you *do* to yourself?'

He shrugged. 'What time is it?'

'Coming on to nine.'

'You have to go home now, it's late.'

'I not going until you more sober than this.'

'Alright.' Silence, dunking, sipping, then: 'Moue?'

She stifled a giggle. 'Yes.'

'I did the thing, you know.'

'What thing?'

'I gave them the food they *needed*. Intiasar child and so. I don't know *why* they needed it. You know, I never do? People think I read their minds, but I can't do that. But they needed *that*. What I gave them.' His head was clearing. A fraction, a little.

He thought her voice softened. 'That's good. So we not cooking?'

'Well, for your children, yes. And Chse. Tomorrow.'

She patted him clumsily. 'Feeling better?'

'A little.'

'Remember somebody here to see you. He been waiting.'

'Look like it setting up to rain.'

'Yes. Macaenus.'

He groaned. 'I *can't*. I have somewhere to go this evening.'

She grasped his hand. 'I don't think so.'

432

Zebediah Remy entered the Torn Poem as if he had been there before; maybe he had. He was a short, fat man, soft all over. Xavier remembered his face from Nya's funeral, at tide. Just when there had seemed nothing else to do or feel, he'd looked up to see a stranger on the outskirts of their group, weeping himself dry. He'd known who he was; a man crying for love.

Perhaps Nya had brought him here. Perhaps they'd sat at a table and held hands and kissed while he was out at market. Perhaps Nya had deserved that.

Perhaps he had deserved it.

Zebediah spoke in an even tone: neither apologetic nor aggressive. He said he was grateful for the welcome, under the circumstances. He was sure Xavier did not want to see him, and truthfully, the feeling was mutual. He'd spent the whole day in his studio, he said, working on a large order of blown glass for the toy factory: embedding black glass beads with even smaller yellow glass globules; shaping white heart-shaped beads and tiny, red glass hibiscus; puffing through a hollow iron tube, swinging and rotating the hot bubble on its end; shaping handfuls of scorching, viscous glass into spinning tops; making eyeballs for dolls. He'd worked without rest for most of the day, without his assistant, or his acolyte. Alone, he would concentrate harder, and not be tempted to think of the day or its meaning. And he would have succeeded, if not for his next-door neighbour's radio.

'So full up of you, macaenus. All day, songs and talk. I think of you, and what I owe you.'

Xavier spread his hands. 'You don't owe me nothing.'

Zebediah looked at him, blinking slowly. 'Nya ghost come see me.'

433

Xavier clutched the top of the table so hard he seasoned it: salt crystals and pieces of nutmeg driven into the wood.

'*When?*'

'Five months ago.'

He could only manage one word.

'No.'

Zebediah spoke on. He did not want to think about why he had withheld the information. Perhaps it was because before she died, Nya had been *his* woman, and Xavier no use to her at all. She'd said so, herself. He'd wanted her visit to be theirs, alone. But as he stretched the glowing, liquid glass into shapes, he'd found himself wondering what he would feel, waiting on her, not knowing.

'In case you *was* waiting,' said Zebediah.

Xavier leaned back in his chair, head entirely clear.

It was a hot day, said Zebediah, and his back was wet with sweat. His two grown sons had come to see him in the morning and brought him lobster. He boiled three in the back yard, grimacing as one shrieked in the water.

Nya was near naked and shuffling. Her face was hard to bear. What flesh remained was going grey, like the belly of a snail, and there were stripes of red at her throat. She smelled like a lychee gone bad. The worst thing was her bones: he could see nearly all her skeleton, or that which remained: half of her ribcage, worn pubic bone and wrist bones clicking. As he watched, one of her few remaining teeth cracked in half and fell down her chest.

He wasn't sure she recognised him. Her eyes were like brown coins: flat and cold. But when he moved closer, wanting to touch her despite everything, she mewled and put her arms out.

He held her; it didn't occur to him then, but perhaps he was

434

able to do it because he'd had children: children who wiped snot on him, covered his house in mud and stool and bled from cuts. As soon as he held her, he realised it wasn't so bad. She smelled, she writhed, she was under his hands a kind of animal thing, but his need to comfort her was the strongest part. She rustled in his arms, and he looked down, to be sure he wasn't frightening her. She nestled into his chest, leaving stains on his tunic.

This close, he realised what he'd thought were bones were not bones at all.

Like so many ghosts, she was rebuilding her body, but what a thing – and here Zebediah sighed so deeply, Xavier wondered if he'd ever been loved as hard as this man loved – what a mad and ingenious woman they'd known!

She'd made herself a ribcage with bright orange love-weed, the kind that strangled flowering bushes. Her pelvic girdle was bamboo. Her green spine was a long, single piece of hollowed sugar cane. Her knee caps were avocado stones and her fingers were shells: rooster tail conch, fighter conch – he bent closer and laughed – she'd even chosen finger coral. Between her legs, she'd wound Battisient parrot feathers in brilliant red and green. He could have stayed there for days; laid her down to admire this new form of her.

In her chest cavity, she'd stuffed a white, fat cloud.

The shell hand reached up, the eyes lit, for a moment. She put her hand on his shoulder, took his arm and wrapped it around her non-existent waist, her intention clear. They'd danced, everywhere they went! She said she'd never danced with a man and let him lead – as soon as she tried, she stepped on his toes, stumbled, lost her balance. It seemed an act of trust too far: to relax, to lean on someone with people watching.

'I just thought she was a bad dancer,' said Xavier, softly.

'No,' said Zebediah. 'My writer-girl could dance.'

They danced for an hour. Up and down his lawn, he praying no one would come and disturb them, but to the gods, he declared, if they did, he would dance on, unashamed. Feet turned just so; pirouette, very careful, basic steps, as if she were an old person. Eventually she stood on his feet and let him take more of the movement. The light in her eyes was dimming. *Crack!* The sound shocked him: her cane spine splintering. Pieces of her were turning to ash, smoke, air. Crumbling. He clutched her, panicked, a handful of vertebrae, but that was dust too, falling into the grass below them. *Crack!* An elbow: the whole arm falling away, shattering when it hit the ground. Zebediah danced on, jaw set, as she disintegrated. *Pop-crack!* His bare feet moved through thick ash where her feet had been, moments ago. There was nothing to hold on to anymore, but she was smiling – he could feel it as she disappeared. He wanted to scream at the heavens: *let her in!* Instead, he danced on, until he was only dancing by himself.

His sons came back for supper and found him sitting on the lawn and kissing the earth.

Zebediah smiled sadly at Xavier. 'So I just did want to let you know.'

★

After Zebediah was gone, Xavier sat down and washed his face again. His head felt strange under his fingers: the bones sharper and simmering in the skin. Around him, the building vibrated. It did that, on some nights. Like it was alive.

He lifted the tray to take it back into the kitchen, which was when he saw the moth that Zebediah had left behind on the dining table.

Through the windows of the Torn Poem, the sky was red.

He was sure the moth would taste like bone and rain.

32

Hah's fingernails appeared on the screen first, tapping the microphone: short and clean and blunt. The screen whooshed and whirred until they could see her face.

'We are back, we are *back*, oh yes. And in one *second*, we going have a result for y—'

Governor Intiasar snatched the microphone away, sending an electrical shriek into the crowd.

'That is *my* job, Miss Hah.'

Anise frowned under her floppy hat. The man truly had no broughtupcy.

'Yes!' yelled a group of young men. 'Your job, baba!'

Hah put her hands on her hips. Intiasar blew into the microphone and brushed the front of his tunic. A woman next to her sighed admiringly.

'Good evening, brothers and sisters,' said Governor Intiasar.

Muttering, in response. Flaccid cheers. Children were still there, some crying, Anise could hear them.

'I want to make *three* announcements before I tell you who has won this year's Miss Pretty Girl International Contest.' Intiasar cleared his throat importantly. 'First and foremost, I have a message from my beautiful daughter. Sonteine want to thank you for all your good wishes and hopes you come by the Temple tomorrow evening to see her come down the steps after she married and walk through Pretty Town with her husband.'

Cheering and nodding and smiling in the crowd for the young bride. Anise rolled her eyes.

'Pretty Town Temple, tomorrow, dusk-time, before the happy couple retire to eat the walkround feast of the macaenus. We even going to provide the recipes, so you ladies can cook it all up for a special occasion.'

There was no way on the gods' green *earth* Xavier would give up a recipe without standing right there to explain it while you cooked it. Furthermore, there were things he could cook that no one else could. How had they convinced him to be part of such a thing?

'What kind of special occasion *I* going to get since you put a drawers-guard on people underneath?'

Yes, her beloved heckler was back, louder than ever.

'I thought you left.'

'I came back,' said the heckler. '*Drawers-guard!*'

Intiasar smiled. 'That is the *second* piece of news, my dear young man. The ban on intimate activity is hereby lifted early.'

Loud and extended cheering, especially from the men.

The heckler looked faintly disappointed.

Hah leaned down into the microphone, frowning.

'I think they need a little more information than *that*, Governor. How do we know it's safe? How do we – ?'

'Gods, lady, give that a *rest*, nah!' someone yelled.

Intiasar smirked. 'I think they right, Miss Hah. You riding me all day. On your little show. This is not the time or place. The last time I check, you wasn't paying no rent on my *mouth*.'

General laughter. Hah was losing a tired and impatient crowd.

Intiasar put his hand over the microphone. His lips moved.

'She better hold her temper,' murmured the heckler.

'Why, what he said to her?'

But the heckler was gone again, his answer swallowed up in the crowd.

439

Hah took a step back.

'Item three,' said Intiasar. 'Popisho, I am very pleased to announce our *general election*! We will all be voting in two months! In usual tradition, any challengers to the office of Governor have three days to name themselves for the ballot and can run a campaign for the entirety of that time.'

A longer, louder cheer, rising up in the air, where the humming-birds had gone. Would Intiasar paint his name on Betti's back if she won the beauty contest, or across Shane's pants suit? She wouldn't put it past him.

'And now the result I know you been waiting for—' said Intiasar.

'*I* have a name.'

Anise craned her neck to see who spoke.

They all did.

It was a quiet and determined voice; it would be good on the radio. It would speak softly in your ear at night-time. A voice that was sure of itself. Rather like Xavier's voice, now she thought about it. But not quite.

Hah's arms swung free, dark lips twitching, biting back what . . . a smile? Almost proprietorial. She knew the owner of that voice, alright.

Anise went up on her tiptoes to see the stranger walking onto the stage and filling the screen.

A limp; benign eyes. People who spoke next day would insist the air around the stage cooled when he arrived. There was a fleck of orange paint on his collarbone, too deliberate to be an accident. Anise could see it on the screen.

She might have expected he'd come with jokes.

The heavy-sandalled guards moved forward, like on wheels, clustering at the edges of the stage.

The man didn't flinch. He came to a stop beside Hah and spoke again into the microphone he was holding.

'My name is Ionosphere Redchoose. I am the son of Pewter. He was a labourer.'

Io and Pewter, she knew those names. Different in colouring, but the same calm, the same clarity. This was Xavier's elder brother. She wanted to hug him and cheer him on.

Intiasar bounced on his toes, pugilistic and smiling.

'I am very happy to run election next to you, Mr – ? Blue Shoes? But you don't hijack an occasion like this, when people want to know about their beauty queen.'

Io's serene gaze stayed on the crowd. Anise pushed forward; others drifted with her. He had that rare ability to make you feel as if he was speaking to you alone. She could see Hah, stage right, finger on her lips, calling for silence.

We all want to be closer to him.

'You *must* listen to me,' said Io. He stepped to the very edge of the stage, looking into individual faces. The people around her smelled like her childhood and riverbanks and hard-back sweat even through the odd, sweet breeze.

'Every year, Bertrand Intiasar employs hundreds of us to work in his factories,' said Io. 'He pays us badly, tells us we should be grateful, and is him-one draw the profit.'

Intiasar smiled wider.

'Of course I draw a wage, along with my business partners, but everything else goes in the public purse. It is Leonard Brenteninton's genius that makes these toys. You want him work for free?'

Io contemplated the crowd, as if Intiasar was inconsequential.

'Last year, the factories showed a profit of 3.64 million.'

Who could have thought so much of anything could exist, let alone money?

'Less than half a million is spent on this land, and on you, the citizens. The rest goes into this man's pocket.'

'That is preposterous,' snapped Intiasar. 'Prove one word.'

'But there is an alternative,' said Io. 'Oh, yes.'

The crowd inhaled. A thrill ran through Anise. Many said that moment was when the sweet storm began, that they felt it in their ankles. Others said it was simply the feeling of people waking up.

'Orange Man?'

'That is him!'

'We been waiting for you, Orange Man!'

Her teeth chattered. The crowd, the words from this man, the sound in the ground, the smell filling her lungs, it was all so very important and connected.

Io held his hands up. 'You *must* believe this last, if you believe nothing else. He is not just a thief, this man. He is murderous. He has sent his people to kill the indigent.' The words trickled through the theatre, through small holes, fissures, cracks and the corners of bolts in the walls. Voices all around her called out into the sky; Anise realised with some surprise that she was calling out with them.

'Kill who?'

'But you can't do that. Them is people, too.'

'Who said he is killing them? Why?'

The screen creaked and swayed. Faces of normal people. The crowd rocked: men and women in one direction and then the other, raising one shoulder and then the other, one sole and then the other, walking sideways like crabs. Intiasar tapped his foot, a small, condescending smile on his face. The clumpy-shoed men were drifting, up-up-up on stage. Hah moved closer to Io, ordering them off, protesting, but this was no longer her space.

Io gestured at Intiasar. 'See these men he have? More are out in the Dead Islands, hunting the indigent. Looking in bushes, curled around rocks, wading through water, for he says they are no better than butterflies. You know why? Anybody get a present, today?'

Intiasar's head snapped up. Guards flooded the stage, circling the couple. Io reached out for Hah, but she pulled away, turning back and forth, yelling at the men to leave them alone.

Io spoke faster.

'You think it was your auntie or your lover leave a box at your yard? Is not them. The indigent went into Intiasar's warehouse today and they took back what belongs to *you*.'

Glee spilled across Anise and through the theatre. Children were held up high, to wave their toys.

'I get a puzzle, made out of blue clay!'

'My boy get a puppet!'

'I don't know what my wife get, we been trying to work it out all evening, but it pretty, you see!'

She wondered if there was a gift on her veranda.

A black crow? A firework? A drum?

Intiasar looked furious. 'This is a criminal act! Any man, woman or a child who have my property must return it today! You will be forgiven! But these things do not belong to you!'

'Forgive my backside! Forgive who?' yelled the heckler.

'Them toys belong to us!'

'What about 3.64 million, you thieving rass?'

'What about the *indigent*?'

A guard grappled with Io for the microphone, but he broke free, still clutching it. 'If he get vote in again, he bringing down factory wages by *half*! When you fighting back, Popisho?'

Cries of outrage from the crowd. Anise struggled to keep her balance as it surged. A guard seized Hah's shoulder and she struck out at him, the flat of her hand moving cleanly across his face. Blood sprayed. The man fell to his knees.

Miss Hah get a strength cors, then.

Men poured around the couple, faster and faster. Anise's belly lurched.

If you caught in a crowd, you cannot be a woman, Anise, her father had once told her. *Accommodate no one.*

Io's determined, straining voice.

'There *is* an alternative. Listen me! If every person who get a toy sell it to the ships when they come, we *all* will have the profits.'

Where is Xavier?

It was like watching a sinkhole in the ocean: pulling the couple down, Hah's patchwork robe at its centre. She could barely see Io, flailing against three guards, Intiasar bellowing commands until the air threatened to splinter. Hah broke free of the deadly sea. She tried to pull Io back through the curtain, but there were too many men in her way, yanking her skirts, hands fluttering around her body, smiling with teeth. Tearing the neck of her robe. Exposing her skin. Io can do nothing, pinned by too many.

The women in the crowd call out, a wounded gospel.

'Don't *touch* her!' screamed Anise. She pushed her way forward, hands fizzing silver. Surely they couldn't do this, in front of everybody, just so?

'*Who is this man?*' thundered Intiasar. 'What qualifies him to speak? What evidence? Miss Hah carry her boyfriend here to make trouble, and who you going to believe? You know how much government money I have to take up, repaint the damn place, 'sake of this man? Alternative, my eye! Bottom eaters and thieves! *Nobody move.*' He jerked his head at Io. 'Man, I am arresting you for lying on a government official. Guards, take him up!'

'*Stop.*'

Anise froze, body crackling.

No one had noticed the little jowled man, shouldering his way onto the stage. A single guard stepped in his way, hesitated, then fell back at his scorn. The other guards abandoned Hah in the corner of the stage. Her chest heaved.

The little man raised his microphone.

'You know, Bertie, you always *did* love a lie.'

Intiasar glared. 'What you doing here? I don't need no help.'

'But I hear you up here with my name.' The little man addressed the crowd. 'Well now. Some of you know me. I am Leo. Samuel's son. Is me who make them toys and stand with this man and sell them.' His mouth turned down. 'Let me tell you, I never see no 3.64. I never see no two million, nor no one million, Mr Governor. And I knowing you since we is knee high to a fenky fly.' He took a deep breath. 'Furthermore. Not two hours ago, I hear you with my own ears, give the order to kill the indigent.' Anise thought he looked close to tears. 'Now how you could do such a thing, my friend? Your son, your *son*, Bertie!'

Secrets, was it the stench of them she smelled?

Our sons, call the crowd. *Our daughters. This must not be allowed. Come, we go Dead Islands. Come, we save them. Somebody. Do something.*

'Gods have mercy,' moaned a woman beside her.

Children, wailing.

Io pushed his way through the guards, pulling Hah with him. Leo gave him the microphone.

'Popisho. Don't cry. They are with us.'

Anise blinked.

So it was, now they were able to look and to see.

Her eyes widened.

That third man in the group, over there. The woman selling baked goods. Here, another woman with two bale of good-quality Dukuyaie linen. The little boy at her elbow, looking up and drowning her in his river-smile. To look into their eyes was to know grass and peace and this place.

The heckler, tall and solemn. How had she not seen indigent in his dear, dark stare?

All hiding their nakedness in stolen blue factory uniforms and their lips moving.

She clutched the walls of the building; felt she might swoon.

Where Xavier?

The indigent were singing, but not as she'd ever heard a song before. This was the dead language of their ancestors, wrenched to life in these throats; lost, found and streaming out of their mouths and down their lips. Singing through the thickening air. In each face she could see terrible compassion and sorrow.

The indigent were praying for *them*.

Anise gasped and retched. The sky turned red. Crackling through it, great plumes of golden electricity.

Intiasar, cursing.

'*Take cover!*' bellowed Io.

Anise ran, trying not to fall as stewards ripped open the theatre gates, as men and women tore at barriers. She saw people pulling the indigent with them: into houses, shops, homes, churches, restaurants, bars. Anywhere to shelter from the burning, cruel rain. Hand in hand.

She ran, raindrops scorching through her robe.

And from across the world, it seemed, the sweet hurricane came for them.

33

Xavier put down the tea tray and picked up the insect. He shook the green notebook free from his bag, along with the two green pencils.

He lay full length on the floor, on his stomach, like a little boy, the book and the moth and the pencils at his head. He used one of the pencils to move the moth around the surface of the notebook, tapping and poking.

It was a Rafter moth. He'd never seen one, but he'd heard about them. They were often mistaken for butterflies. Bright green wings, splotched with white, edged with gold, thorax dark as a vanilla pod.

What *was* he, now he know Nya ghost never seek him out?

He knows the things that he *does*. Chop and boil and grow flowers and feed chickens and watch diners, watch their faces. Tell people things: move that, polish that, arrange that, make that better. He knows how to fashion a shelf for his kitchen, built at the perfect angle to hold a new-baked coconut cake, so the smell hits diners just at the right moment. How much cod liver oil for the hens, when they're egg-bound. He recognises the season's first ripe courgette, slicing it, tossing it in hot olive oil, adding nine chilli seeds exactly. He'd taken it to Nya, excited: *taste this, taste it!* And she: *Xavier, I don't want to*, and he—

Sulking.

Until she took his courgette and ate it and said she liked it.

He knows how to war in a house.

He stroked the wings. Green scales filtered onto his fingers. It would be sour on his tongue then punch the back of his throat. Moths this good tasted of their colour. The tang of green, a dirty brown stain on your lips, like the one he threw away.

He rifled through the notebook, fingers vibrating, ticking things off. See here, look here: things he *is*, things he *knows*. Remember to plant two seeds instead of one to compensate for the slugs. Learn how to catch a mongoose so Moue don't have to catch all the mongoose-them. He knows how to salt water to lock in the colour of vegetables, because here it *is*, an item on his list to do. He knows his stoves, they're like old ladies, squat and hot, except for the left-hand far-side one, which warms at a different pace on rainy days. Chilli in chocolate dishes. He knows how sore his arms are: crackling and flexing elbows. He knows not to play games when you tell a man about his dinner. Mushroom was mushroom and meat was meat. It was rare that a diner expected something, got something else and felt happy about it. Des'ree told him so.

He knows he will never meet another like her.

The most recent entry in his notebook is a record of last week's barter: Mas' Prekeh offered two good pigeon a day for a barrel of Moue's otaheite apple syrup.

Outside, thunder barroooomed and he shuffled closer to the moth, curling himself around it.

He knows how to write a recipe.

And Nya hadn't come to him.

What was he, if not a man squaring his shoulders, to do his best by a woman? Making sacrifice.

Nya liked to write inside his notebooks because it was the best way to get his attention: *desecrating your blessed texts*, she'd sneered, crossing out an important ingredient or a sketch he needed. She'd called them poems, her writing in his notebooks, but he'd never been able to agree, not because he knew better than her about such things, but because he knew the poetry she usually made. He'd not understood all of it, especially when they were young, but he'd appreciated its ambition, its joy. How clever it was.

These scribbles were just ways to die.

He read her lists out loud to the Rafter moth.

machete in the garden
swim until too tired to swim back
eat manchioneal berries
puffer fish or
green ackee pods
climb one of the foreign ships and
jump off the front
into the motor
fast motor
invite a beat
ing
feed my shark to a throat
cut
run
starve until hipbones split the skin
fly off Temple roof
wrap myself in coral reef
embrace a stingray
die BAD
slice my belly off
scorpion fish
wrists on barbed wire

tangled in a net
rat rum
bite

What would she have done, if not for Zebediah? Wander forever, better than coming to him?

Of course she couldn't trust him, to help her. How could he have expected it?

She'd finally killed herself, because nothing made her better. Zebediah knew. Had the balls to face it.

And what was *he*?

A moth eater, always that. Every day. There were green moth scales on his hands, so he rubbed them across the bridge of his nose and lay on his back, licking his lips.

He knows that he misses moth euphoria, the sweating, the mad energy, especially the hallucinations, so dark and lost.

The eventual nothing-at-all.

Shouldn't he just take it now, gorging, tasting the silk and the green? Walk out into the thunder and lose his mind on the side of the road, like a dog? Like Zebediah Remy wanted him to? He put his head back, baring his neck to the air. It would be good, eating moth in a storm; like his day-god, eating his own lips. The rain screamed around the house. He was dimly aware this was no normal storm. He should bring the storm shutters down. He should do many things to make himself safe.

Nya had wanted to die for so long, eventually he'd ignored her.

The last time he'd craved like this was in Anise's yellow house. Five days' abstinence: he had never been an adult without moth. His life seemed meaningless. He could not remember the feeling of his first walkround, nor the taste of anything; even his love for Anise felt submerged. He couldn't trust any decision he'd ever made. He was a person with no clear and reliable feeling. He'd not known the extent of his *uselessness*. He imagined the faces of people who loved him. But what had they loved? He slept; screamed into his hands; clutched his belly; stank. Anise could not make him eat anything more than cornbread he rolled between his fingers and nibbled like a mus-mus. He couldn't stop thinking about the old house he'd bought, with its yawning cliff edge. He considered his body coolly, imagined the meaty sound of it hitting hard sand, the moment of stepping free into the sky. He got out of his hammock and pulled on his tunic. Moved through the small house in the dark. Anise was asleep in the day room.

Xavier? She lit a candle. Her hair was thick, eyes heavy. *What are you doing?*

He told her simply. The cliff. The freedom. And so. Her face was solemn. He thought she'd say nothing was beyond him, that he had to fight for life, but she didn't beg or try to argue him out of it. It was a trick, to shock him out of his resolve. She sat, looking at him.

I will explain to people who love you that you couldn't stay.

The air was warm.

I will do that for you. But be sure, Xavier. Because you cannot take it back or change it.

He had needed someone to see him, to understand; to astonish him, like the sky.

He cupped the Rafter moth in his hands.

✳

451

Have the maids changed the curtains or moved the furniture?
Nya asked, once. It was the year before her suicide. *There is
something different about your face.* She sat, staring into the
bedroom mirror. *And mine, too.*

No, Nya, he'd said. If he chose the wrong words, she would
rage and not sleep, and what was wrong changed every day.

It isn't the room, she said. There was incredulity on her face.
It's us. She put her hand on her jaw. *The glow of youth is gone.
Don't you see that? And around us, everywhere, young people
blazing.* She walked over to him.

We getting older, she laughed. *Isn't that wonderful?*

✳

She was right, not to haunt him. He would not have been able
to dance.

He picked up the green moth and wrenched open the restaurant door.

✳

Anise climbed the hill above Carenage beach, lungs bursting.
The rain cut her scalp. She sluiced energy down her arms, across
her cheeks and her legs.

This was the way her father said she would die. Most parents
told sweet hurricane stories at night, a scary tale to make bad
children good, but no one told it like Pastor Lati.

*One day those gods you love going murder you in a sweet-
sweet storm for jokes, and then you going know I was right.*

The people on the beach below congealed into dark clumps,
like ants, then scattered in sprays of panic. The smell was so

thick she might chew on it. She strained: chest, eyes, ears, anybody, anybody, *anybody* left, anybody in danger?

You.

She watched the sea swell, rise, lapping the rim of the moon.

Her mind screamed for there to be nobody in danger, but of course there was. One little girl with lungs on her hips, sheltering under a rattling lean-to, a place where women went to shower off the salt and leave their children in the shade. Crouching, bewildered.

Anise began to run down the hill. She felt like the smallest thing in the world, a seed or an atom against the wind and the rolling ocean. She stumbled on a root and fell, grazing her hands and knees, fighting upwards. Despite the rain, she felt dry: saliva dried, pores crumbling.

The child was no more than ten feet away, the old lean-to peeling apart above her. Anise fought forward: biceps, triceps, thigh-bone, ankle, skin like tearing, flailing, *wanting* the girl into her arms, terrified but safe and *yes*, she had her, clutching the warmth of her, wind pushing them back towards safety, her strong legs see-sawing through the murk, triumphant.

She would stuff the child with Xavier's plantain syrup tarts and a lamp would be lit for her and games would be played. Because of course she was going to the Torn Poem – it was where she'd been heading all day.

But that wasn't what happened; no saving of any child, for her.

Anise felt the wind pick her up and put her down. Wicked, zooting, shooting wind, a thing of shapes: triangular wind, rhomboid wind, loop-de-loop wind, cube wind, spheroid, and she wondered if the gods had come down to make things extra impossible. She could hear the creaking of the sea, imagine its shark carcasses, its millions of tiny, sharp stones and jellyfish corpses, their dead, stinging tentacles enough to make the heart contract and each piece of coral enough to spear a belly. The wind, flinging her backward, making it impossible to reach the little girl.

She struggled to her feet in time to see the heel-back and hand-middle of the man, bundling the girl onto his back, where she clung like a clam. The man ran along the beach, back into Pretty Town. She'd seen pictures of horses from foreign and he reminded her of them: head up and snorting, the child a jockey.

Her arms and face stung.

Run, Anise!

She ran towards the Torn Poem. Swallowing sand and groping forward. If you were watching her, it would seem she was running on air, the wind holding and rolling her. She thought of her mother and where she might be, of how strong her father was, but how slow. Bonamie, who'd never seen a danger she didn't run towards, primed for battle, where was she? And Tan-Tan, o you gods? One pink house full of whore and a baby.

Let them be well.

Below her, the salt water took its first chunk of the beach.

✳

The man who saved her from the storm reminded Olivianna of her grandfather. Both of them had sad eyes and white in their hair and beards. But this long-legged man moved much faster. By the time he put her down on the lady's big veranda and kissed her cheek, she was sorry to see him go, turning away, making whooping noises and heading for the sea.

She was very sure he was the lightning bolt of the world.

She knocked on the door and the lady came out with a blanket and water to wash off the rain, so her skin wasn't so stinging and sore. Oliviana hoped her mamma was safe and that the grandpa kind of man could swim.

★

Around the Torn Poem and through the queer light, the wind was tearing the garden apart, in the way of lovers who have waited too long. There would be bruising in the morning and love bites in unexpected places and things that would never be said again. Orange creeper stalks tossed up together with magnolia vine; plum-coloured stamens; ripped white mountain roses; contorted, lichen-covered tree branches; ginger lilies; silken cherry leaves. Xavier stood, astonished, as a red shrimp plant tore free of its moorings, its odd crustacean blossoms exploding in the air, bouncing down the cliff and into the sea. The kissing almond trees were tilting, half uprooted, and as he watched, they went the way of everything else, pulled up, whirling around the house in a vortex, gifted with bizarre locomotion by the storm.

How can one hear a single breath, during such a storm? How does the sound make its way through roaring of wind and a sea that threatens the horizon? But still, he thinks he hears her breathing, and there she is, struggling up the steps.

He lets go of the moth.

She sees him fighting towards her, through the remains of his garden. He doesn't have far to come; she is already there, near screaming at the rain and the petals.

Her skin is hot when he grabs her up.

Inside, he runs a bucket of water and pours it over her, then does it again, flooding the kitchen floor, rubbing her skin to get rid of the caustic, sweet rain. He sluices himself the same way as she dries off with towels he's brought. Somehow, they aren't looking at each other, but he can feel her up his back and neck, and she can feel him.

She finishes drying her feet.

He rubs his mouth-corner free of water.

They look.

He sees that she's no longer as young as she was and perhaps she's better.

She sees that he is still sad.

He sees her fine, thin shoulders; the even yards of skin. That backside.

She sees his mouth.

'What you doing, running around in the rain?' he says, then thinks, what way is that to greet an old friend?

She thinks the same thing, except for the old friend part because they're not old friends. But o, she wants to be.

He thinks she's beautiful with pieces of his garden stuck to her robe.

'I need your bathroom,' she says.

'Stay,' he says. He wants to be still with her, for a moment.

She laughs. 'I need to *piss*, Xavier!'

When she comes back, he puts a hand on her arm, then a hand on her cheek. She touches the hand on her cheek. Light pools around them as she heals his bruised skin and sore arms. She catches a fever, before it can bloom. He catches her mouth with his mouth.

'Look like I skip your line,' she says.

456

EPILOGUE

'Hello, caller.'

'Greetings, Miss Hah.'

'Yes, Mamma. Where you calling from?'

'I am over in Pluie district. What a time we having with the clearing up, but everybody pulling together. I glad you make it through the storm, sister. Many was worried for your safety. If hurricane never get you, them blasted beauty contest guardie might of do you something.'

Hah chuckled. 'I am here and well. The twenty-four days long, eh? Who you sit out sweet hurricane with?'

'My two good friend. We play, you see! Jacks and skipping and dress-up.'

'That sound good to me.'

'We board up everything, but the rain was bad-bad. I have two child suck down some when I wasn't looking, and all they could do is doo-doo all week.'

'They recovering, Mamma?'

'Yes, look like they getting better. We turned our hand and made the best.'

'Thank you for calling.'

'I did know there was something else. I wanting to say howdy and good greetings to Mrs Intiasar, lose her husband. I hear many people feeling all kind of ideas about that man. Saying since as how he is the only one who dead in the hurricane, he the only one deserve it. But I don't think so. Is only one we lose, give gods thanks and praises, but he was everything to her.'

'True thing, Mamma. We feel for her.'

★

Xavier Redchoose walked through the town, nodding at people.

The early morning beach was glimmering and fresh. People came out of houses, holes, out of themselves and each other. Still recovering. Work still to be done. They looked at the sea. A week since sweet hurricane pass, but from early morning until late night, the sound of hammer and saw and chisel.

And no fish in the sea. Not even a little eel. It was worrying.

Clip-clap-trap of the bread on the hearth fire as he walked.

He'd spent most of the week trying to help: moving heavy things, filling in roads, tiling roofs, securing power lines, collecting water, mending generators. Leading community meetings next to Io. But small things were even more important: a kindness on the street; the way an old person looked at you and you felt your worth. He could not recall hugging so many strangers.

'Let them take strength from you,' said Anise, healing his pains in the evenings.

Romanza said his mother spent the whole hurricane making pudding. She'd started making it on about day four of the storm and she and Olivianna didn't stop until they were completely out of every pudding ingredient. When she slipped yet another in the oven, he'd creep over to her and let her stroke his head and told her someone he loved might be dead.

'But his lover survived,' Anise said.

'Yes,' said Xavier.

★

Pilar spent the sweet hurricane inside the yard of a man with five children between the ages of one and twelve, whose mother had run down the road for cocoa-tea and fresh eggs. The husband, who'd objected to her leaving even for a little twenty minutes, found himself facing childcare alone for who-knew-*how*-long. Pilar was leaving a parcel of stuffed animals from the toy factory on their stoop when he found himself hauled inside by the desperate father.

Pilar was no good as a storyteller for the older ones because it took him too long to say anything. The roof banged and the children complained, and they changed dirty nappies and washed them and fed five and muttered about how woman was *very* suited to this, but not so much man. The father talked about chi-chi man on the seventh day and then most of the eighth day was taken up with Pilar cursing him very slowly and quietly, so the children couldn't hear. It was one of the finest cursings ever heard in Popisho, rich in metaphor and simile, all in between the food that had to be prepared and learning to tell stories *much* more quickly because something had to be done to amuse them all and send the baby to sleep.

'Don't want no bottom eater hold my childs,' muttered the father.

'I will put him down here right now if you like,' said Pilar.

'Gods, you don't see the child have gas? Clean it, man.'

And so on.

★

The sky was pink. It had not been blue since the hurricane passed. Xavier wondered if it would ever be blue again. He waved at a boatman and climbed into his canoe. As they drew away from the shore, he looked back at the people meandering down the beach, as if the ocean had some kind of answer.

Des'ree called him to say she and the boys spent their hurricane time in the local jail, which was the closest place she could find when the heart-a-claps broke loose; thank all the gods that the boys had insisted on coming to see Miss Pretty with her. There were eighteen prisoners in the jail and one prison guard to keep the peace, and she'd found them full of wisdom. They taught her how to steal the best of a man's catch without him noticing, milk a goat quick o'clock, pick a lock, start somebody else's putt-putt and make a very good watermelon pickle.

When Sonteine and Dandu turned up at the family compound, it was already so obvious that she was happily pregnant that her mother didn't tell her about her father for several hours. When she did, Sonteine walked with Romanza for a very long time, until they found a surviving tree to climb, then sat in it with her brother and cried.

★

Anise came to meet Xavier at the front door of the Torn Poem, completely naked. They hadn't worn any clothes for so long that the first time he put some on they felt heavy and rough. The grass was beginning to grow again in the flat bare yard. He was too impressed by the surgical nature of the devastation and her belly button to be sad.

'Sadness will come again,' Anise said when she'd looked up one day and seen him watching her with shiny eyes.

'I know,' he said.

He began seasoning parrot fish for supper; she made him a cup of adami tea and stood, an S-shaped curve, beside the window. Even the hills were stripped. These days people looked at her nearly as much as they looked at him; she said she didn't care.

'Imagine, Miss Hah, what a disgrace! I hear that healer run all the way over to him yard, make sure she lock inside with him.'

'Well, you never know with these things. Best we mind our own business.'

Anise picked an orange hot pepper for Xavier.

'Give me another one. Remember Hah like pepper.'

'Remember Chse don't.'

Io found his backside up to the Torn Poem the very minute sweet hurricane seemed done with them all, Chse under his armpit and a gorgeous woman out in front. The fact that she was Hah the radio-lady troubled Xavier at first, but she'd brought him chrysanthemum seeds, several orchids, some fast-growing trees and several well-considered arguments about privacy, responsibility and partisanship.

When Moue arrived fifteen minutes later to check her chickens not dead, Io and Xavier hugged her until she squeaked and protested, which gave the brothers an excuse to embrace each other, and they all turned various colours of the rainbow.

★

Mixie spent the time alone. She smoked out a large stock of bush weed and wrote a play, which was later staged with small success in Mampy district for two weeks. She heard Archie was engaged to be married and was surprised to find she didn't mind.

When Pilar found Romanza, he drew him out into the sunshine of the twenty-fifth Dead Island and shared his body so deliberately and slowly that Romanza had to look away, because he couldn't meet his gaze, but smiled into his shoulder. When they orgasmed together, it was as natural as music and from then on, they made a habit of it.

During the hurricane, Leo worried about his son and lit a candle for his friend.

✳

'I hearing you, caller.'

'Miss Hah, you know what I did see in that blasted hurricane?'

'Talk and tell me, man.'

'Ghost running in the rain. Not one or two! Dozen of ghost, I see them through my window. Now what you think about that?'

'I hoping they feel a little happiness.'

The man grunted assent.

'I swear I did see Intiasar in that rain with them, you know. Running good.'

'True-true?'

In the end, Bertrand Intiasar found time as a ghost the best experience of all.

Io called the radio stations repeatedly to discuss the election, the state of the roads, the way for matters to best be fixed, the promises he had made and intended to make, and argued splendidly when Mrs Intiasar called up to argue splendidly. He and Hah both agreed that Intiasar's widow was shaping up to be a worthy adversary in the election, governance stating that a family member could stand in on the untimely death of any elected official, and everybody knew that Romanza and Sonteine had no interest in any of that.

Lyla darned the hole in her dress and made several more, including one for Anise, and in different sizes to accommodate her own growing belly. She sent the frock with a note inviting Anise over to talk if she ever had the time. Anise went for a very good roast chicken and steamed vegetables and took Bonamie with her. Much merriment ensued, and when Anise found herself sobbing uncontrollably because she missed Tan-Tan, Lyla and Bonamie held her, and said there were some sadnesses you just had to live with, and everybody agreed that the cheating fool would have made a good father.

Romanza went back to listening to women in rum bars.

'Time for one more before I done today. Listen next for the places you can pick up fresh water supplies, and if you have river round back, make sure you share with neighbours, but only after them come into your community and test for contaminant. Yes, who on the line, talk quick!'

It was Betti Ovaltine, relieved there was finally a decision about the winner of the Miss Pretty International Contest. She really wasn't sure she could accept it though, because Governor Intiasar had suggested some bandooloo business before he passed and maybe that was why she win.

Hah summoned Des'ree on the line.

'No,' said Des'ree. 'In the end, we all did agree it was you. You just don't have to fuck anybody for it now.'

'Gods, Des'ree, language on my show! You don't turn over no new leaf?'

'I never promise anybody that.'

Shane called up to say she not feeling too dusty, since as how she think she did well in the competition, turn down Intiasar slackness all-to-complete, though not to speak ill of the dead, and *also* she wanted to say she proud to lie down with woman and she have all quality kind of hair dye for sale, if people want to know.

'Take care of that oxtail-with-a-side-a-butter-bean body, I beg you,' says Hah.

'But must,' said Shane.

✷

The only thing Anise had wanted to do during the hurricane was say *exactly* what she meant, never forgetting kindness, of course. Xavier said *he* thought the whole saying-exactly-what-you-meant-though-never-forgetting-kindness was a good idea and he might try to practise it too. He also announced he was in love with her, had been from the very first minute, planned to be until whatever killed him killed him, but also what killed him might be moth, because it was still a thing in his life he was trying to find peace with and what did she think of that.

Anise said she'd factored the moth in – and the macaenus thing, which mostly meant she had to be famous, too. None of it was simple, but she found the voice inside her head had become more relaxed and playful after being stuck with him for twenty-four days and so what to do, except wait and see what might become of them.

'You could always get up and walk through another wall if I vex you,' said Xavier, because she'd told him all about that on day three.

'I could,' said Anise. 'You better watch yourself.'

The next morning she watched him unlace Nya's hammock, hold it for a while and then store it away.

After the storm, Zebediah bound and published a small collection of Nya's love poetry and distributed it door to door.

Xavier went and found the fisher-boy and took him out to a rum bar with Romanza, where they danced very badly to very good music. He also gave the boy a purse with ninety-five coins, after Romanza inveigled the cost of the moth out of him. Xavier didn't ask *which* indigent was running moth so very fine and fat, because after all, he was trying to have a different life.

Very late at night on the way home and tipsy, the fisher-boy, whose name was Jassen, asked *mastercanIsitbyyou* very prettily indeed and there it was, braps! his first acolyte.

They cook with the indigent in the Dead Islands; at the edge of Bend Down Market; at the lip of a temple; help teach egg-cookery to bored nine-year-olds, because all the grown-ups busy.

Jassen salts the cod these days.

*

Anise was willing to chop onions; when Xavier told her she wasn't doing it properly, she told him not to be so fussy about onions. Xavier put wine vinegar on the badly cut onions and pepper and sifted flour in his hands until it was suitably salted, battered the parrot fish, then lost his concentration when Anise said he might follow her upstairs because there was something she'd forgotten to show him.

They only pause in their lovemaking when someone comes to yell up at their window that the Fatidique are in the sea-oh!

'What,' says Xavier.

'What,' says Anise.

They drag on clothing and run out of the house barefoot, she with flour on her scalp and ankles where he parted them.

The sky has recovered itself, is once again oyster-blue, Popisho-blue, girls-in-Sunday-ribbons blue, and where the sky meets the ocean they can see a fuzzy, dark and chanting line of obeah women, hundreds of them, wading in the kick-back waves, waist deep, palms up.

Can you give me your heart, ask the obeah women, and the fish come into the shallows. Fish the size of fingertips, nothing more than tail and teeth; fish like tangled underbrush that taste of seasoned butter; fish with long tails like birds; fish that howl.

People gather on the shore, delighted. A wave trips a man complaining about his storefront being blocked.

They splash; they laugh.

They think of love as a reddening of the earth under the sun.

Acknowledgements

My deepest respect and thanks to Hannah Bannister and Jeremy Poynting, at Peepal Tree Press, who beautifully saved me from obscurity; to my formidable and wise agent Nicola Chang; to the king of advocacy, Nikesh Shukla; to my 'midwife' Louisa Joyner at Faber and Faber and the editorial team at Farrar, Straus and Giroux; to Eleanor Rees, the best raaasssclaaht copy-editor ever.

Nobody would be reading this book without you.

To those who helped me carve this novel out of a mountain: my beloved Stacey Barney, the first editor who believed, for whom I rewrote Anise at least twice; the *tour de force* who is Jamie Smythe, the only one who could bear to read it when it was over 230k long; and Louise 'make sure you haven't already written it' Tondeur, the smartest human I ever met. Blessings on Troy Lopez, whose mushrooms I brushed and kitchen I invaded. And Patience Agbabi, who never doubted, not for one second.

You are my friends.

The Crew Who Abides: you're like a field laid out before me, a sky, my Lepidoptera – my sister Soroya Nosworthy, Carol Russell, Jameela Kassim, Judith Bryan, Jenne Liburd, Okeiliah Williams, Sola Coard, Joshua Idehen, Bobby Joseph, Jehan White, Mahdis Keshvarz, Ricky McKenley, Amba Chevannes, Sarah Manley, Stu Nathan, Taitu Heron, Abena Chevannes, Ancil McKain, Jose Sarmiento Hinojosa, Anne Morgan, Alan Flynn, Carla Dixon,

Carol Moses, Marion Bernard-Amos, Rose Rainford, Marilyn Ng A Qui, Richard Frankson, Kirk Henry, Mauricio Passer, Lesley Gordon, Dr Leslie Kelly, Martin Redwood, Pauline Smith and Colin Bell . . .

Each time we sit down, we see each other.

Keep your heads up, mutha-effers: giving thanks to my family, from whose magic, imperfections and nuances I come; in particular, my various parents – Neil, Joan, Marianne and Maurice – and our littlest ones – Jai, Inara, Ethan, Zora, Oliver and Cairo.

To Sid & Tim & Janis & Shaka, who have returned to being ideas in our heads.

My grandparents.

Alexander Nevermind.

Trixie Rosanna Taylor, for a Spanish mountain and a swimming pool. Thanks to Anna and Beth, for a magic forest to heal inside. Shane, for all the hot Cannonball chocolate.

To comrades in this word-struggle: Bernardine Evaristo, Kei Miller, Musa Okwonga, Niven Govinden, Vicky Arana, Kadija George, Dorothea Smartt, Nicholas Royle, Sharmaine Lovegrove, Melanie Abrahams & all the Renaissance One crew, Sunny Singh, Rob Shearman, Michael Hughes, Marlon James, Sarah Sanders, Sharmilla Beezmohun, Irenosen Okojie, Catherine Johnson, Naomi Woddis, Monique Roffey, Maggie Gee, Courrtia Newland, Joy Francis, the Spread The Word staff, and Inua Ellams.

Vania & Leah.

You've helped me remain and believe and grow.

To the lovers who taught me all the flavours: bitter, spicy, sour, sweet, umami, oleogustus.

Love to my soul-daughter, Steph Elliot Vickers, who sits in the evening light and in the sunshine, scribbling. And to my partner, Malc Wells – fuckface, you better still be here, by the next book.

I acknowledge . . .
    The fibromyalgia.
    The eating disorder.
    The dreaming.
    The moth.

Walk good.

Leone Ross
July 2020